MW00659070

Carnage

For more information about the author and her books, visit her website— https://shanteltessier.com/

You can join her reader group. It's the only place to get exclusive teasers, first to know about current projects and release dates. And also have chances to win some amazing giveaways- https://www.facebook.com/groups/TheSinfulSide

Editor: Jenny Sims

Cover Designer and Formatter: Melissa Cunningham - Book Love Designs

Carnage

USA TODAY & WALL STREET JOURNAL BESTSELLING AUTHOR

SHANTEL TESSIER

WARNING

For those of you who choose to go in blind, please remember that this dark revenge romance is a work of fiction, and I do NOT condone any situations or actions that take place between these characters. This book is not to teach you BDSM, so please do not take it as a how-to. There is a lot of bondage without aftercare. My FMCs (female main characters) love their Heroes as they are—unapologetic. If you need a groveling Hero, this book is not for you. With that being said, every character does go through some kind of trauma (physical and emotional) at some point in this story. If you've read any of the previous Lords (not required to read Carnage), then you have an idea of what their world is like. But I promise you, they have nothing on the Spade brothers. They wrote the book and then sold it to the devil. So buckle up and get ready for one hell of a ride.

Feel free to continue to the prologue if you're like me and have no triggers and like to be surprised, but just remember that I warned you. If you do NOT want to go in blind, please read the trigger warnings & kinks listed below.

Carnage may contain triggers for some.

Trigger Warnings include but are not limited to:
Murder and torture (both in graphic detail), CNC (consent-non-consent), blanket consent, dubcon (dubious consent), kidnapping, forced drugging, claustrophobia, somnophilia, branding, BDSM, bondage, blackout contacts, deepthroat training, face and throat fucking, forced orgasm, orgasm denial, anal, punishment clothing, humiliation, degradation, cockwarming, drug and alcohol use, forced proximity, miscarriage, rape.

If you have any questions, feel free to email me, and one of my assistants or I will get back to you. shanteltessierassistant@gmail.com

AUTHORS NOTE

Nothing about this is to be taken seriously. It is strictly a work of fiction and for your smut pleasure.

Carnage is an all-new dark standalone romance from the USA Today & Wall Street Journal bestselling author Shantel Tessier. Carnage is based in the Lords' world and can be read as a standalone**.** But please know that if you have not read any previous Lords book(s), Carnage may contain spoilers for you.

Things to know about ***Carnage***

This is not an RH
Secret society
MF
J/P (jealous/possessive) Hero
OTT (over the top) Hero
Can be read as a standalone
Told in dual POV
Virgin h

PLAYLIST

“cult leader” by KiNG MALA
“This Is Gonna Hurt” by Sixx:A.M
“M.I.N.E. by Five Finger Death Punch
“love me” by Ex Habit
“I can Tell” by 504 Boyz
“I hope ur miserable until ur dead” by Nessa Barrett
“Hallelujah” by No Resolve
“NUMB” by Ryan Oakes

Part One

PROLOGUE

L.O.R.D.

A Lord takes his oath seriously. Only blood will solidify their commitment to serve those who demand their complete devotion.

*He is a **Leader**, believes in **Order**, knows when to **Rule**, and is a **Deity**.*

A Lord must be initiated in order to become a member but can be removed at any time for any reason. If he makes it past the three trials of initiation, he will forever know power and wealth. But not all Lords are built the same. Some are stronger, smarter, hungrier than others.

*They are challenged just to see how far their **loyalty** will go.*

*They are pushed to their limits in order to prove their **devotion**.*

*They are willing to show their **commitment**.*

Nothing except their life will suffice.

Limits will be tested, and morals forgotten.

A Lord can be a judge, jury, and executioner. He holds power that is unmatched by anyone other than his brother.

Chosen one:

A Lord must remain celibate during his first three years at

Barrington University. Once he is initiated into the Lords, he is gifted a chosen for his senior year.

A Lady:

After they graduate from Barrington, they are to marry a Lady—a wife to serve him. If he shall die before her, she is then gifted to another Lord to ensure the secrets are kept within the secret society.

A Spade brother:

A Lord is placed strategically out into the world. But no Lord is safe from their own if they break their oath. If you don't believe in hell, the Spade brothers will change your mind. They are a special kind of Lord. They will sit on their thrones and watch you burn to death for eternity with the fire they started. They give no fucks and have no limits. They collect the names they are given, and erase you from the world as if you never existed, and make you wish that was the truth.

ONE

SAINT

INITIATION

LOYALTY
Freshman year at Barrington University

I was born into a secret society. They say we're the lucky ones. That the world will bow to us and we'll never go without anything. As long as we pass our initiations, we'll know riches beyond our wildest dreams.

I'm a Spade brother. To anyone on the street who hears that, they would think I have siblings, and in a sense, I do. Our last names aren't Spade, and we don't share the same parents. But we might as well be blood brothers. We grew up together. And one day, we'll graduate from Barrington and run **Carnage** together.

Just like our fathers.

And their fathers.

And their fathers.

We're a long line of Spade brothers. It was some bullshit title that the Lords gave our families centuries ago. Someone has to run their hell, and we were the unlucky ones.

Is it what we want? Doesn't fucking matter what we want. We serve the Lords, and as a servant, you do as you're told.

I've known that we're different since as far back as I can remember, and my father won't let me forget it. He told me I'd have my chance to make him proud. That time has come.

It's my freshman year at Barrington University. My first year of initiation. Even though we were born into this world, we're forced to earn our spot. *Kill or be killed* would be the Lord's motto if they had one.

I kneel with a black hood over my head, keeping me from seeing where I'm at or who else is in the room with me. My wrists are shackled in front of me as they rest on my jean-clad thighs. I'm shirtless. My right eye is starting to swell shut, and I'm pretty sure my nose is broken. I can't breathe through it, but I can taste the blood covering my lips that runs down my face. The lack of light takes everything I have not to pass out. At this point, I'm not sure how many days I've been awake fighting. I've been fed bread and water. That's it. They want us to be weak and vulnerable.

All Lords go through initiations, but as a Spade brother, ours are different. More intense. There are countless Lords throughout the world. But a Spade brother? We're limited. See, I only qualify because my father is one. And one day, if I have a son, he'll be one.

We must all prove that we can do what is needed for the society.

It's our purpose.

The Lords test you so they can toss the weak out early on. You're born into this world, but they can deem you inadequate at any time. So you show up and kill whoever your target is.

If I had to explain a Spade brother to some Joe on the street who doesn't know that the Lords exist, I'd say we're the hit men of the society. But instead of killing, we capture and torture. If we're sent to retrieve you, you will not escape us.

We are the hunters in a world full of prey. It's not like we hurt the good guys. If you ask me, everyone in our society is bad. But we're all willing to do what must be done in order to survive. It's a man-eat-man world.

"Saint Beckham Carter." I hear my name over my pounding headache. "You have been called to serve, son. Do you wish to proceed?"

"I do, sir," I answer without hesitation, but I don't even recognize my voice because my tongue is swollen. I bit the fuck out of it when I got a fist to the mouth.

Fight. Win. Fight. Win.

That's what we train for. Over and over until one of us kills the other. Honestly, I think most of them give up too soon. They realize this life isn't worth your soul. But I've never been known to need one. What does it get you?

Into heaven?

I don't believe in that shit. When you're raised in hell, heaven is a fairy tale that doesn't exist.

"Let's see what you've got, son," the man states. "String him up."

Hands grab at me from behind, yanking me to my feet. I don't even try to fight. Have to save my strength for what's to come. My cuffed wrists are brought above my head, pulling on my shoulders. I grind my teeth so I don't make a sound at the pain that shoots up my back in this position.

The hood is pulled from my head, and I take a deep breath, blinking several times, waiting for my eyes to adjust to the bright light.

I'm not sure where I'm at exactly, but I know it's Carnage. It's an open arena. Two stories. A quick look lets me know Lords pack the place on the upper level in stadium-type seating. A look over my shoulder tells me it's all the way around. I've been thrown into a shark tank, and I'm the bait.

All the Lords wear black masks and matching cloaks. I'm center stage, lower level, on a platform. Like a witch being burned at the stake, I'm strung up to a metal structure with a pole on either side of me and a third across the top. I'm six foot five, and my steel-toed boots barely touch the floor. My body is pulled so tight that the new position makes breathing even harder.

I look up and feel my hands already going numb from the position. My skin splits from being so tight in the metal.

"We will begin." The man's voice from before calls out, walking in front of the platform. Then he turns to face me and lowers his voice. "If you survive this, son, you will live to see another year." With that, he walks out of my view.

If I could, I'd panic at his choice of words, but I just don't have the energy to do so. I have to save it for what's to come.

The squeaking wheels make me cringe. It's as bad as nails on a chalkboard. A man enters the arena from the opposite side. He pushes a cart, but I can't see what he has on it because my vision is blurry.

But it doesn't matter because he's heading right toward me. I get a better view once he reaches the platform. He picks up a syringe and a vial that sits on top of the cart.

I start to fight the restraints. I hate drugs of any kind. I don't like feeling out of control of my body or my thoughts. Drugs slow you down and make it harder to focus on what's in front of you. Especially since I haven't eaten a real meal in days. It'll probably make me sick.

Once the plunger sucks back all the liquid, emptying the vial, he walks up the three stairs in front of me and stands to my left.

I try to adjust my arms once more, my shoulders fucking screaming at the stretch. They fucking burn like I've been lit on fire. And the sweat that runs down my skin stings where I've been cut from the previous fights.

"Open wide," he orders, and before I can even comply, he shoves something into my mouth, pushing my head back in the process. It's hard to fucking breathe since my nose is broken, but I make do. "You'll feel a pinch," he states as he places a hand on my bare chest. I scream into the cloth as the most excruciating pain shoots through my body, taking what little breath I had away.

It's over in a flash, and I feel a rush. Like a dead car getting jump-started. He yanks the cloth from my mouth. "I'd say you have about twenty minutes." He smiles at me, and I have no fucking clue what he's talking about.

He leaves the platform and pushes his cart across the arena. Once I no longer see him, my wrists are freed, and I fall to my knees. I don't even feel the blow. I take a deep breath through my nose, and it feels healed. My sinus cavity is wide open.

I stand to my feet, jumping down off the platform. The lights are all of a sudden brighter. My heart pounds in my chest like a drum, and my pulse races. I could run for days. I no longer feel any pain. Just pure fucking power. I'm energized.

He injected me with adrenaline.

The question is why? What am I supposed to do with it?

My muscles tense and flex on their own. I fist my hands and can feel the blood rushing in my veins. Fuck, I feel invincible.

I hear a sound behind me and spin around just in time to see a man rushing me. He knocks us both down, and I roll a few times before I jump to my feet. But then I'm hit from behind, knocking me to my knees.

Fuck, there are two of them.

I get up and turn in time to see his fist flying to my face, and I manage to block it as I shove mine into his. He doesn't even budge.

They're on adrenaline too. Not surprising. The guy said I should have about twenty minutes. Before what? I crash? Get killed?

I'm hit from behind, knocking me into the guy I just punched in the face. He grabs me, spins me around, and shoves me into the other one.

I grind my teeth, getting angry. My patience is on a shorter fuse than usual. I take a step to the side, putting some distance between us, needing a second to think. I reach down and undo my belt. They let me keep it on. I grasp it with each fist and jump on the guy closest to me, wrapping it around his neck from behind and pulling on it.

He loses his footing from me choking him and dropping my body backward. We stumble back, and he falls on top of me. I wrap my legs around his stomach and squeeze as hard as I can, locking my ankles together while I hold the belt tightly around his neck.

I hold on with everything I have as he tries to fight me, rolling side to side and grabbing at my hands. His nails dig into me, breaking the skin, but I ignore it.

The second guy leans down and tries to pry the man in my grasp away, but it doesn't work. The man on top of me grows heavier and softer. His body loses the battle with strangulation as he begins to asphyxiate. He taps my arm instead of digging his nails in, and I snort. This isn't a tap-out scenario. This is a kill-or-be-killed situation, and today isn't the day that I die.

The guy who stands over us grabs my boots and yanks me and the dying man across the floor. But I refuse to let go. I'm too close now.

When the man on top of me finally goes limp, I wait another second before I release him. Then I push his corpse off me.

I get to my feet and sway a little. I'm losing the adrenaline. The rush is falling away.

The man across from me notices and smirks. He didn't use all of his while fighting us. I'm going to have to run on backup. To further my point, the guy runs away from me, making me frown. But he rushes up the stairs to the platform, jumps up onto the bar that my arms were tied to and swings his large body up and over it, doing a flip around it.

What the fuck? Is he some kind of gymnast? Acrobat? Where did they find him, the goddamn circus?

He lands on the platform and turns to face me, smirking. He lifts his hands and motions for me to come to him. Any other time, I'd make him come to me, but I don't have an extra second to spare. All he has to do is keep me running in circles until I crash, then hit me a few times to win.

I won't make it that easy for him.

Instead, I take a deep breath and run for him. I jump the three stairs onto the platform. He stands to his full height in surprise. And I take the opportunity to jump as well, gripping the metal bar he just spun around. I lift my knees, kicking him right in the chest, knocking him clear off the back end of the platform.

Letting go, I fall to my feet and pick up the chain and cuffs that lie where I was released. I then jump off as well as he rolls to get up on his hands and knees. I position myself over him, one leg on either side of his back, then wrap the chain around his neck from behind and yank him to his feet. I drag him back onto the stage and thread the end of the chain through both cuffs, pulling tight and securing it around his neck.

He goes frantic, trying to get it off. I jump up, toss the end of the chain over the bar, reach up and grab it, and let my legs go limp and yank on it, hanging him by it.

My vision goes in and out like before. My body is starting to give up on me. That headache returns tenfold. I feel a sharp pain in my side, and I'm not sure if I've broken a rib or if my nose is the reason I can't breathe.

The man continues to dangle from the bar. He thrashes around, fighting the chain around his neck, and I tell myself I can't let go. Not yet.

"Just...a little more," I grind out. I'm pretty sure I have lockjaw because I can't open my mouth, and it's getting harder to breathe. Or maybe I'm grinding my teeth. I can't tell the difference.

I watch his arms drop to his sides, and his body sways back and forth. My sweaty hands slip from the chain, unable to hold myself up anymore, and I drop to the stage. My legs are like Jell-O, so I lie there as the man slumps next to me as well. His open and vacant eyes on mine.

I can't move as mine grow heavy. Hands grab me, pulling me from the man and off the stage. If there's more of them, I just won't survive because I have nothing left.

I'm placed on a soft cushion and wheeled out of the arena. The last thing I see is my father running up next to me. He's smiling, and I blink, vision blurry. "Good job, Son." He slaps my chest, making me flinch.

My head falls to the side, and I get a glance at Lords pulling the dead guys from the arena before everything fades away and I'm covered in darkness.

TWO

SAINT

INITIATION

DEVOTION
Sophomore year at Barrington University

I'm leaning up against a concrete wall in the basement under the courtyard at Carnage. I was instructed to be here, and when I arrived, they immediately ushered me down here. I think that was yesterday, though I'm not 100 percent sure. There is no window in here. Just concrete walls and a door with a slot where I was fed water and a piece of bread hours ago.

I have no clue what my initiation consists of—we never do. We just show up and do what must be done.

I was left fully dressed and allowed to keep my combat boots on, which threw up more red flags than anything else. I've seen my father and the others strip men naked, brand them, and throw them in a cell. If they expect me to go crazy and kill myself with the use of my clothes or shoestrings, they'll be disappointed. I'm not suicidal.

The door opens, and my father enters with another Lord, whose identity is disguised. Nothing new. The Lords love their masks and cloaks. It makes them feel superior. As if running the world isn't enough.

"Give me a second with my son," my father tells him.

The man in the mask nods and steps out, closing the door.

I cross my arms over my chest as he runs his hand through his dark hair. Lords are intended to breed after graduation, so the fact that they have kids at a young age is common.

"Do I get conjugal visits?" I ask, my mind going to a specific woman who is brunette with blue eyes. She's the twin sister of Adam —another Spade brother—and everything I want. And one day, I'll get her.

His eyes narrow on me. "This is serious, Saint." He huffs. "This test..." He pauses, rethinking what he was about to say. "I'll see you afterward." With that, he turns, knocking on the door, and it opens, allowing him to exit.

I stay where I'm at, and this time, three Lords enter the confined space, making my heart race as I look over their cloaks and masks. One holds out what looks like a cap to a two liter of some sort. It's full of clear liquid.

Taking in a deep breath, I take the offered cap and hold it up. "Bottoms up," I say and toss it into my mouth, knowing it's going to fuck me up. But it's not like I can say no.

It drops to the floor before I even have the chance to blink and stumble back. My legs no longer hold me up, and I fall into the back concrete wall. My eyes grow heavy, and I watch the three blurry figures walk toward me as my eyes fall closed and blackness takes over.

I GROAN, A THROBBING IN THE BACK OF MY HEAD HITTING LIKE A drum. I go to roll over onto my side but can't. "Fuuucckk," I slur, trying to get my bearings straight. Where the fuck am I? How long have I been out?

Opening my heavy eyes, I see blurry figures right in front of my face. Lines run down the length of my body, and I realize I'm lying on my back. I fist my hands, trying to get feeling into them. They're cold and numb. Lifting my head, I hit it on something and curse myself.

Fuck, Saint! Now the front hurts as much as the back. I lie still and close my eyes, taking in a few deep breaths to let myself adjust to wherever the fuck I am before I hurt myself.

Once I can move my fingers, I realize my arms are down by my sides, and I'm still dressed because I feel the roughness of my jeans on the palms of my hands. I go to touch my face, but my arms don't make it far because they come to a stop when my elbows hit something hard.

Opening my eyes, they adjust to see the blurry lines I saw initially are metal bars. My breathing picks up when I realize exactly where I am—the pits.

The best way to describe them is that they resemble shallow graves in the center of the concrete floor. I've watched my father place men in here and then they lock them in with bars across the top. There's not much room for movement, let alone escape.

I turn my head from side to side to see both concrete sides only inches from my face. The tight space smashes my shoulders and arms down to my sides. My pulse races, and I move my hands to rest on my belt and try to move them up my stomach and chest to see how far I can go. But they can't go any higher than my belt because when I go to bend my elbows, the concrete sides stop them.

I try to calm my erratic breathing. "Don't panic," I tell myself. They don't want to kill me. That won't benefit them.

I feel around the best I can down by my sides, trying to see if there is a key anywhere underneath or beside me. But I've seen how the pits work. The key goes in from the top where the feet go. There's no way I'd be able to reach that. I have no clue what the point to this is. Am I supposed to free myself? Or is it to see how long I can last in a concrete box?

A ticking sound gets my attention, and I look around the ceiling the best I can through the five bars. Lifting my head, I allow my forehead to press against the bar in the center and see a timer hanging on the wall outside the pit. It's large in size and has big red numbers. It's counting down from what I'm guessing is five minutes because it's currently at four and a half and dropping.

"What the fuck happens once it stops?" I ask myself. I've never seen that before with previous men put in here. They have to serve time, but it's way more than five minutes.

"It comes in waves." A voice speaks.

I tilt my head back, trying to look around, but can't see shit. "What does?" I ask, thinking that maybe it was one of my *brothers*—Kashton, Adam, or Haidyn—but I didn't recognize the voice.

"The timer," he answers, and I can tell by the softness in his voice that he's weak. There are three pits in the floor here so he could be in one next to me. "The first wave is tolerable...the second gets colder..." He pauses before whispering, "The third is the coldest."

The blood rushes in my ears and I try to bend my knees and get frustrated when they hit the bars. Lifting my head as far as I can, I see I'm down to two minutes and fifty seconds. "After the third?" I rush out.

He coughs, and it sounds like he's been smoking all his life, but it's probably just the shit Carnage has put him through. "I've never seen anyone make it past that." He gets out before coughing again.

My fear rises, and I try to shake it off. No. I won't fucking die in here. There has to be a reason as to why this is my initiation. Instead, I lift my head, letting the bars push against my pounding head, and watch the timer count down the last twenty seconds. When it gets to zero, an alarm sounds, and I feel a rush of cold air down by my legs before water begins to fill the hole.

FUCK!

My fear is drowning to death. This is why this is my initiation. My father knows this. He found my mom once trying to drown me in the bathtub. She hated my father, and I fell into that category by association.

I take in a deep breath and let it out, trying to calm my nerves as the water fills the confined space, soaking into my clothes, making my limbs feel heavier than they did already.

Lifting my head the best I can, the water comes to a stop at about my ears. My neck strains, and I slowly lie down, the water coming up to my cheeks. The only sound I can hear is my own heavy breathing.

My body is tense, hands fisted, and I remind myself not to panic as I shiver. The water is cold, and the slightest movement makes it splash around my face.

Then as fast as it filled the space, it's sucked out, leaving me shivering and teeth chattering. I take in a deep breath. The guy said three times. That means I've got two more. Lifting my head, I see the clock reset to three minutes this time.

My chest feels heavy, my wet shirt sticking to me, and my legs are already restricted to the space so the fact that my jeans are soaked makes it harder to move them. My boots feel like my feet are in concrete.

I close my eyes, trying to ignore the blood rushing in my ears. It's nothing. Just another day, another chance to prove myself. They kept me in the cell for so long to make me weak from lack of food and water. They wanted me weak, then had me drink whatever the fuck that shit was to knock me out to put me in here. They wanted the panic factor to set me up for failure.

There is no word to call out or signal that a Lord can do or say in order to stop an initiation. Not like I would anyway. So there has to be an endgame. Because this isn't a kill-or-be-killed situation. It's a mind game. An illusion meant to push you to your limits. To see how far you can go before they get to throw you away. The Lords only take the best, and they want you to prove your worth.

I hear the sound of the alarm once again and the rush of cold air before the water enters. It's colder this time just like the guy had said. Almost freezing, making it worse since my clothes are already wet.

I'm shaking uncontrollably, lifting my head to let it fill all the way. Once I know it's done, I lower my head into the water to see how far it comes up this time. It covers my eyes, making me close them along with my lips, but I'm able to breathe through my nose. I arch my neck instead of lifting it, allowing my lips to part and suck in a ragged breath. A little bit of water enters my mouth, and I choke on it, making my body press against the bars above me.

I count in my head as a distraction, knowing that sending myself into a panic attack won't do me any good. Possibly just kill me.

Once I get to forty-five, the water is pulled out, and I readjust my head, trying to relax and open my eyes, blinking rapidly because water covers my face and lashes. It burns, which makes me think it's salt water. It's denser than fresh water so it anchors a person more. Another test.

I'm freezing. My body shakes uncontrollably, but my clothes feel like they've shrunk in size. The salt water makes them feel like compressions, then the added weight has them pinning me to the concrete floor. Not like I could move anyway.

My throat burns like my eyes, and my chest is so heavy that it's getting harder to breathe. My teeth chatter so hard they ache. My head falls to the side, and I blink at the concrete wall. How many times did the guy say it did this? Three? I don't know if I can survive one more. I wouldn't say I'm scared anymore, just getting sleepy. Is it the shit they gave me? Or the cold water?

That's what hypothermia does to you. Slows your heart rate; numbs the body.

"Don't pass out." I hear that voice again.

I blink my heavy eyes and try to talk, but I'm not sure anything comes out.

"You've got another wave in one minute." He goes on. "It's going to come up higher. You won't be able to breathe at all. So take a few deep breaths and get ready."

"Why..." I lick my numbing lips. "Are you helping me?"

"Let's just say one day I might need a favor."

I roll my head so I'm looking up through the bars once again, and his words make me laugh. Or I'm becoming delusional.

"Five seconds," he warns.

I blink. My burning eyes are so heavy.

"Two seconds."

I take in a shaky breath, and a loud noise hits my ears. The back of my mind registers danger, but I'm not sure from what. Then a cold gust of air hits my wet clothes before I feel it. The water. It comes up faster this time. It's also colder. Freezing cold.

I take a deep breath as it covers my face completely. I can't move. The weight of it too heavy and my body too weak. It's so cold that it almost feels like I'm burning at first before the chill sets in.

I can't lift my head, and I open my eyes, and they burn, but I can see the bars. I'm so close to life but closer to death. It's like when I was five, and I'm back in the bathtub once again with my mom's hands on my chest, holding me down. I kicked and fought with everything I could, but I was too weak to fight her off.

She was screaming at me, but I couldn't understand what she was saying. Just saw her mouth moving while she cried tears into the water that was drowning me. My father heard the commotion, pushed her to the side, and pulled me out. I never saw her again, and I never asked why. She didn't want me, and my father didn't want to lose his only son. It wasn't because he loved me; it was because he would have no one to take his place once the Lords decided he needed to hand over Carnage to his child.

It's the only reason I'm still alive to this day. I blink slowly, my throat burning as I watch the water splash out over the edges of the pit I'm locked in.

My eyes close, and I arch my neck, needing to breathe. My body fights the confined space, pressing against the bars. I thrash back and forth, hoping to splash some of the water out so I can breathe, but it feels as if it continues to fill itself.

Unable to take it anymore, I part my lips and try to breathe, swallowing some. Pain explodes in my chest. It causes my body to jerk involuntarily. The panic forces me to try and breathe again, and I swallow more of the salty tasting water. I'm pretty sure I'm seizing from the harsh movements my body is doing on it's own.

Drowning has always been my greatest fear, and the Lords chose to use that against me. All I can do is accept it now.

Just when I think I've decided I'll die in the pit, the water is sucked out, and I begin to cough up water onto my face while gasping in cold air that burns my throat. I hear the loud sound of the locks unclasping and the scraping of metal before the bars disappear and hands grab at me. I'm yanked from the pit and tossed onto my stomach.

A hand beats on my back and I convulse lying on the cold concrete. Hands all over...pulling and yanking. I'm being stripped of my wet clothing.

"Good job, Son." I hear my father's voice over my coughing and gasping. "I knew you could do it."

I pull away from him but fall to my face. I lift my heavy eyes to see a figure hanging over in the corner. He's got a head of dark hair that falls over his forehead. He's naked and covered in dirt. He hangs by his cuffed wrists above his head. His eyes closed. I'm not sure if he was the one helping me or if it was my mind playing games with me. But his eyes crack open and meet mine before I pass out.

THREE

SAINT

INITIATION

COMMITMENT
Junior year at Barrington University

"Get in and get out," Haidyn speaks, checking his Patek Philippe watch for the fifth time in the past minute.

Kashton grunts. "You act like I want to hang out and have a beer." He straightens his suit jacket, eye-fucking the bleach-blond waitress who walks by and winks at him.

Haidyn shoves Kashton's arm, getting his attention. "Out of the four of us, you're the one who would make us stay longer than we should."

Kashton nods in agreement. "If only." He winks back at the blonde when she chooses to walk by once again.

"He can't fuck you, darling." Adam waves her off. "His dick doesn't work." Her eyes widen on a gasp before she spins around and takes off. He looks over at Kashton, who only laughs at him. "I'd like to get out of here before the sun comes up," Adam adds.

I hate to break it to them, but we'll be here for a while. "Everyone has their card memorized?" I ask, tucking my hands into the pockets of my black dress slacks.

"Yes, Dad." Kashton smiles at me.

Adam nods, and Haidyn taps the side of his head to acknowledge that he remembers it.

"Then let's go."

We were each given a card with a name, location, and time. For this initiation, we must work together. If you ask me, the Lords are fucking with us. They want us to fail, get angry with one another, or toss each other off the side of the megayacht we're currently on. Or get caught so they can set us up to be killed as well.

"Anyone else feeling seasick?" Kashton places his hand on his chest and sways back and forth.

"It's like three hundred feet long. I can't even tell we're on water," Adam answers him.

"We've been on the yacht for an hour," Haidyn reminds him.

"I've never done well with water," Kashton snaps defensively. "You remember that summer before freshman year at Barrington when we took Adam's father's boat out and I puked all over the bow?"

"That's because you drank an entire bottle of Jäger and had nothing to eat that day." Adam laughs. "You also slapped your dick onto a cheese spread and were offering women your 'cheese stick.'"

"Hey, I wasn't going to get pussy for the next three years. I was living my best life." He grunts, grabbing his slacks as if he can't wait to get to use his cock again.

We all feel that way.

Haidyn checks his watch again and fixes his backpack on his shoulder. "I'm out. See you guys soon." He turns, giving us his back and walking through a set of doors.

"Me too." Adam tosses a piece of gum into his mouth and does the man handshake hug with Kashton and I nod to him before he leaves as well.

"Are you going to get sick?" I ask Kash. We didn't come this far for him to fuck it up by puking everywhere.

He shakes his head. "Nah, I think I'll be okay."

Kashton and I make our way through the megayacht. It belongs to a Lord, but no one really knows what he does. He keeps himself secluded. Once a year, he throws a party on *Isabella* in the Atlantic when he spends the weekends in the Hamptons. He's pissed someone off, and it turns out it'll work in our favor.

We have four names to check off our list tonight. Each of us has to take one out as a team. If one of us fails, we all fail is how the Lords see us, but it makes me laugh.

"Fuck me," Kashton exclaims loudly, and an older woman dressed in a black cocktail dress gasps, clutching her pearls next to us.

"I apologize." I place my hands on his shoulders. "First time on the water. He's feeling ill."

Her face softens, and she pops open her clutch. "I understand. This will help. I always carry them for my husband." She hands him a piece of gum for nausea, and he pops it in his mouth, mumbling a thank you.

She walks off into a crowd, and I turn to face him. "Keep it down," I say, scanning the room. When my eyes find his, I follow them to see why the outburst.

He's staring at a profile view of the woman out on the deck with bleach-blond hair standing with an older man. I'm guessing her father or *daddy*, however you want to see it. She's sipping on a glass of champagne with her hair in a tight bun at the nape of her neck, wearing a red dress that fits tightly, showing off every curve. She looks over in our direction, and Kashton practically falls over himself. "Goddamn..."

"Like Adam said, you can't use your dick right now," I remind him, grabbing his suit jacket and pulling him up a set of stairs and out of sight of the woman.

"I can jack off while I watch her fuck herself," he adds, trying to look over his shoulder. "I can fuck her with things other than my cock. Record it and watch it over and over."

We get to the top of the stairs and step on the platform. A private elevator is in front of us with a man dressed in an all-black tux standing at it. He looks from me to Kashton and moves to stand in front of the door, blocking our entrance.

"Name?" he requests.

"Hart," I answer, and he checks his clipboard.

"Unzip the bag," the man orders.

I turn to face Kashton and unzip the duffle bag he carries for me. Stacks and stacks of hundred-dollar bills is all you can see. It's what's underneath that matters. I zip it back up when he stands and steps out of the way. "Good luck, Mr. Hart."

I give him a curt nod as the elevator opens, and we step inside. "This shit is heavy as fuck." He drops the bag to his feet and starts bouncing up and down, chewing away on the gum. Not only is he horny as fuck but he's also hyped up on energy drinks because he's been up for over twenty-four hours. "You good?" I ask.

He nods.

The elevator dings, and the door slides open. Soft music plays as we step off into a large circular room that sits on the upper level of the yacht. I bet the view would be gorgeous during the day, but right now, all the glass just showcases the dark night.

To the left is a full bar setup with six barstools. One of the bartenders looks up at me, and I catch a faint smile at the corner of his lips.

To the right is a lounging area filled with two couches and a chair. Six TVs hang on the wall all currently displaying poker games around the world. The Lord who throws the party is a known gambler. It doesn't matter what it is, he will bet on it. His private poker games are talked about all over the world and that was our in.

The carpet is pristine white, with rich brown and gold accents. Wealth always likes to be flashy. I've spent so much of my life at

Carnage that I forget not everything is made out of concrete and shackles.

To my right, next to the lounging area, is a cashier. A young brunette stands behind a glass window. She looks up at me and smiles. "Are you going to play, Mr. Hart?" The security guard who checked my name and bag obviously informed them we were coming up.

"Yes," I answer, and she looks past me, smiling at Kashton. Turning to look at him, his eyes are on her tits that are pushed up in the black corset.

"How much would you like, sir?" she asks.

"One million, please." We'll start there and see where it leads.

TWO HOURS LATER, I'VE LOST THREE HUNDRED THOUSAND. THE man who sits to my right is up over a million, and the one to my left, I'm pretty sure, is having a heart attack. He's sweating profusely and breathing heavily. He's been sucking down drink after drink to ignore the fact he's lost his large fortune over the past year. But it wasn't his to lose.

He's been digging his hole deeper and deeper for twelve months now, and he already owes a lot to someone tired of waiting. That's why I'm here.

Gamblers get greedy. It's never enough for them. I'm not much of a gambler, but I get it. The want for more...power, wealth, pussy. Is there such a thing as too much? I don't think so.

The man to my right laughs as he wins another hand. "Well, boys, it was fun." He gets up from the table, collecting his winnings, and walks off.

Another hour and he's been too busy losing that he hasn't been paying attention to me. My signs, my tics. He only has himself to blame.

As a Lord, we've been trained to lie and cheat to win. So making him believe I have three queens, with two sixes already on the table, gives me the better full house.

The room is eerily quiet as everyone watches. He takes a deep breath and tosses his cards down onto the table, folding.

I lay mine down, and he jumps to his feet, slapping his hands on the felt. "What the fuck?" he barks out. "You made me believe you had the winning hand."

I didn't.

Sitting back in my seat, he storms over to the bar and gets another drink. I wait for him to return. Because a desperate man is a predictable man.

Kashton still stands behind me with my duffle bag at his feet. I make no move to get up. The dealer patiently waits as he too watches the man drink down another. He knows he's going to return and ask me to play him again. I've hurt his ego. Made him look like a fool in front of friends and colleagues.

"Everyone out," he commands from the bar, and I hide my smile while taking a sip of bourbon.

Eight men usher themselves out along with two waitresses and the cashier. I push my chair back to stand, buttoning my suit jacket.

"Not you." He points at me.

"I'm done for the evening," I say, stepping from the table.

"One more game. Three million." His eyes drop to my duffle bag that Kashton holds, licking his lips. He's hungry. Desperate. He was given a deadline, and he's past it.

I take a quick look around. Haidyn is still at the bar, eyes on me. Adam is by the exit; arms crossed over his chest and gives me a nod. He's locked the door, and Kash remains behind me.

I reach up, rubbing my chin to contemplate if I want to play, but it's a signal. "Alright." I give him a nod. "One game. Three million."

We get seated once again, and before the dealer can even touch the cards, Haidyn comes up behind him, grabs his head, and twists his neck, breaking it.

His head falls to the felt, and the guy next to me jumps up, shouting. I grab the back of his neck and slam the side of his face into the poker table, making him groan.

He goes limp and starts to fall to the floor, but Kashton helps me get him onto the table. Laying him on his back, I jump up onto the felt and straddle his stomach. Adam reaches into the duffle bag and pulls out the rope.

"What—?" The guy groans, looking around aimlessly.

Haidyn shoves a bar towel into his mouth to silence him. I'm not sure how much time we've got, but the clock has started, and we've still got three more names to cross off before we can get off this yacht.

Kashton makes quick work tying the guy's wrists together with the rope from the bag, and then he plops down in a chair, restraining them above his head.

I rip his button-down shirt open to expose his chest to the room as Haidyn hands me a pair of serving tongs, and the guys eyes widen. "This is going to hurt." I say before I press it to his chest and squeeze the tongs into his skin over his brand.

He throws his head back, screaming into the bar towel. Pulling the skin as hard as I can, I take a pocketknife and slice off his brand.

His body bucks and thrashes, and I squeeze him with my legs to keep him in place. "I need a bag," I shout, and Haidyn rushes over to the bar and grabs a small baggie. Coming back, he opens it up for me and I drop the bloody piece of skin covered with the Lords crest into it.

I jump up, standing with my feet on either side of his hips. "Turn him over."

Haidyn and Adam flip him onto his stomach while Kashton undoes the rope around his wrists. We've got to switch things up. Falling to my knees, I straddle his back this time and help Kashton reposition his arms behind his back and tie his wrists in place while Haidyn and Adam tie his ankles together and then to the bag.

Jumping down, I walk around where his head hangs off the edge of the blood-covered table. I yank the bar towel from his mouth, and spit flies out as he starts to shout.

"I was told to give you this." I shove a piece of paper into his mouth, and he gags as I shove it to the back of his throat. "That's it." I press further, and he chokes. "Swallow it. All the way." When I feel his throat work, I remove my hand and tap the side of his face. "Good boy."

He's gasping and tears run down his face. "You son of a bitch. I'll have you killed..."

"We're all going to die," I tell him and shove the bar towel back into his mouth to silence him again. Haidyn hands me the duct tape, and I wrap it around his head, making sure he can't spit out the towel. "But today is your day."

Once he's ready, Haidyn and I grab him while Adam grabs the dead dealer, and Kashton collects the duffle bag off the floor. We exit the sliding glass door out onto the private balcony. It's windy and cold outside as the yacht continues farther and farther out to sea. It's an all-night party and won't return to the marina until morning. We'll be long gone by then.

We lay him on a chair and connect the excess of rope around his ankles to the leather handles, securing him to the duffle bag. I had lead pipes hidden underneath the money in the bag. We needed the added weight and the bag to not look suspicious.

He's shaking his head furiously as he screams into the tape and bar towel. "Don't worry, I've included your money in the bag as well." I smile at him.

"What are we doing with him?" Adam kicks the dead dealer.

I take my pocketknife, bend and cut the guy down his stomach and chest. Blood pours out of the now open wound and the other guy starts to gag as it bathes him in it. "Hand me another rope." I hold my hand up to no one in particular, and Haidyn gives it to me. I wrap it around the dead guy's neck a few times and tie it off and wrap what's left around the other man. "The weight should hold both. And if not, I'm sure something will eat them."

It takes all four of us to lift them both and get them over the railing to throw them into the ocean. I lean over and watch to see if they surface. It never happens. Either they sank to the bottom or the yacht sucked them under and the propellers got them. Either way, one down and three to go.

"Clean up," Haidyn says, dropping his backpack next to us. "Onto the next."

A Lord isn't a coward. And only a coward would hide who they really are. A part of our point to prove is that we are untouchable. You can't fuck with us because we fuck back. And where anyone else would end up in jail for such a crime, we'll be walking the streets, as free men.

FOUR

SAINT

INITIATION

ONE OF THEM
Senior year at Barrington University

I breathe heavily into the hood that covers my head. It's too thick to see through, but by the heat on my chest, I can tell I'm outside in the sun. I'm shirtless but dressed in jeans and my boots.

There's a wooden post at my back, and my arms are tied behind it, the rope tight and cutting into my wrists. I can feel the post cutting up my back with the slightest of movement. There's rope around my neck securing me to it along with my ankles. The less movement we're allowed the better.

My heart pounds in my chest, and sweat runs down my exposed skin. I've been like this for quite some time. It's the waiting that they want to terrify you. The unknown.

I thrive off it. Surprise me. Give me something to look forward to. When you're forced to hunt and kill, the chase gets old. Sometimes you have to offer yourself up as bait, and that's when the true fun begins.

The smell of smoke fills my runny nose, and I know they've started the fire. The heat will soon follow.

The hood is yanked from my head, and I blink rapidly as my assumption was right and the sun blasts my sensitive eyes. I try to bow my head, but the rough rope wrapped around my neck prevents it.

"Lords." I hear a man's voice, and I pry them open to see a Lord standing on the other side of a large fire pit. Four branding irons waiting to be used. To be a reminder of who we are and what we'll do.

A quick look out of the corner of my eyes, I know that I'm not alone out here in the courtyard at Carnage. So are my brothers.

"Today is the day that you take your oath. And with that oath comes great responsibility." His voice carries out and over to the balconies of Carnage where Lords stand. They're not dressed in their usual cloaks and masks. Today is the day they get to be seen. Their chance to show their respect to those of us who are being given the gift of their world. "As a Spade brother, you will be the ones who must punish those who disobey their oath. You will show them that we do not take our life for granted. You are their jury and executioner. Do you understand?"

"Yes, sir," the four of us say in unison.

He nods and takes a step back from the now raging firepit.

My father comes into view, standing in front of me. His arms are crossed behind his back, and his chest bows out with pride. "Saint Beckham Carter, you have completed all your trials of initiation. Do you wish to proceed?"

"Yes, sir," I say, trying to stretch my neck, but it just tightens the rope. The heat from the growing fire makes me hot, and the sweat that covers my skin burns where the rope has rubbed me raw.

He clears his throat and straightens his shoulders. "A Lord must be willing to go above and beyond for his title. He must show strength and have what it takes. If you fail your position as a Lord, your brother will take what you earned." He gives me his back and picks up the end of one of the brands that's dipped in the fire.

I swallow nervously, the rope feeling like it's tightened around my neck. He turns to face me. "Gag him."

Someone comes up behind me, and my mouth is pried open. Something is shoved into my mouth, filling out my cheeks. It's large and rubber. I clench my jaw, biting down on it, and my body hums with anticipation as my nose runs. Breathing is getting harder.

"Saint Beckham Carter." He calls me by my full name. "Welcome to the Lords, son. For you shall reap the benefits of your sacrifice." Stepping into me, he places the crest into my already hot and sweaty skin, forever reminding me that I was born a Lord and I will die a Lord.

FIVE

SAINT

We're officially Lords. The brand that burns my chest is a constant reminder that the only way out is death.

We've all been raised not to fear death. It's what you do with your life that should terrify you. Once you're dead, you'll no longer give a fuck about anything. But being alive? That's a rush.

I pull up to the house and park my Lamborghini Veneno in the street. Some girl attending Barrington is throwing a party at her daddy's house. She's entering her freshman year and wants to make a good impression. They always do, but it doesn't matter. Daddy's money can't buy her everything—not in this town or in our world. Her father owns several businesses, but he's not a Lord. Therefore, he's a small fish in an ocean littered with sharks.

"Hey, man," Haidyn calls out. I turn to see him getting off his blacked-out R1 parked behind me. "Where's Kashton and Adam?" He unzips his leather jacket, but I notice he doesn't have his helmet tonight. Instead, he's got a baseball cap on backward.

"They're meeting us here," I answer, stuffing my hands into the pockets of my jeans.

He nods, walking toward me. "Let's go in and see what kind of trouble we can get into." He throws his arm over my shoulders and laughs.

I'm only here for one reason. Surprisingly, it's not to start trouble.

We enter the house and make our way through the throngs of people. It's packed. With social media these days, you can fill a large house in a matter of minutes. It's been going on for a few hours already. Empty beer cans and broken bottles are everywhere. People making out in hallways and practically fucking on whatever surface they can find.

"ARMY OF ME" by In This Moment blasts throughout the house. They've got the lights dimmed and strobes on, giving the illusion that I'm constantly blinking.

We head to the kitchen and each grab a drink of our own and then make our way to the back of the house. Walking outside, I take a sip of my beer when I spot her. I've been watching her on a fake social media account for the past few hours. That's how I knew she was here.

She's in the pool on some guy's shoulders, and my hand tightens on my beer can. Her perky tits are only covered by white triangles. Her dark hair is wet and sticks to her back, neck, and shoulders. The guy grabs her hands and goes underwater. With her head barely above water, she readjusts herself on his shoulders before he pops up and tosses her across the pool.

The sound of her landing on her back makes everyone cringe before a few laugh.

Gasping for breath, she breaks the surface and pushes her hair back from her face, blinking. "Are you okay?" he asks, swimming over to her.

She nods, laughing. "Yeah." I don't need to see her to know she's drunk. I've seen her posts tonight. It wasn't hard to tell by the way she was misspelling words as if she was slurring her speech. I curse myself for not getting here sooner, but my father needed to *talk* to me. His idea of urgent differs from mine. It could have waited. Anything regarding her comes first in my world.

"You sure? That sounded like it hurt." He goes on, grabbing her arm and pulling her into him.

I step forward, but Haidyn grabs my shirt to stop me. "Not now, man," he mumbles under his breath so only I can hear.

Ashtyn Lane Price belongs to me. She just doesn't know it yet. But she will, very soon. And once I make her mine, the world will know it too.

She pushes off him and goes underwater. When her head pops up again, she's over at the stairs. It's dark outside, but the light on the back patio illuminates the area along with the pool lights, giving us all a view as if it's midday.

She slowly climbs them, one hand on the railing, the other pushing her hair back from her gorgeous face. Water falls off the curves of her body, and I want to lick every inch of her. The bathing suit bottom covers very little of her bubble ass, leaving nothing to the imagination. I've seen her naked before. I've watched her undress and crawl into bed from her closet when she thought she was alone.

I've watched her sleep and touched her face while hoping she was dreaming of me. I'm a man obsessed with a woman I haven't been able to have. Some would call it creepy or pathetic. I call it devoted.

Walking over to a table, she picks up a pink beach towel and wrings out her long dark hair. Then she begins to dry off her legs, stomach, and chest. The little bikini she wears makes me hard and jealous. Once she's mine, she'll be under my arms with my name carved into her skin. And then I won't care about her lack of clothes. I'll show her off to anyone who wants to look at her.

But if I had my way, I'd keep her chained up in the basement until then. Right now, I can see all the guys have their eyes on her ass. Including Haidyn.

I slap his chest, and he just chuckles before sipping his beer. "We all know she'll be yours, Saint," he mumbles.

Wrapping the towel around her shoulders, she turns away from the table and walks toward us. Looking up from her cell in her hand, she spots us. Coming to a stop, she gives me a drunken smile before dropping her eyes to the porch. I love that she's innocent because I can't wait to ruin her.

"Hey, guys," she says softly, looking up at us through her wet lashes.

"What's up, baby girl?" Haidyn asks, his eyes dropping to her exposed chest that the towel doesn't cover.

I don't mind him looking. I just want to be the one that shows her off. Like right now, I want to tie her up out here for all to see and offer her to him. My terms. My way. I want to see her beg me to let him get her off. It's sick, I know. To be so jealous of other men getting to look at her while also wanting to share her. I can only chalk it up to what love and hate feel like. Both are very powerful. I want to control what she feels and when she feels it.

"Not much. You?" She licks her lips, and my already hard cock reminds me just how bad I crave to feel them wrapped around me.

Ashtyn is five-five and currently barefoot. Haidyn and I are both over six feet tall, and we've got boots on. She's got small breasts and a tiny waist with narrow hips and a nice round ass. I love her size. Most women would call me a pig for having a type, but she's exactly what I want, and I compare every woman I see to her. Not a single one even comes close.

"Where's your brother?" Haidyn asks.

She frowns as if not expecting him to want to know that. That, just maybe, we had wanted to see her. If she only knew why I was here. "He was inside playing beer pong with Kash last time I saw him."

"Ash?" a girl calls out, stepping outside. She squeezes between Haidyn and me, and hands Ashtyn a drink in a red Solo cup. "Here you go."

Ashtyn takes it and brings the rim of the cup to her lips, but I rip it from her hand and throw the cup to the patio. The alcohol splashes her feet and legs.

"Hey?" her friend shouts. "What the fuck, Saint?"

"She's not drinking that shit. Who knows what's in it." You can't trust those who attend Barrington. They're just as dirty as anyone else but have the money to get out of trouble. Girls get drugged, raped, and killed here just like anywhere else. But the only difference is their faces don't end up all over social media because the wealthy daddies pay for their families' silence. It's sad what the price for a human life is. Being a Lord has taught me that I'll fight for my life, but a daughter of a Lord isn't allowed that same courtesy.

Her friend rolls her eyes, but Ashtyn smiles at me. "You're always a gentleman."

Me? A gentleman? She has no clue that I'm going to turn her into a dirty whore who will beg to be treated like a toy.

Her plump lips softly smile and then she surprises me by leaning up on her tiptoes to kiss my cheek. "But you worry too much." Pulling back, she nibbles on her bottom lip, and my eyes drop to see her nipples are hard through the thin material of her bikini. I want to rip it off and tie her up with the strings. Make her a doll that I can play with in front of everyone. "See you around, boys." And with that, they take each other's hands and walk into the house to get a new drink.

ASHTYN

I CAN FEEL HIM BEHIND ME ONCE I ENTER THE HOUSE. MY hands grip the towel to pull it up in the process to give him a better view of my ass. I want Saint to want me. To want it.

I've always been one for a challenge. I was raised to be competitive. And getting the man I want is no different.

A part of me wants to drop the towel right now and see what he does. Would he remove my bathing suit or would he cover me back up?

Probably the latter. He can't touch me. Or any other woman, for that matter right now. But soon, he'll be given a woman to use, and I hate how much I pray it's me. Especially considering I don't believe in God. It's crazy what we choose to believe is real and fake.

A God? He doesn't exist in our world.

The devil? Absolutely.

Evil will always outshine the good because it will do whatever it takes in order to survive. The good doesn't have what it takes. That's why it's considered good. It won't cheat or deceit you. It believes that what happens is what's meant to be. I want a man who will do whatever it takes to make what "he" wants to happen. Saint comes to mind when I think of that. What would he do if I tried to take another guy home tonight just for fun? Due to circumstances out of my control, I can't fuck anyone, but I can pretend.

The flashing lights have me stumbling more than I already was outside as I sing along to "cult leader" by KiNG MALA.

We walk up to the island in the kitchen to get me a new drink, and out of the corner of my eye, I catch the back of Saint walking past. My shoulders slump that he didn't stay. But I know he's looking for my brother and Kashton.

I know exactly where they're at. "Surprise me," I tell the guy holding a new Solo cup in his hand.

"God, Saint is such an ass." Whitney huffs. I know her from Barrington. We're friends, but I wouldn't say we're best friends. We hang out every now and then. She understands what it's like to be a woman growing up in the Lords world.

I smile. "I like the way he is."

She rolls her eyes. "Please. He's a piece of shit who thinks he rules the world."

"You just described every Lord out there." They're raised to believe that. I've seen it firsthand with my father and how he's raised my brother. A Lord can do no wrong. They're rewarded for being evil. The more creative they can be, the more they are praised.

"They're not all the same," she argues.

I snort. "Okay." Not believing that. She has a sister and a brother. I don't feel sorry for Miller. He's just another Lord who thinks he can do no wrong. But her sister? That's a different story. Laikyn is a couple of years younger than her, and Whitney's two years younger than me. I'm going into my senior year at Barrington, and Whitney will be a sophomore. Whitney isn't as sheltered as her sister is, though. I feel sorry for Laikyn. She has no clue what her life will be like once she attends Barrington. My mother has never hidden my future from me.

You will belong to a Lord, and if you're lucky, you'll die young. She once said that to me after finishing off an entire bottle of wine one night when I found her crying at the kitchen table because my father didn't come home for dinner. I'm always confused as to why she cares about what he's out doing because they hate one another. They married because their families told them to. Not for love. That's how relationships work in my world. Two families are combined for power. Marrying because you love someone is unheard of.

"Here you go." The guy hands me my new drink, and I don't miss the way his eyes drop to my hard nipples. I'm still wet from the pool, and it's freezing in this house.

Thoughts of Saint have me looking around to see if he's in the kitchen, and I'm disappointed when he's not. He looked so fucking good. He always does. And the way he ripped my drink from my hand? *Whew.* Maybe I wanted to take the chance of it being laced with something? Bet he never thought of that. It'd give him a reason to take care of me. I'd do anything to be in his arms, even if that meant being unconscious and unable to remember most of it.

There are more ways than one to accomplish that. I toss it back and take a gulp, gasping at the strong taste of vodka and ...blackberry? "Fu...ck," I breathe.

The kid winks at me. "It's an Aunt Roberta."

As if I know what the fuck that is. I take another drink, and it throws me into a coughing fit.

Whitney slaps my back. "What the fuck did you give her?" she growls at him.

"An Aunt—"

"I heard you the first time, jackass," she snaps. "What the hell is in it?"

"Straight alcohol," he says in a duh voice.

It runs down my chin and onto my chest, forcing tears from my eyes. "I'm...fine." I gasp, coughing once more. Hitting my chest, I take a deep breath, and the burn intensifies.

"Jesus, Ash, are you trying to kill yourself?" Whitney mutters.

Shaking my head, I cover my mouth with my free hand while the other still holds my drink. Whitney tries to take it from me, but I step back, gripping it tighter. "I'm fine," I tell her. Getting under control, I quickly look around for Saint, but again, there's no sign of him.

I'm not the type of girl who waits around for a hero. Or wants a Prince Charming. They're the good guys—boring. I want someone who I know will fight for me. Even if they have to cheat to win. And that's exactly what a Lord is raised to do—fight. It's in their blood. All they know.

I take a sip this time and smile at the kid staring at me expectantly. I nod. "Good. Thanks." Then I turn and head toward the stairs as Whitney hollers at me. I ignore her, pretending that the music is too loud to hear her. She doesn't understand what I want or need. Just like me, her future is already set in motion. We can't stop it, so we might as well make the best of what we have now.

School starts in a couple of days, and I have three weeks before I become someone's bitch. I hate to think that I might not be Saint's chosen.

A chosen is given to a Lord. She is his reward for going three years without pussy. She will serve him sexually no matter how depraved his fantasies might be for his senior year. But no one knows just how dirty my thoughts are. How much I crave for him to use me. In our world, we're brought up to be needed. Most won't understand it, and that's okay. But no matter what a Lord says or does, he needs a woman. Those three years of initiation are like you pulling a rubber band taut and holding it. Once you let it go, it's going to fly. Telling a man he can't have sex for those three years and then giving him someone to use is just like that rubber band.

Making my way upstairs, I suck down a few more drinks. Each one is so strong that it makes me think I'm going to vomit, but I manage to keep them down. I enter the room and am thankful there's no strobe light in here. Just dimly lit with blue lights that trim the walls and along the baseboards. Men and women sit around drinking, and smoke fills the large space from those getting high.

I spot Saint immediately over by the pool table. His back is to me. I drop the towel and toss it to a kid sitting in a chair. Haidyn sees me first, and he chokes on his beer. I've grown up around all the Spade brothers because of my brother. I've spent many summers and vacations with them because our dads are close friends. I'd be lying if I said I haven't thought about all three of them in my bed with me. But Saint is the one I think of the most. In my dreams, he's the one who ties me up and lets his friends have their way with me.

Haidyn slaps Saint's shoulder, who turns around to see what he's staring at. His green eyes drop to my legs and slowly run up over my body. Goose bumps cover my skin, making me shiver, and my nipples harden. When his eyes meet mine, his already sharp jaw ticks, and I can't help but smile.

I take another gulp of my drink, and he rushes over. Grabbing my free hand, he yanks me from the room. I giggle when he pulls me into another one across the hall. It's just the two of us.

"Something wrong?" I ask.

"Jesus, Ash. You can't walk around in just your bathing suit," he growls. "Where are your clothes?"

"It's a pool party," I counter, sucking down more of my drink. I want it empty and barely able to stand. The thought of falling into him sounds like a good time.

He crosses his arms over his chest, and I begin to drool at the way he glares at me. Heat rushes up my spine, and butterflies fill my stomach. I want to feel his hand wrapped around my neck, choking me. I want him to make me beg to breathe while my legs are wrapped around his waist.

I take another drink.

"Where did you get that one?" he demands.

I take another; it's almost gone at this point, and it doesn't burn as much, but I still feel that I might vomit. If not now, it'll happen later for sure. "Found it on the counter..."

"Fucking hell." He takes it from my hand and sets it on the dresser to his right.

I start laughing, and his eyes narrow on mine. "Last time I'm going to tell you...put some fucking clothes on." His voice wasn't as commanding that time, and his eyes are now on my chest.

I like that he thinks he can control me. My already wobbly legs step forward, pushing my body into him, and he stiffens. "Want me to take off my bathing suit?" I arch a brow. "Maybe you can help me." I turn, giving him my back, and I hold my wet hair for him to untie it.

"Ashtyn." His low and threatening tone makes me shiver.

"What?" I ask, looking at him over my shoulder. "I didn't bring anything else to wear."

He runs a hand down his face, letting out an annoyed breath, and the sight of his Lords ring makes my heart race. It's their crest—a circle with three horizontal lines through the middle. It's a reminder of how much power they hold. Every Lord wears them while attending the university. No one outside of the society knows what it means, but I do, and I wish I could explain how much it turns me on. "Find something else to wear, or I'm taking you home."

I smile, turning back to face him. The alcohol that I've consumed tonight makes me more daring than I've ever been before. I go to lean into him and stand on my tiptoes, but he stops me when his hand reaches out and wraps around my throat.

A moan escapes my lips when they fall open.

He yanks my face so close to his I bet he can smell the liquor on my breath. His pretty green eyes glare into mine, and I imagine us both naked, him underneath me as he fucks me on the floor, bent over the dresser, or on the bed. My pussy clenches at the different positions he could force me into. "Put some fucking clothes on. Now."

I manage to smile, but I'm sure it's lopsided. My lips have gone numb. "What if I don't want to?"

His eyes slide to the dresser to look at the drink mostly gone, and then back at me. "What's in that?"

"Not sure." I shrug, my hands coming up to wrap around his waist. My hands dig into the fabric of his shirt, feeling his muscles, and my eyes grow heavy.

"Goddammit, Ash," he grinds out.

I lick my lips, tasting the lingering alcohol. "Going to babysit me, Saint? Make sure no one takes advantage of me?" I arch my brow.

He lets out a deep breath, his green eyes dropping to my lips.

"Unless..."

"Unless what?" he asks, his voice now rough. I push my hips into him, feeling how hard he is. My knees threaten to buckle. I crave him so much that it hurts. His fingers are still around my neck, and I wish he'd just squeeze a little harder. Force me to my knees, and I'd open my mouth for him to use.

"You...want to take advantage of me?" I whisper.

The door opens, and he doesn't release me, but he looks over my head at whoever just entered the room. "Am I interrupting something?" Haidyn asks.

"No," Saint snaps as my shoulders slump. *If only.*

Haidyn speaks, "We gotta go."

"I agree." Saint releases me, and I take in a shaky breath as he grabs my hand. "I'm taking you home."

I roll my eyes, but he yanks me from the room, down the hallway, and out the front door. I don't even get the chance to tell Whitney goodbye. I'll message her tomorrow.

My brother stands outside next to Kashton, waiting for Haidyn and Saint. He spots me, and his jaw sharpens. "What the fuck, Saint?" he barks. "She's not going with us to the house of Lords."

"She's not," Saint agrees, opening his passenger car door for me.

He shoves me into the car. "I'm dropping her off at your parents' and will meet you guys there." With that, he slams the door shut, and I cross my arms over my chest, letting out a huff. But the smell that fills his car makes my thighs tighten. Fuck, I've wanted him so long that I've imagined him fucking me a thousand ways. And each one ends up with me on my knees begging for more.

I watch him open the trunk at the front of the car and remove something from it. Moments later, I see what it is when he opens his door.

A hoodie. "Put that on," he orders, tossing it into my lap.

"I want to go to my place," I inform him when he drops into the driver's side, ignoring the hoodie.

"Your parents are closer to where I'm headed," he states, pulling away from the curb.

"My car is here." I go on. "I drove."

He gives me a quick look, his eyes going to the hoodie before placing his green eyes back on the road. "I'll drop it off later."

Huffing, I lean my wet hair back against his seat, knowing it'll piss him off even more. The air conditioner is on full blast, and my nipples are hard. I'm no longer soaking wet but definitely not dry and very drunk. A part of me wants to reach over and unzip his jeans. But he'll just push me away. I'm sure as fuck not putting the hoodie on, though. I'd rather freeze to death first. If he wants me to wear it, he can dress me.

My heavy eyes close as "This Is Gonna Hurt" by Sixx:A.M. fills the confined space inside of his car.

SIX

SAINT

I pull up to her parents' and place my car in park. Looking over at her, I see she's got her eyes closed, head tilted to the side. Her pouty lips are parted, and her chest rises and falls as she breathes deeply. She's passed out.

It's for the best. My car smells like her, and it's had me so fucking hard. My hoodie is still in her lap, and my teeth grind at the fact I'm going to have to pick her up and carry her inside. I wanted to just drop her off. Watch her stomp into the house mad at me.

Shoving my door open, I slam it, hoping it'll wake her up. But when I open hers, she's still out.

Fuck!

Bending down, I place my arms underneath her and lift her from the car. I carry her up the stairs and into the house, then climb the grand staircase headed for her room. I lay her down in her bed, and she moans, her hips lifting off the bed slightly.

"Saint."

The sound of my name on her lips makes my legs weak. I sit down on the side of the bed, and unable to stop myself, I reach out, running my knuckles over the thin white material of her bathing suit top, brushing them against her nipples.

"Yeah, sweetheart?" I ask, my voice rough. My phone vibrates in my pocket, but I ignore it, knowing it's one of the brothers wondering where the fuck I am.

She arches her back, taking a deep breath. "I want you." Her pretty blue eyes flutter open, unfocused and heavy.

I smile, my hand cupping her face, and she leans into it, eyes falling closed. "You'll be mine soon, Ashtyn. I promise."

She's out once again, and I take what little strength I have, stand, and walk out of her room, knowing I have to do whatever it takes to make her mine.

I ENTER THROUGH THE OPEN GATE AT THE HOUSE OF LORDS. IT'S fifteen minutes from Barrington University. It was once a hotel that was given to the Lords. It's a weekend, so the gates are open because they're throwing their usual weekend party, getting ready for the ritual where all the seniors take their chosen. Otherwise, the gates remain closed to outsiders.

I take the long and curvy entrance faster than I should and come up to the renovated hotel. It's white brick with black shutters and has six columns on the large front porch. I follow the roundabout that has a pond and fountain in the center. Staying right, I drive under the breezeway and park in the back. I see Haidyn's bike, Kashton's car, and Adam's G-wagon. I bring mine to a stop next to them.

All Lords are required to live here throughout our years at Barrington. They're pretty strict on it up until your senior year. Then we're allowed a lot more freedom. Especially us Spade brothers because we spend so much time at Carnage.

I enter the building through the back and jump on the elevator, taking it down to the basement. Once I step off, I walk down the hallway and stride into the room. It's more like a bunker. Racks on the far wall display guns and knives of various sizes. The others already sit at the large table in the center of the room. All three of them look up at me.

"About time," Adam snaps, checking his watch. "What the fuck took so long?"

"I'm here." I avoid his question.

"Should have left her at the party," he bites out.

I choose to ignore him. He's been treating Ashtyn like shit lately. I don't like it, but it is what it is. The door opens behind me, and I plop down next to Haidyn.

Lincoln—a Lord who runs the house of Lords, enters the room with another man I've never seen before. He wears an all-black suit with a matching tie. His dark hair slicked back. He can't be more than twenty-five.

"Brothers, I called you all here for an important meeting." Lincoln steps back and gestures to the man that I notice he didn't introduce to us.

"Hello, gentlemen." He tosses us each a manila envelope.

I open mine up to see a woman lying on a bed. She's naked, her head hanging off the side, her neck slit from one side to the other. Blood runs down the edge of the bed and puddles onto the floor. Her ankles are tied together with barbwire. I'm guessing her wrists are too since her arms look to be secured underneath her.

"Over five months last year, twenty girls went missing. Five of those were found raped and murdered," he announces.

"The other fifteen?" Haidyn asks, scanning the picture.

"Still missing," the man answers.

Adam slams his folder down. "What does this have to do with us?"

"Did they attend Barrington?" Kashton questions before he can answer Adam.

"No." He looks at Kash. "All were still in high school—seniors—but none of the five were connected to one another. As far as we can tell, they didn't know the Lords existed."

"The ones who are still missing?" I ask.

He shakes his head. "Not that we have found."

"I'm with Adam," Lincoln adds, scanning the folder Adam put on the table. "What does this have to do with them?" He means the Spade brothers.

They have to think a Lord is involved and want us to step in and take care of it. The question is, why? What the fuck can we do?

The man opens up a briefcase and pulls out a single picture. His eyes meet mine before he drops it in front of me. I keep mine on his when he speaks. "The girl in the first picture was my sister." Deafening silence falls over the room. "The woman in this photo"—he taps the one that still lies in front of me—"was the last person seen with her."

Swallowing, I drop my eyes to the picture, and my heart races at what I see. "You said..." I clear my throat. "That none of them were connected to the Lords." My eyes raise to his once more.

"None were. Until now..."

ASHTYN

"Ashtyn?"

I ignore the woman's voice behind my back. It reminds me of nails in a blender. Makes your skin crawl and is annoying as fuck. And she repeats herself over and over. If she asks me how I feel one more time, I'm going to scream.

Maybe throw something. It'll give them a reason to think I'm crazy. I'm pretty sure my mother wants to send me away. Not sure why, though. It's not like she's actually raised my brother and me. In our world, the Lady—a Lord's wife—sits in the corner looking pretty while the nannies are the true parents. It's because of them that I've actually survived this long.

"Ashtyn!" my mother barks my name this time.

I turn around to face the two women. Leaning back against the floor-to-ceiling window, I cross my arms over my chest. She's been making me come here for years with her. You can say I'm in denial all you want, but she's the one who needs professional help. Not me.

"See what I mean?" my mother whispers through clenched teeth as if I can't hear her.

The woman gives me a big fake smile, pretending she didn't hear her. "How was your weekend?" she asks me.

I go to answer, "Fine," and my mother huffs.

"I caught her watching porn. Again." She reaches into her Louis Vuitton and pulls out a piece of paper. I'm not surprised she took a picture and then printed it off. Evidence, she calls it. At least that's what my father said he needed when she told him I was a sex addict.

You have to actually get fucked in order to be one. But whatever. My father understood that I'm not a sex addict. Do I think I could become one? There's always hope. I'm also twenty-one years old. How many women my age haven't watched porn?

Her therapist looks at the paper and frowns. "I thought we talked about this?" Her eyes meet mine.

I give them my back once again and look out the floor-to-ceiling windows. As a child to a Lord and Lady, they've been throwing sex in our faces since we were kids. Yet when we want it, they reprimand us for it.

Make it make sense.

I mean, I know the logic behind it. It's a test. They're always testing us. The Lords are made to remain celibate for their first three years at Barrington University while going through their initiations. Their senior year they get a chosen—a girl to fuck.

I don't know about you, but I think that sounds amazing. Fucking use my body. Show me what it's made for. Instead, I've had to get myself off.

My father is a Spade brother. All Lords have to offer their children to the Lords. That's why they reproduce in the first place. Their sons go through initiations, and their daughters must serve the men who make it.

But a daughter of a Spade? I'm given to another Spade brother. The next generation. In three weeks, my father will gift me to a Spade brother as an offering to his Lords. I don't know who it will be, but I know who I want. And the way he looked at my body at the party when I was dripping wet out of the pool, I'd say he wants me too.

Saint is the one guy I dream about at night. He's the one I imagine fucking me when I watch porn. He just has this way with his eyes. Like he's always undressing me. I knew he was going to the party. I overheard my brother talking about it on the phone. So I made sure to go, and I wanted to be in the pool when he arrived. Am I poking the bear? Yes. Do I want to see what it'll do once provoked? Also yes. But it backfired. I passed out when he drove me to my parents, and I woke up in my room all alone this morning. My car parked in the driveway without a text or call from him. Not like I expected one. I'm not his friend; my brother is. So I decided to watch some porn and try to relieve the pain between my legs that Saint left me with last night.

"Ashtyn!" my mother growls. "This is serious."

"I'm a virgin, Mother," I remind her. A part of us being a gift is that we have to bleed. The Lords are all about control. You spread your legs when you're told to. You kneel when you're told to. And you shut your fucking mouth when you're told to. "Not sure why watching porn is so intolerable for you." Lords kill people, and this is the hill she wants to die on? Sex? Pathetic.

"See..." she hisses. "This is what I'm dealing with. She has unrealistic expectations."

I roll my eyes and turn back to face them. I'd say that Saint will fulfill my expectations and even raise them.

"Tell her," my mother urges. "Tell her what to expect."

The therapist sits back in her seat, her eyes meeting mine. "What do *you* expect to get out of sex?" she asks frankly.

"Off," I answer, and my mother gasps. "From what I see, if he fucks you right, you get to come all over his dick."

My mother rushes over to me and slaps me across the face. It's not hard. She's too weak to make it hurt. She'd have to actually eat a meal that isn't liquid to have any strength. "You little bit—"

"It's okay." My mother's therapist interrupts her. "Ashtyn." She looks at me. "You understand porn isn't real, right? It's scripted just like anything else we see on TV."

"She was watching a gang bang." My mother grips her pearls. For being such a slut, she's really an uptight bitch. I know she's had her fair share of men. My father doesn't care who has a piece of his wife. Anything to keep her out of his hair. They both fuck others. All my father cares about is his loyalty to the Lords. Nothing else matters. If he were required to set me on fire in front of them, he'd do it. Thankfully all I have to do is spread my legs and get fucked. "A gang bang," she cries, covering her face with shaking hands.

"Better your odds. At least one dick has to be good." I shrug.

My mother's face turns red as can be, and she takes in a deep breath.

I mean, they can't all be fake, right? I've watched so many women come on my phone and laptop. I'm sure an FBI agent has my name at the top of his list. I make sure all the sites I watch are legit, and the actors are of age, but it hasn't helped my craving. The more degrading shit I find, the deeper I dig. I've heard porn can desensitize you. I believe it.

I just want to be touched, held, and feel skin to skin. I'm starving for something I've never even tasted. And I just know that once I'm able to get it, life will be better.

"Ashtyn, I'd like a moment with your mother, please." The therapist gives me a soft smile.

I don't need to be told twice. I walk out of her office and sit on the bench out in the hallway. My thighs clench, but I've never even touched myself. I've gotten off, of course, but it's been with vibrating toys. Only on the outside. Nothing inside.

Not all chosens have to abstain from sex for her Lord. But I'm a chosen for a Spade brother. We have different rules. And one of them is I have to bleed for my Lord. Prove I was worthy of him. He's gone three years without pussy. But the fuckers were able to fuck before then. I'm not sure which is worst. Never experiencing it or knowing what it's like and having to go without.

"Let's go." My mother huffs, exiting the office and slamming the door shut behind her.

I follow her to the elevator, to the first floor and out to her Bugatti that my father bought her for Christmas last year. Once we're in, I press my forehead to the warm glass.

"This isn't about you, Ash." She sighs heavily.

"Then why do you take me to see her with you?" I wonder.

"No. I mean the sex. A Lord—" She pauses. "A Lord takes what he wants when he wants it. It's not up to you to enjoy. It's up to you to serve."

"Is there a difference?" I mumble. We're raised to be needed. Being used sexually should be something we get out of it, if you ask me. I mean, without us, the Lords wouldn't exist. We're the ones who give birth to their children, adding to their numbers. The thought of being Saint's sex toy sounds pretty satisfying to me.

Bringing the car to a stop, she grabs my shirt and gently pulls me to face her. Giving me a soft smile, she pushes my wild hair behind my ear and gently touches my cheek where she slapped me. "You don't understand. And you won't until it's too late. Sex makes you feel things."

Isn't that the point? From what I've read, it's euphoric. An out-of-body experience if done correctly.

"I just hate it." She lowers her voice. "The fact that you have to be a virgin. If you'd experience it before, maybe it'd be different."

I sit up straighter. "Why?"

"He's not going to love you, honey," she states bluntly.

My shoulders fall, and I look down at my hands. "I'm not looking for love," I say softly. I understand that love doesn't exist in our world. It's sex, money, and power. Love is unheard of. Your own parents don't love you; you're made for a purpose not any other reason.

"Everyone deserves to be loved. I'm just sorry you'll never experience it."

I look up at her and see unshed tears in her eyes.

"I'm sorry," she whispers once again, and I have a feeling she's talking about something else now.

I swallow, all of a sudden uncomfortable. We don't have heart-to-hearts. She yells, and I say stupid shit to get slapped. That's how it's always been. "For what?" I can't help but ask.

"For having you."

My stomach sinks, and my throat closes up, making it hard to breathe. She just spoke the words I've always known, but she never dared to speak. If I were a boy, it'd be different. I'd be celebrated for getting a pussy to fuck soon.

"If you ever get the chance, Ashtyn, you run. Run like hell and don't ever look back. Do you understand me?"

I don't know where she expects me to go, but the fear in her eyes has me nodding. "Ye-ah."

"I mean it. You will never be enough for a Lord." Sitting back in her seat, she mumbles, "No woman ever is...and you're nothing special."

SEVEN

SAINT

I sit on my bed at the house of Lords, watching her on my phone. I have cameras in her room at her parents' house and her place. They've been there for over a year now. I was up all night last night with the Lords and finally dropped her car off at seven this morning. I wanted to go inside and see her so badly but made myself leave.

I forced myself to go home and get a few hours of sleep. When I woke up, I couldn't help it. I pulled up the footage of her in her room and watched her wake up this morning.

She left an hour ago to go to her mother's therapy session that I know she makes her attend. But on my cell, she's lying on her bed watching porn on her phone. I can hear the woman moaning and gagging as she gets fucked by what sounds like several men.

Ashtyn rocks back and forth on top of her duvet. Her teeth sink into her bottom lip, and her left hand massages her breast. She's so fucking needy it's adorable.

I imagine my sweetheart on her hands and knees crawling across the floor to me with tears in her eyes begging me to fuck her. To let her come.

"Saint," she moans my name, and I groan.

Fuck, I've never heard anything so desperate, and I've watched grown men beg for their lives. Nothing can top her.

I push my sweatpants down and grab my hard cock in my hand. I imagine her on her stomach lying between my open legs with her lips wrapped around my cock. Pretty blue eyes full of tears looking up at me as she gags. Drool running from her perfect lips as tears fall down her cheeks. It's a sight to see, and I can't wait to record her on my phone so I can show her how pretty she looks being my dirty whore.

Her head falls back, and she pinches her nipple, pulling on it slightly, making herself gasp. But she doesn't let go. Instead, she pulls harder, her teeth sinking into her lip to stifle a cry.

She likes pain. I've watched her push herself over and over the last year on the hidden cameras I have in her room.

Reaching over, she grabs the vibrator that lies next to her, and her room fills with the buzzing sound. She spreads her legs wide and places it on her pussy over her nude color underwear. She's never naked when she gets herself off. I think the thought of touching herself makes her nervous. Too afraid she'll go too far and end up fingering herself.

"Oh...God..." she moans, her hips bucking as she sinks further into her mattress.

I'll be the one she fucks soon, and she'll understand that God won't be able to help her.

Her phone falls from her hand, and she lets it lie next to her as she rides the vibrator. Her voice rises, and she slaps her free hand over her face. My hand tightens on my hard cock when she pinches her nose, restricting her air.

"Oh sweetheart," I whisper, loving that she's showing me what she likes. She's not afraid to experiment. She has no clue just how good it can be.

I'm not a virgin. I fucked in high school. The thought of having to go three years without sex during college was a challenge that I was more than ready to accept. But the moment I realized that the one I desired wanted me back was when I almost said fuck the Lords. But the thought of anyone else having her won over.

If I fucked her, I'd be kicked out, and she would be a used-up whore since she has to be a virgin for her Lord. I refused to take that chance. If anyone else fucks her other than me, it'll be because I'll allow them to.

I watch her hips buck, and she shakes her head while still holding her hand over her face and pinching her nose. She stiffens, and her neck arches as she comes in her underwear.

Removing her hand, she gasps and turns the vibrator off. She's panting as she throws it to the floor, and I look over the now wet stain that covers her pussy. If I were there, I'd tear them off and shove them into her mouth so she could taste herself while I bury my face between her shaking legs and force her to come again on my face.

After a minute, she gets up and puts her vibrator away and walks to her bathroom. The woman still getting gangbanged on her phone is the only sound I hear.

Moments later, her door opens, and I release my dick and sit up straighter. Her mom walks over to her bed and picks up Ashtyn's cell. Her mouth drops open at the sound of the woman gagging.

Just then, Ashtyn exits her bathroom now fully dressed, and her mother looks up at her. "Mom?" she shrieks.

"What in the fuck are you doing?" her mother demands, holding Ashtyn's cell up.

She crosses her arms over her chest and rolls her eyes. "It's just porn, Mom. Not like I'm fucking anyone."

Her mom huffs and stops the video before throwing it onto her bed. "Get ready. We're leaving in twenty minutes."

"Where are we going?" Ashtyn asks, stepping forward.

Her mother storms out without answering, slamming her bedroom door, and Ashtyn huffs. She knows where they're going and so do I. Her mother is taking her to see her therapist. She swears she's a sex addict.

She doesn't like that Ashtyn is curious.

My cell rings, interrupting the video, and I see it's a Lord. I take a deep breath and hit answer. This is the call I've been waiting for. He better hope it's the news I want.

ASHTYN

My mother and I enter my parents' house, and my father's right-hand man stands in the foyer. "Your father wants to see you in his study," he says to me.

I nod and begin to walk that way. My mother's heels clapping on the marble floor lets me know she's following.

"He wants to see Ashtyn. Alone," Dean calls out.

"I'm her fucking mother and will accompany her," she snaps at him. Grabbing my upper arm, she drags me down the hall and bursts through the double doors.

My father stands at the floor-to-ceiling windows overlooking the woods at the back of the property. "Altus—"

"Leave us," he commands.

She straightens her stance. "I will not..."

"Get the fuck out before I have you thrown out." His voice is calm as he swirls his scotch in the glass. He takes a sip, and I see Dean standing at the double doors with an "I told you so" look pointed at my mother.

She lets out a huff, and I drop my eyes to the floor. The doors slam shut moments later.

"Ashtyn?"

"Yes, Father?" I raise my eyes to meet his.

"The vow ceremony is soon."

"I understand what is expected of me." My mother has made it very clear she does not want me offered to a Spade brother, but it's out of her control. My father is a Spade brother, and since he has a daughter, I must serve the next generation. I'm currently the only daughter of a Spade brother among the Lords. The other three women who are chosens are from high-ranking Lords. The Spades only accept the top tier when it comes to pussy. And the Lords are like anything else—some hold more power than others.

A Spade brother is a Lord, but they have their own rules, initiations, and ways of performing the ritual when taking on a chosen. Other chosens have the option of accepting their Lord. I do not. I'm given away no matter what.

He finishes his drink before setting the empty glass on his desk. Pulling back his suit jacket, he places his hands in the pockets of his dress slacks. His cold stare meets mine. "You won't disappoint me, will you?"

"No, Father," I rush out. "I'm still..."

He holds up a hand to stop me, and I bite my lip. Running his hand down his face, he sits in his chair. "Your mother thinks you're out whoring around." He glares at me, and the way he says it, I feel he's still on the fence. "That fucking therapist she takes you to said you're too advanced for a virgin."

I flinch at his words. Sex is so openly discussed in our society, yet they don't want us to have it. It's like dangling a feast in front of a starving man. Most fathers in the world would never mention the word sex to their daughters. Yet my father is going to watch another man fuck me for my first time. "I don't understand what that means," I say honestly. "But I assure you, she's wrong."

"I guess we'll see, won't we?"

I swallow nervously. I've done my research, and I may not bleed my first time for several reasons. Like when I was twelve and spent my summer away at horse camp. Nonintercourse trauma is a thing. I've read up on it before.

"You may go." He drops his eyes to his computer, dismissing me.

I turn around to leave and see Dean open the door for me. Of course, he didn't leave when my mother did. I softly thank him for holding it open. Once in the hallway, I run to the grand foyer and rush up the stairs into my room. I'm going to grab a few things and head to my house for the week. I've had about enough of my mother for the day. She'll be watching me like a hawk now.

My black curtains are closed, so it's giving the illusion it's nighttime. I make my way to my nightstand and flip on the small lamp. Seeing a box sitting on my bed below my pillow makes me frown.

I untie the white lace and remove the lid. Pulling back the tissue paper, I find a folded piece of paper. I open it up.

> *I vow.*
>
> *You vow.*
>
> *We vow.*

Six words and fifteen letters that everyone in my world knows by heart. The vows we must take in order to give us purpose. They are what a chosen must speak to her Lord. Some even say it in their vows for marriage. It is an oath, a promise to serve.

My hands shake, and I drop the letter to pull back the black tissue paper. Inside the box sits pieces of leather of various lengths and widths.

Two are longer and wider than the other two. There's a fifth one thinner in width with a silver ring in the middle.

A collar.

I'll be a Lord's pet.

Something to be used and played with. The thought has my breath hitching and my pulse racing.

A light turns on, illuminating the room, and I jump back with a scream when I see a man sitting on the small couch by my bay windows.

He's leaning back into the cushions, arms fanned across the top, legs spread wide. He's dressed in dark jeans, a black T-shirt, and a Lords mask—white with gray lines on it that resembles cracks. The eyes and lips are black as if a bottomless pit of darkness.

I place my hand on my pounding chest and take a step back from the side of my bed as he gets up and walks toward me. He's in no rush, and I swallow nervously. I turn to face him as he rounds the end of the bed. When I step back, my ass hits my nightstand, and I whimper.

Coming to a stop, he stands silently in front of me. My heart hammers in my chest as my pussy clenches. My breathing fills the room. I'm terrified and turned on at the same time. I've felt this way while watching scary movies, but to experience it firsthand is like nothing I've ever known.

He just stands there, and I can feel his eyes on me. I shuffle on my feet in the silence, wondering who it is and what he's thinking.

Slowly, I reach my hands up and quickly pull them down. When he makes no move to stop me, I do it again. I lick my lips, and my fingers touch the tip of the mask on the chin and start to push it up.

A part of me hopes he stops me. I like surprises. The unknown. Another part is terrified that it's not Saint. And if so, I'm going to cry. Don't get me wrong, I love Haidyn and Kashton, but Saint is it for me.

Taking in a shaky breath, I push it up. The mask pops off his head and falls to the floor, and I look into a set of bright green eyes. I've seen them a million times, but they've never looked like this. Hungry. Forbidden.

"Saint." I manage to whisper his name, and a whimper escapes my parted lips when his knuckles touch my face.

"Sweetheart." He smiles down at me.

My thighs clench. This has to be a dream. "You're my..." I swallow. "I'm your chosen?"

"You're mine." He nods once, his eyes roaming my face.

I look over at my bed, and his hand drops from my face. "Are these from you?"

"They are."

My pulse races at his confession, and the blood rushes in my ears. Suddenly, the room is too hot, and I tug at my shirt, needing some fresh air.

"I can't wait to see you dressed in nothing but them."

I never understood the meaning of butterflies in your stomach until now. Nothing about his words are vulgar, but the thought of standing in front of him naked makes me nervous. Terrified actually. I've always wanted this, yet I'm still afraid of what's to come. What he'll do to me once I'm his. Last night, I was drunk, but now I'm sober and realize he'll be able to do whatever he wants to me in three weeks.

Avoiding his stare, I pick up the leather straps. I hold two in my hand. "What are these for?" I ask, although I have an idea.

"You'll wear these for the vow ceremony," he answers.

My eyes snap up to his. That butterfly sensation intensifies. "Ceremony?"

He holds the one in his hand out, and I give him a nod, like I'm curious. I've watched some fucked-up shit when it comes to porn. I know damn well what they are. But I'll let him think he's teaching me something. I have no problem dumbing myself down for a man who wants to feel superior. Especially if it's Saint. Sacrifices must be made in our lives.

He wraps the rough leather around my small wrist, buckling it in place. Then he turns it to where the small silver ring is at the top.

I pick up the second one that matches it in the box and hold it out to him with shaky hands. He places it on my other wrist as well. The leather that lines the insides, rub against my skin and make my arms heavy. "And these?" I point at the ones just a tad longer in length.

"They're for your ankles."

A tingle runs up my spine. I'll be strapped down when he takes my virginity. For some reason, that thought never crossed my mind. Did I expect it to be on a bed of roses with candles lit all around us while soft music played in the background? No. But I didn't think it'd be a BDSM scene either. Is he going to whip me too?

"So..." I stop myself, unable to finish my question. My breathing comes quicker and quicker. I'm excited but also nervous. I've read where fear can feel the same as excitement. So the fact that my underwear is soaked, I'd say both turn me on.

"It's going to hurt." My pussy clenches, and he reaches up, pushing my hair from my face. "But I promise to make it feel better later."

Translation—*when we're alone.*

"We've got to give them a show," he continues at my silence.

A show? "You want me to fake it?" I ask. Maybe my mother was right. She's been through this before and knows exactly what will happen.

"You won't ever have to fake it, sweetheart." He smirks. "If I want you to come, you'll come. If I don't want you to, you won't."

I frown, not understanding. "Why wouldn't you want me to come?" I've never seen a video where a woman doesn't get off. Usually, they come over and over. They make it look like the best type of torture.

He chuckles. "I have so much to teach you." Leaning in, he gives my forehead a gentle kiss and then turns to walk toward my door.

My pulse races, and I step forward. "Teach me something now," I rush out.

Stopping, he places his hands in his pockets and turns to face me once again. I hold my breath, waiting for him to leave. We're not allowed to do anything together. We've both gone this long, what's three more weeks? But the fact that he's here in my room, and I now know that he'll be my Lord, I don't want him to leave. I'm desperate to keep him here for as long as possible.

I look down at the box, desperately trying to find something. A shiny silver thing gets my attention. It's got a latch on either side. There are four of them, but I pick up one. "What is this?"

He takes it from me, answering, "It's a double-ended bolt snap."

I frown. Sounds like it belongs in a garage, not in the bedroom. "Will you show me what it's for?"

Stepping back, he slowly looks me up and down. I want to ask if he wanted me to be his chosen or if he got stuck with me. But does it really matter? No. He's the one I've hoped to serve, and I won't ask why I was so lucky.

"Get undressed," he orders.

I lift my eyes to meet his, and I stare at him in disbelief, but my nipples harden at the way his voice changes. Authoritative. Commanding. I have the urge to disobey to see if he rips them off me, but I don't want to take the chance of him leaving.

I'm not as drunk and as ballsy as I was last night at the party. I'm sober and terrified now.

He arches a dark brow at my hesitation.

Afraid he'll leave, I take a shaky breath and grab the hem of my T-shirt. I pull it over my head, toss it to the bed, then undo my bra. I let it fall and instinctively shield my chest with my hands.

"Modesty is something you'll learn to get over, sweetheart."

My wide eyes go to his, and he stares at me expectantly. He waits for me to follow through on my end.

Slowly, I drop my hands from my chest and undo my shorts, kick off my shoes, and lower them along with my thong. I stand naked in front of him, and my heart hammers in my heaving chest.

"Turn around. Hands behind your back," he orders.

I gladly turn my back to him and take a deep breath, doing as I'm told. He jerks on the leather around my wrists, bringing them behind my back, and places his hands on my shoulders, turning me to face him. "Better." He smiles, his eyes dropping to my bare chest.

Pulling on my arms, I realize the silver thing he held in his hand is now gone. It must connect the cuffs to one another with the silver rings attached to the leather. I get confirmation when I try to pull my arms apart from behind my back. They're tied together, and the inside of the leather rubs harshly against my wrists.

I bite my lip to keep from moaning, but my pussy throbs, loving the lack of movement. I've never wanted to touch him more than I do right now, knowing that I can't.

He walks over to the couch where he was when I entered and sits down on it. "Come here," he commands, and wetness pools between my shaky legs.

I slowly walk around my bed and over to him to stand in front of the couch. This is what I've dreamed of—Saint and I together. Me naked and begging him to fuck me. But my heart is racing. I never expected it to play out this way. And he's fully dressed.

"Spin around for me, sweetheart. Show me what I've waited to see."

Dropping my head, I do a slow spin, trying to calm my breathing and ignore my racing heart. When I get to face him, he pats his jean-clad thigh. "Have a seat."

It's hard, but I manage to straddle his right thigh. His hands go to my waist, and the touch burns my skin. "Push your ass back, hips forward. Open your legs," he commands as he spreads his wide, giving me room to do as he says.

"I—"

He slaps my outer thigh, and I yelp in surprise as the lingering sting makes my pussy clench.

"It wasn't a question or a suggestion. Do as you're told, or I'll gag you."

I moan, not even realizing it before it's too late, and he smiles at the sound. My cheeks heat with embarrassment, but I manage to position my hips, pushing them forward while I arch my back and push my ass back. My head drops forward when I realize why he wanted me in this position. The roughness of his jeans rubs against my swollen clit.

"That's it, Ash." His fingers dig into my thighs, pinching the skin.

I lift my head and move my hips back and forth. "Oh God..." I swallow and gasp in a breath as my hips pick up speed, rocking back and forth on his thigh.

"Look at how fucking needy you are, sweetheart." He lets go of my thigh and slaps it again.

I'm gasping. All hesitation I had a second ago is now gone.

Both of his hands leave my thighs, and he grabs my hard nipples and pulls them forward.

I cry out, hips now bucking in response to the pain.

"You like that?" He pulls harder, and my shoulders shake at the sting. "Fuck, you're a needy whore. Aren't you?"

"Y-es," I say, nodding. The friction of his jeans rubs in just the right spot. "God—"

He slaps the side of my breast, cutting me off. "There is no God here, sweetheart. Make no mistake, you will kneel for me, but the things I have planned for you are anything but holy."

I moan, knowing that I'll devote my life to him. I'll be his most trusted servant.

"You're going to beg me for it, aren't you? Like a good girl needing to be treated like the slut she is."

I already knew that, but I love how he makes it sound like a promise I'll make him keep. "Yes...please..."

"Please what?" His hand goes back to my nipples, and he pinches them harder than before. I find myself pulling away, liking the way it stings.

"Please, may I come?" I ask, knowing I'm so close. I've never come without a toy before. I didn't even know it was possible to get off without touching yourself in some way.

"Not yet," he answers.

"Saint," I gasp, "please..."

He slaps me across the face this time, and my pussy pulses. It wasn't like when my mother hit me. It felt different...sensual. I imagine it's what a kiss feels like, and I lick my lips.

His hand then grips my chin, my hair wild in my face. His free hand pushes it back, and I'm gasping for breath. "Did I say stop?" he asks, and I realize I'm no longer moving.

"No," I choke out, pulling on the leather cuffs that bind my hands behind my back. My shoulders burn, and my hands fist. I just want to touch him. To kiss him. Run my hands through his dark hair and pull his face to mine. My lips are parted, and his eyes are on them like he wants to taste me.

"Keep riding my thigh, sweetheart. Show me how desperate you are."

I start again, and my pussy is so swollen. I'm wet, dripping for him.

His one hand remains gripping my chin while the other pushes two fingers into my mouth. I suck on them but gag when they hit the back of my throat.

"We'll work on that. You'll spend a lot of time on your knees, sweetheart, while I fuck those pretty lips."

I whimper, loving the idea of that. "Yes, sir." I don't know why the breathless words come out of my mouth, but they do. I've seen it in the videos I watch, and it just felt right. Fuck, I'll call him Daddy if he wants.

"That's a good girl," he growls, slapping me again, and my hips buck involuntarily. "You're just a toy begging to be played with, aren't you?"

"Yes." I nod frantically. Tears sting my eyes, and my thighs clench both sides of his. "Please, play with me," I beg, shamelessly pushing my chest closer to his face, wanting him to pinch my nipples again.

"In time, sweetheart. In time." His fingers wrap around my throat, forcing my head back.

I stare up at the ceiling while tears fall from the corners of my eyes, and my hips move back and forth. When I swallow against his hand, it tightens, and my lips part, but there's nothing to breathe in.

My chest bows out, my thighs clenching the one I'm grinding my swollen pussy on. Stars dance across my vision as if they're falling across a dark night, and heat rushes over my skin like I'm on fire. My nipples are hard, and my tied hands fist. I stop, my body stiffening as a wave washes over me, drowning me in an endless ocean.

He releases my neck, and I suck in a deep breath. My body shakes, and he cups my face, forcing my head down to look at him.

He's smiling, but I can't even feel my lips right now. "You came all over my leg, sweetheart. Such a good little whore."

I blink, and fresh tears run down my face. My head spins, and my heart races. I'm high. I've smoked weed before, and it didn't feel this good. I'm giddy, like a schoolgirl who has a crush. I'm ready to beg him to give me another one. Saint can tie me up and play with me for hours if he wants.

Leaning in, he kisses my forehead tenderly and picks me up off his thigh. He places me on my shaking legs. Turning me away from him, he undoes the cuffs, removing them from around my wrists.

I let out a sigh of disappointment when my hands are free, and he places his on my back. "Bend over," he orders.

I drop my head and place my hands on the cushion of the couch, my already heavy breathing going erratic, scared and excited to see what he'll do to me next. My thighs clench while I stand on shaky legs.

"Don't move," he orders, and out of the corner of my eye, I watch him walk over to my desk. He picks up something and then comes to stand behind me once more. He places a hand on my back, and I frown when it feels like he's drawing on me.

"Saint—?"

He slaps my ass. "You're mine now, Ash. That means I can do whatever the fuck I want. Understand?"

"Yes, sir," I say breathlessly when his hand drops to my left thigh before going to my right. When he finishes doing whatever the hell he's doing, he grabs my hair and yanks me to stand. My lips part, and I gasp as he spins me around. His free hand goes to my neck once more.

Fuck, I knew he'd be this way, and I'm already drooling for him to tie me up and play with me again.

"Say it," he demands.

My heavy eyes search his. "I'm yours." I know exactly what he wants to hear, and I'm more than willing to do whatever it takes.

"Goddamn right, you're mine, Ashtyn." He steps into me, his

hand around my throat forcing my head back to stare up at him. "And from here on out, no one sees your body unless I want them to. Do you understand?"

I nod, sucking in a deep breath. "I understand." I want him to show me off. Be proud of me.

Letting go of my throat, he runs his knuckles down my heaving chest and over my breast. "I'll see you soon, sweetheart." With that, he exits my room like I didn't just ride his thigh like the needy slut that I am.

I fall onto the couch, staring at the now closed door, breathing heavily and covered in sweat. My mother was right. Sex makes you feel things. I've always been in love with Saint, but after what I just felt...I realize I'd crawl across the floor and ride his shoe while vowing to be his "good girl" to have that feeling again. It wouldn't matter who the fuck wanted to watch me.

EIGHT

SAINT

Goddamn!

I've never experienced something so fucking sexy before. And I've seen hundreds of Lords fuck their chosens over the years. At the vow ceremonies and at the house of Lords when they have parties every fucking night of the week. The porn I've watched. It was better than watching her come on my phone when she didn't know anyone was watching.

I didn't go against any rules. I didn't fuck her. But fuck, it took everything in me not to throw her on the floor, pull her ass up in the air, and fuck her wet cunt.

Reaching down, I adjust my hard cock as I walk toward the front doors of her parents' house.

"Saint?"

I come to a stop and close my eyes. *Fuck!* "Yes, Mr. Price?" I turn to face her father. He knew I was coming over after he called me earlier. He interrupted when I was watching her on my phone to congratulate me. I was to have his daughter. I grabbed the box I had stashed under my bed and rushed over here to beat her home so I could set up. I didn't expect anything to happen, though. Not that I'm complaining.

During our phone call, he informed me he wants me to be with his daughter as much as I want her. And I was excited to tell her that it would be me who fucks her at the vow ceremony.

He stands in the middle of the foyer, hands shoved into the pockets of his dress slacks. His eyes drop to my hard dick, and my teeth grind. The wet spot where his only daughter just rode my thigh until she came all over it is clearly visible. "Call me Altus."

I nod but say nothing.

"After all, I'll be handing my daughter over to you in a few weeks."

I'm going to take these vows very seriously. I'm going to carve them into her flawless skin, so she has a reminder of who owns her for the rest of her life. In case she ever tries to forget. "Did you need something, sir?" I ask, getting to the point.

He chuckles. "I just want to make sure you're aware of...well, my wife considers it a problem."

I frown. "With what?"

"Ashtyn."

"What about her?" I step forward. He didn't mention anything about a *problem* during our earlier phone call.

I know how her mother feels about the situation. I also know she can't do shit about it. It's a tradition. The Lords and Spade brothers have been doing things a certain way for hundreds of years now. It will never be changed. Do I agree with it? No. If I ever have a daughter, I'll have to offer her up as well to another generation of Spade brothers. The thought makes me sick to my stomach, but I'll burn that bridge when I get there.

"She's been seeing a therapist," he says tightly. Obviously, it's against his wishes. "And well, from what I've been told from reports, she's not a virgin."

I laugh, and when his eyes narrow on mine, I cough to cover it up. "You can't be serious." Ashtyn hasn't fucked another man. I would know. If he knew of all the times I've watched her, he'd understand just how obsessed I am with her.

Something catches my attention, and my eyes shoot to the top of the stairs just in time to see her step back from the second-story balcony.

"Ashtyn has assured me that she is." He straightens his shoulders, obviously uncomfortable with our conversation. "But I don't have to tell you what will happen if she's lying."

I stiffen at his words. "She's not."

He takes a step closer to me, and my heart beats wildly in my chest. "If she's lying, you will take care of it. Do you understand me?"

Chosens who do not bleed for their Spade brother are considered whores. But they do not get paid to spread their legs. They are used for those who do not know the Lords exist. They are drugged and fucked. Thrown to the streets. Given to pimps. They are shunned by their families.

He wants me to take his daughter and drop her off, hand her over to a pimp where he will sell her body to whoever wants a piece. Over my dead body. I will make Ashtyn a whore, but she'll be mine. And the only cocks she'll fuck other than mine, are those who I'll allow. "I understand, sir."

He turns, giving me his back, and walks down the hall. I exit the house and head toward my car in their roundabout driveway. Getting in, I start it. As I pull out of their driveway, my cell rings.

Sweetheart lights up the screen on my dash.

I hit answer, and my Bluetooth picks up. "Hey—"

"I swear, Saint." She sniffs. "I've never had sex."

I sigh. I was hoping she didn't hear the conversation, but it wasn't like we were quiet. "I know. I believe you," I assure her.

"But what if I don't..." She sniffles again.

It's fucked up that they expect them to bleed. Because I've slept with virgins while in high school who didn't. "I'll take care of it," I promise her.

"What do you mean?" she asks.

"Don't worry about it, sweetheart." I've waited years to have her. She's mine. I refuse to let the Lords take the one thing I want away from me. Not when I've already given them so much. They can have whatever I have, except for her. She's off-limits. "In the meantime." I change the subject. "I don't want you touching yourself."

"What?" She gasps. "Saint—"

"I mean it, Ashtyn," I growl.

She's silent for a second. "Are you...are you punishing me?"

"Do you want to be punished?" I avoid her question. The silence that lingers makes me smile.

I felt the way she grounded her pussy harder on my thigh when I dug my fingers into hers. Or the way she moaned when I slapped her. How she pulled away when I pinched her nipples. My sweetheart likes a little pain with her pleasure. I'm going to push that to see how much she can take. How much pain she'll get off on.

"No," she finally answers. Her voice so soft that I barely hear it over the roar of my car. We both know it's a lie. "But why can't I?"

"Because I don't want anyone getting you off other than me. That includes yourself." It's that simple. I'm going to make her beg me to come. I know she's been seeing a therapist. She's been seeing her for years. As for watching porn? My girl is curious, and I'm going to teach her things that will make her blush from embarrassment and cry for more.

"But the vow ceremony is three weeks away, Saint," she whines.

I imagine her on her knees, batting her long dark lashes, pushing her bottom lip out while she begs me not to make her wait. Fuck, it's a sight to see. "I didn't say you had to wait until then. I just said you couldn't do it."

"Oh," she breathes, and I adjust my dick inside my jeans.

I'm still so fucking hard. I can't wait to fuck her. I'm glad our first time together will be in front of a crowd. I've always been one to show off what's mine. And Ashtyn will be no different. Everyone will know she belongs to me.

"So..." She trails off, and I chuckle. "When—?"

"I'm pulling up to the house of Lords. I'll call you back in a couple of hours." I interrupt her and hang up, knowing exactly what she was about to ask yet refusing to answer. She'll get off when I decide to get her off.

ASHTYN

I'LL CALL YOU BACK IN A COUPLE OF HOURS?

Does he really think I'll lie in bed just watching my phone, waiting for him to call? If so, then he doesn't know me as well as I thought he did.

My cell rings, and I pick it up to press ignore, thinking it's him, when I see it's a friend of mine. "Hello?" I answer.

"Get ready. We're going out," she says in greeting. By the sound of the music blaring in the background, I'd say she's already out.

"How long do I have?" I ask, thinking some alcohol is exactly what I need. As much as I want Saint, I don't belong to him yet, and I refuse to let him keep me waiting on him.

"You at your place or your parents'?" she asks.

"Parents'."

"I'll be there in thirty."

We hang up, and I jump in a quick shower. I don't have time to wash my hair or anything, so I throw it up in a high pony. It's hot outside anyway. I just soap up, get out, and quickly throw on some clothes and a little bit of makeup. Not like I need to impress anyone.

Checking the clock on my phone, I see Saint left my parents' almost four hours ago, and I haven't heard a word from him. I'm not surprised, but it does piss me off.

I can't get off, and I'm supposed to wait around for him to call? What kind of test is this?

The thought of my mother being right pisses me off more than anything. He won't love me. It'll be all about sex. I don't mind him using me for sex as long as I'm the only woman he sleeps with. The thought of him being with anyone else makes me sick. But that's crazy, right? Lords aren't faithful. Once we take our vows, he's free to fuck whoever he wants. I'm the one that'll be tied to him, not the other way around. And he can pass me around to anyone he wants, so why would he only fuck me? I'll be the best fucking whore he's ever had. I'll make sure he never needs another woman. No matter what I have to do to show my devotion.

After I finish getting ready, I hide the box he left me underneath my bed so my mother doesn't find it. I wouldn't put it past her to snoop through my room.

I start to walk down the stairs, but stop when I hear my father's voice. "What the fuck happened?" he whisper-shouts. I can tell he's trying to be quiet, but he wants to yell.

"I didn't do it," someone responds tightly.

It's Adam. My twin brother.

We look nothing alike. He has my father's green eyes and lighter hair. I got the dark hair and blue eyes just like our mom. Except you'd never know because she bleaches her hair these days.

"Well, I received a phone call that you were last seen with her." Our father goes on. "How do you explain that?"

Adam sighs, and as I slowly start to descend the stairs to try to get a better vantage point to eavesdrop on them, the front doors open.

"Hey, hottie." My friend enters, spotting me on the stairs. "Hey, Mr. Price." She looks ahead down the hallway and winks at my father.

I roll my eyes. She's obsessed with every man she sees. But I'm jealous. I envy her. Her father isn't a Lord. She attends Barrington University. We're both seniors this year, and she's been sleeping her way through school since freshman year.

You don't have to be a Lord to attend Barrington. Men and women from all around the world come to the university. It's where the wealthy and elite send their children for what they consider the only acceptable education. It's a lie, really. The parents pay millions to make it look like their kids are smart. But they really skip their classes and party nonstop while the professors give them A's.

"I'm out," my brother announces, taking the opportunity that Marie just gave him to end his conversation with our father.

"Son—"

"I'll see you tomorrow," Adam calls out, rushing out the double doors.

I come to a stop and turn to see my father. His eyes look me up and down in disappointment. I overheard his conversation with Saint. It was embarrassing. To hear your father tell another man that you're a whore. Would I be if I didn't have to be a virgin? Most likely.

But I've wanted to give my V-card to Saint for years. I just wish it didn't have to be this way. I hate the world my parents have forced us to live in.

He steps forward. "Ashtyn..."

"I'm going out with Marie, and I'll be staying at my place tonight," I inform him, giving him my back and also rushing out. Marie doesn't know about the Lords, and I'd rather she didn't find out about the sick and twisted rituals that make up the secret society.

Rushing down the steps to her car, we both fall into it. We sit for a second until she looks over at me. "Everything okay?"

I nod. "Yep. Where are we going?"

Smiling, she answers, "to the woods."

I GREW UP IN PENNSYLVANIA. BEEN HERE ALL MY LIFE. So I might be biased, but it's gorgeous. There's nowhere I'd rather live. I'm not really sure what I want to do with the rest of my life, but it doesn't matter anyway. I'll be married off to a Lord of my father's choosing and then I'll be his faithful Lady. I'll cook, clean, suck his cock, and raise his children. It's what's expected of us. We don't get to have a career or drive to succeed. We serve our Lords just like the Lords serve their society.

We take the winding roads and climb the hills as she takes us to the spot where everyone parties. Senior year has officially started at Barrington, and everyone is ready to party it up. Every night of the week. It doesn't matter that classes have started. The professors get paid to pass us, not teach us. Most students have families that already run multibillion-dollar companies, so they don't need the education. They need the diploma to put on their wall once Daddy hands them the company to make it look like they worked hard for their position.

She pulls onto the road, her headlights shining on the gravel. So many cars are parked on both sides that it's hard to get through. Finding an opening, she darts into it, pulling her car to a stop in a grassy area.

We get out and make our way over to where the bonfire is. "You need a drink," she laughs.

"Yeah," I agree. Between my parents, Saint, and now my brother, I need to get out of my own head. The fact that I can't get off is eating at me. Is this how they feel when they're told they can't fuck?

I mean, how will he even know? It's not like I live with him. We've got classes, and he's always got meetings at the house of Lords. Not to mention, he has to go to Carnage most days. My father spends most, if not all, of his time there. I'm not sure what the fuck he actually does, but I'd rather not know.

We make our way over to where a few tables are set up. Rows and rows of liquor sit out. A few guys stand behind them with a cooler by their feet. They're filling Solo cups full of ice, then pouring the drinks.

Others who walk around have their own drinks. "Hey ladies, what can we get you?" asks a guy I know from Barrington. His eyes drop to my chest, and I try to ignore the ache between my thighs that Saint left me with earlier. I wanted him to get me off again. A part of me wants to test how many times in a row my body can handle it.

"Surprise me." I give him a smile.

"Hey, isn't that your brother?" Marie taps my arm, pointing over to a group of guys.

He has his back turned to us, but it's definitely him talking to a couple of guys. One I know better than the other. Tyson Crawford is a sophomore at Barrington this year. I've seen him hanging out with Saint at the house of Lords when I attended parties last year. The other guy is a senior. I only know him as Hooke. I'm not sure if that's a last name or a nickname. But he's a senior with the Spade brothers. "Grab my drink. I'll be right back," I tell her and don't wait for a response.

I make my way over to them and interrupt their conversation. "Hey?" I say, yanking on Adam's arm.

He turns around, looks down at me, and sighs, annoyed that I'm here. We've never been those twins you hear about who are so in tune that we can tell what the other feels or hear each other's thoughts.

We don't hang out very often. Even less so in the past few years. His life has always been devoted to the Lords, even before he started initiations. Then he had to move into the house of Lords our freshman year. No one in our family spends time with each other, though.

"What are you doing here, Ashtyn?" he asks, looking around over my head.

Hooke and Tyson stare blankly at me, and I avoid eye contact. Being around any Lord can be intimidating. They always make you feel small. Nonexistent. Especially the ones I'm not around normally. Makes me nervous. "I overheard you and Dad arguing back at the house," I say, ignoring his question. I don't have to tell him why I'm here. I'm an adult, and he doesn't own this land.

Hooke and Tyson dismiss me and carry on with their previous conversation, and my brother runs his hand down his face. "Always being a snoop."

"What was it about?" I place my hands on my hips.

He looks down at me, his green eyes narrowed with annoyance. "That's none of your damn business." Adam goes to walk off, but I follow him.

"Is it regarding the Lords?" I dig. They never tell me anything.

Just enough to keep me guessing. I wonder if that's what he was talking about with Tyson and Hooke. I should have listened before I interrupted.

"Fuck off, Ash," he growls over his shoulder.

I place my hand on his arm. "Tell me—"

"Get the fuck away!" He spins around and shouts. Everyone who heard stops their conversations to stare at us.

"Are you...are you in trouble?" I ask softly. The Lords have no problem eliminating you if they feel that they can't control you. He doesn't meet my stare. Instead, he looks over my head, jaw clenching. "Can Dad help you?" I go on at his silence.

He gives a rough laugh. "No, Dad can't help me." His eyes drop to mine. "Just like he can't make you a virgin again."

My mouth falls open on a gasp, and his laughter grows. "What? Like it's a secret that you're a whore."

"I am not," I say defensively, and I wonder if Saint already told him what I did earlier in my bedroom at our parents' house. I'm not dumb. I know guys brag when they fuck a girl. And although we didn't fuck, I did act like a fool and ride his thigh. I was exactly what Saint wanted me to be—his needy fucking whore.

"Whatever." He pulls his cell out of his pocket and types away on it. I stand staring at the grass until he puts it away. "You worry about your problem, and I'll worry about mine." With that, he turns and gives me his back, storming off into the crowd.

"Here you go." Marie comes up beside me and hands me my drink. I take a big gulp, trying to ignore the pit in my stomach. I know I'm a virgin, but that still might not be enough when it comes time for the vow ceremony. I don't know what I'm more afraid of—the punishment I'll receive or the fact that Saint will have to throw me away.

NINE

SAINT

I've been watching her for the past hour. Adam texted me that she was here at the party. His exact words were:

Your whore is here. Get her off my back.

Adam doesn't give a fuck that Ashtyn is to be my chosen. When I told him that I was picking her, he didn't even bat an eye. He knew a Spade brother would have her one day. And my day is coming soon.

I hit call on my phone for the tenth time and watch her press ignore while grabbing a new drink. I've seen her down three so far. At this point, she's pretty far gone.

I've stood back and watched her drink with her friend while they laugh and stumble over their own feet. It's cute really. That she thinks she can ride my thigh, and come on it, and then ignore me like it never happened.

She'll never be able to escape me. Not anymore. As much as I've wanted her, I've never let her know. Now I'm going to make sure she understands just how serious I am.

I send her a text.

If you don't answer my call, I'm going to take a belt to your ass.

She's laughing with her friend when she removes her cell from the back pocket of her jeans.

Reading over my text, I watch her start to type. My phone dings.

You'd have to actually touch me in order to do that.

I smirk and type back.

I can touch you all I want. I just can't fuck you...yet.

I watch her read it and then put her cell away in her back pocket. Grinding my teeth when she doesn't text me anything, I call it. Straight to voicemail. The bitch turned it off.

That makes eleven calls.

"I'm going to need your assistance." I snap my fingers at Haidyn and Kashton who are talking to one another next to me.

They both nod, not even caring what the fuck it is. My sweetheart is about to find out just what we're all about.

I sip on my drink while I watch her for the next twenty minutes. She's so drunk, and I wonder how she got here. Surely, she didn't drive, and I know she didn't come with Adam. He already left. He's got some shit going on with the Lords right now. I'm not sure what it is exactly, but it's not looking good. It's also not my problem. His sister, on the other hand, is my only concern right now.

I can't take her to the house of Lords until after the vow ceremony. So I'll have to take her to her house. I might just spend the next three weeks there with her.

Watching her stumble away from the party, I observe her friend going back over to the table for another drink as Ashtyn goes the opposite way. She shouldn't be walking around all by herself out here. I only trust about five men at this party. And two of them came with me.

"Let's go," I tell the guys as I start to follow her. She passes a few groups of people, a bonfire, and then proceeds to the cars parked out in a field. Walking up to a black Camaro, she tries to open the passenger door.

"Shit," Ashtyn hisses when she realizes it's locked. Spinning around, she goes to head back, but I put myself in her way, making her yelp when her body hits mine.

"Hello, sweetheart," I say, smiling down at her.

"Saint," she gasps, her wide eyes going to both Kashton and Haidyn, who stand on either side of me. She then looks to the crowd to see just how far away she is from anyone helping her. "What are you—" Her face hardens. "House of Lords, my ass!" She pushes her hips out with her hands on them.

She's so cute. "Let's go for a walk." I grab her upper arm and pull her from the car.

"I don't think—"

"I don't care what you think," I interrupt her. She tries to pull away, but I yank her to me. Bending down, I wrap my arm around the back of her legs and toss her over my shoulder. I walk farther away from the party behind us, into the tree line on the opposite side where the partygoers have made the field a parking lot.

"Saint," she squeals as her hands hit my ass. She yanks on my jeans like that's going to do her any good. "I'm going to puke," she whines as she bounces up and down.

"Then puke."

The guys laugh, and she lets out a growl, but her body slumps, no longer fighting. I stomp on branches, looking for the right spot. Thankfully, there's so much going on behind us that we have enough light to see over here.

Finding what I want, I set her down on her feet, and she sways a little. "Hold her." I push her into Haidyn, who wraps his arm around her neck from behind. She fights him, her nails clawing at his arm, and he laughs at her pointless attempt to escape.

"Calm down, baby girl. We're not going to hurt you...much," he tells her, and Kashton just laughs as she lets out a frustrated growl.

I undo my belt and nod to the tree behind them. "Place her arms above her head," I order.

He drags her over underneath the branches that cross low between two trees. Kashton grabs her arms and holds them up above her head while she kicks and screams. I step up to them and wrap my belt around her small wrists above the low-hanging tree branches. Tying them together, I secure her up on her tiptoes.

"Saint?" Her head falls back, and she looks up at her tied wrists above her head. She pulls on them, but she's not getting free. The branches are thick enough that even if she were to hang from them, they wouldn't break. "What the fuck?" she hisses, glaring at me.

"I told you what would happen if you didn't answer my phone call." She can't say I didn't warn her.

She's panting from her struggle with Haidyn and Kashton. I hold my hand out to Haidyn. "Give me your belt."

He smirks, staring at her as he lifts his shirt, unbuckles his belt, and pulls it free from his belt loops.

A whimper leaves her parted lips. I lick mine. I can't wait to taste her. "Let's get you more comfortable, sweetheart." Stepping into her, I undo her jeans and yank them down her tan and toned legs. I remove them and toss them to Kashton, who hangs them over the back of his neck and shoulders.

Without warning, I slide my finger into the tiny white lace thong and run it along her pussy. When I feel how wet she is, I push it into her.

She bucks her hips; her head falls back, and she moans. It's the sexiest sound I've ever heard. "Saint." She gasps, "Don't...please..."

"Still horny, sweetheart, even after you came all over my thigh earlier?" She's afraid I'm going to make her bleed if she hasn't already. But I'm not worried about that.

Haidyn widens his stance, crossing his arms over his chest. "She came on your thigh?" He arches a brow, watching the way her body rocks back and forth as I slowly tease her clit with my thumb. "That's something I'd like to see."

"Tell him, Ash. Tell him how you rode my leg like a horny bitch in heat."

She sucks in a deep breath. I smile when she spreads her legs wider for me. A not-so-subtle hint she wants more. "You were begging to come, weren't you?"

"Yes," she breathes.

I remove my hand from the material, and her body sags. Reaching up, I grab her knitted white crop top. I grip the collar and tear the material down the front to expose two white triangles. It's the same bathing suit she wore at the pool party over the weekend. I push them out of the way, exposing her tits to the warm night air.

"Saint!" she cries out, her body trying harder to pull her tied hands free from above her head while she twists from side to side.

I grab her hard nipples, pulling her body into mine, and place my face to hers. She's panting, and I can smell the cinnamon on her breath. "What did I tell you about being shy?" She whimpers, closing her heavy eyes. "They're going to watch me fuck you, sweetheart." They spring open and widen. "Once I get to use this body, they'll watch whatever I do to you. I might even let them play with you too."

Her pretty eyes well with unshed tears as I pinch her nipples harder. I have her right where I want her. If only I could fuck her cunt right now. It'd be the perfect night. "I think you'd like that."

She shakes her head, sniffling.

I smile. "It's okay, Ash. We're all adults. You like the idea of them both fucking you? Or maybe you like the idea of the three of us fucking you at the same time?"

She sniffs again, and I release her tits, lowering my hand to her pussy once more. Sliding my hand into her thong, I get my answer. "You're soaked now."

I yank the underwear down her shaking legs and wad them in my hand. "Open wide," I order and shove the material into her mouth before she can even comply. I grip her cheeks, pushing her head back, and a muffled cry falls from her lips. "It's time to get on with why I dragged you out here. I still have to teach that ass of yours a lesson. You don't want anyone to see you get punished, do you?"

She mumbles through the thong and tries to shake her head. *That's what I thought.* She wants to be experienced. She wants to be fucked. But she's still a little shy about it. And I like that. "Then keep these in your mouth." I release her face, and it falls forward as her heavy breathing fills the air around us.

I step behind her and look over her ass and legs. I wrote on her earlier, and I'm not even sure if she's seen it yet. "Kash, take a picture of this." I lift my hand, motioning for him to stand beside me.

Pulling his cell out of his pocket, he chuckles as he takes a picture of her restrained body hanging from the tree branches.

I take his cell and hold it out in front of her face. "Did you see what I did to you, sweetheart?"

Her watery eyes widen, and she mumbles nonsense into her thong when she sees **Saint's** written across her lower back—tramp stamp—in Sharpie and **good girl** written below each ass cheek. "I wanted to make sure you remember who this belongs to." I give her ass a tap and return his phone to him.

"Now, where were we? Oh, yeah. I've called you eleven times tonight, sweetheart. So you're going to get eleven swats." She shuffles from foot to foot, trying to pull free, and I like how her body struggles.

I take Haidyn's belt, double it over, and swat her ass. She screams into her thong. I do it again across the top of her thighs, unable to help myself. I love the way her skin instantly turns red. The black letters look even more prominent.

"That's two."

She's kicking her legs up, the heels of her feet hitting her thighs as she tries to use them to cover herself from me.

I slap her ass cheeks, making them red as well. She pushes her ass back, her legs clenching shut, and I get an idea. "Spread your legs."

Her shoulders start to shake. When she doesn't do so, I slap her ass again. "Now."

Tears fall from her bottom lashes, and I look at Haidyn. "Help her out."

He uncrosses his arms and steps in front of her. She twists and turns, trying to kick him out of the way. But he spreads her legs wide open with his, planting his shoes on the inside of her bare feet.

I reach between her legs again, unable to help myself. "Fuck, sweetheart. Your pussy is so wet." I press my front to her back and look over at the people partying not far from us. "Which part turns you on the most? The fact that anyone can come over and catch you tied up and at my mercy? Or the pain from my belt to your flawless skin?" I slide a finger into her, and she pushes back against it. "Or is it that Haidyn and Kashton are hard while watching me punish you?" A strangled moan comes from her stuffed mouth when I thrust in two. "Let them all watch you beg me to let you come." I remove my fingers, step back, and swat her ass once more.

She throws her head back and cries out, but it's not loud enough for anyone to hear.

Haidyn's eyes meet mine, and I nod, telling him he can step back. I can force her to get what I want, but I'd prefer her to give it to me. To submit and obey.

Standing in front of her, I grab her cheeks, and her heavy eyes meet mine. The tears run freely from her pretty blue eyes. "Are you going to listen to me from now on?"

She nods the best she can, sucking in a deep breath through her nose. "Spread your legs. As wide as you can," I order, testing her.

Sniffing, she places her legs out, causing her to arch her back and press her chest forward. Her arms strain above her head.

I tap the belt between her inner thighs, gently hitting her pussy, and she closes her legs with a cry.

Arching my brow, I tsk. "Did I say you could close them?"

When she closes her eyes, fresh tears roll down her face, and she opens her legs once more. "That's a good girl," I say, and she whimpers. "Leave them there, or I'll have the guys do it for you."

I tap her cunt once more with the belt, and her body jerks. I do it again, harder this time, and she cries out so hard that part of her thong falls out. "No. No." I shove it back inside, filling her tear-streaked cheeks. "Next time I gag you, I'll make sure to tape those lips shut."

Her shoulders go side to side, trying to relieve the pressure, and I tap her cunt again with the belt. She flinches but doesn't make a sound that time. She expected it, so I do it harder. Her hips buck. I do it again even harder than the last. Her head falls back. Again. This time, the pain forces a scream into the thong.

Her inner thighs and pussy are red from the smack of the belt. I would give anything to drop to my knees right now, throw her legs over my shoulders, and lick it better.

I drop the belt to my side and reach between her legs. "Goddamn, Ash. Just look at you. Tied up and dripping wet." She moves her hips, trying to ride my fingers, so I remove them. "This is a punishment, sweetheart. You won't be coming tonight."

She cries, tears rolling down her face to her exposed chest. I walk behind her, and she tries to look over her shoulder to see what I'm doing, but her arms are in the way.

"Now...where were we?" I slap the belt across her ass as I continue to remind her who the fuck owns her now.

ASHTYN

I WAKE UP, GROANING. MY THIGHS ACHE, MY ASS STINGS, AND my pussy is swollen. I'm naked but alone in my bed.

Thoughts of the night before come crashing back, and I bury my face into my pillow. Saint was at the party. He took me over to the trees, tied me up, and spanked me with a belt. Haidyn and Kashton watched like paying customers. It was humiliating, yet I loved every second of it.

My phone ringing makes me flinch as I sit up and see it lying on my nightstand.

My Lord lights up my screen, and I roll my eyes. Someone got into my phone last night and updated his contact. "He—" I clear my throat. "Hello?"

"Good morning, sweetheart." Saint's voice fills my ear.

"Morning," I mumble, rubbing my heavy eyes. Fuck, I need some water and something to eat. Not to mention pain medication. I have a pounding headache, and my wrists are sore. The skin around them is irritated where they rubbed against the tree branches they'd tied me from. I couldn't help but fight, even if I didn't want to be free.

I can feel the burn on my ass and thighs from the belt last night. I ache all over. My hand falls from my face, and I open my eyes. I scream when I see a figure standing in the doorway of my room. "Jesus, Saint." I fling my cell toward him as I lie on my back. "I have a headache," I say, covering my face with my hands to avoid the bright light coming into my room from my windows. "What are you doing here?" I don't even bother to look at him.

The bed dips beside me, and his hands pull mine from my face. "I'm disappointed, sweetheart," he says.

"I've gotten drunk before." I try to roll away, but he places a hand on either side of my chest, caging me in on my bed.

"I wanted you to ignore that call so I could tie you face down on your bed and take a belt to your ass again."

My thighs clench at the reminder of what he did last night. I swallow as his eyes drop to my chest and run over my body, remembering I'm naked. He's fully dressed in the same clothes as last night, letting me know he stayed here at my place with me.

"I should do it anyway after what you tried to pull last night."

My wide eyes meet his. "What did I do?" I don't remember past being spanked in the woods. Everything goes black after that. Who knows what I did.

"It took everything I had to stop you from sucking my cock in the car while I drove you home."

I can't help but laugh at that, and he arches a brow. "Funny, huh?"

"You make it sound like a bad thing." I'm still laughing. "You saying you didn't want it?"

He places his right hand on my face and leans down. His lips almost touch mine, and my laughter dies completely. I hold my breath, knowing it smells awful. "I want nothing more than to fuck this pretty face, sweetheart," he says softly, his eyes drilling into mine. He moves his fingers to run over my trembling lips. "And I'm going to. But when I do, it won't be in a car with you drunk off your ass."

I take a shaky breath, and he sits up, pulling his hands away. Pushing myself up as well, I lean my back against the headboard. "I hate this," I whisper. "Will it always be this way?"

He sighs, running his hand down his unshaven face. "The Lords have rules for a reason," he deflects.

"They don't make any sense," I growl.

"They don't have to make sense to us. We just have to follow them."

I roll my eyes and bow my head, rubbing my temples.

"It's only three more weeks," he reminds me, and I snort. It might as well be three years.

The sound of my phone going off with a text gets our attention, and he stands to pick it up off the floor where I threw it at him. He reads it and then hands it to me.

> MOM: Tomorrow afternoon at 3. I'll pick you up at 2:30. Be ready.

"Fuck this day," I say, tossing it back on the floor without responding.

"What's tomorrow at three?" he asks.

I curl up onto my side, facing him. "Therapy."

"Want me to go with you?" he asks, his fingers gently pushing the hair off the side of my face.

"No," I rush out, and he frowns. "God, no. You'll only make it worse."

"I just want to help."

"I know, but she'd just try to convince you that I'm a whore addicted to sex and watching porn." Aren't I? I've let him call me his whore. Fuck, I want to be his anything. He can call me whatever he wants as long as he lets me come. I kind of even like the fact that he doesn't allow me to. It makes it much more exciting and confusing.

"You make that sound like a bad thing." He smiles, throwing my own words back at me.

I pull on the covers, yanking them up to my neck, suddenly self-conscious that I'm still naked and he's fully clothed. "No man wants a whore," I say.

That's what my mom and her therapist tell me. Not one who actually enjoys sex anyway. We're supposed to do it because it's expected of us. You're supposed to do as you're told but hate it at the same time. It's all a fucking mind game that no one is supposed to figure out.

He gets up off the bed, and I roll over, giving him my back. I'm tired. I need more sleep and for this headache to go away. The text from my mother just made it worse. Yawning, I close my eyes, but they spring open the moment the covers are yanked from my body. I'm turned onto my back as Saint's knee digs into the bed beside me. He shoves my hands above my head, and I scream out, legs kicking as he secures them in place. "What the...?"

Positioning himself between my legs, he easily spreads them wide open, and I pant, looking up at him. "Saint," I breathe, yanking on my hands. "What are you doing?"

"Let's get one thing straight, Ashtyn," he says. Both hands grip my hips, and he holds me pinned to the bed. The soft sheet underneath me hurts my ass and thighs that he took a belt to last night.

"There's nothing wrong with watching porn. Or wanting sex. And there's sure as fuck nothing wrong with wanting to be *my* whore."

My breath catches at his words. The reminder of *Saint's good girl* in Sharpie makes my thighs tighten around his waist. He could write it on my neck for all I care. Let him show my mom that he wants me.

"Because I'm going to make you exactly that." His hand moves over my pelvic bone and between my legs. "They've got you brainwashed if you believe that shit." His thumb runs over my clit, and I moan, lifting my hips off the bed. "And although I don't like what they've made you believe, I have no problem undoing it. So, starting today, right now, I'm going to train your body and your mind to be my whore. And I'll continue to do so. Do you understand me?"

I nod quickly, trying to catch my breath.

"Say 'I'm going to be your dirty little whore, Saint.'"

Sucking in a deep breath, I whisper, "I'm going to be..."

He wraps his hand around my throat, cutting off my words and my breath. He lowers his face to mine and speaks. "Louder, Ash. Make me fucking believe it." He sits back up, but his hand remains around my throat, though it no longer cuts off my air.

I cough, sucking in a deep breath now that I'm able to, and arch my back off the bed. "I'm going to be your dirty little whore, Saint."

"That's a good girl." He smiles, satisfied. Letting go of my throat, I unwrap my thighs from his waist, and he gets off the bed.

I lie naked with my hands tied above my head while he reaches into my nightstand. He grabs a vibrator, then removes his belt from his jeans. He places it underneath my lower thighs, and cinches it tight, pinching my skin. "Saint?" I try to pull my knees apart, but it doesn't do any good.

"No penetration, sweetheart," he reminds me, and I groan, my clit throbbing.

"Then what are you doing?" I wonder, my back arching.

"You're going to lie here tied to your bed while I sit here and watch you get off over and over. We're going to train your mind to enjoy coming for me like the good whore I want you to be."

Turning the knob of the vibrator, he places it between my legs on top of my pelvic bone and turns the knob to high. My hips buck, a cry of surprise coming from my lips. "Saint..." I pull my tied legs up, bending my knees, knocking his hand and vibrator out of the way.

He turns it off, and I slump into the bed. "This won't do," he mumbles to himself.

I take a second to collect myself while he walks out of my room, leaving me alone.

I yank on my hands and twist my body from side to side, trying to free myself, but there's no such luck. It feels like he leaves me here for hours, but he returns with a rope dangling from his hand in probably what was more like five minutes.

Coming to the side of the bed, he undoes his belt from around my legs, and I pull my knees up as he goes to the foot of my bed. He bends down on the other side of my footboard and then pops up after a second. Reaching over the bed, he grabs my ankle and yanks it down, pulling it out to the side, wrapping the rope around and tying it off.

I yank on it to find he secured it to the bed somehow. "Saint... please," I beg, pulling on my arms as tears start to sting my eyes. I just want to touch him. Yank his clothes off and see him naked.

"I know, Ash. I know," he says as he grips my other ankle and ties it off to the opposite side. My arms are above my head, my legs spread wide open as he comes back over to the side of the bed and sits down next to me.

The sound of the vibrator fills the room again. It's turned up all the way when he places it between my open legs. I fight it, trying to pull my legs closed, needing to roll from side to side, but I have no choice but to take it. His eyes are on mine as I try to breathe through the first orgasm that rocks my body.

My lips part, but nothing comes out as my back arches off the bed, yanking on the ropes. He places two fingers in my mouth and orders, "suck on them."

I wrap my lips around them and do as he says, my body trembling and sweat beads dotting my heated skin.

"Good girl," he praises me, and I blink, tears falling from my eyes.

He begins to move the wand of the vibrator up and down my swollen clit, and I feel the sensation again. I try to shake my head, but he shoves his fingers farther down my throat, making me gag.

"You're doing so good, sweetheart." His green eyes are on mine as he smiles.

I blink, fresh tears falling from my eyes, and I suck on his fingers as he pulls them free from my mouth. He slaps my face, and my thighs clench. "Say it, Ash. Who are you?"

"Yours," I gasp, trying to wiggle my hips free from the vibration. I need a second to get myself together, but he keeps it in place.

He slaps the side of my breasts harder than he slapped my face, and my hips buck, that feeling between my legs becoming stronger. My breath hitches, and a cold sweat covers my exposed body. My lips open on a scream, but he shoves his fingers into my mouth once more. And I wrap my lips around them, sucking.

"That's it." He smiles down at me. "Suck on them, sweetheart. That's what a whore does."

My eyes grow heavy as they roll back into my head. My toes curl, and my breath is taken away as I come again with his fingers down my throat.

TEN

SAINT

I turn off the vibrator and toss it to the side. Looking down at her, I watch her heavy eyes dart around aimlessly. "Five times," I tell her. "I'll give you ten minutes, and we'll go again."

"N-o," she chokes out, shaking her head. Big tears run down her wet cheeks.

"Yes." Something like this takes time, but it's doable. People don't understand just how powerful sex can really be. How easily a body and mind can be trained. Manipulated. Our world is built off it.

It's like anything else. They train us for years to be what they want us to be. Why would sex be any different?

Fuck. Fuck some more. And then fuck again. Over and over until the body needs it in order to survive. It's like oxygen. You breathe without having to even think about it. The need to have human contact in some capacity is the same. Those who go without wouldn't understand it. Their bodies and brains don't think the same as those who do. And that's okay. But they're missing out if you ask me.

I get up off the bed, leaving her tied there and listen to her heavy breathing fill the large room as she shakes uncontrollably.

Picking up her cell, I place it on her nightstand. Nothing is wrong with wanting sex. Or watching porn. It's human nature. A natural instinct. Hell, even animals do it.

Sure, women are meant to be toys in our world, but that doesn't mean they can't enjoy it.

I get it. It's not hard to see her world from a woman's point of view. You show too much cleavage, you're a slut. Don't show enough, you're a prude. You tell a guy no, you're playing hard to get. You let him fuck you, you're too easy.

Ashtyn was made to be mine. I've always felt that way about her. And any man would be lucky to have her. That's why I'm going to take her. I saw her first and wanted her first. I'm in it for the long game. Even if that means I have to chain her up in my basement to keep her away from the world that seems to want to take her from me.

Her phone dings with another message, and I pick it up and read over it. Her mother again.

> MOM: We're going to discuss the vow ceremony. You need to understand the consequences of your actions, Ashtyn. My job as a mother is to prepare you for what's to come.

Translation: they don't think she's a virgin and want to make sure she's aware of what will happen to her when she doesn't bleed for me.

I close the screen and place it back on the nightstand before sitting down next to her. She's got her eyes closed, her breathing has evened out, and her body is relaxed. She's passed out on me.

"Wake up, sweetheart." I turn on the vibrator and push it between her open legs. She's so wet it slides easily now, and I love the sound of her cries when her eyes spring open. Her hips immediately start to buck the best she can since I have her tied down as tightly as possible.

Her neck arches, and she sucks in a deep breath before a cry rips through the room.

We have a long night ahead of us.

. . .

ASHTYN

I FEEL WORSE TODAY THAN WHEN I WOKE UP HUNGOVER yesterday. My body is fucking Jell-O. I have aftershocks from all the times Saint made me come yesterday and then again last night. I was so useless that we ate lunch and dinner in my bed.

When I woke up this morning, I was disappointed yet relieved that I was alone. I showered and got dressed. I didn't do my hair or any makeup. I threw on some cotton shorts and a tank top and called it good. I managed to get through my classes at Barrington. Thankfully, I only have three today. I feel like a zombie. All I want to do is go home and pass the fuck out.

Who knew getting off so much would be this exhausting?

I sit in my mother's therapist's office, staring at nothing, when a hand hits my arm, making me jump. "What?" I ask.

"She asked you a question." My mother growls at me.

"What?" I look at the therapist, who seems more annoyed today than usual.

"The vow ceremony is in three weeks. How do you feel about it?"

I shrug. "Not sure it matters. It's happening no matter what."

Her lips purse at my answer. "What about afterward?"

"When I'm no longer a virgin?" I arch a brow.

They're setting me up to tell on myself. It's only to save them from the embarrassment, and I won't do it. If I don't bleed, I at least want them to know what it feels like to be ashamed. They're allowing me to be fucked in front of a crowd, so they might as well get second-hand embarrassment.

I've heard of women in the past having sex and breaking the rules on purpose. They want any other life than this one, and it's their way out. But it only works if you're given to a Spade brother. A chosen picked for the vow ceremony doesn't have to be pure for her Lord.

That's why they dunk them in the baptism pool—to clean them of past sexual partners.

"I think..." She pauses, frowning. "You're twenty-one, Ashtyn. You go out, party, get drunk. I think that maybe you experienced more than you are aware of."

"Maybe you were raped," my mother adds, nodding to herself.

I run a hand down my face. "Mom..."

"It's happened, Ashtyn. Women go out, get drunk, and wake up the next day with no memory of what happened."

I know. I did that. Apparently, I was trying to suck Saint's dick the night he took me home from the bonfire party. Do I believe him? Absolutely. I would have let him fuck me a long time ago if it had not been for the Lords and their stupid rules.

"Men take advantage of girls in situations like that. Maybe we should call the doctor. Have him check you," my mom offers.

You can't check for virginity. I've googled that before to see. And there's no way you can tell. "Did both of you bleed your first time?" I ask.

"Of course." My mother huffs. Otherwise, she wouldn't be my mother. My father would have given her away, and her family would've shunned her. Then he would have gone on to marry another woman, and I would not exist. A Spade brother doesn't have to marry his chosen, but my father did end up marrying my mother.

The therapist, however, I don't know her past or her personal life. I understand it's none of my business, but if she wants to get personal, then let's get personal. "This conversation isn't about us." She refuses to answer my question.

I stand, and my mother does as well. "Ash—"

"I'm leaving, Mom. I'm going home. I'm tired, and you guys can't tell me anything that I don't already know." With that, I walk out of her office and get in the elevator. I make my way down to the first floor and out to my car.

When I woke this morning, my mother texted me yesterday that she would pick me up. I told her I'd meet her here because I was staying late at Barrington to do some research and didn't have time to go to my place. It was a lie. I wasn't about to be stuck in the car with her again after another session.

I drive to my place in silence, and it doesn't help me any. If anything, it makes me even more on edge. They're making me doubt my body and myself.

Pulling up to my house, I get out and walk in through the front door. I drop my purse, keys, and phone on the floor, not caring about any of them. I make my way to my bedroom and push the door open. I come to a stop when I see Saint sitting on the edge of my bed.

My eyes scan the piece of rope laid out. Day two of my training, and honestly, it's exactly what I need. Force me to come over and over until I can't speak clearly and just pass the fuck out.

When my eyes meet his, the smile drops off his face. "Ashtyn." He jumps to his feet and rushes over to me. "Hey." His voice softens. "What's wrong?" His bright-green eyes search mine, and I don't realize I'm crying until he wipes the tears from my face.

I shake my head, the knot in my throat keeping me from forming a word. He wraps his arms around me, and I cling to him as he holds me.

"I'm going to take care of it," he says as if he knows why I'm upset.

I'm not even sure why I'm crying. The rules, the society, the pressure. Hell, it could be my damn period for all I know. Maybe I just need a nap or a stiff drink. I feel like I'm yelling in a room full of people, and no one is listening to what I have to say. Seriously? How many times do I need to have the same conversation with my mother and her therapist? I guess the answer to that is until Saint fucks me in front of the Lords. That day will change everything. My future, my chance at being with him. I have a fifty-fifty shot of spending the next year with him or being sent away for the rest of my life.

"I'm going to take care of it," he repeats, but I feel like he's trying to convince himself more than me.

I manage a nod, but I don't believe him.

ELEVEN

SAINT

I stand next to her bed while she lies tied to it. She's naked, and her body shakes from spending another night coming for me on her vibrator.

She needed out of her own head. Her mother and her therapist have spent years brainwashing my sweetheart. I've only been doing it for a couple of days, but I'm going to win. I'll make sure of it.

Putting the vibrator back in her nightstand, I then begin to untie her. Once her legs and arms are free, I crawl onto her bed, and she rolls into me, burying her face into my chest. She sobs, and I wrap my arms around her. I'm not sure if it's from overstimulation or her session with her mother's therapist. It could be a combination of both, really.

I lie on my side, fully dressed while she clings to me naked until her sobs subside and her body softens.

I gently roll her onto her back and run my knuckles down her soft cheeks. They're still wet from her tears that she cried while she begged me to stop. I didn't. It's for the best. I want her to know it's okay to want something that others see as inappropriate.

If she were to wake up right now and tell me that she wanted me to tie her down and line men up to fuck her, I wouldn't judge her. I'd tell her fuck no, but I wouldn't think any less of her.

My cell rings, and I stand to remove it from my pocket. ***Dad*** flashes across my screen, and I answer. "Hello?"

"I need you at Carnage," he says in greeting. "Now."

Sighing, I look over her sleeping body, knowing she's had enough for tonight. "Be right there."

He hangs up, and I pocket my cell. Leaning over the bed, I give her forehead a soft kiss, then cover her sleeping body with the covers.

I exit her house, locking it up and placing my key into my pocket. She has no clue I made one when her dad bought her the house last year. As I walk down the steps, my cell rings again, and I growl, pulling it out. *What now?*

It's Haidyn. "Hey—"

"Where are you?" he demands, sounding pissy.

"On my way to Carnage." I avoid telling him I'm at Ashtyn's. It's none of his business where I am.

He hangs up without saying another word, and I pocket my phone once more. Approaching my bike parked in her driveway, I remove my helmet from where it hangs off my mirror. Usually, I take it with me everywhere I go so no one can steal it, but that won't happen at her place. It's a gated community. They have two guards who are at their gate twenty-four seven.

After I slide it over my head, I fasten it under my chin. Then I pick up my leather jacket that I had lying over the seat and pull it on as well. It's not for safety, more for the fact that it hides who I am while on it.

Lords are raised to wear masks and cloaks most of the time. We're placed in a world where no one knows our power. We've had to hide our true identity for years. It's a hard habit to break.

Starting up the bike, I put it in gear and take off out of her driveway. I'm headed to Carnage to find out what the fuck is going on.

Carnage is a city of its own, covering hundreds of thousands of acres in the middle of nowhere tucked into the mountains. Although we're Lords, we are meant to be secluded. One day, we'll run this place that no one knows exists, and although I never wanted it, I've accepted it.

I stop at the gate, pressing in the code, and it opens, allowing me entry. I rev the engine on the bike before taking off through it and lean into the curves more than I need to on the winding road lined with trees. I come up to the circle drive when the main building comes into view. But I take the side road, going behind it.

I park my bike at the back and get off, then remove my helmet and jacket, leaving them both with the bike. Rushing up the steps, I enter the back entrance and take the elevator down to the basement. If our fathers want us here, it's only for one reason.

Stepping off the elevator, I suck in a breath of cold air and walk down the hallway to the open room. Haidyn leans against the wall, arms crossed over his chest. Kashton sits in a chair, leaning back comfortably. Adam stands in the middle, glaring at his father, who stares at me like he knows I've spent the past two days tying his daughter to her bed and forcing her to come for me until she's a sobbing, blubbering mess.

I want her mind filled with me. Every thought she has consumed by me. I'm going to erase everything and anything her piece-of-shit mother has put into her head. All she'll know is begging, crawling, and coming for me.

"Boys," my father states, entering behind me.

"Is there a reason we're here?" Kash asks with a sigh, looking down at his watch. He was obviously in the middle of something when he received his phone call to come here.

"Yes." My father claps his hands once. "And it's going to take all night. So cancel whatever plans you have."

ASHTYN

It's been a week since Saint started *training* my body. I'm always sore. My body is weak, but it's working. All I think about is when he'll show up and tie me down and force me to come.

I look forward to it. I go to classes during the day, then rush home, get naked, and shower so I'm ready for whenever he decides to show up. It's been less and less the past few days. I've been getting texts about him having to be at Carnage. I don't know why, but I feel my father has something to do with it.

My mother has been blowing up my phone. I've missed two appointments with her and her therapist this week because I was coming all over myself while Saint told me I was his *good girl.*

So when he canceled on me again tonight, I decided to call Whitney. She's always up for going out and getting drunk. I'm on my third drink and feeling pretty good. We're out at the field with bonfires, and I stand in the center of it, looking over at the woods and remembering how he tied me up, stripped me naked, and spanked my ass in front of Kashton and Haidyn.

The Sharpie words have almost faded completely, and the marks from the belt have healed. It no longer hurts to sit down or shower. I want him to do it again. Maybe I'll ignore him the next time he calls so he'll punish me.

"Here you go." Whitney comes up next to me, handing me a new drink.

"Thanks," I mumble.

"Why are you in such a funk?" she asks, taking a sip of hers. "Don't tell me it's over Saint?" When I don't answer, she rolls her eyes. "He's not worth it, Ash. I promise you, there's someone better out there for you." She takes another sip, and her eyes zero in over the rim of her cup as Tyson Crawford walks by with a group of guys from Barrington.

I take a drink from the cup and then another. My body is begging to get off tonight. In less than a week, I've become a needy slut for Saint and my vibrator just like he wants. I can't imagine what it'll be like once he can actually fuck me, but I'm looking forward to it.

My cell rings, and I pull it out of my back pocket to see it's my mother. I press ignore and go to put it back, but it immediately rings again. "Hello?" She's not going to stop.

"Where are you at?" she demands.

I look around at the party in the middle of nowhere and take another sip of my drink. "Home."

"Don't lie to me, Ashtyn. I'm at your house right now."

I can't help but laugh. I'm not wasted, but I feel pretty good.

"ASHTYN!" she screams in my ear.

"I'll be home later." I hang up and turn off my cell, knowing she won't stop. I'll call her tomorrow. Maybe.

I lift the cup to my lips, and instead of taking a sip this time, I suck it down. Holding my breath, I swallow as much as I can and gasp when I pull it away. Looking into the cup, I find it only has a little left, so I down the rest.

Walking over to the table, I set my empty cup down and ask, "Another, please."

"Have you seen this?" Whitney asks, holding her phone out to me. She's got her social media pulled up. It's a picture of a bleach blond. She's smiling while wearing a black and gold cheerleader uniform. Her bright blue eyes shine, and her bleached teeth sparkle.

"No. Who is it?" I ask, waiting for my new drink.

"She's gone missing." She slides to a video, and it shows the girl walking through a parking lot and getting into a white BMW. "This was the last place she was seen." Whitney goes on. "Found her car two miles down the road from the football field. Abandoned. No purse. No phone. Nothing. It was still running, and the driver's side door was wide open."

"Here you go." The guy hands me a fresh drink, and I thank him.

When we start to walk away from the table, she speaks, "I heard that Adam was the last one to see her."

I come to a stop with my drink paused at my lips. I frown, shaking my head. "Don't believe everything you hear." My brother is a douche, and I hate him most days, but he doesn't kidnap women. My father would kill him if that were the case. The Lords are too important for him to be fucking his chances. And a Lord involved with something like this would get the Lords' attention.

A thought hits me, and I think back to the argument my father was having with my brother the other day at their house. And my pulse begins to race. Surely, he's not involved. I don't believe it. Adam would never...

I throw back my drink and gulp it down.

Hours later, Whitney pulls up to my house, and I stumble inside. I'm dying of thirst, so I make my way to the kitchen to grab a water.

Flipping on the light, I blink rapidly at the harshness. I come to a stumbling stop when I see Saint sitting at my kitchen table. He's dressed in his black hoodie, dark jeans, and his mask. The rope he uses to tie me to my bed sits on top of the table in front of him.

As much as I want to do a training session, I'm too drunk for that tonight. "You..." I hiccup. "Can leave." I reach down and remove my shirt, tossing it across the room. Then I stumble from foot to foot as I kick off my shoes. While I make my way to the fridge, I undo my jeans.

Opening it up, I lean over and grab what I want. I close the door to find him now standing beside it. "I mean it..."

He wraps his hand around my throat, squeezing and taking away my air. My hand drops the water, and I go limp. My eyes instantly grow heavy as my vision goes in and out while staring into his black eyes on the mask. I've drunk too much; my body can't fight him, and it doesn't want to.

My lips part, and I try to suck in a breath, but all it does is make my pussy throb when I get nothing. Hands grab my body, and my arms are pulled behind my back. Something is placed around them, and I can't pull them apart.

He lets go of my neck, and I fall to my knees, unable to hold myself up. The room spins, and I suck in a breath that burns my throat. I begin to cough. A fist grabs my hair, and my head is yanked up. I see three blurry figures. Two stand in front of me, and one at my back holds my head up.

I blink, my eyes so heavy. "Not tonight, Saint," I slur, my tongue heavy. "I...can't." I'm too tired; I drank too much. The thought of his fingers down my throat makes me want to gag. I'm going to get sick soon.

The hand in my hair lets go, and my head falls forward. Unable to stop myself because I no longer have use of my hands, I fall face-first to the floor and shiver at how cold the marble is. My eyes close as I'm lifted into the air.

TWELVE

SAINT

I pull my bike up to Carnage and put in the code, opening the wrought-iron gates. Then I'm driving down the curvy two-lane road before the trees open up, and it comes into view.

I've spent more time here in the last week than I've wanted to. But it is what it is. The Lords are very strict on what we can and can't do. And right now, I can't abandon my responsibilities no matter how much I want to. Especially for pussy.

We graduate with honors from Barrington University without even attending a single class. Because the Lords already know where we're going to be placed out in the real world.

There are judges, doctors, attorneys, teachers, and those in law enforcement. You name it, we've got a Lord on the payroll. Some of us are just more successful than others. It all has to do with your bloodline and where you fall in the Lords world.

Getting off my bike, I run up the stairs and through the double doors that squeak, announcing my entrance.

I make my way over to the elevator and take it up to the seventh floor. I enter the Spade brothers' office. "You wanted to see me," I say to Mr. Price.

He looks up at me from his desk. He's the only one here, thankfully. Otherwise, my father would want to know what I'm doing. I don't even know what the fuck we're doing. He had sent me a text this morning to meet him here first thing. Alone. I wasn't about to turn him down when the chosen ceremony is so close.

"I need to show you something," he says, straightening his suit jacket.

"Okay," I say slowly.

"But first I need you to understand that you can't act on this."

I cross my arms over my chest.

"Saint," he growls. "You have to promise."

What could be so important that he's making me promise? Surely, he doesn't take that shit seriously? What's next? Make us cross our pinkies like we're little girls agreeing to keep a secret? "You have my word." I lie. I'm not agreeing to shit when I don't have all the facts.

Sighing, he picks up the remote and turns on the TV that hangs on the wall.

I step closer as a video begins to play. The sound of Ashtyn's soft sobs fills the room as the video shows me with his daughter tied to her bed with my fingers down her throat while she comes all over the vibrator that I hold between her shaking legs.

"Did you really think I'd buy her a house without placing surveillance inside?" he questions.

I take a deep breath and turn to look him in the eyes. "I didn't break any rules," I say through gritted teeth. The fact that he watches his daughter in her room on a daily basis should be the sick part. But add the fact he's also watched me get her off? But then again, a part of me isn't all that surprised. He'll be watching me fuck her soon in front of an audience anyway.

"I'm aware." He nods. "But this one tells a different story." He presses play once more, and this time, there is no audio.

But I can see it all play out in front of me like a scary movie. Only it's not scripted. It's real.

My breathing picks up as I clench my hands. "No," I manage to say, shaking my head, not believing my own eyes. It ends, and the TV shuts off.

I realize I'm shaking when a hand lands on my shoulder, and I jump back.

"Son," he says. "Remember the conversation we had at my home the other day?"

I nod. It's all I'm capable of.

"You know what to do, then?"

Another nod.

"You keep my secret, and I'll keep yours."

ASHTYN

I'M SITTING ON MY BED, AN EMPTY BOTTLE OF WINE IN MY HAND watching a documentary about a serial killer who murdered over fifty people in a ten-year span. My first thought is that he's a Lord. To get away with that many murders in this day and time? They have to know who he is, where he's been, and who his victims are.

That tells me they're letting him get away with it. Or maybe the detectives on the case are the Lords and they're told to stay one step behind. Either way, someone involved has the Lords crest branded on their chest.

I turn the channel, and it's the news. I sit up when I see a brunette on it. Another missing girl. She's nineteen and just started her freshman year at college. Her mother last saw her for lunch three days ago. Her mother called her that evening, and she never returned it. The girl's car was also abandoned and empty, with the driver's side door open.

It shows her mom and dad at a press conference. They're holding up a picture of her. The mother is too distraught to speak while the father pleads for her to come home. If someone has her to just let her go. I hate it for them. For her. But a part of me wishes I had a family like that. One that would care if I went missing. Instead, my family will toss me to the side when I don't do what my body is "required" to do.

My door opens, and I look over to see Saint enter my room. It's been three days since I saw him. No call, no text, nothing. Which tells me one thing—he's been at Carnage.

My father does the same to my mother. Goes off the grid. Then he comes home, and she yells at him until he leaves again. God, that has to be such a miserable life. Always so unhappy or having to fake it. No wonder she hates it so much.

"What do you want, Saint?" I ask, lifting the wine bottle to my lips, but I frown when I'm reminded it's empty.

He shoves his hands into the pockets of his jeans. Fuck, he looks delicious. He's wearing a white T-shirt and combat boots with a black leather jacket, which tells me he rode his bike over here. He's got a hat on backward that his dark hair peeks out from underneath. I hate that he's seen me naked, yet I haven't seen him.

"How drunk are you?" he asks flatly.

I frown, wondering if he's mad at me, and that's why he's ignored me. What happened to our three weeks of training? I've been looking forward to being tied up and forced to come all over myself. "Not drunk enough." I toss the bottle on the floor, and it rolls along my white carpet until he places his boot out to stop it. I mean, really what else is there to do?

His eyes drop to the empty bottle and then rise to meet mine. "Looks like you've had more than enough to me."

I get up off the bed, and he looks over my bare legs. All I have on is an oversized T-shirt. It's his. I've had it for several years. He left it at my parents' one night after he and his friends came over when my brother had a swimming party. I've never worn it around him until now.

Reaching down, I grab the hem and pull it up and over my head, tossing it to the side. He arches a brow at me. I've become quite comfortable with being naked around him in the past week and a half. When the man you're in love with strips you naked, ties you down, and gets you off with a vibrator between your legs while he stays fully dressed, you no longer have the urge to cover up your body. And then add the times he's stripped you in front of his friends...He was right; modesty no longer matters.

"Ashtyn." The way he growls my name was meant as a warning, but all it does is make me shiver with anticipation.

I've never seen this guy naked, and all I want is for him to use me. "What?" I place my hands out wide. "You're here for a reason, right? To play with me."

He shakes his head and crosses his arms over his chest. I have a feeling it's to fight the urge to touch me. At least that's what I tell myself. I want to be irresistible. I want him to lose control. He's so close.

"Not tonight," he finally speaks, his eyes still on my chest.

I lick my lips before pushing my bottom one out. He thinks I'm drunk, but I'm not even close. "Why not?" Before he can even answer, I pretend to trip and fall into him. His arms wrap around my hips, and I throw mine around his neck. Lifting on my tiptoes, I push my lips to his and kiss him.

His arms release me to remove mine from his neck, and he pushes me back. I open my heavy eyes and look up at him. He's frowning at me as if disappointed. "What are you doing, Ashtyn?" He growls.

"Just fuck me," I say.

"Ash—"

My hands drop to his belt, and I undo it. Then I fumble with the button on his jeans and zipper.

"Ash! Stop," he barks out, stepping back.

I start to get angry. "What the fuck, Saint? Just fuck me already."

"I can't do that, and you know it."

I roll my eyes. "We both know that I'm not going to bleed when you fuck me. So just do it now."

"I can't," he says through gritted teeth. "And I told you I'd take care of it."

"You can't make me a virgin, Saint!" I slap the side of his face. We both know I am, but if I don't bleed, everyone will think I'm not. It's a lose-lose situation at this point.

He wraps his hand around my throat, slams my back into my closed door, and steps into me. I take in a shaky breath as his pretty bright-green eyes glare down at me, but I'm not afraid of him. This is the reaction I want out of him.

"I'm going to fuck you, sweetheart. I'm going to strip you naked, tie you down, and fuck you in front of everyone in that room. I'm going to humiliate you while you cry for me. But don't doubt me, Ash. I will make you bleed. Even if I have to hurt you to do so, it will happen. You will belong to me."

My thighs clench as my pulse races under his tight grip. Hurt me? Why does that sound exciting? I'm still sore from whatever he did to me in my kitchen last time I saw him. It makes me wonder how far he'll go to ensure he gets to keep me. Whatever it is, I'm willing to take it. I can't imagine a life without him.

"I've waited too long to get to where we are, and I've done too much for the Lords for them to throw me out now," he grinds out through gritted teeth.

"They won't find out," I add. My voice barely a whisper because of his hand tightly gripping my throat.

"I'll know, and that's enough," he growls.

Tears sting my eyes, and I push my hips into his. He's hard. I wish I had the strength he does. Because I would do anything for him to push me to my knees right now.

"But make no mistake, sweetheart. Once you're mine, I'm going to make sure the world knows it. Lord or not, men will know that I own you." He lowers his forehead to mine. "Now be a good girl, crawl into bed, and get some sleep. You're going to need your rest, Ash. Because once the vow ceremony is complete, you won't be getting any." With that, he pulls me from the door and exits my room, slamming it behind him.

THIRTEEN

ASHTYN

It's been three weeks since I learned Saint will be my Lord. It's gone about how I expected it to. Slow as fuck.

After my drunken outburst, he never came back to see me again. We've talked on the phone, and he's texted me, but it's not the same. He's been distant, and I've been losing my mind.

I should be mad at him, but instead, it makes me even more greedy for him. I've accepted my fate tonight. Being fucked in front of a group of men is the least of my worries.

My mother has had me go to therapy every day this week with her. I sit there and zone out, ignoring them both. What's done is done.

I go to my classes, but I don't pay attention to any of my professors. Whitney asks me nightly to go out, but I avoid her. If I'm not with Saint, I want to be alone.

I'm sitting on the edge of my bed, wrapped in a towel fresh out of the shower. My hair is still wet, and I haven't started my makeup yet. I have an hour before my mother picks me up to head to Carnage.

She insisted on driving me, which I found odd, but whatever. She wouldn't let it go. I don't know if she plans on waiting in the car once she drops me off or what. It's not like she can come in and watch the show. The only women allowed to be present are the ones handing their lives over to their Lord.

My cell rings, and I look to see it's Saint video calling me. This is the first time I've heard from him in three days. I want to press ignore, just to piss him off, but doubt fills me, and I worry he's calling to tell me he changed his mind. He believes my mother and her therapist, and no longer wants to make me his. If I'm not innocent, then I don't deserve him. That'll embarrass him and his family.

I nervously wipe my sweaty hand on my towel and answer. "Hey?" my voice is soft to try to cover up the hesitation I feel when my heart begins to race. If he tells me not to meet him at Carnage, I'll do what my mother said to do and run. I'm not sure where I'll go, but anywhere will be better than staying here and seeing him with someone else.

"Go to your nightstand," he orders.

I frown. "Saint—"

"It wasn't a suggestion, Ashtyn."

I look around to see where he's at and notice he's propped up against a black headboard. But it's not the one at his parents' or the house of Lords. He must be at Carnage. He's also shirtless, and I can see his brand on his chest. The Lords crest is a circle with three horizontal lines through the middle of it. It represents power. All of them receive the brand at the beginning of their senior year at Barrington. You can tell it's fresh by the raised and reddened skin.

I walk over to my nightstand. "Now what?" I ask, staring at the white wood.

"Open the bottom drawer and grab the black box."

Doing as I'm told, I pick it up with my free hand. "Okay."

"Now grab the chair by your window and take the items into your closet."

"The closet?" I question. "Saint, what the fuck?"

"Now, Ashtyn," he barks.

I slam the bottom drawer shut and walk over to the table by my windows. I set everything on the cream leather cushion, including the phone, and slide it across the white carpet over to my walk-in closet. I wanted this house strictly for the closet. It's like another bedroom on its own, and I'm obsessed with it.

Once inside, I go back and pick up my towel off the floor that I lost along the way because I couldn't hold it up under my arms. "Okay. All in the closet."

"Now shut the door," he commands.

I do it and show him with my phone. "It's shut. Now, are you going to tell me why I'm hiding out in my closet like there's a burglar about to break into my house?"

"Face your floor-to-ceiling mirror and lay your towel flat on the floor in front of it." He ignores my question, but I didn't expect an answer.

Laying the towel down, I stand to face the mirror, showing him with my cell once again.

"Prop the phone up on the chair facing the mirror. Then kneel in front of the mirror, facing it as well."

I get into position and slap my bare thighs. "This game is fun and all, but I'm short on time," I inform him. Now that I know he's not ditching me, I need to get ready.

"Open the box," he commands.

Knowing he's not going to stop, I pick up the box he had me get out of my nightstand and pull the lid off. My breath hitches, my eyes rising to the mirror to look at my phone propped on the chair behind me. I have it at an angle so he can see me clearly. "Saint...no."

His eyes are on mine as he speaks. "Pour the lube on it, spread your legs, and slide that plug into your ass."

I shake my head, my pulse racing. "I can't..."

"Yes, you can," he assures me.

"I—"

"Come on, sweetheart." He softens his voice, and I lick my lips. "You can do it. Do it for me. Show me how much you want to be my good girl."

I swallow the lump in my throat, and with shaky hands, I remove the black butt plug from the box and the lube. I pop the lid and a few drops drip onto the pointed tip as my heavy breathing fills the room.

"More," he urges. "Cover it. You can't have too much. The more you use, the easier it'll slide right in."

I squeeze the bottle, and it comes pouring out. It drips off the sides, covering my fingers as well and onto the towel underneath me.

I hold it up with a shaky hand to show him, and he nods. "Good girl. Now spread your legs wide, reach between your legs and rub your fingers along your ass. Spread the lube on it."

With a deep breath, I do as he says, and I whimper when my ass clenches.

"You've got to relax, Ash. Deep breaths. I promise it's not as bad as you think it'll be. I'll make it feel good."

"Okay." I nod, my eyes starting to sting with unshed tears.

"Do it again and slide a finger into yourself this time. Make sure to get the lube inside your ass."

SAINT

She shifts on her knees and sniffs. Closing her eyes, she puts her hand back between her legs, and she runs her fingers over her ass, sliding a finger into herself. She bows her head with a whine.

"Again," I order.

I need her to relax in order for the vow ceremony to go how I want. I'm going to have to hurt her in front of everyone. So I need her mind elsewhere. I can't see her before the ritual. Our fathers have had us at Carnage for the last three days, so this was my only option. Thankfully, I already had this stuff set up because I planned on doing it to her yesterday.

And I needed to hide her in her closet because now I know her father has cameras inside her house. Hopefully, there aren't any in the closet. It was the best option I could come up with on such short notice.

"I can't..." Her tear-filled eyes meet mine in the mirror. "Saint—"

"Again," I command.

She sniffs but places her hand between her legs and cries out as she fingers her ass.

"In and out, Ash. Don't stop. Count out loud for me."

"One," she whispers. "Two...three."

"Push it farther inside that ass, sweetheart. Make it feel good."

She nods, tears now spilling over her bottom lashes. I'm so fucking hard right now. I imagine myself on my knees behind her with one hand fisted in her hair, the other guiding my cock into her ass while I kiss the side of her face, tasting her tears as she begs me to stop.

"Sa-int." My name trembles on her lips, and she removes her hand from between her shaking legs.

"Turn around and face the chair," I say, sitting up straighter.

When she's in position, I say, "Bend over. Spread your legs, put your ass up in the air, and reach between your legs."

She swallows nervously. Her pretty blue eyes beg me to let her stop. "Please?"

"Begging isn't going to get you out of this, Ash," I say sternly.

She drops to her forearms and spreads her legs, arching her back, her ass, and pussy up into the air, giving me a great view in the mirror. "You're wet, sweetheart."

She quietly sobs, embarrassed and ashamed. *I love it.* "Reach between your legs and fuck your ass with your finger."

She repositions herself, placing the side of her face and upper chest on the floor so she can arch her back more to reach between her spread legs. She slides it in. Just enough so that her short and manicured fingernail enters before she pulls it out.

"I said finger yourself, Ash. Not tease it." If I was there, I'd take my belt to her ass for that.

She whimpers but pushes it farther into herself this time.

"Again."

She pushes it in just a little more. "All the way," I say. "Bury it in your ass." Her hands are much smaller than mine, so I know she can take more.

This time, she pushes it up to her knuckle and cries out, shifting on her knees.

"Good girl. Pull it out and do it again. Faster this time."

She does, and sobs begin to fill the large closet.

"Enter a second one." We don't have time to go slow.

She's got the side of her face buried in the carpet while doing as she's told. They slip in and out easily, but she's being too gentle with herself.

"Two at a time. Count out loud until you get to ten."

She counts between sobs.

"Good girl. Now faster."

She picks up the speed, pumping them in and out, and I hear her cry turn to a moan. I smile. "That's my good little whore. Come on, sweetheart. Fuck your ass for me."

When she reaches ten, she goes to stop, but I say. "Add another."

She shoves three fingers into her ass for me. "Good girl. You're doing so well. I wish you could see how pretty you look."

She pushes them back into her ass, and she cries, trembling. Lube runs down her thighs, and her pussy is dripping. Fuck, she's a sight to see.

She cries out each number, and I praise her as she does it.

Once done, she drops her hand from between her legs, thinking she's finished.

"Now grab the butt plug, pour more lube on it, and slide it into your ass."

She sits up on her legs and looks at the phone. Her face is soaked from tears, her eyes red, and her pouty lips tremble. Fuck, I wish I was there to kiss her. "Now, Ash," I command. *We don't have all night.*

She pours more lube on the plug and leans back over, her ass now in the mirror once more. "Do the same thing with the tip of the plug that you did with your fingers. A little at a time."

She places the tip at her tight ass and pauses.

"Push your hips back while pushing the plug in."

She does and cries out, "Saint...please."

"You can do it, sweetheart." I coax her. "You've done so well. You're almost there."

She pushes it in a little more.

"That's my girl. Look at you. Push it more."

She's sobbing but manages to do so. "Saint." She cries out my name, stopping it from going farther, but she doesn't pull it out. She holds it in place.

"Fuck, Ash." I groan. "If only you could see yourself right now. Fucking beautiful, sweetheart."

She whimpers, and her thighs shake. I want to lick up her legs and bury my face in her throbbing cunt.

"Just a little more. Rock your ass back and forth, applying pressure to the plug. Come on, sweetheart. Fuck your ass for me. Show me that you're my good little whore."

She begins to rock back and forth, applying pressure with her shaking hand, and more disappears into her ass. It's opening up for her, and I can't wait until it's my cock. I'm fucking every hole she has tonight. I'm going to own her. The ceremony is for the Lords. But she's mine. I'll put on the show they require, but nothing is off-limits once I get her in my room afterward.

"That's it," I say, watching her rock back and forth. She spreads her legs wider, her back arching more. She's so close. "Almost there."

She begins to sob once again, and I can see she's at the base. "Push it in, Ash. All the way. It's going to hurt, but I promise it'll feel better."

She takes in a deep breath and then pushes it in as a cry rips through the closet. Her hands fall from her legs, and she lies flat on the floor.

"That's it, sweetheart. It's in. Fuck, you did so good for me."

She buries her face in the carpet, crying.

"We're not done," I inform her.

"N-oooo," she sobs.

"Sit up," I command, needing to do one last thing.

Doing as she's told, she bows her head, unable to look at me this time. Humiliated and ashamed. *Fuck, she's so goddamn gorgeous.* I can't wait to see her kneeling in front of me like this instead of over the phone. "There's one other thing in the box you brought into the closet with you. Pull them out."

Tears drop to her shaking thighs, and she reaches out pulling the box to her. She removes the last remaining item and holds it up.

"Cuff your hands behind your back." No questions asked, she places the right cuff around her small wrist, and I smile at the clicks when she tightens it. Then she places her arms behind her back. It takes her a second, but she manages to grab the left one and get it on as well. Then she sits there with her knees tucked underneath her and arms cuffed behind her back. Her wet hair is stuck to her tear-streaked face, chest, and back. My eyes drop to see the black rubber plug that's in her ass, and my hard cock jerks inside my sweatpants.

"Bend over like you were before, legs spread and ass up in the air. I want to see all of you in the mirror, sweetheart."

She gets in position, eager to hide her face from me.

My eyes look over the floor-to-ceiling mirror with the plug in her ass and her hands cuffed behind her back, which is arched high in the air. I want to bury my face in her pussy. I can taste how fucking sweet it's going to be. I want my girl on display in front of a crowd to show her off to the world.

"Your pussy is swollen, Ash. It's begging to be filled like your ass." Her cries grow louder at my words. It's beautiful. "Don't move. Stay just like that. Do you understand?"

"Ye-yes," she answers softly.

I pick up my cell and open the app, turning it on. She screams as the buzzing sound fills the closet. Her body thrashes on the floor, but she keeps her legs spread for me as she yanks on the cuffs that hold them hostage.

"How's that feel, sweetheart?"

She's gasping, her hips rocking back and forth.

I smile. "You look so good fucking yourself."

Her legs spread even wider, and her cries grow to moans.

"Feels good, doesn't it?" I turn the second button on, and she's fucking squirming on the floor. The plug isn't overly big. I plan on fucking her ass later, so I'll have to stretch it after the ceremony more than she just did. This is just a start. A distraction.

"Saint... oh God..." She gasps. Her knees spread so wide. "Oh—"

"Fuck, you're gorgeous, Ash." I can't help but tell her. "I can't wait to be buried deep inside you while you come all over my cock."

"I'm going..." Her body stiffens, her knees shaking as she brings them together, arching her back more into the air.

I watch in the mirror as her pussy throbs. "Come for me, sweetheart. I know it feels good. Come all over yourself."

She cries out, and it's nothing like it had been before as she stiffens, and cum leaks from her wet cunt.

"Good girl, sweetheart." Fuck, that was hot. Goddamn, she's amazing. "Sit up and look at me," I command, turning it off.

Slowly, she rises, and her heavy, bloodshot eyes meet mine on the phone. "The key to the handcuffs is in the same box you got them from."

She nods.

"You will arrive at Carnage with nothing but a dress on and that plug in your ass."

She swallows.

"I'm going to strip you naked, so you don't need anything on underneath it. Do you understand?"

She nods, sucking in a deep breath. Her chest is heaving, and her pretty pink nipples hard. My mouth waters just thinking about sucking on them.

"That's my good girl. I'll see you soon." I end the video call and run a hand down my face. *Fuck!* I have ten minutes to jack off to the show she just gave me, and then I have to dress and be downstairs.

FOURTEEN

ASHTYN

I lie on the closet floor, still shaking with my hands cuffed behind my back and a plug in my ass. I'm exhausted, and my ass is sore.

I had no clue you could get off on just a butt plug, but my body did. I didn't even think about modesty or embarrassment once it started to vibrate. It was degrading, and my body liked it.

"Ashtyn?" my mom calls out.

I sit up, my ass on my legs, and clench my teeth not to moan at the way the plug pushes deeper into me.

Shit! She's early? How do I explain I'm cuffed and naked while wearing a butt plug in my closet?

"Ashtyn?" she snaps.

I turn around to where my back is to the box and tip it over to drop the key to the handcuffs. Then I scoot over closer to the mirror, stifling a moan. Fuck, this plug shouldn't feel this good.

Looking in the mirror over my shoulder, I try to get the key in the lock but drop it.

Fuck!

"Ashtyn, where are you?" she barks, and my pulse races. She's going to see me.

Taking a deep breath, I tell myself to calm down and try again. Moving to lie on my back, I bring my knees to my chest and slide my hands down my legs so they're at least no longer behind me. Now, I can see what I'm doing. I pick up the key and slide it into the lock, then I twist it. The left one pops open. I quickly undo the right, then toss them and the key along with the lube into the box I found them in and shove it under some clothes I have folded on the floor.

I stand and almost fall over due to being down on my knees for so long. The blood still rushes to my feet. I grab the towel, not caring that it's got lube on it and wrap it underneath my arms and tuck it into itself.

My door swings open, and I jump back with a scream as my mom enters my closet. "I've been hollering at you. Why didn't you answer?"

"I, uh, sorry. Had my earbuds in." I lie, trying to calm my breathing. I look like I just got off. My skin's flushed, and body trembling. I can feel the lube and cum that covers my ass and thighs. Plus, I have rug burns on my knees from when I rocked back and forth while fucking myself with my fingers and the plug.

She looks me over and tilts her head to the side. "You're not ready. We need to leave in fifteen minutes."

Have I been in here that long? "I'll be ready," I assure her.

Her eyes drop to the chair, and she frowns. "Why is this in here?"

"I needed it," I say defensively. Why does it matter? This is my house, and I'm a twenty-one-year-old adult. If I want to put a chair in my closet, then I can.

"For what reason?" She goes on.

Looking up, I search for an excuse. I know I'm running out of time, and she won't quit asking. "I needed to use it to reach the top shelf."

She looks me up and down. "Hmm."

I pull the towel tighter around myself. Surely, she won't tell me to remove it and bend over. Could you imagine if she knew I just uncuffed myself? It would just add to her thoughts that I'm a sex addict and make for very awkward therapist sessions.

"Get ready. We're leaving in thirteen minutes now." She grabs the chair and pulls it from the closet, slamming the door shut.

I let out a shaky breath and drop to my knees once more. My body trembles, and my ass clenches around the plug. *Jesus!*

"READY?" MY MOTHER CALLS OUT, ENTERING MY ROOM ONCE more exactly thirteen minutes later.

"Yeah," I answer and exit. I don't even grab my cell. I have nowhere to put it or any use for it tonight.

"Ashtyn—"

"Can we not do this, Mother?" I say as she gets on the highway. "I'm not in the mood."

She lets out a huff but thankfully remains silent. Thirty minutes later, we're pulling up to Carnage.

The Lords have a cathedral in the middle of nowhere where they perform all their sick and twisted rituals, but Carnage also has one. It's a smaller version. This is where they perform theirs. I guess I can thank God because not all the Lords will watch me get fucked for the first time. Just a select few. Most of the Lords who attend Barrington will be at the other location tonight.

My mother brings the vehicle to a stop in the roundabout and turns off the car. "Ashtyn..."

"Goodbye, Mother." I mean it in more ways than one. I'm aware that I may never see her again.

I get out and slam the door shut. We've never had a close relationship, so I'm not sure why she seems to care what happens to me now. She knew when she got pregnant that she might have a daughter, and this would one day happen.

As I walk up the steps, my legs shake in my six-inch heels. I run my sweaty hands down my bare thighs, taking in a deep breath.

This is it. They tell us from a young age that this is what we're made for—to serve a Lord. We should feel privileged to be a chosen. I don't feel that way. Do I want Saint? Yes. But I want him more than someone who I know has to devote his life to a secret society that thinks I'm worthless.

I've seen Lords drop their chosens, or their wives for the Lords without thought. They don't marry for love. They marry for convenience. To merge names that will give them more power. And then the Lady is supposed to give them children. A son to rule the world or a daughter who will one day serve.

The sad part is that I would give Saint a child and that makes me a sick person knowing what they're born into. I would expect my kids to hate me as I hate my parents.

As I enter the double doors, a man stands in a tuxedo. He's been helping Carnage out for years. I can only imagine some of the shit he's seen.

"Hello, miss." He nods to me as if I haven't known him my whole life.

"Hello, Jessie," I whisper.

"This way, ma'am. They're waiting for you."

My heels clap on the floor as I follow him to the elevator and up to the fifth floor. My legs shake and my breathing accelerates as he comes up to another set of double doors. They're stained glass with black roses and skulls all over them. They'd be beautiful if not for the meaning.

He pushes them open, and I wish I'd had more to drink as I enter. Six rows deep of pews are full of Lords. They all face forward, dressed in black cloaks, and their signature masks cover their faces. The thought that my father and brother are among them makes me sick to my stomach.

The lights are dimmer, and candles are placed on sconces along the back wall, framing a stained glass window. It's not for religious purposes. The Lords don't gather here to worship any god other than themselves. Instead, the window has a black spade in the center with flames around it as if giving it the image it's on fire. The numbers 666 are written across the bottom. A large Lords altar is at the front of the room.

The box that was on my bed three weeks ago is now in the center of the altar. I make my way down the aisle, and a man stands next to it. It's Saint, but I can't see his face.

He turns to open the box and pulls out the cuffs, laying them out on the surface. I come to a stop, and his voice commands. "Undress."

This is the part of what he said he was going to do to humiliate me. We have to willingly give ourselves to our Lord. Even though we never really had a choice.

I reach down, grab the hem of my dress, and pull it up and over my head, exposing my body to the room. I did as I was told and wore nothing underneath.

He stands there; the only sound in the room is my heavy breathing, and my nipples go hard, wondering what he's looking at or what he's thinking.

Reaching out, he takes my right hand and places the leather strap around it, buckling it to fit tightly on my small wrist. He repeats the process with my other wrist and both ankles. Then he grabs my hand and walks me to stand behind the altar to face the crowd.

He bends down next to my legs and spreads them wide. Rope is already tied at each end, and he threads it through the silver rings on my ankle cuffs, securing my legs wide open. His hands grab the back of my neck, and he pushes my face down onto the altar.

I shiver, a whimper leaving my lips from the coldness of the concrete surface. Two Lords from the front pews rise and walk to stand in front of me. Each one takes an arm and pulls them out wide, securing them to each end with the rope already attached to the leather bindings around my wrists.

A new man comes to stand on my left, and I take in a shaky

breath when he begins to speak. "Do you give yourself to your Lord?" he asks, and I don't recognize his voice.

"Y-yes," I answer.

His mask nods to Saint, who I can feel standing behind me. He's discarded his cloak because the roughness of his jeans presses against my bare ass.

A hand fists my hair, and he yanks my head back, making me cry out. My voice echoes off the walls of the cathedral. "Recite your vows, sweetheart," Saint commands in my ear.

"I vow," I say eagerly. Any doubt about not bleeding for him has left my mind. Even if I'm only his for the next ten minutes, it will be enough.

"You vow." His voice rings out.

"We vow." We both say at the same time. His voice louder than mine.

He lets go of my hair, and I drop the side of my face to the altar, closing my eyes.

He steps back, running his fingers over my pussy, and I try to push my ass back against it, but I'm tied down too tightly to reach him.

"So eager to be my whore, sweetheart." The Lords chuckle at his words, and I bite my tongue to keep from making any noise.

He knows how much I want him. His hand comes down on my ass, and I yank on the rope that ties me down. Something pushes against my pussy.

"Saint," I gasp as it enters me.

"You're wet, Ash," he muses, and I realize it's his finger when he pushes a second one into me.

I cry out, pulling harder as the pain has tears stinging my eyes. That along with the feel of the plug in my butt is overwhelming. "Please..."

He pulls them out and pushes them in again. I'm on my tiptoes, crying and shaking uncontrollably. It hurts more than I thought it would.

"Shh." He rubs my bare back. "This is what you want, sweetheart. To be fucked like a whore in front of everyone."

I bury my face into the altar, gasping to breathe. He told me he would humiliate me. I hate how wet I am because it's turning me on.

"You chose to me be mine, Ash. That means I get to use you." He pumps his fingers in and out of me faster and faster.

The plug begins to vibrate on a much lower setting than it did in my closet earlier, and a moan escapes my lips as my body rocks back and forth on the altar. I'm sweating like a literal whore in church, which makes it easier for my body to move along the hard and cold surface I'm tied to.

Something enters my pussy that sends a shrill scream from my lips, my face rising, and my hands fist. I yank on the rope that holds me down.

Then his weight is on top of my back, his hand around my throat from behind. "Watch them, sweetheart. Let them see how pretty you are when you come on my dick."

His hips slam forward, and my lips part, but nothing comes out this time. A paralyzing pain seizes my body, taking my breath away.

He starts to move. In and out. His cock rams my hips into the side of the hard surface of the altar. The masks and cloaks staring at me fade as Saint's heavy breathing fills my ears. Or maybe it's mine. I'm not sure.

Am I even able to breathe? The way the room spins, I'd say no. His dick hits the right spot, and I make a noise that even I can't comprehend. The plug vibrates more than before, or maybe my mind is playing tricks on me.

"That's it, sweetheart. Moan for me." Saint growls in my ear, and I realize I'm crying when I taste my tears. "Do you know how long I've waited to fuck you, Ash? Too long. Now be a good girl and come for me. Show them all how much you enjoy pain."

SAINT

I can feel her body shake underneath mine. But I can also feel how soaked her cunt is.

Fuck, her pussy feels amazing. It's so tight, and the warmth...like a fucking oven.

Letting go of her throat, I lean up and watch my cock fuck her pussy. A smile plays on my face. "Will you look at that?" I pull out, and she slumps against the altar. I wrap my hand around my cock and run it up and down, smearing the blood on my hand and then shove it back into her.

I slap her ass with my bloody hand. "You're such a good girl for bleeding on my cock." She whimpers, her shoulders shaking. I want her to know that she did exactly what I told her she'd do.

I'm on a mission tonight, even if that meant hurting her. If I had to rip her open, she would prove to the Lords that she's mine. Forever.

She can heal later.

Reaching up, I grab a fistful of her hair, and she doesn't even scream. The cathedral is full of her heavy breathing and soft cries. I've still got my mask and jeans on. All I did was remove my cloak and unzip my jeans to pull my cock out.

We don't have to be naked.

The Lords have humiliated us enough. Tonight is the night we get to reap the rewards of our loyalty. Tonight is the night I get to claim my sweetheart in front of everyone who wishes they were me.

"Saint." My name falls from her lips, and I smile, loving the way it sounds.

"That's it, Ash. Tell them who is fucking you. Who fucking owns you." I slam forward, and she shudders. Her cunt tightly hugs my bloody cock. I've only ever dreamed of her like this. It felt like it was never going to come true. My hand drops between us, and my thumb presses on the vibrating butt plug. I have it turned down somewhat. Just enough to give her a little extra.

"Saint!" She cries out this time when I pull my cock out and push forward.

Her pussy is soaking wet. This is what this life is about—control. Dominance.

Her hands fist, her thighs shaking as her cunt clenches down on me like a vise. I smile as she comes all over my dick. "That's a good girl," I praise, and she gasps, trying to catch her breath. "Coming for me like the whore you are." I push the mask to the top of my head, lean over, and kiss the side of her tear-streaked face. "Now it's my turn." Letting go of her, I stand to my full six-foot-five height, grip her hips, and slam into her over and over.

So hard that I'm sweating and breathless by the time my balls tighten. I push forward one last time, holding myself balls deep, and come inside her. I'm proud of myself that I lasted that long. I already came twice today jacking off.

When I pull out, cum and blood drip from the tip of my cock, and she lies bent over the altar, crying and spent like a doll I just used. "That's just the beginning, sweetheart." I slap her ass that already has my handprint on it and leave the plug in.

FIFTEEN

ASHTYN

The next hour is a blur as I sit in the front pew with Saint next to me. I'm glad I'm too fucked up to witness my brother take his chosen.

I feel drunk—more than I did earlier when I arrived. I'm not sure if that's the orgasm or the actual liquor hitting me.

I bled.

I want to scream it to the world. Is it weird that I want to rub it in my mother's and her therapist's faces? Probably. But when you've been told you can't do something, you want to show them that you can, in fact, do it, and I did.

I also got off. Saint made the pain feel good. I have never experienced anything like it. It was more than what I ever thought possible.

My heavy eyes fall to my thigh, where Saint's hand rests. His ring with the Lords crest on it feels cold against my burning skin. I have bruises. They cover my wrists and dot my thighs. I'm sure there are more that my dress currently covers.

After he finished with me, he untied me and slipped my dress back on, leaving the cuffs in place along with the plug. I can feel his cum inside me. My thighs are slick with a mixture of both of our cum and sweat. They still shake.

It was like an earthquake hit my body. If I had been standing, it would have put me on my knees. Hell, he had to help me to my seat.

Saint taps my thigh before standing. I look up, and my heavy eyes scan the room to see that Haidyn is done with his chosen. He was the last to go. I know of her from Barrington, but we're not close.

All the Lords stand from the pews and make their way out of the cathedral. I stay seated, afraid my feet won't be able to hold me up. They hurt from my heels, not to mention my legs are Jell-O.

Saint stands in front of me, softly talking to Kashton. His chosen kneels on the floor behind him. Her arms are tied behind her back, and she's still naked. I don't know her. Never seen her before.

The Lords have different rankings within their society. Only the best of the best is gifted to the Spade brothers, so she has to be someone important. Or at least her father is.

Take my brother's chosen, for example. Her father is a congressman. She's an only child, and as far as I know, she hates my brother. I've only met her once at a party, and she told me she hated me and my family. I wanted to apologize but couldn't bring myself to say the words. I hate my family most days too.

"Come on," Saint orders, grabbing my hand and pulling me to my feet. The heels making it ten times harder to stand on my shaky legs.

"Where are we going?" I ask. I honestly wasn't prepared to make it this far. So I have no clue what happens now. Do we go to his place? Mine?

He cups my cheek, and I look up at his mask-covered face, but he doesn't answer. I'm only greeted with silence. This is how it'll be from here on out. I'll ask questions, and he'll keep things from me.

He ushers me into his room and shuts the door behind him when I hear a lock. "Saint—?"

Turning around, he places his lips on mine, and I moan into his mouth. His hands grip my shaking thighs, and he picks me up. I wrap my legs around his hips as he spins us around, and he shoves my back into the door.

I pull away from the kiss, gasping, and cry out. His lips drop to my neck, and I lean my head to give him better access. "Please..." I beg him to fuck me again.

He pulls me from the door and walks me to his bed. Tossing me onto it, he shoves my dress up my body, not even bothering to take it off, and crawls onto the bed, spreading my legs. He goes to put his head between my legs, and I grip his hair. "Wait."

He looks up at me. Green eyes shining and a naughty smile on his face. "Are you about to tell me no?" He runs his tongue along his upper teeth in the sexiest way that makes my cum-filled pussy clench.

"A chosen isn't allowed to tell her Lord no," I say breathlessly.

Softly chuckling, he lowers his lips to my neck. "You can use whatever words you like, sweetheart, but just know I'm going to do whatever I want to you." He gently kisses my flushed skin, and I arch my back, my nails digging into his back, pulling on his shirt.

"But..." I gasp when his hand moves between our bodies, and he plays with my pussy.

"But what?" he asks, trailing kisses along my jawline. This is what I've wished for for so long. My body vibrates with joy.

"I bled." Swallowing, I add, and his fingers stop. He sits up and stares down at me. The coldness in his eyes makes me nervous. No more playful Saint.

"What about it?" he asks. His voice now flat.

Swallowing nervously, I say, "The blood. You were going to ..."

A smile spreads across his face, and he laughs once more. I wonder about the change of attitude all of a sudden. "Sweetheart, I don't give a fuck about that. If I want to fuck your cunt with my tongue, I'm going to do so."

Heat rises up my neck, and my cheeks flush at his words.

He stands off the bed, grabs my arm, and forces me to sit. He removes my dress and then pushes me onto my back. Spreading my legs wide, he places his lips to my inner thigh and kisses his way up my sensitive skin.

I'm shaking uncontrollably with nervousness and from the orgasm he gave me during the vow ceremony. I should be embarrassed, but I have no control over my body right now. It's wanted him for too long.

"Oh god." I pant, my hands digging into his hair as I feel his lips cover my pussy. A deep suction has me bucking my hips. "Saint." I fist his hair, and his fingers dig into my legs, pinning them down painfully, and I lift my head to look down at him. His eyes are open and staring up at me over my pussy. Slowly, he licks upward, and my heart races at how fucking sexy he is. "Please." My head falls to the bed, and I push his head down again, needing to feel that suction again.

But he's stronger and pulls back. "So greedy." He slaps my pussy, and my legs close as I cry out, jerking on the bed.

The lingering sting has me panting. "Fuck, Saint..."

He shoves my legs open and does it again. I scream, heat rising along my skin, and my nipples harden. "Keep your legs open for me, sweetheart. Can you do that?"

I nod quickly, taking in a deep breath. "Yes."

"Good girl." He places my hands on my inner thighs and tells me to, "Hold them."

He slaps his belt on my pussy, and I arch my back, a cry ripping from my throat as my pussy throbs. He does it again, and I bite my trembling lip. He slaps it a third time, and I'm practically convulsing as tears fall down the side of my face.

"So pretty." He rubs his fingers up and down my swollen and throbbing pussy. "You're so fucking wet, Ash. I'm going to spend every fucking day inside you."

A wish come true.

My eyes are closed, and I'm sobbing from the sting, the pain, the pleasure. It's all too much at once. As if I'm a rubber band pulled tight that needs to be released.

I feel his lips on my pussy again, but he's soft, tenderly kissing and licking it. "You taste amazing, sweetheart." Then he's sucking and biting. I'm gasping, my skin on fire as I hold my legs open for him to torture me in the best way.

"Saint," I gasp, and my back arches off the bed when I feel it again. Same as before. "I'm..." I'm unable to finish the sentence because my breath is taken away when I feel the wave.

"Come on my face, Ash," he growls before he's unable to speak because he's buried between my legs, and I explode.

SAINT

I LICK MY LIPS, LOOKING OVER HER SHAKING BODY. SHE'S gasping and crying. Rolling over onto her side, she brings her legs up to her chest, and I open the top drawer of my dresser and grab what I need.

Pushing her onto her stomach, I yank her arms behind her back, and she doesn't fight as I fasten the double ended bolt snap in place, securing her arms behind her back. She still wears the cuffs on her ankles and wrists from the ceremony. They won't be coming off this weekend.

I roll her onto her back, crushing her arms underneath her, and position myself between her shaking legs. I push them farther apart and reach down to her butt plug. I pull on it, and she starts screaming my name.

"You're okay, Ash. Just relax."

"Please, don't." She begs.

My girl is overwhelmed. I expected this, though. She was forced to fuck in front of a crowd full of people, two being her father and brother. She's come twice since she arrived at Carnage and once in her closet before she got here. And I've been rougher than you should be with a virgin on her tight cunt. And now I'm going to take her ass. After this, I'll clean us both up in the shower and then take her mouth. She will pass out eventually. But that won't stop me.

I twist the plug before slowly pulling it out, and she whimpers. Grabbing the lube I had pulled out of the nightstand, I pour it over my cock, and some drips onto the bed as I make a mess.

I close the lid and put it to the side, not wanting to toss it on the floor. I'm going to need it again before the night is over. "I'm sorry, sweetheart," I say, leaning over her shaking body.

Her heavy eyes open to look up at me, and she sniffs. "For what?" she asks softly.

"I'm going to fuck your ass now, Ash, and it's going to hurt."

Her eyes widen, and she shakes her head. "Saint, please..."

I push the head of my cock into her tight ass, and her screams fill the room while I groan at how fucking good it feels. I've been dreaming of this day. Every fucking time I saw her, I imagined this. "You're doing so good." I push farther, and she arches her neck and back. "The more you fight, the tighter it is, Ash, and it just makes me force it," I tell her although I'm not complaining. "Fuck, it feels good sweetheart. So fucking good." I look down to watch my cock slide out before I push into her again. The plug wasn't enough to stretch her as wide as I needed, but it was better than no prep at all. "Look at you, sweetheart," I say over her cries. "Your ass is taking my cock so well. Look at you being a good whore."

I let out a deep growl when I slide in deeper. "More than halfway," I inform her, and she gasps.

Placing her shaking legs over my shoulders, I lean over her trembling body and place one hand over her mouth, and the other slides underneath her neck, reaching up to her head and gripping a handful of dark hair. I yank her head back, exposing her neck to me, and I start to move.

Her face is wet from tears and drool, making my hand slippery, so

I dig my fingers into her cheeks to hold it in place. "Your cunt is full of my cum, sweetheart, and soon your ass will be too."

She breathes heavily from her nose because I allow it and mumbles unintelligible words into my hand. I move my hips back and forth, getting more and more forceful as her ass opens up for me to take it as hard as I want.

SIXTEEN

ASHTYN

I enter the elevator and ride it up to the fourth floor with a smile on my face. It dings before the door slides open, and I step off it. I make my way to the office door and enter. My mother looks up at me from her seat while her therapist stands from her desk.

"Ashtyn." She nods, gesturing to the seat that I sit in every time I've been forced to attend these godforsaken sessions. "How are you feeling?" she asks, lowering herself to her seat.

"Great." I give her a big smile.

Her eyes go from mine to my mother's. "How was the ceremony?" She gets right to the point.

Saint has been using my body as it was intended. It hurts to even sit down; my ass is so sore. And my pussy? Fuck, it burns when I pee. I've had so much sex in the past forty-eight hours that I have a UTI. I didn't even know that was possible until I began to cry after I peed. Saint had come running in, asking what was wrong. He then explained to me what it was. I thought something was seriously wrong with me. And don't even get me started on my throat. It hurts to swallow. Last night, I was brushing my teeth and noticed I had bruises on the back of my mouth from Saint's cock fucking it. But no matter how much it hurts, or how sore I am, I can't get enough of him. The man is unstoppable. I never stopped to think about what he'd be like when told he can't fuck for three years. I've been tied to his bed back at Carnage for two days now while he made good on his promise of making me his whore.

"It was good. I'm no longer a virgin, so there's that," I decide to say with a shrug, leaving out the details. They know how sex works.

They look back and forth at one another again, and my mother turns in her chair to face me. "Meaning?"

"I bled." Did my father not tell her this? I figured he would. The way they both look at me, they seem surprised I'm even here. So maybe my father hadn't said anything, and she thought he left me on the streets.

"That's—"

"Good." My mother's therapist interrupts whatever my mother was about to say. "Congratulations, Ashtyn, you're officially a woman now."

"Does that mean I no longer have to attend these sessions?" I ask. What do you know, I wasn't a sex addict. I will be now, though.

"I think—"

"I'd like to continue seeing you." She interrupts my mother once more. "Once a week should be enough." Averting her eyes, she looks down at her pen and paper and writes in her notebook.

I refrain from sighing. "Why?" I ask.

She frowns, looking up at me. "I think it's best that we save that for our next session." Her eyes go from mine to my mother's briefly, and I wonder if I'm going to start seeing her on my own? My mother won't like that at all. She's too nosy to let me come by myself. But if I start coming alone, does that mean she can't tell my mother what we discuss? I'll ask her that next time.

I remain silent throughout the rest of my mother's session, tuning them out. I have nothing else to say and unlike my mother, I don't care what her issues are that she needs to discuss with a therapist. I'd rather not know so my father can't question me what is said between them. Not like he'd ask anyway. Pretty sure he doesn't give a shit about my mother.

We're riding the elevator down after her session when her cell rings. I catch sight of an unknown number before she can decline it. "You can get that if you need to," I inform her.

Ignoring me, she shoves her cell into her Louis Vuitton and straightens her shoulders. She's mad. I'm pretty sure it's at me. I'm not sure what I can and can't do anymore to make her happy.

Once outside, I walk toward my car not even bothering to tell her goodbye when she grabs my arm and turns me to face her. She's got her sunglasses on, shielding her eyes from me. "Remember what I said, Ash."

"About what?" I need her to explain what she means exactly.

"About Saint..." It's the first time she's referenced him, and it makes me wonder which Spade brother she would have chosen for me to be with. "A Lord in general."

I nod. *Ahh,* "He'll never love me. I remember." When I turn back to my car, she spins me around again. "Mom," I snap, yanking my arm free.

"I—" Her cell rings again, and she huffs. Digging it out of her purse, I see unknown on her screen. And as she takes a second to decline it once more, I jump into my car and speed off. I'm supposed to meet Saint back at Carnage, and I'm already late.

SAINT

I SIT IN MY PARENTS' HOME THEATER ROOM. THE LIGHTS ARE off, and *Titanic* plays on the screen before me. I'm relaxed back on one of the large couches. My back is propped up on pillows with one arm behind my head. The other absentmindedly rubs Ashtyn's thigh over the Hermes blanket she's wrapped up in.

We had planned on going swimming earlier, but the storm hit, so she suggested watching *Titanic*. It's her favorite movie of all time. I don't hate it, but I've watched it more times than I care to.

My cell lights up next to me, and I pick it up to see it's a text from Haidyn.

I'm at your parents'. Where the fuck are you?

I type back my reply.

In the media room.

The one place I didn't look. Be right there.

My eyes fall to her, and I slowly pull the blanket back to see she's still dressed in her swimsuit from earlier. We've been in here maybe thirty minutes, and she was out almost immediately. We didn't get any sleep last night. Well, I didn't. I kept her up for most of it. She passed out a couple of times, but I didn't allow her to stay asleep.

Being told for three years that you can't fuck and then getting the one thing you've always wanted means I'll use her every chance I get. Any way that I can. I'll sleep when I die. She's been mine for two weeks now, and I still can't get enough of her.

I type out a quick message to Haidyn.

Will you stop by my room and grab a few things?

Sure. What do you need?

I respond and place my phone back down next to me. Feeling something dig into the side of my leg, I reach down and see it's the sucker she brought in here with her. Mine is next to my cell. Both still wrapped and untouched. So are the peach rings that she loves.

A few minutes later, the door opens, and I watch to see if the soft light coming in through the hallway fazes her. She doesn't move.

Haidyn walks around to the front of the couch we're sitting on and smirks when he sees she's passed out. My eyes drop to his hands, and he tosses the things that he picked up in my room onto my lap.

"Have a seat," I tell him.

He removes his black leather jacket, which I see is wet, letting me know it's still storming outside. He tosses it to the side, then crawls onto the couch and sits opposite of me, getting comfortable. His right arm placed along the back of the cushions. His left hand reaches down and pushes her dark hair from her face.

She's on her right side, her back to the screen. Both knees are bent to her chest, and she's tucked into a ball, softly snoring away. I love to watch her sleep; she looks so peaceful. I almost feel sorry for what I'm about to do to her. Almost.

"Help me roll her over onto her back," I say, and he sits up, pushing her shoulders to lay her flat. Her head falls to the side, and her chest rises and falls from a deep intake of breath.

The first thing I do is untie both knots that sit on her narrow hips before removing the black bikini bottoms. Then I take the rope that he brought me from my room and begin to tie it around her upper thighs—making my way down to her ankles. It doesn't have to be precise or pretty.

Then I pick up her legs and push her knees to her chest. "Hold her legs." I nod to her sleeping body, and he grabs her thighs, pulling them to rest on her chest. A soft moan comes from her parted lips, but her eyes remain closed.

I bring her arms down and cross her wrists behind her knees. Taking the remainder of the rope, I tie them together. "Put her back on her side." We roll her onto her right side, facing the inside of the couch once again. I then undo the knots to remove the last bit of her bathing suit and toss it to the floor so that she's now naked.

I have her ass and cunt right next to me, and her head is next to Haidyn. He picks it up while moving closer to me, so her head can rest on his jeans-clad thigh.

She begins to stir, fighting the rope, but her eyes remain closed.

Haidyn gathers her long dark hair into his left fist and jerks her head back, making her eyes flutter before they close.

He leans farther back into the couch cushion and bends his knees, bringing his legs up a little. Her head is now centered in his lap. I run my fingers over her pussy before I force one into her. She's not nearly ready, but she will be soon. "Wake up, sweetheart," I say, pulling it out before pushing it into her once again.

Her eyes flutter open, and she stiffens, taking in the scene. We've had this conversation before—sharing her with the guys. I brought it up the other night how turned on she was at the vow ceremony when everyone watched me fuck her. I then asked how she felt if I were to let Haidyn and Kashton fuck her. Her cheeks turned red, and she couldn't look me in the eyes. It was adorable, and all the answer that I needed.

I didn't plan on it happening today, but here we are. I love to show off what I have, and what better way than to let them have a little taste? I'll limit them of course to what I allow them to do to her, but I'm excited to see how much she enjoys it.

"Saint?" she questions sleepily.

I lean over, running my knuckles down her pretty face. "You're going to be a good girl for me, Ash."

She nods, swallowing nervously. "Yes," she whispers, and I give her a proud smile.

Righting himself, he unzips his jeans and pulls out his dick. He rubs the tip against her pouty lips. "Open wide, baby girl," he orders.

Her eyes may be open, but they're heavy and unfocused as she looks around aimlessly. Her mind tries to catch up with what she sees and why she can't move.

I slap her ass hard enough to leave a handprint, and she gasps. He takes the opportunity to shove the head of his dick into her mouth.

Her eyes start to focus, and her body wiggles in the rope. He slides his knuckles down the side of her face as she looks up at him and begins to realize his dick is in her mouth. She moans around it, her hands fisting trying to straighten out her legs.

"Sucking my dick is such a whore thing to do, Ash," Haidyn tells her, and she blinks, confused by his words.

I adjust myself to lie on my side so I have better access to her ass and pussy. I slap it, making her jump. She begins to mumble incoherent words around his dick, and his free hand grips her neck. She fights harder when he takes away her air. "Just hold it," he tells her. "No licking. No sucking. Just fucking lie here and drool all over my cock, baby girl. Keep it nice and warm for me."

She blinks rapidly as I remove the finger from her cunt and pour lube directly on her ass.

He lets go of her throat, and she opens her mouth wider to take a deep breath, but he pushes her face farther down, more of his cock entering her mouth. "Breathe through your nose," he commands, tapping the side of her face, making her flinch. "Or you won't breathe at all."

She wiggles, lying on her side, knees up to her chest, arms tied behind her knees. I pick up the sucker that she had brought with her in here and unwrap it. I place it in my mouth and suck on it for a few seconds. I don't swallow to get it nice and wet. I pull it free from my lips and place it at her cunt. I turn it in a circular motion before pushing it into her. Just enough that the cherry sucker disappears. After a second, I pull it out and pop it back into my mouth.

"Cherry and pussy. My favorite flavors," I say, sucking her off it.

Haidyn laughs. "You just can't help yourself, can you?"

I snort, popping the sucker from my lips and putting it back into her wet pussy, loving the way she tries to pull away. She's not going anywhere. I'm in the mood to share my toy. "That's all you isn't it, sweetheart?" I push it a little farther until my fingertips are at the entrance of her wet cunt before I pull it free. "She loves a cock in her mouth." I stick my tongue out and twist the sucker as I run her juices along it, moaning around the taste.

His fist gripping her hair, shoves her head down, and she gags as his cock hits the back of her throat while his free hand goes back to her neck once again. Her hips buck, and her body tenses.

I sit up and place a hand on her hip, pinning her down to the couch while my free hand slides between her legs and pushes two fingers into her.

"Suck it," he orders, looking down at her. "Come on, baby girl. You want to suck my cock so bad. Then fucking suck." He pulls her mouth off his length to shove her down onto it again. Her pussy clenches on my fingers as she makes slurping and gagging sounds around him.

He holds her head in place once again, and I push a third finger into her. "You're getting wetter, sweetheart." I remove them only to shove them back in. My fingers dig into her hip, holding her down, knowing they'll leave bruises. I might share her with my friends, but there will be limits. They can have her mouth and her ass. Her cunt is mine.

She blinks, tears running down the side of her face as it turns dark red from lack of oxygen. He releases her neck and pulls his cock back enough so she no longer gags.

She lies there breathing heavily through her nose, and he begins to run his hand through her hair. "Good girl," he praises her while her small body trembles. "That's what I want to see. My cock resting in your warm and wet mouth. If I want to fuck it, I'll fuck it, do you understand?"

SEVENTEEN

ASHTYN

I lie on my side as Haidyn's hand slowly runs through my hair. His cock fills my mouth as drool runs out of the corner. His jeans and the side of my face are wet.

My hips gently rock back and forth as Saint plays with my pussy. His thumb makes small circles on my swollen clit. Two fingers slowly go in and out.

They're playing with me.

My legs are tied with rope that is rubbing against my hot and sweaty skin. I fist my tied hands and try to stretch out my legs, but it's no good. I'm sandwiched between them on the couch.

Haidyn's cock fills my mouth. I've only got maybe two inches. I've seen all three of them, but right now, it just feels bigger than usual. Maybe because it's just resting there.

I've never done this before. Not like this anyway.

Of course, I've sucked Saint's dick since the night of the vow ceremony. But just held it in my mouth? My natural instinct is to suck. My tongue runs along the head. The skin is so soft, I wish he'd push it to the back of my throat.

Something enters my pussy, and I moan around Haidyn's dick.

His blue eyes drop to look at me, but he doesn't say anything. I sniff, my nose running as bad as the drool out of the corner of my mouth. My eyes sting from unshed tears. My body is begging, but I have no voice.

I tense when I feel something at my ass.

"Relax," Saint says, his hand slapping my ass before he rubs circles over the lingering sting. "I want to watch you come with Haidyn's cock in your mouth, sweetheart."

I whimper, eyes closing as I try to breathe through my runny nose. Haidyn's hand touches my forehead, and this time, when he goes to run his hand through my hair, he grabs a fist of it. Pinpricks spread across my scalp, and it makes my pussy wet.

He uses it to push my head down, his thick cock filling my mouth just as something is rubbed on my ass.

It's more lube.

I open my mouth as wide as I can to breathe, but Haidyn just shoves my head farther down. His cock hits the back of my throat, and I gag.

"Take it, baby girl," Haidyn says softly. "Open your throat and let me fuck it. You know you want me to."

I do, and I can't deny it. My pussy is soaked, my pulse racing, and if I wasn't gagging on his dick, I'd beg him for it.

I thought I was dreaming when Saint woke me up, and I saw him and Haidyn. He mentioned sharing me with Haidyn and Kashton the night in the woods when he took a belt to my ass in front of them. Then he brought it up again the other night while lying in his bed, and I couldn't find my voice to tell him that I wanted it. Too ashamed and embarrassed. I didn't want Saint to think he wasn't enough for me.

My hips are grabbed, and a mumbled cry is forced from my full mouth as I'm rolled over onto my knees, and my ass is shoved into the air. The new position pulls on my shoulders since my wrists are tied behind my bent knees.

Haidyn lets go of my hair only to gather it all in both hands. He pulls my head up as my legs now smash my hands underneath me.

My breath is taken away when Saint's cock pushes into my pussy, spreading me wide. Haidyn doesn't give me a chance to cry out when he shoves my head down onto his dick.

They use me. I lie on the couch, tied up with tears running down my face as Haidyn controls my head, forcing me to gag and choke on his dick while Saint kneels behind me and fucks my pussy. The sound of his body slapping mine fills the room with their heavy breathing. I'm not even sure who I am anymore.

My neck hurts, and my jaw is sore.

I stare at Haidyn's wet jeans as drool and snot fall from my face. I feel light-headed. My vision fades in and out as something enters my ass. It's Saint's finger, and my pussy clenches around his dick as he pounds into me.

Something cold runs down my ass, and I know it's more lube when he pushes two fingers into it. It hurts and feels good at the same time. A strangled cry is ripped from my lips, and Haidyn's hips lift, forcing his cock down my throat and turning the sound into a gag. Fresh tears fall from my eyes as my body rocks back and forth while they both fuck me like I'm a sex doll.

Hard and fast.

It's just as good as I always imagined it would be. As I'm about to lose consciousness, my body heats, and my toes curl. White lights flash across my vision, and I realize my mother and her therapist were wrong. Those women being used in the porn I watched weren't acting. They were having the best time of their life.

SAINT

My balls begin to tighten as I slam into her cunt, and Haidyn pushes her head down on his cock, lifting his hips off the couch. His eyes close, and his head falls back, a growl coming from his parted lips as he comes down her throat.

My fingers dig into her hips, and her pussy clenches down on me while she comes on my dick.

He yanks her head from his dick, and she gasps. Sobs immediately follow when I slam into her, filling her pussy full of my cum.

"Fuck, baby girl." He breathes heavily, pushing the wet strands of hair from her drool-covered face.

Her pussy pulses around me as I slowly pull out and watch the cum drip from her swollen cunt.

He helps me place her shaking body onto her side, but neither of us attempts to untie her. A quick look at the screen shows the movie isn't halfway over yet.

"You guys are having fun without me?"

Haidyn and I look up to see Kashton standing next to the couch. His eyes are on a shaking Ashtyn. When did he get here?

"Where the fuck have you been? I called you on my way over," Haidyn asks, stretching his arms along the back of the couch, getting comfortable. His wet cock still out of his zipper.

"Had to take Melony home," he answers, and my eyes drop to the outline of his hard dick when his hand reaches down to adjust himself.

I lean over Ashtyn, my hand cupping her tear-streaked face. "You did so good," I tell her, and she sniffs. "But you're not done, sweetheart." She blinks fresh tears from her beautiful blue eyes.

"Sa-int." My name is spoken roughly as she takes a deep breath. "So tired..." She pulls on the rope.

"I know, Ash. And you'll get some rest soon. I promise." I push the wet hair from her cheeks as I hear Kashton unzip his jeans, already knowing where this is going.

"Be my good girl and open your mouth," I order.

She shakes her head, her eyes looking up through her wet lashes to see Kashton push his knees into the side of the couch, getting in position. His hard cock already in his hand.

"He's going to fuck your mouth, and you're going to come for me again."

"No...I can't..." she cries, her body shaking uncontrollably.

"You'll come as many times as I want you to, sweetheart," I inform her. Looking up at Kash, I nod. "Plus, you need the practice."

I'm going to teach my girl to be the best at sucking dick because if I had a choice, that's what I'd pick. I'm going to use her until she craves it. Then I'm going to show her off to anyone who wants to watch her on her knees.

Kashton reaches over, grabs her shoulders, and yanks her to where her head hangs off the edge of the couch. Her voice rings out into the room over the surround sound before he pushes his cock into her open mouth.

I pick up the vibrator that I had Haidyn bring me earlier and coat it in the lube before I push it into her soaked pussy. I pick up my cell, go to the app, and turn it on.

Her body tenses. Kashton throws his head back and groans. "Fuck...that's a good girl, sweet cheeks. Suck my cock."

I begin to finger her ass as the sound of her gagging and sucking fills the room. He adjusts his hand and moves it behind her neck to tilt it back for a better angle.

Her body tries to rock back and forth. He lets go of her neck, wraps his arm around her tied knees, and pulls them toward his body. The new position forces her back to arch, putting her ass up in the air.

I remove my finger from her ass, only to add a second. Then a third. I get more forceful, watching her body tighten. I know the moment she comes because her body relaxes for just a second before she tries to fight the vibrator once more, cum now dripping from her pussy.

Kashton pulls out of her mouth, and the sound of her trying to catch her breath follows. "Fuck..." He sighs heavily before pushing back into her. He's slow this time, going deep with long thrusts that force gags out of her.

Her body shakes due to the vibrator that's on high. I'm gentle with her ass, not wanting to be too rough on her. It's going to be another long night.

It only takes a couple more minutes, and he's coming down her throat just like Haidyn did.

He falls down onto the couch, and I pull her over to me. Picking her up, I sit her on my lap, and her watery eyes blink up at mine. "You're okay, sweetheart." I push her hair from her wet face. "You did such a good job. You're my good girl."

I rock her tied body back and forth as her cries fill the room.

"Pl-ease..." She sobs.

I ignore her and go back to watching the movie. I'm not untying her or removing the vibrator. She'll come for me until I decide she's had enough. After all, a whore should be rewarded for her generosity.

EIGHTEEN

ASHTYN

I've been staying with Saint at the house of Lords for three weeks now. It has been hell and bliss. The things I have experienced are just as earth-shattering as I thought they'd be. But I never imagined how exhausting it would be.

Being a whore isn't easy. Who knew?

But I wouldn't give it up for anything.

This morning, I woke up and came home to grab a few things. He had a meeting at Carnage anyway, and I really don't like being there with all the other Lords while he's not. I'm lying in my bed watching TV when my cell vibrates next to me. I pick it up and read the message.

MY LORD: Get dressed. I'm on my way.

Jumping to my feet, I rush to my closet and throw on some jeans and a tank top. It's still fairly warm here in Pennsylvania. I put on my tennis shoes and rush downstairs. I've learned that when Saint says he's on his way, he's almost at his destination.

I'm running out the door when I hear the sound of the bikes

down the street. Seconds later, three roll into my driveway. Saint is first. I can tell by the black-and-white skull helmet. It looks like there's smoke coming out of the black eyes. Haidyn is second. His helmet is a deep red. Kashton's is solid white. I wonder why my brother isn't with them.

Saint comes to a stop and places both feet on the ground to hold the bike up. He doesn't even bother to remove his helmet. He just gestures for me to jump on the back. I slide my helmet on along with the leather jacket he got me. Buckling it under my chin, I place the ball of my shoe on the back foot peg and hands on his shoulders while I throw my leg over and sit on the back seat.

He revs the engine on the crotch rocket, and the seat vibrates between my legs. I smile and tap his thigh to let him know I'm ready.

He takes off down the driveway and through the gate. I close my eyes, wishing I could feel the wind on my face and in my hair, but Saint won't allow me on his bike unless I have a helmet and jacket on.

We get onto the freeway, and we ride between Haidyn and Kashton. Kashton slows down, and I watch him over my shoulder to see he's weaving across all three lanes, forcing the cars behind him to slow down as Haidyn revs up his bike. He yanks the front wheel up off the road and rides a wheelie past us.

I hold on tighter, expecting Saint to do the same, but he speeds up to catch up with Haidyn who sits his front tire down and slows to be next to us. Kashton comes up on our left once more.

I love it when Saint takes me for a ride, but it doesn't happen all that often. Whenever we go out, it's in the car. He says it's safer. As if the way he drives on four wheels is any different from when he's driving on two.

I don't know how long we've been riding, but my ass is numb, and my back hurts. I adjust myself, and Saint reaches back, placing his hand on my thigh.

A little while later, we're pulling into a gas station, and we all get off the bikes. I stretch my sore legs as Saint removes his helmet. He places it to hang on his mirror and then turns to face me. I tilt my head back so he can undo the buckle underneath my chin, and he takes mine off.

"My cell has been going off like crazy," Haidyn growls, unzipping his jacket and pulling his phone from the inside. "Fuck," he hisses, looking down at it. "We've got to go."

"Where?" Kashton asks, already putting his helmet back on.

Haidyn looks at Saint. "Carnage."

My eyes widen as he looks at me. We've spent a lot of time together lately—practically every day—but we've been at the house of Lords. "I can't..."

"It'll be fine," Saint assures me.

"But—"

"I don't have time to take you back home and then go the opposite way to Carnage. It'll be fine." He grabs my face and kisses my forehead before placing my helmet back on and fastening it.

SAINT

We pull up to the gate of Carnage, and Kashton keys in the code before it open, allowing us to enter. I can feel her body stiff on my back. Her father has worked here since before she was born, and she can probably count on one hand how many times she's been here. Once was recently when we took our vows at the ritual.

We take the curvy road, and I reach down and grip her thigh. I give it a little squeeze to try to ease her concern. I had a few missed calls from my dad but no texts. So I have no clue as to why we're here, but hopefully, it won't take very long.

Pulling up to the back, I place the kickstand down and get off the bike before helping her off as well. I remove her helmet and place both of ours to hang on each mirror.

"Come on." I grab her hand and pull her up the stairs and through the double doors. "Give me ten," I tell the guys, and they nod, heading to our father's offices that they share. I take Ashtyn up a flight of stairs to the third floor. Pulling her down a hallway, I enter a door at the end.

"Saint—?"

I turn her to face me once we're in the room. "Stay here, Ash. Do not leave this room. Do you understand me?"

She bites her bottom lip nervously while staring at her feet.

I grip her chin and force her head back so she has to look at me. "Ashtyn. This is serious. Do you understand me?"

"Yes," she whispers. "I won't leave this room."

"That's my good girl." I lean in and press my lips to hers, and she kisses me back. Her arms wrap around my neck, and she pushes herself into me.

I groan when I have to pull away. "I'll be back." Giving her my back, I exit the room and rush down the hall to the staircase to the basement. It's always cold down here.

I make my way through a set of doors and come to the open room. Our fathers sit at the table. Kashton and Haidyn stand behind them. "What'd I miss?" I ask.

My father checks his watch. "Where the fuck were you?"

Before I have to come up with some lame excuse, Haidyn's father stands from his chair. "They're here now. Let's get to work."

I look at Kashton, and he softly shakes his head. They didn't tell them why we're here. Not surprised. They never do.

We follow them out of the room and down the hall. My father pulls out his cell to make a call. When the person on the other end answers, he speaks. "We're ready. Bring her in."

NINETEEN

ASHTYN

I pace back and forth in his room. At least, I'm guessing it's his room. It's where he brought me back to the night of the vow ceremony.

My heart races that he brought me here. The night of the ritual was different. My father and the rest of the Spade brothers knew I was here. I'm hiding out now, and my father will be pissed if he knew Saint brought me with him.

I have no phone on me because I left it at home. No purse or ID. Coming to a stop, I look at the closed door and walk over to it. I twist the knob and am surprised he didn't lock me in here. That's something Saint would do.

Stepping out into the hallway, I softly close the door behind me. I make my way back to the door that I know leads to the stairs. Leaning over the railing, I look down over the stairwell and listen to the silence, making sure I'm alone. I'll head back outside. Stand next to the bike and wait. At least if I'm caught out there, it won't look so suspicious.

I start to make my way down to the first level when I hear a shrill scream. I slam my back into the wall, and my heart races as I look up to make sure someone didn't see me. But I'm still alone.

It comes again, and I realize it's from the basement. Making my way down to the bottom floor, I push open the door and look down at a dimly lit hallway to see it's empty.

I step through the door, closing it behind me and quickly take a few steps. I hear a door squeaking and jump into an open one. It's a small rectangular room with a concrete floor and walls. There's a square glass in front of me, allowing me to see in the next room. It reminds me of the shows you see where the cops watch the criminal get interrogated for the crimes they commit.

That shrill scream comes again, and I press my back into the corner as I look at the open door. *Fuck, I should have closed it.*

"Got her?" someone barks.

"Yeah," another one answers.

The scream echoes, and I place my hands over my ears because it's getting closer. I bend my knees, sliding my back down the wall as I catch sight of a woman being dragged across the floor in the hallway outside of the room. Blue eyes meet mine before they quickly disappear.

I crawl across the floor and shut the door as quickly as possible but also as quietly as I can not to bring any attention to the room. Standing to my feet, I look through the glass to see they have her in the room across from me.

Two men dressed in cloaks and masks pull the woman across the floor. They drag her with a rope that is wrapped around her neck. You no longer hear her scream, but her hands grab at it, trying to loosen it.

They bring her to a stop, and she rolls over onto her stomach, coughing and grabbing her reddened neck. Rope burns already show on her pale skin. One of the guys yanks her shorts down her legs and underwear while the other rips her shirt off her chest, exposing her fake tits to the room. She wasn't wearing a bra.

One of them grabs the rope that lies next to her and yanks her back to stand with it around her neck. He holds it tight while she fights until her body goes slack, and her eyes roll back into her head. He allows her to drop to the concrete floor once more, and he pushes her onto her back while the other grabs a white straitjacket that hangs on the wall.

They slide her arms into the front of it easily and then turn her onto her stomach, fastening her inside it. It has a zipper that goes all the way up to the base of her neck and five buckles across the back. They bring two more straps between her legs pulling them tightly as they buckle those in place as well. One last strap for her forearms attaches to the front.

One grabs her hair and yanks her to her feet before throwing her into a chair in the middle of the room. A large red ball gag is shoved into her mouth and fastened at the back of her head.

Her eyes are heavy as she looks around aimlessly. She's not fully conscious yet from them choking her out, but she's starting to come around.

She blinks, and fresh tears fall from her eyes as she sobs. She thrashes the best she can in the straitjacket while two men kneel at the front of the chair. They yank her legs wide apart, and each one fastens an ankle to the front legs of the chair, preventing her from closing her legs.

Thrashing back and forth, she continues to sob, and drool runs from her lips. The door to their room opens, and I duck the moment I see someone new enter. Pressing my back to the wall below the mirror, I try to calm my racing heart.

My eyes shoot to my closed door. I wonder how the fuck I'm going to get out of here without being seen. What if Saint is back in his room looking for me?

Turning around, I get to my knees and lift my head to look through the mirror, knowing they can't see me, or they would have already been in here to get me too.

I count four men now dressed in cloaks and masks. I have no clue who they could be. The door opens again, and my pulse races when I see Saint enter the room.

What the fuck is he doing in there?

He goes to the far wall and leans back against it. Crossing his arms over his chest, he places one combat boot on the wall bending his knee as he stares at the woman. Not an ounce of emotion in his cold eyes.

I've grown up in this world. I understand what a Lord is about, but I never stopped to think what Saint was capable of. Don't they say love is blind? That women ignore the red flags when they see a pretty face?

How could I have missed so much? Is he going to stand there and let them hurt her?

I get my answer the next second when a man enters the room. The woman sees him and begins to scream louder and thrash harder. One of the cloak and mask walks behind the chair and attaches a hook into a silver ring at the back of the gag and pulls on it, forcing her to lift her chin to stare at the ceiling.

SAINT

THE LORDS HAVE AN UNDERSTANDING. A CODE THAT WE LIVE BY. And that is the Lords come first. No matter what. Even though we're all supposed to be "brothers" within the society, someone involved always wants more than what they're given. Those Lords are punished. Some killed immediately. Others are brought here to Carnage to live out a lifelong sentence of pain and humiliation.

Women in our world are no different. Their treatment is to fit the crime.

The woman sits tied in the chair in the center of the room while the Lord stands before her. My eyes go to the mirror that's on the opposite wall from me. I feel like we're being watched. But that's just me being paranoid. I'm ready to get this over, get back to Ashtyn, and get the fuck out of here. Being at Carnage tonight was the last thing on my mind. I'm not sure why our fathers wanted us here in the first place.

The Lord gets my attention as he slaps the woman. Her mumbled sobs follow. She shakes her head the best she can as he shoves his hand between her now naked and open legs. Her upper body is covered with the straitjacket. But her lower body only has the two straps that go between her legs, leaving her pussy wide open.

"Want to be fucked, bitch?" he asks her.

Spit flies from her mouth as she tries to wiggle free, but she's not going anywhere.

"I'm here to grant that wish." He smiles down at her. "I chose a straitjacket as your punishment. I hear that after long periods of time, it can be quite painful. Your blood pools in your elbows, leading to swelling. Your hands will go numb of course from lack of circulation. Depending on how long I decide to have them keep you in this, you may start to experience bone and muscle stiffness in your upper arms and shoulders. You also run the possibility of overheating if I have them turn up the temperature in here." He taps the side of her tear-streaked face. Looking up, he addresses the rest of us in the room. "I want her to have the full treatment. Do not go easy on her."

My father nods in understanding.

"Give her a pregnancy test. If she's knocked up, terminate it," he commands. "And I want a hysterectomy performed regardless." She sobs into the gag. "I'll come back to visit you, darling. Just to make sure you're getting what you deserve." He exits the room and slams the door shut.

My father looks at me. "You two get her prepped." One by one, they each filter out of the room, leaving Kashton and me alone.

I walk over to the far end of the room where the cabinets are. Opening up the top one, I grab what we need and place it on the counter. The door opens, and I turn, expecting it to be Haidyn, but it's Devin. He has a rolling cart that has a metal bowl with hot coals dumped in the middle.

"Here you are, sir." He nods, stepping back and exiting the room.

She screams into the gag, trying to free herself, but there's no use. No one can escape that. Kashton takes the lighter fluid and pours it into the bowl, soaking the coals in it. Then he removes the Zippo from his back pocket. It's chrome with a black spade in the center, and inside, it has a skull with 666 across the bottom. Lighting it, he drops it into the bowl as well, starting the fire.

It doesn't take long to heat. I take the 666 branding iron and hold it over the fire, slowly turning it to make sure all sides are equally heated. I'd hate to have to do it more than once.

When it's burning red, Kashton and I walk over to her. "Where do you want it?" Kash asks her.

Snot, drool, and tears cover her face as she screams so loud, she begins to choke around the gag. "This is only the beginning," I tell her, knowing that our fathers will make her life a living hell.

Kashton undoes the latch attached to the ball gag harness at the back of her head that forces her chin to the ceiling. He grips her hair and shoves her head down. I press the brand to the back of her neck. The smell of burning flesh fills the room and so does the sound of sizzling skin and her gagged scream.

TWENTY

ASHTYN

I'm shaking as I watch the naked woman in the chair. She's thrashing as Kashton holds her hair down, and Saint brands the back of her neck. My watery eyes widen, and my heart hammers in my chest. How can they do this to her? Hurt an innocent woman just because another Lord told them to?

Saint removes the brand. Kashton yanks her head up, and she's shaking uncontrollably. Her bloodshot eyes are on mine as if she can see me, and a chill runs up my spine.

I push off the glass, stepping back, and hit something...no someone. My body stiffens, and a hand covers my mouth while another wraps around my arms, pinning them down to my side.

"Shh," a voice whispers in my ear, and I'm paralyzed—unable to move. I might as well be in the straitjacket like the woman in the other room. "Don't make a sound, baby girl. They can't see you, but they can hear you."

It's Haidyn! I blink, and a tear rolls down my cheek.

He removes his hand from my mouth, and I take in a shaky breath. I spin around as he pulls his cell from his pocket and watch him type away on it.

"Hai-dyn?" I whisper. God, I hope he's not doing what I think he's doing. Please...no.

His eyes meet mine, and he places it back in his pocket. "Sorry, Ash," he says, not sounding a bit remorseful.

My heart hammers in my chest as I look back through the glass and see Saint pull his phone from his pocket. A lump lodges in my throat, making it impossible to swallow. His bright-green eyes snap up and look directly at me, and my stomach sinks.

He starts walking toward the door, and I run to the one in the room I'm in. It's already open. I was too busy watching what was happening to the woman to even hear Haidyn open it and join me. I hit the hallway and run to the stairwell.

I make it up to the first floor and rush outside into the dark night. I'm shaking, my side's burning, and I'm trying to catch my breath. It's like one of those bad dreams where you know something evil is chasing you, but you can't get away fast enough. I almost trip over a loose branch on the ground, and my hair is stuck to my tear-streaked face as I shove limbs out of my way.

I jump over a branch, but I'm hit from behind as I land. I scream as I'm shoved to the uneven ground. Rocks dig into my chest and stomach. I'm yanked and tossed onto my back, and a hand covers my mouth. I slap at whoever is on top of me. I can't see anything because my hair covers more than half my face, stuck to my tears. I can't breathe with his hand over my mouth, so I try to free it by digging my nails into his skin, but it does no good.

My hands are ripped from the man and pulled above my head, pinned to the ground. I kick my legs and arch my back, but it's useless. Someone is on top of me, and they're too heavy.

The hand is removed from my mouth only to be replaced by some kind of cloth shoved into it, filling my cheeks. I cry into it, my body shaking.

"Shhh," a voice says softly. My hair is pushed from my face, and hands grab my wet cheeks. "You're okay, sweetheart. You're okay."

Saint is on top of me. I arch my neck to see Haidyn kneeling above my head, pinning my arms down.

A sob wracks my body.

"You're okay." He repeats, and I shake my head. "I'm not going to hurt you, Ash, but you've got to be quiet." He looks over his shoulder before his eyes come back to mine. "Can you do that?"

I nod quickly, taking a deep breath through my nose.

He reaches into my mouth and removes the cloth, and I sob. "Shh." He covers my mouth once more. "Deep breaths, sweetheart. Come on, calm your breathing for me."

I take a deep breath and blink the fresh tears from my eyes.

"That's it. Good girl. Again," he says softly.

I manage to take another breath through my nose, and he slowly removes his hand from my face. I lick my wet lips, and he smiles down at me. "You're okay. Nothing is going to happen to you."

Haidyn releases my wrists, and I bring them to my chest, trying to shield myself from Saint.

"Take her home." Haidyn gets to his feet. "I'll cover for you." He stands and walks away from us, heading back toward Carnage.

"Come on." Saint gets off me and grabs my hand, pulling me to my feet. I stumble back from him, and he stands before me, staring. I blink the fresh tears streaming down my face, trying to stabilize myself on my shaking legs. He steps forward. "Ash—"

I take another one back.

Reaching up, he runs his hands through his hair. "I need you to understand something..."

"Don't touch me." I manage to get out through the knot in my throat.

He places his hands out wide. "You can't stay here, sweetheart. I have to take you home."

I shake my head, wrapping my arms around myself.

"Listen to me, Ashtyn," he commands, his voice so harsh it makes me flinch.

My watery eyes lift to meet his dark stare.

"Either you willingly leave with me, or I tie you up, gag that pretty mouth of yours, and drag you from these woods."

Drag? As in with a rope around my neck? The blood rushes in my ears. How did I not know what Saint was capable of? How could I have ever felt so safe around him? How many women has he hurt? Killed? What will it take for him to do the same to me? I remember my father telling me what he must do if I didn't bleed for him. I never stopped to think about it until now. That only due to pure luck, he hasn't done to me what he just did to that woman.

He reaches down and undoes his belt, and my heart leaps in my chest. "Ok-ay...okay." I swallow. "I'll leave with you." If I allow him to tie up and gag me, I won't have a chance.

SAINT

Haidyn had tossed me the keys to a car that he has here because the last thing I wanted to do was put her on the back of my bike to take her home.

She follows me back to Carnage, and we get into his car. She sniffs. "Where do you want to go?" I ask. I can't take her to the house of Lords because I have to come back here, and I don't want her there without me.

"My place," she whispers.

I'm not sure how much she saw. Haidyn just messaged me that he was with her, and she was in the observation room. I want to ask her, but I'm just going to assume she saw all of it by how she reacted.

Reaching over, I touch her thigh, and she jumps. "Ash—"

"How could you do that to her?" she asks softly.

I sigh. "We have no control over what our fathers order us to do." It's true. When we run Carnage, we'll have full say, but until then, we will do as we're told.

"How long will you keep her in that?"

"I'm not sure." Again, that's up to her husband. He was the one who brought her in tied up in his trunk.

"What else will our dads have you guys do to her?" she wonders.

I run a hand through my hair. "They..." I stop myself, unable to finish that sentence. The truth is our fathers won't touch her. It'll be everyone else who gets their piece. I can't say I feel sorry for the woman. She deserves it. The innocent aren't sent to Carnage.

"That was her husband, right?" she whispers. Again, I don't answer. "What if she's pregnant?" she asks softly.

"Carnage is no place for a child." That's the only way I can think to respond to that question. I'm not saying it's right, I'm just saying that if she is, I can't save her or the baby. It's up to her husband since he's the one who turned her in.

"How could he do that to her? He's supposed to protect her."

"Lords don't marry for love." Some do, but it's rare, and she already knows that. She's just trying to justify what she saw.

She doesn't ask any more questions. Instead, she sinks further into the passenger seat. I pull up to her house, and she's out before I can even open the driver's side door.

"Ash?" I call out as she runs toward her house.

I rush up behind her and grab her arm, turning her to face me. She whimpers in my arms, and I hate how terrified she is of me. "You're okay," I say and force her eyes to mine. "I'm not going to hurt you, okay?"

She nods, crossing her arms over her chest, not believing a damn thing I just said. I look at her house and then back at her. "You can't tell anyone what you saw."

Her watery eyes meet mine, but she says nothing. "No one, Ash."

"I under—"

"I don't think you do," I say, tightening my hands on her upper arms. She tries to pull away, but I maintain my firm grasp. "No one. Not a soul."

"I understand," she snaps, pulling away from me, and I let her go.

With a heavy sigh, I watch her turn away from me. She runs up her steps into her house and slams the front door shut.

TWENTY-ONE

ASHTYN

I sit straight up in bed, the covers falling to pool in my lap. Straining my ears, I hear a sound in my house, and I jump out of bed, grabbing my cell from beside me. I had fallen asleep after I finished a bottle of wine and cried into my pillow.

A look at the clock tells me that Saint dropped me off five hours ago, and it's still dark outside.

Getting out of bed, I pull up his name and hover over the call button when I hear water running in my kitchen. Maybe he's come back, and that just pisses me off. How dare he think I'm just going to forget what I saw? Or that he doesn't have to answer my questions?

I make my way in there, expecting it to be him, but I come to a stop when I see someone else standing at my sink filling a glass of water. "What are you doing here?" I ask, taking a step back.

The man turns to face me, his eyes dropping to my bare feet and running up my oversized T-shirt. He sets the glass down and leans back against the counter, crossing his arms over his chest. "Ashtyn—"

"How did you get in?" I demand.

He reaches into his pocket and removes a key. "Dad gave me a key when he got you the house." Then he drops it onto the counter.

I roll my eyes. "Leave." I don't want anything to do with any Lord right now—especially my brother. I didn't see him there, but there were several in cloaks and masks. He could have easily been one of them. I turn and walk out of the kitchen, but he grabs my arm, yanking me back. I spin around and slam my fist into his face. I'm not in the mood to play games at the moment. Or be touched by anyone.

"Fuck, Ash." He covers his nose with his hand.

"Don't touch me!" I scream.

He holds his arms out wide, taking a step back. "I'm here to check on you," he states.

"Bullshit," I spit out.

Sighing, he removes his cell from his back pocket, unlocks it, and sets it down on the counter. Saint's voice fills my kitchen. "Hey, man. Where the fuck are you? Your dad is pissed that you're not at Carnage. Speaking of which..." He sighs heavily, sounding stressed. "I took Ash with me, and she saw...some shit. I just dropped her off at her house. She was pretty upset. I wasn't able to stay with her because I have to head back. If you get a chance, can you stop by and check on her, please? I'm really worried." He pauses. "I have to go. Kash is calling me." *Click.*

"What did you see?" my brother asks, pocketing his cell.

I drop my eyes to the marble floor. "Doesn't matter."

"Ash—"

"You want me to believe that you came by to check on me in the middle of the night because Saint asked you to?" I'm not buying it. They're testing me. Saint told me not to tell a soul what I saw. Although I'm pissed at him right now, I'm keeping my mouth closed. I won't give the Lords a reason to kill me. That would be them taking the easy way out.

"Look, I know I've been a shitty brother. But..." He looks away from me. "There is some shit going on that I'm trying to make sure you stay out of."

I step forward. "What do you mean? Does this have to do with what Dad was talking to you about the night of the party in the woods? The girl who went missing?"

His silence tells me enough.

"So you are in trouble with the Lords? Is that why you're avoiding Carnage?" I can only imagine how mad our father is right now if Adam is supposed to be there like the others, and he's not.

"I'm trying to find who is setting me up," he growls. "And I can't do that if I'm having to babysit you." His eyes narrow on mine.

Babysit me? "You haven't been a brother for years, Adam. I don't need you to start now." I roll my eyes and turn to walk away.

"Don't blame Saint."

I whip around. "He's a Lord. He's part of the problem." Fuck him and what he thinks about my opinion of Saint.

He rounds the island, and I take a step back as he advances on me, but my ass hits the counter, stopping my escape. "Listen, Ash. Whatever you think you know, I promise it's not the truth, and whatever you saw is a very small fraction of what the Lords are capable of. This..." He holds his hands out wide, gesturing to my house. "Is what the Lords want the world to see. Money and power are what they want us to think they will give us. But the dirty truth is Carnage."

"What about it?" I ask nervously. I'm getting a sickening feeling after what I saw earlier this evening there. My father never talks about what goes on at Carnage, and my mother never asks. Either she knows or she doesn't care.

"Carnage is a prison. It's where the Lords send their own that do them wrong. We, the Spade brothers, are the ones that run the Lords' hell."

"Saint—"

He steps into me, cutting me off, and I tilt my head back to look him in the eyes. My stomach tightens at the look in his. "Saint is the only one who can protect you. He's the only one who cares about you."

I flinch at his harsh words.

"So whatever you saw, or whatever he did, just know any other

Lord could do the same to you. Saint will be the only one to ensure it doesn't happen." Placing his hands on my upper arms, I stiffen. "I'm going to go away for a little while."

"What? Where are you going?" I rush out.

"It's better that you don't know."

"Adam..."

"Go home," he snaps. Letting go of me, he steps back.

"I am home."

"No. To Mom and Dad's. Do not stay here alone. I had a key, but the next person who comes over might not. I've called Saint, Haidyn, and Kashton. All of their phones are off." I swallow nervously as he runs a hand through his hair. "I'm not going back to Carnage, so I don't know what's going on..."

"Do you think he's okay?" I can't help but worry, and my pulse races at the thought that they might be doing the same thing to him that he did to that woman.

"Saint can hold his own, but you need to get the fuck out of here. Go stay with Mom. Saint will call you when he's able to." He goes to exit the house.

"What about you?" I ask, hating how worried I am for him. We've never been close, but that doesn't mean I want him killed. The Lords preach brotherhood, but they're as shady as they come. They're raised to fight for the smallest amount of money and power. You can't just undo that once you're initiated. If they feel threatened, they attack. And no law or rule states that they can't get "rid" of their own. If they think you deserve it, then they allow it.

"I'll come back for you and Mom once I find what I'm looking for." With that, he turns and exits my house, leaving a chill down my spine.

I run upstairs, grab a few things along with my cell, and throw it all in a bag. Then I'm hurrying to my car in the garage and rushing to my parents' house, wondering if my father knows I was at Carnage tonight. If he does, what will he do to me? Would my mother stop him from trying to kill me? No. She wouldn't step in and jeopardize her life for me. Even Adam knows that. He said Saint is the only one I can trust.

I don't want to believe him, but that little voice in my mind screams that he's right. Saint has never hurt me. Not in the way I saw him hurt that woman. Does that mean he's incapable of hurting me? No. It just means I haven't pushed him that far yet.

Pulling up to my parents' house, I get out, grab my bag, and enter the house. It's almost four in the morning, so I quietly make my way up to my room. I'll let my mother know I'm here in the morning. But when I go to open the door, I hear her voice in the foyer below.

"Don't come back here."

Pausing, I stare at my door, trying to listen over the sound of the blood rushing in my ears.

"I've tried calling you." A male's voice growls.

"I was ignoring you for a reason," she snaps. Then she adds in a softer voice, "You know you can't come here."

The sound of the front door opens, and just when I think I can walk into my room, I hear the man say, "Why is Ashtyn's car here? I thought we were alone."

Fuck! He just saw me parked in the driveway. I didn't pull it into the garage. Who the hell is this that they know what I drive?

"She must have come home earlier," my mother adds. "It's fine. I'm sure she's asleep."

"Go check," he commands.

My pulse races.

"I'm not—"

"Go fucking check," he snaps, interrupting her.

I twist the doorknob as softly as I can. I rush to my bed as I rip the shirt up and over my head, throw my bag across the room, and kick off my shoes. I yank my duvet back and jump into bed, pulling it up to my neck, my back facing the door, and bring it up over my face so only half of my head can be seen.

My door opens, and I hold my breath as light filters into my room.

"See, I told you," my mother whispers, and my heart hammers, knowing a man I don't know is looking into my room.

The door softly closes a moment later, and I let out the breath I was holding but don't dare move. Instead, I lie in the dark staring at nothing, trying to figure out what the fuck is going on and who is actually on my side.

I feel like I can't trust anyone anymore.

SAINT

It's been three days since Ashtyn ran out of Carnage, and I took her home. She's avoiding me. I've called, texted, and left voicemails, but they've all gone unanswered.

I'm not sure what to do at this point. How much time does she need to come to terms with this life? She grew up around this. The woman who she saw wasn't innocent, but she didn't give me the chance to explain that. It's not like we choose random women in the mall parking lot and kidnap them before torturing them. I hate to say it, but there is a method to the madness.

I've been watching her on camera. She's staying at her parents', secluding herself from the world. She mainly drinks and stays in bed, sleeping quite a bit. She's going to classes, but not all of them. She'll leave for an hour or two and then come home and crawl back in bed. It makes me mad that she's being this way. That she's so shaken up over a bitch who doesn't deserve it. And the way she looked at me. Pulled away from me. Does she really think I'd hurt her? I've saved her. Of course I can't tell her that. There's no scenario where I'd come out as the good guy.

"Saint?" my father calls out.

"Yeah?" I walk toward him in the basement at Carnage.

"The woman isn't pregnant." He shoves some papers into my chest, and I reach up to take them so they don't fall to my feet. "Take her to see Devin. He's expecting her." With that, he continues down the hallway.

I make my way to the woman's room that she was placed in the night her husband brought her in. Unlocking the steel door, it creaks, letting her know she has a visitor. She lies on a black operating table that has wheels. Usually, you don't get anything to lay on when sentenced to a cell, but her husband wants her strapped down at all times.

A white and brown medical restraint runs across the bottom of the table with her ankles buckled into them on each end. Another runs from side to side on her upper legs, strapping her thighs down, which force her legs wide open. She has a catheter that hangs on the side. The third and final strap runs underneath her neck, also fastened on her throat to keep her head down. The ball gag has been removed and replaced with bondage tape now over her lips and chin. I'm not sure who removed the gag, but they replaced something inside of her mouth by the way her cheeks expand.

When her wild eyes see me, she begins to scream into her gag and thrash around. She's still got energy. It'll take a few more days to lose hope. For her to understand that this will be her life now.

I drop the papers onto the straitjacket that she's still strapped in and unlock the wheels. Then I begin to push her out of the room and down the hall.

The woman continues her worthless fight. She's just wearing herself out. But it won't matter. Devin is going to knock her out and perform a hysterectomy. I must say I'm relieved that she's not pregnant. I don't want to have to explain that to Ashtyn if she were to ask me. I think she plans on never talking to me again, but that's not how it's going to work. She's just lucky right now that Carnage has kept me busy and away from her.

When I get the first chance, I'm going to her parents' house and making sure she remembers who she is—mine. And that I'm not playing this silent game anymore. She can hate me all she wants; it's not going to keep me away.

I enter the double doors of the hospital, and Devin waits for me. He is our main doctor here at Carnage. Has been since I was little.

I bring the table to a stop, and he takes over. I watch him push her into a room as her muffled cries and screams fade to nothing when the doors close behind them.

She's a mother...was a mother. She traded her only child in for a life that she thought was better than this. Her husband was informed that his daughter was found dead of an overdose in an alley last week. She had never done drugs a day in her life. So he said. He had went through his wife's cell and their banking accounts to find where she had set it up to have their daughter killed. Paid five grand to an old boyfriend of the daughter's to make it look like a suicide. He had messaged his ex that he missed her and talked her into going out on a date with him. After they finished dinner, they went to a friends of his house where they shot her up with drugs and raped her before tossing her into an alley once done.

I knew of their daughter. She would be a senior at Barrington next year, and her mother didn't want her living the life that her husband had planned for their daughter.

I grew up in this life around death and torture every day, so I'm desensitized by all of it. But this one gets to me because that could have been Ashtyn. Her mother has been so hell-bent on her not being my chosen that I know just how far she went to keep that from happening. I was lucky that Altus shared what he knew with me.

Now we've each got a secret. And that's what bothers me the most. My hands are tied, and I can't do shit about it. Not now anyway and maybe never. It's eating at me, and I hate to let shit go.

"Hey, man."

I turn to see Kashton walking toward me with an ice pack in his hand. "What the hell happened to you?" I ask, seeing the blood dripping from his busted nose.

"Trying to help Devin earlier with a patient. The bastard knocked the shit out of me."

I laugh. "It happens."

We both turn and exit the hospital to head back to the basement, and he looks around and sees we're alone before he speaks. "Has anyone said anything about Ashtyn?"

"Nope." Haidyn and I filled him in on what happened, but none of our dads have said anything to me. And as far as I know, Altus has been staying here at Carnage.

I haven't told my brothers what Altus showed me, but I know that he's on Ashtyn's side. If the other dads found out, they would probably force his hand, but for right now, she's safe. And I intend to keep it that way.

TWENTY-TWO

ASHTYN

I've been staying at my parents' house for five days, so my mother knows something is up. I never choose to stay here. She hasn't mentioned anything about the stranger being here the other night and spotting my car.

I've also noticed that my father hasn't been home since I've been here either, which makes me think he's been at Carnage. I haven't had any contact with Saint either, and I'm not sure how I feel about that just yet. He's tried, but I've ignored him. I'm not sure what to do or how to proceed at this point. Too many moving parts that I just can't trust.

One minute, I worry if he's okay. Then the next, I remember him branding a woman tied to a chair in a straitjacket.

"Honey, I made us an appointment tomorrow," my mother says, entering my room.

I'm on my third pint of Ben & Jerry's mint chocolate cookie and my second bottle of wine. I close my eyes, and I see the woman begging them not to kill her. I see Saint just watching, not an ounce of emotion in his cold eyes. And I hear Haidyn telling me to stay quiet or they'll replace the woman with me. "I'm not going," I tell her.

The last thing I'm going to do is tell her fucking therapist what I saw. One, they won't believe me, and two, they won't fucking care.

She huffs, her hands on her narrow hips. "You're going, and that's final." She turns and exits my room, slamming my door shut.

I look at my cell and see that it's almost dead. I haven't charged it the last couple of days.

Rolling out of bed, I decide I need a shower to try to get out of this funk that I've fallen into. Maybe I'll feel better if I clean myself up.

An hour later, I stand in my bathroom, drying my hair, when I hear a sound. I shut the blow dryer off and lay it on my counter. "Mom?" I call out. After a few seconds of silence, I exit my bathroom and enter my adjoining bedroom. Walking over to my closed door, I twist the knob. "Mom—?"

It's shoved open, hitting me so hard that it knocks me on my ass. "What the...?"

"Hi, sweetheart," a man says, entering my room.

I know him. Miles Hopper. He's a sophomore this year at Barrington University. I've seen him at the house of Lords. He's a couple of years younger than Saint. "Get the fuck out of my room." They're not friends, so I'm not sure why the hell he'd be here. Unless my brother sent him. But I don't remember Adam being close with him.

He reaches around into his back pocket and removes a zip tie. The smile he gives me makes my stomach sink. "Come on, baby. You love it when Saint ties you up and plays with you."

I scream, trying to get to my feet, but he's faster. Grabbing my hair, he yanks me over to the side of my bed and pins me to it. I try to push myself up, but it's useless. He grabs both of my arms, his fingers digging into my skin as he yanks them behind my back and secures my wrists together tightly with the zip tie. Then he wraps his arm around my upper arms and drags me out of my room, down the stairs and to the living room. Letting me go, he shoves me forward. I trip, falling to my knees.

A set of black boots steps in front of me, and the tip of a knife on my chin forces me to look up at him. "Where is your brother?" Tyson Crawford demands.

I knew this would happen. *It's better that you don't know.* Adam said that to me when he told me he was leaving. "I'll never tell you," I say through gritted teeth.

He sighs, crouching down in front of me. His elbows rest on his thighs. "You understand I have to hurt you if you choose to protect him, right?" He runs the blade over my heaving chest.

"Do what you have to do," I spit out, refusing to give in. I won't die for a Lord, but my brother? I have to give him time to find answers. I don't know what's going on, but he was physically shaken up. I'd never seen my brother like that before.

Standing, he shakes his head. "What a waste."

"You're the waste." I pull my lips back with a growl. "Doing whatever the Lords tell you to do. You're nothing but a fucking puppet." The Lords think they have power, but they don't. It's a joke. They do as they're told when they are told to do it. I never understood how much they control them until I became Saint's chosen. He's always being called to Carnage. Or ordered to do something that he can't tell me. And what he did to that woman...

Tyson throws his head back, laughing. "What's that make your brother?"

"He had the balls to stand up for himself," I snap, not really knowing what else to say. But the longer I keep him talking, the more time I have that he won't kill me. "To get away from them."

He smiles. "Why didn't he take you and your mother with him?"

"He'll come back for us when the time is right." I lift my chin. I believed Adam when he said he'd be back. I'm just not sure when that'll be.

Tyson steps over to my mom, lying on her stomach with her hands tied behind her back. She screams into the duct tape over her mouth when he grips her bleach-blond hair and jerks her up. He stabs her in the chest and yanks it out.

"MOM!" I scream, jumping up and rushing over to her body that lies on the floor.

But he steps in front of me, wrapping a hand around my neck, lifting my feet up off the floor. Our faces almost touching, he says, "Still want me to do whatever I have to do?" He arches a brow.

I'm sobbing, my body shaking in his hand as I look at my mother lying dead on our floor. Tyson loosens the grip on my neck, and I choke out, "I ... don't know anything." Why would he think that I do? I'm no one. Just a woman in a man's world. A fucking chosen that a Lord gets to use.

Miles enters the room, and he holds up my cell phone. "Let's see if we can get him to come to us."

Tyson tightens his hand on my throat once more, and I thrash in his hold as he chokes me. I try to fight, but there's no use. My body is shutting down, betraying me. My eyes start to roll into my head, and he lets go, taking a step back. I fall to my knees, coughing and spit flying from my mouth, sobbing once again.

He moves to stand behind me and grips my hair, yanking my head back as Miles stands in front of me and holds up my phone. "Smile for the camera," he tells me as I try to breathe through the sobs.

After capturing a picture, he types out a message while Tyson tugs me to my feet and drags me over to the couch, forcing me to sit. He sits down across from me on the coffee table and grips my chin. "You better hope he's as loyal to you as you are to him."

My cell rings, and my heart leaps in my chest. *It's going to die soon.* "Blocked number," Miles announces.

"That's not a good start," Tyson states, and my shoulders shake as I begin to rock back and forth.

Miles hits answer and places it on speakerphone. I hold my breath. "What the fuck?" Adam's voice demands.

"Help me!" I cry, jumping to my feet.

Tyson leaps forward, shoving me onto my back on the couch,

straddling my chest, and places a hand over my mouth. I scream into it as he pins my tied arms underneath me.

"Who the fuck is this?" Adam shouts. "What the fuck do you want?"

"You," Tyson answers, but his eyes are on mine as tears run down the sides of my face. I arch my neck and back the best I can, trying to fight him off.

My brother goes silent as my muffled cries get louder.

"The Lords sent us to collect you," Miles says. "Either you're here in an hour or your sister is dead like your mother." He hangs up the phone and turns it off, tossing it into the vase filled with red roses on the end table by the couch. I close my eyes, sobbing, knowing that they just destroyed any chance I had of surviving this. Now I can't even try to call Saint to save me. I'm going to die here.

Tyson gets up off me and goes back to sitting on the coffee table. I slowly get up and try to stretch my tied arms behind my back.

"Don't worry," Miles begins, walking behind the couch. The sound of him cocking a gun makes me tremble. "If he doesn't come to your rescue, we'll show you mercy and make it quick." He grips my hair, pulling my head back, and pushes the end of the barrel into my temple.

I'm gasping for breath. "Please ... I didn't do anything." I swallow. I feel like the woman I watched at Carnage beg for her life in front of a group of men who did nothing to save her. But I have a feeling they won't keep me alive like she probably is. I'll be dead in a puddle of my own blood like my mother very soon.

Tyson gets up, and I try to do the same and run, but Miles has me by my hair, holding me in place. Tyson opens up a bag that they must have brought and then walks back toward me. He falls down onto the couch, straddling my legs, and I scream at the top of my lungs.

"Please..." I sob, trying to throw him off me, but Miles still has my hair, my arms are tied behind my back, and Tyson has my legs pinned down. I have no chance.

Tyson shoves a cloth into my mouth, silencing my cries for help and then rips off a piece of duct tape with his teeth and shoves it over my lips. My watery eyes meet his blue ones, trying to plead with him to let me go.

Saint can protect you. My brother lied. Saint can't do anything to help me right now. But when he finds out I've been killed, he'll do something alright. He'll make sure these two pay for my death. At least that much I know.

Tyson gets up off me, and I try to calm my heavy breathing. I have to think this through. Try to figure out how the fuck to survive this.

Miles lets go of my hair, and I watch him out of the corner of my eye pull his cell out of his pocket. Tyson's back faces us as he stands at the fireplace. It's the only shot I have.

I jump up to my feet and make a run for it. Fucking bastards didn't tie my ankles.

"Fuck!" Miles hisses, and my heart races as I head toward the hallway. "Goddammit," he growls throwing me face down onto the floor next to my dead mother. "Fucking bitch." He straddles my back, fists my hair, and yanks my head up off the marble floor.

My eyes find Tyson as I suck in a breath through my nose.

"I was going to make it quick," Miles announces. I feel something cold against my neck, then a sting follows as he cuts me with the pocketknife. I close my eyes tightly as the warm blood runs down my skin. "Now I'm going to take my time. Split this little body of yours open one slice at a time. You'll be begging for us to kill you soon."

"Look at me," Tyson commands.

I open my watery eyes, and he's crouching down in front of me with his phone out, and I know he's taking a picture. Probably to prove to whoever ordered the hit on my brother that I'm about to die because Adam is a coward. I've never hated him more than I do right now.

"Just a little something for us to jack off to later." Miles laughs, and he reaches around with his free hand and pinches my nose.

I buck wildly as panic sets in that I can no longer breathe, and his laughter fills my ears.

SAINT

I'M SHAKING. MY HANDS HAVE A DEATH GRIP ON MY CELL WHILE I look at the picture. It's a close-up of a brunette.

Ashtyn.

She's positioned on her stomach in the middle of the family room I know all too well. A man straddles her back, but his face isn't included in the picture. I can tell by her shoulders that her arms are tied behind her back. There's a knife at her neck. He's already cut her because blood trails down her perfectly tan skin and onto the marble floor.

Her baby-blue eyes are bloodshot from crying. Tears run down her pretty face, snot leaks from her nose, and duct tape covers her plump lips.

My chest vibrates, my blood boils like a forgotten pot of water on the stove. It's overflowing and sizzling onto the burner.

I scan the text.

You want her?

She's already mine. Ashtyn belongs to me. She's my girl.

Fuck yes, I want her!

My fingers fly over the letters, replying as quickly as I can. I had received the picture of her minutes before I even opened it up. If she's already dead...

You've got ten minutes.

My phone alerts me of his response, stopping that thought.

"We'll make it." Kashton slaps my shoulder as he sits behind me in the SUV.

I can't stop looking at her. I haven't spoken to her since I dropped her off at her house five days ago. We've been locked at Carnage taking care of shit for our fathers while they're out of town. I just happened to turn my phone on right before I got the text. I haven't even had the chance to check the cameras in her room today.

"Why the fuck does Tyson have her?" Haidyn demands, taking the curves fast in the middle of the night.

"The Lords," Kashton answers when I don't. I can't seem to form a single fucking word. The world is black, my vision impaired other than the picture of her on my phone. My mind clouded and my body so energized, I could jump start a car.

I'm vibrating with rage. An animal waiting to be set off its leash to attack. Destroy.

The car comes to a screeching halt outside of the mansion. I'm out of the passenger door before Haidyn can even put the car in park. Running up the stairs, I shove both doors open to the house so hard they hit the interior wall with a bang.

I rush into the family room where I know she is. Tyson sits on the couch, his arms fanned across the back looking as comfortable as can be. He's lucky I don't blow his fucking head off. I would ask him why the fuck he's even here at Ashtyn's parents' house, but I already know. Kashton was right. The Lords are the only logical answer my head can come up with right now.

Another Lord by the name of Miles Hopper jumps up from the couch. "What the fuck are you doing here?" he demands. When we don't answer, he spins around to look at Tyson. "What did you do, Tyson?"

Tyson also ignores him.

I catch sight of Ashtyn lying face down on the floor, hands zip-tied behind her back and duct tape over her mouth. I've had her in this position plenty of times. But she's always been naked.

To see her in such a vulnerable position that another man put her in makes me fucking feral. Explosive. The blood rushes in my ears when she lifts her head off the floor, and her watery eyes meet mine. Her body fights the restraints as she rolls side to side and begins to mumble unintelligible words behind the tape.

Hang on, sweetheart.

I remove the pocketknife from my back pocket and flip it open as I storm over to her. Leaning down, I cut the zip tie around her wrists and grab her arm, yanking her to her feet more forcefully than I mean to. I rip the tape off her lips and remove the cloth inside her mouth, and she sobs, immediately throwing her body into mine and wrapping her arms around my neck, standing up on her tiptoes.

I wrap my arms around her protectively, feeling her tremble against me.

"You can't take her," Miles growls, then turns to face Tyson once more. "We have a job to do."

I knew it was for the Lords. They're only sophomores this year. They are both here because this is their initiation. The question is why?

"And we did it." Tyson nods to her mother who lies dead on the floor next to where I found Ashtyn. The blood that has pooled around her tells me that she was stabbed or shot.

"She's supposed to be dead," Miles snaps. "Everyone in this house must be taken care of. If her brother isn't here in thirty minutes, I'm going to fucking gut the bitch."

Adam? Why am I not surprised this has to do with him?

I pry Ashtyn's arms from around my neck as she protests and push her to the side as Miles turns back to face me. I bury my knife into his neck and then yank it out. Ashtyn covers her ears as Miles makes gurgling noises before dropping to his knees.

Fucking bastard. Over my dead body will I let him touch what's mine, let alone kill her. He got off easy. Only because I want to get her out of here as soon as possible.

Kashton pulls her into his arms to comfort her as I wipe the bloody knife on my jeans.

Tyson stands from the couch. "You understand what this means?" he asks me, his eyes going to a sobbing Ashtyn. Haidyn takes her from Kashton. Gripping her thighs, he picks her up, and she wraps her legs around his waist, burying her face into his neck. Her sobs fill the room. Tyson's eyes come back to mine, waiting for a response.

I nod, closing the knife and shoving my now bloody hands into my pockets. "I owe you." Looking over at her, I've never seen her this terrified, and the thought of losing her is maddening. What if Tyson hadn't sent me that picture? What if Miles had killed her before I arrived? I tell myself not to think about that right now. He did send me a picture, and I did make it in time.

I saved her.

Walking over to Haidyn, I rub her back, and she pulls her face from him to look at me. She removes her arms from around his neck and reaches for me like a child needing to be comforted. I take her from him and hold her shaking body to mine as we turn and walk out of her mother's house, knowing she will never come back here.

Tyson saved her from the Lords. The very men I vowed my life to. Life as she knows it will never be the same. She will depend on me for everything. Not like I was ever going to let her go anyway.

I crawl into the back seat of the SUV while Kashton closes the door behind me and then gets in the passenger seat, and Haidyn starts the Cadillac.

She's straddling my waist, arms wrapped around me, and continues to sob. "You're okay, sweetheart." I rub her back. Poor thing is trembling. I can only imagine what she went through. Did she watch them kill her mother? I mean, if you ask me, she was a piece of shit. Whether she deserved to die or not, I hate that it might have happened in front of Ashtyn. "I've got you now," I tell her. "You're safe."

"Where to?" Haidyn asks, his eyes meeting mine in the rear-view mirror.

"Carnage," I answer for more reasons than one. If the Lords want her dead, I have to hide her. To the world, she no longer exists, and thankfully, I have the right place to keep her. Plus, her father will be there. He'll tell me exactly where Adam is, and we'll figure this out.

"No-ooo." She pulls away from my neck and shakes her head quickly.

"Ash, sweetheart..." I reach up and push the hair from her tear-streaked face. "We have to."

"Please?" She gasps. "Not there." She blinks, and fresh tears run down her gorgeous face.

"It's going to be okay. I promise." I pull her into me once again and nod to Haidyn, who is still staring at me in the mirror.

Thirty minutes later, we arrive at Carnage. I carry her inside. She hasn't said a word, but she's quit crying. I'm pretty sure she's gone into shock.

I place her on her feet, and she sways. I remove her shirt, bra, shorts, and underwear. I run a hot bath for her and look at her neck. It's not deep, and it's quit bleeding. "I'll call Devin to look at it," I inform her. I don't think it'll need stitches, but I'm not a fucking doctor.

Taking her hand, I help her into the tub, and she sinks into it. Crossing her arms over her chest, she stares straight ahead.

"Saint?" Kashton pokes his head in and nods to me.

"I'll be right back," I tell her, stepping out into the adjoining bedroom where he and Haidyn wait. "What?" I ask tightly. I'm not in the mood for any more surprises tonight. I want to get her cleaned up and in my bed, where I can hold her for the rest of the night.

"Altus isn't here," Haidyn announces.

"Meaning?" I snap.

"Meaning...her brother and her father are both missing..." Kashton trails off.

I run a hand through my hair. "Maybe he's..."

"His wife is dead. His son is MIA, and his daughter is supposed to be dead. All ordered by the Lords. You think the fact that he wasn't home or not here is a coincidence?" Haidyn snorts at his own question. Our fathers have been gone for three days, but they came back this morning. I just saw her dad two hours ago in his office. Where the fuck has he gone in the meantime?

"I..."

"Saint."

The soft sound of my name cuts me off, and I spin around. Ashtyn stands before me, arms crossed over her chest. She's naked and parts of her wet hair stick to her heaving chest. Tears fill her pretty eyes, and she sniffs. "He said he'd come back for us."

I step closer to her. "Who? Adam?"

She nods, her eyes dropping to her bare feet.

"When did you talk to him?" Kash asks her.

"Five days ago. After Saint took me home, Adam came by my house."

I had asked him to check on her, but I never got a response from him, so I figured he hadn't seen her.

"Did he tell you where he was going?" Haidyn asks.

She shakes her head.

"Did he say why he was running?" Kashton speaks.

Licking her trembling lips, she speaks softly. "Something about being framed." I look at Kash before I turn to Haidyn. He shrugs, also not sure how much of that is true.

"What did Tyson and Miles say?" Kash goes on.

I can always call and ask Tyson, but I want to see if what he tells me matches what she says. I trust her more than any Lord.

Her eyes drop to the floor. "Tyson texted him a picture of me... Adam called my cell. I begged him..." A sob erupts from her throat. I wrap my arms around her, holding her shaking and wet body.

I look up at Haidyn, and he sighs heavily while Kashton watches her closely. When his eyes meet mine, he nods, telling me he's thinking the same thing I am. "If he's got his cell, he can be tracked."

"He called from a blocked number," she mumbles into my neck.

The guys both stand there staring at me, and I bend down, picking her up in my arms, and carry her back to the bathroom. I set her down into the warm water that fills the tub and push the hair from her face. "I'll be right back," I tell her, stepping back into my bedroom and shutting the bathroom door.

"What do you think?" Kashton asks.

"I think Adam is on the run to save his own ass." Haidyn snorts. "And if we can't track him, we'll never find him."

"He could be anywhere by now. Ashtyn said she saw him five days ago," Kash adds. "Adam can cover a lot of ground in five days' time."

My bedroom door is shoved open. "What the fuck is going on?" my father demands, entering the room.

I place myself in front of the bathroom door, knowing Ashtyn is in the bath naked. He watched me fuck her in front of the Lords. That was required in order to solidify that she belonged to me. Now things have changed.

"Saint?" he snaps. "I just got a phone call. Ashtyn and Adam are missing, their mother is dead, and Altus isn't answering his cell."

None of us says anything.

He crosses his arms over his chest. "Saint...where the fuck...?"

The door behind me opens, and my father trails off. I don't have to turn around to know that Ashtyn just walked out of my bathroom. The way Haidyn bows his head and Kashton's sigh tells me all I need to know. Spinning around, I see her again with a towel wrapped around her, wet hair stuck to her reddened skin from the hot water.

My father's eyes go from her to me, and then he looks at Haidyn and Kashton as if he wants one of us to explain how she got here and why she's practically naked in my bedroom.

"I—"

"Father, give us a minute." I interrupt whatever she was about to say.

His eyes slowly look her up and down before he meets mine. "My office. Ten minutes," he orders before turning and rushing out, slamming my door shut.

I turn to face her. "Ashtyn—"

"Are they all dead?" she asks, her watery eyes meeting mine. "My father too?"

Placing my hands on her upper arms, I lie, "No. He's fine." The poor thing has already lost her mother and possibly her brother. I don't need her thinking she has no one left. Not when she has me. "I'm going to go talk to my dad. I'll be right back."

She nods as if I asked for permission. "A moment." I gesture to the bedroom door, and the guys follow me out into the hallway. Closing the door behind me, I turn to face them. "Stay with her. I'll be right back." I turn my back to them and head toward the office when Haidyn's words stop me.

"He's never going to let her stay here."

My teeth grind, but he's right. I'm trying to find an excuse for what to do about her. She's hidden from the Lords here, but then again, Lords run it. We don't have any say over Carnage. Not yet. Not until our fathers hand it over to us.

"There is something you can do," Kashton says, getting my attention.

I look at him, and he smiles. "It was going to happen anyway." He shrugs carelessly.

It's my only option at this point. And he's right, it was going to happen anyway.

Entering my father's office, I find not only him but Haidyn's and Kashton's father as well. They're having a fucking meeting, and I bet I can guess the topic of the conversation—my girl.

"Have a seat, son."

"I'll stand." I cross my arms over my chest, widening my stance.

"Saint—"

"I'll handle this, Garrett," my father tells Haidyn's dad.

Kashton's father just stares at me. He's a man of few words. I think that's why Kashton is the jokester in our group. He had to always entertain himself.

"If this is about Ashtyn, she's not going anywhere."

"Her family is dead," Garrett snaps, confirming what I already assumed.

"I'm her family," I state. "If they want to take her, they'll have to kill me."

Kashton's father's smirk gives me an eerie feeling. "We'll see about that."

"What the fuck does that mean?" I snap, stepping forward.

My father speaks. "She can stay, but she must be initiated." His words make my stomach knot. "Adam is no longer here, and she doesn't *belong* to a Lord." Meaning, she's not a wife—Lady. My father goes on. "Therefore, we have authority over her."

I fist my hands, hating how true they are. If we had control of Carnage, it'd be different. "We are willing to give her to you, but in order to do so, you must do what needs to be done," he says vaguely.

She must become a prisoner...my slave. But in doing so, I have to hurt her. They have no clue what I've done to keep her safe. To make her mine. She'll hate me, and that thought makes my chest tighten. Does it matter what she thinks of me? Not really. She'll be alive and all mine. That's all I've ever wanted.

"Told you he couldn't do it." Haidyn's father gives a dark chuckle at my silence. "I say we go with my plan. Throw her in a cell in the basement. No one's going to be looking for her..."

"No!" I shout. "You're not—"

"Those are your two options, Saint." My father interrupts me. "You take her, or we do. What's it going to be?"

"Me," I growl through gritted teeth. It's not even a fucking question. Like hell I'll hand her over to them. I'm too selfish to let her go. I'd rather have her. "When?"

"No time like the present." Haidyn's father gives me a cold smile, and I grind my teeth. I've always hated him.

I turn to leave when my father speaks. "I'll have Jessie bring you everything you need to get her ready."

That tightening returns to my chest. It means I'm not even going to get to choose *how* I do it. They'll place an order for what they want me to use and send it to me.

I exit the office and rush back to my room. Haidyn and Kashton stand by my bed. No Ashtyn. "Where is she?" I snap.

"Still in the bathroom," Kash answers.

I run a hand through my hair. "Change of plans." They both frown. "Well, I'm still going to do what I had planned, but I just have to do something else before."

"What now?"

"I have to initiate her into Carnage."

"Fuck," Haidyn growls.

"You can't be serious?" Kash snaps. "Saint, you can't..."

"I don't have a fucking choice!" I shout. "You either help me or get the fuck out." I point at the door. I've made up my mind. There's no going back.

Our fathers wanted me to hand her over to them. They knew I'd never do that, so they gave me an option that would leave her hating me. What they don't understand is that I can live with that.

Kashton lets out a huff and walks to the door. Yanking it open, Jessie was about to enter with what I'm going to need. Kashton looks it over and then to me. Turning his back, he storms down the hall.

My stomach sinks as Jessie delivers what our fathers ordered. He leaves us without a word. "Do you believe in coincidences?" Haidyn asks, his eyes scanning over everything.

"No," I answer softly. It's a warning.

"Me either." Haidyn turns to look at me, straightening his shoulders. "What do you need me to do?"

TWENTY-THREE

ASHTYN

I sit in the bathtub, the water cold. My mind on my mom...her body. The way Tyson stabbed her. No emotion. The Lords are trained to do as they're told. They're puppets to a master. Every day of their life before they're even born is mapped out. Who they'll fuck, who they get to marry. Where they'll work.

A part of me wishes Tyson had just killed me. My family is gone. I know it. No one wanted to tell me. A Lord doesn't want to deal with a woman, much less one who's alone now. My bloodline is gone. I'm the last of my family. You'd think I'd be important. But I'm not. I've got a cunt. Not a dick.

The door opens, and I stare straight ahead at the glass shower that stands next to the tub. My knees pulled up to my chest and my arms wrapped around them. The water is bloody from washing my body and hair. I don't know what's mine or my mother's. It's crazy that this is all that's left of her.

"Come on, sweetheart. Your water is cold." I hear Saint's voice, but I don't acknowledge him in any way. What's the point?

He grabs the towel off the side of the tub and then his hands are on my arms. I allow him to lift me to stand and when my legs give out, he picks me up. Getting himself wet in the process as water drips from my trembling body.

He sets me on the edge of the tub and begins to dry me off. "You should have let him kill me," I whisper.

His hand stops, the towel pausing on my legs. He's kneeling in front of me but drops the towel. He stands to his full height, grips my chin, and shoves my head back, forcing me to meet his stare. "I took a vow to protect you."

I snort at that bullshit lie. A Lord will tell you anything he wants you to hear and make you believe it. It's one quality they have that makes them like any other man in this world. "You just don't want to lose your toy."

His hand lowers to my throat, and his grip tightens, restricting my air. He pulls me to stand. My lips part as I watch his eyes grow cold, sending a shiver down my spine.

"Sweetheart, I've been going easy on you. But that is about to change." Letting go of my neck, I cough as he bends down and picks up the towel and continues to dry me off.

I stare at myself in the mirror in front of me where the his and her sinks are. I'm covered in bruises from Tyson and Miles. From being choked, slapped, and restrained. I feel as hollow as I look.

He tosses the towel to the side and runs his hand up into my hair, gripping it tightly. Then he opens the bathroom door and shoves me into his room.

I stumble to a stop when I see what looks like a smaller version of a hospital bed now by the window and something that resembles a gown wadded up on top of it. I spin around to face him. "Saint—"

"I'm sorry, sweetheart." Reaching out, he cups my cheek. "But I'll do whatever I have to do to keep you."

"Wh-at?" My voice wavers due to the lump in my throat.

He looks over my head and nods, signaling to someone. Before I can react, an arm wraps around my throat from behind. I reach up to grip it, my nails digging into the muscular arm that takes my air away.

I'm lifted off my feet, and I kick and squirm as I'm spun toward the king-sized bed. They fall onto it, me underneath them. Their free hand covers my mouth and face, pinching my nose.

I buck and kick trying to get them off but they're too heavy, suffocating me. "I'm sorry, baby girl." I hear a familiar voice rasp in my ear. "I always thought you deserved better."

My lungs burn, tears roll down my heavy eyes, and my hand fists the sheets. I'm trying to crawl away but can't get anywhere. My feet kick nothing but air as he lies on top of me.

My body jerks involuntarily, trying to breathe. Dots start to dance across my vision. A soapy taste fills my mouth. My limbs grow heavy, my body abandoning the fight and giving up.

"That's it, Ash," Haidyn says softly. "That's a good girl. Just relax, baby girl."

I try to breathe, but all it does is suction his large hand to my wet face.

He rolls over onto his back. I think he's going to let me go, but instead, he wraps his jean-clad thighs around mine, locking my legs in place.

I stare up at the ceiling while his arm tightens around my throat now that he's got me in a better position like a snake and his hand remains covering my face.

My heavy arms begin to tingle, and they fall to my sides. My body sinks into his muscular one that lies under me. Fresh tears roll down the sides of my face before my eyes close. A calmness washes over me, accepting my fate. Maybe this was the plan all along. To kill me themselves.

SAINT

Haidyn slides out from underneath her, and Ashtyn's head falls to the side. Her eyes are open but unfocused, and she sucks in a ragged breath.

"You could have sedated her," he offers.

I shake my head. I know our fathers… "They want her awake." I knew she'd never agree to what I have to do. I had to force her hand. It was my only option. I promised her after what she saw that I'd never hurt her. I didn't think I'd break that promise so soon.

Picking up the heavy straitjacket that Jessie delivered, I walk over to her where she lies nearly unconscious. "Help me get her dressed."

We place her arms into the front sleeves, and he jumps onto the bed to kneel behind her while we sit her up and secure her arms around her chest. She's gasping, still trying to breathe but her body isn't fighting. I didn't want to hurt her. I knew the moment Ashtyn saw the straitjacket, she'd be reminded of what happened to the woman brought in by her husband. Having Haidyn choke her out was better than broken bones. They take too long to heal. Plus, she's already going to have a long road to recovery, mentally and physically. She's lost all of her family in one day. She thinks I'm all she has left, and I'm about to prove I'm not here to save her.

"Done," Haidyn states after he's finished buckling all the straps in the back. He gets up off the bed and I look over her.

The straitjackets Carnage uses are of the strongest material—both canvas and duck cloth. It's not meant to protect those who wear it from themselves. Ours are meant to torment. The inside is made of burlap linings—to drive our prisoners crazy. So the more you fight, the more painful it will get.

We carry them in multiple sizes. They sent me the smallest one, and I made sure we put it on as tight as possible. Leaving it loose won't do her any favors.

I had to put her in naked. Our fathers will know if she has clothes on. As much as I want her fully dressed, it just wasn't an option. If our father's think I'm going soft on her, they'll take over. And I won't let them harm her. I'd rather I do it than them. They'll kill her because they don't need her. At least, I'll keep her alive.

Haidyn helps me lay her down on her back, and I grab the two straps between her legs out from underneath her. I pull them up tightly on either side of her cunt, buckling them below her crossed arms to the front. We have both styles: open crotch—two straps and closed—one strap. It just depends if we want it to keep something inside the person wearing it or leave it open for use.

Then I do the last one that runs vertically across her arms. She won't be able to move.

"Come on, sweetheart." I pick her limp body up and carry her over to the stretcher that Jessie also delivered while she was in the bathtub.

Once I lay her down, Haidyn spreads her legs wide to each side and buckles her ankles into the built-in medical restraints. The stretcher has a total of ten restraints. Her ankles, knees, and upper thighs, along with her chest and neck. She doesn't need the wrist option since she's in the straitjacket.

I do one across her chest and then one that wraps around her neck.

"Sa-int?" She coughs, body jerking.

I lean over, cupping her tear-streaked face and meet her heavy stare. "I love you, Ashtyn." It's the first time I've ever said those words out loud, to anyone. But I've felt it for years.

She arches her back the best the restraints allow and begs. "Please..."

"Remember that, sweetheart. I love you so much that I have to hurt you."

She shakes her head, tears filling her pretty blue eyes. She's starting to come back around, and my chest tightens. She'll survive. But I can't promise my love won't be what kills us both. The Lords have taught me to fight until death to get what I want. I'll do the same for her.

"Let... me go." Her voice is rough from Haidyn choking her out. So she coughs trying to clear it. "Please...Saint. I just want to go home."

My stomach knots at her words. This is her home now. There is nowhere else for her to go.

"Just let me go." The stretcher shakes as she fights harder.

"Don't hurt yourself."

"Let me go." She arches her neck, screaming before she breaks into a sob.

Haidyn taps my shoulder, and I look over at him to see he's holding out the last piece of her outfit.

Taking it from him, I shove the large black rubber mouthguard into her mouth, making sure to position her lips around it. It's to protect her teeth and tongue. It has a tube that sticks out the front so she can breathe through if need be.

"Help me out." I bark at him as she goes feral. I'm afraid she'll hurt herself. That's for me to do.

He holds both sides of her face as I rip off the end of the duct tape that they obviously wanted me to use. He holds her head helping me as I wrap it around her head, covering everything from her chin to underneath her nose, making sure not to cover the hole in her mouth guard. Once done, I toss the tape to the side and go over to my nightstand and pull out what I need. Then I go back over to her, grip her taped cheeks, and bite the lid of the Sharpie and write on the tape.

They want me to make her mine? Then I'll do just that.

I grab the blanket and toss it over the lower part of her body, so no one sees her as we push out of her room.

TWENTY-FOUR

ASHTYN

One, two, three, four... I count the buzzing fluorescent lights that pass by as I stare up at the ceiling, trying to ignore the burning of my skin. I have no control over any part of my body. I'm strapped down to a bed as Haidyn and Saint push me through Carnage.

My vision has finally returned, but they took away my voice with the gag. It's bulky and rubber, filling my mouth. My teeth dig into it as saliva runs down the back of my throat and every now and then, I gag on it. They ignore me. The tape that he wrapped around my cheeks is pinching my skin.

I love you, sweetheart.

His words keep echoing in my head like a song on repeat. It's what every girl wants to hear, right? I've heard others at Barrington say love is hard. I never believed them. Loving Saint has been the easiest thing in my life.

Until now. Why does it have to be so painful? Why do I have to be so stupid?

It's a game of lose-lose. I mean love is like anything else—temporary. People fall in and out of love just as easily as people pass away.

You just wake up one day and no longer feel anything for them. I've seen it. Not in my world, but the one that doesn't know we exist.

They bring me to a stop, and I hear the metal squeak of a heavy door. I can't breathe. My arms are secured tightly to my chest. My legs are also strapped down and I try to yank them free, but there's no use. The leather straps I'm buckled in just rub against my skin, and I feel like I'm covered in razors. It burns so bad. But why am I so wet?

My pussy clenches, and I cry into the gag, hating how fucking wet I am right now.

Saint looks down at me, and his eyes soften. I close mine as a sob wracks my body. This isn't about pleasure. He's going to hurt me. But he knows I like pain and get off on it.

Is that his plan? Humiliate me? Have me beg him to fuck me? I'm naked and my nipples are hard rubbing against the itchy inside of the straitjacket. My arms are crossed right underneath my breasts and my body gently rocks back and forth with the movement of the bed they've got me tied to.

They wheel me forward, and the sound of a door latching behind us has my heart racing. Looking around aimlessly, I see nothing but concrete walls. I'm strapped in a straitjacket sweating my ass off with a blanket over me, yet coldness sets over me. The room is freezing.

They place me in the center and rip the blanket off.

I buck, thrash, and scream into the gag. I can't stop trying to escape. But do I want to? I'm not sure. I pull my thighs to close to hide my wet pussy, but of course, it doesn't work. I'm wide open for him to see, and my face heats up with embarrassment.

The bed I'm strapped to is adjusted where my head is lifted and my feet lowered, tilting me so I'm more upright than lying down. The new position has me sliding down just a tad, pushing the already tight belt around my neck pushes deeper against my throat.

My eyes catch sight of the mirror in front of me, and suddenly, I can't breathe.

I'm the woman. The one on display for whoever is on the other side of the two-way glass.

My eyes shoot over to the back of Saint, and I see him at a counter, but he's standing in the way. I can't see what's in his hand. Haidyn stands next to him. "Adrenaline?" he asks, but it's muffled over the blood rushing in my ears.

"No," Saint answers. "I don't want to kill her."

He doesn't want to kill me? Isn't that what I'm here for? To die? Everyone else in my family is dead. I'm the last one they must get rid of. He said he was going to hurt me.

"I'd prefer her to pass out." Saint goes on.

"And if she doesn't?" Haidyn asks.

"She will," he assures him. "Her body won't be able to handle it." Reaching over, he flips a switch on the wall, and a red light comes on up in the corner. There's a speaker next to it. Whoever is in the observation room is now listening to us.

I yank on my arms and pull on my neck, trying to free it, but the leather wrapped around it chokes me in the process. I cough and sputter as saliva shoots through the hole in the middle of my gagged mouthpiece.

Saint turns to face me, and I plead with my eyes for him to stop. His eyes stay on mine as he walks over to me. I flinch when something cold wipes across my exposed pubic bone. I'm naked from there down. I can tell by the way the cold air from the vents in the ceiling touch my skin.

He does it again, and I close my eyes trying to hold in a sob. He's cleaning me. Yeah. I'm that woman. They're going to brand me. The question is will he leave me like this afterward? If so, how long until my arms go numb? Isn't that what her husband told her? She'd lose feeling? That could be a blessing right now, considering how much my skin burns.

I'm gasping, trying not to panic. It feels like my heart races in my chest. Can you have a heart attack at twenty-one? I'm sure it's possible.

Saint comes to stand in front of me once again, and this time I see the burning end of the brand. My eyes are too blurry from unshed tears to know what's on it. It doesn't matter, really. I said my vows in front of the Lords. In our world, they're more binding than blood. I'm his to do as he pleases.

"Take a deep breath, Ashtyn."

His words are as cold as this room. I know they're for whoever is on the other side of the mirror, but they make my stomach drop, nonetheless.

Snot running from my nose, I take a shaky breath and brace myself, praying he's right, and I pass out.

SAINT

SAINT'S WHORE IS WRITTEN ACROSS THE DUCT TAPE THAT COVERS the bottom half of her face. I thought it'd be a nice touch to my *fuck you* attitude toward our fathers for forcing my hand to hurt her like this.

Ashtyn's gasping for breath; her body shakes uncontrollably, and her eyes are squeezed shut as tears run down her face and tape.

"Are you sure?"

I look up at Haidyn who stares at me. His eyes say everything that I feel. What if she doesn't pass out? I've been branded. It hurts like hell. But I chose that. She's being forced. Am I willing to take that chance?

"No." I answer his question. I can't guarantee that she'll pass out. Even if she did, she'll still feel it. I nod to the counter to my left. "Go ahead and give her the adrenaline."

Ashtyn's wide, red-rimmed eyes meet mine, and she starts shaking her head, thrashing around on the stretcher. Her cheeks hollow out, and the tape wrinkles from scrunching her features.

Haidyn walks over to the counter, opens a drawer, and fills a syringe from a clear vial. Pulling the plunger back, he draws it out and then tosses it to the side, where it rolls onto the floor and breaks.

She's screaming into the tape as he walks back over to her. He unbuckles the belted strap that pins her neck to the stretcher, and she goes to lean up, but he grips her taped face with his free hand, forcing her neck back at an angle, exposing it to the room before he sinks the needle into it, administering the liquid.

She instantly goes limp, and her eyes close. He didn't really give her adrenaline, but since our fathers were listening and would only allow that to be administered, I had to say that. It's better that she's sedated and doesn't remember this.

I press the end of the brand to her pelvic bone. It's the longest five seconds of my life even though I know she's out. I've branded plenty of people in the past few years, but I hate to have to do it to her. The smell of burning flesh fills the room.

I remove the brand and look over the reddened 666 that will forever be there because of me. Because of our life.

I toss the brand to the side and turn to face the mirror. I can't see them, but I can feel all of their narrowed eyes on us. They're mad that we sedated her. Fuck them!

Walking over, I flip the switch, turn off the intercom system and go back over to her. They just wanted to hear her scream. It was all about torturing her. Forcing her to give what Carnage requires—your soul. Your fucking life. She'll forever belong to it. And me.

"Call Devin," I order Haidyn. "Tell him to meet me in my room." She needs to be looked at anyway for what Tyson and Miles did her to earlier this evening.

"On it." He pulls out his phone, and I rip the tape off her mouth, unwrapping it from around her head, pulling her hair and skin. Prying her mouth open, I remove the mouthguard.

"I'm so sorry, sweetheart," I say even though she can't hear me. I really am. She didn't deserve this, and when I find Adam, I'm going to fucking take my time killing his ass.

I undo the buckle over her chest. I yank off the ones that pin her legs down. I take the blanket that I had her covered in and place it over her and then pick her up, not even bothering with the strait-jacket. I'll take it off when I get her back to my room.

I'm lying in my bed with the TV on but muted. She lies next to me, naked. Devin came and saw her as soon as I got her back to the room. He placed some ointment on her brand and bandaged it up. Her neck was fine. Nothing too serious and it didn't need stitches. A bandage was all it needed.

She's been in and out for the last few hours now. Haidyn has come by to see her, but I still haven't spoken to Kashton. He's mad at me for the decision I made, but what did he expect? Did he truly think I was going to hand her over to our fathers? To this hell? I stand by my decision. A Lord does what needs to be done.

Ashtyn begins to stir, and I watch her heavy eyes open and then close. Reaching up, her hand goes to her neck, and I grab her wrist. "It's just a bandage, sweetheart."

Her eyes spring open at my voice, and pretty blue eyes meet mine. She stiffens next to me, and I let go of her wrist to cup her cheek. She flinches, and my chest tightens. "Ash, I'm—" I stop myself from saying I'm sorry because I'm not. I'd brand her five more times if I need to if that meant I got to keep her.

She stares at me unblinkingly as they start to fill with unshed tears. My eyes lower to her chest, and her skin is still red and irritated from the straitjacket. I can't help myself and run my knuckles over her soft nipple to watch it harden at my touch. I'm not going to fuck her, but that doesn't mean I don't want to. I always want her. Always have. I think she's experienced enough pain for one day.

"W-hy?" she asks in her soft voice.

I watch the first tear fall out the corner of her eye. "I had a choice to make." That's my only answer.

She swallows and closes her heavy eyes, forcing another tear to fall free. When she looks up at me this time, I cup her cheek, and she pulls away, sitting up and pushing her back into the headboard.

I sit up as well and cup her face with both of my hands, not allowing her to pull away. "I love you, Ash."

"No," she whimpers, gently shaking her head. Her bottom lip starts to tremble when she sucks in a deep breath. She's not 100 percent herself yet. The drugs are still in her system, so it's going to fuck with her emotions for a few more hours. Plus, given the day she's had...

"Yes." I nod. "I've been in love with you." She sniffs, and I run my thumb over her parted lips. "And when forced to choose—keep you or let you go—I will hurt you before I live a life without you."

Her wide eyes swim in tears before they spill over her bottom lashes, falling down her face. She doesn't have to love me. I don't need that kind of acceptance from her.

I know that makes me a bastard. The villain in her story. It sounds like I'm heartless and cold. And I might be, but I sure as fuck don't care.

Letting go of her face, I get up out of bed and walk over to the edge she sits on. "Come on, sweetheart." I pick her up in my arms, and I'm surprised she doesn't fight me. Instead, she buries her head into my shirt, and her cries fill the room while I carry her into the bathroom. I'm going to bathe my girl. Get all the adhesive off her face from the tape and wash her body free of the lining of the straitjacket. Then I'm going to put her back in my bed where she will stay for the rest of her life.

TWENTY-FIVE

ASHTYN

It's been two days since Haidyn choked me out and helped Saint place me in a straitjacket for him to brand me.

I woke up confused hours later back in his bedroom naked and feeling drowsy. I cried a lot. Then Saint gave me a bath. While he bathed me, Saint explained that Haidyn had knocked me out and Devin had dressed it with cream and a bandage. He took it off for my bath and put on a new one afterward. I have a fresh one on now. I haven't seen it nor do I want to.

They branded me. A part of me no longer feels anything. My family is dead, my life just ...gone. What else is there to do?

Rolling over in Saint's bed, I stare at the empty spot next to me. He wasn't here when I woke up this morning. It's not the first time this has happened, but he didn't leave me any information as to where he's at, and I don't have a phone. Mine was ruined when it got placed in a flower vase and something tells me I'm not going to get a new one. Everyone that I'm allowed to talk to is here. Why would I need to reach the outside world? I'm dead.

A knock on the door has me sitting up, the movement making me flinch as the bandage pinches my skin over the brand. "Yeah?" I call out, and my voice cracks. I haven't said much in the last two days. Saint keeps feeding me pain pills that either make me sleep or drowsy. He's bathed me the previous two nights, brought me food, and keeps me in bed. Says I need to relax and let the brand heal. Devin comes in to check on me and changes the bandage. My neck looks better and no longer needs one.

The door opens, and my pulse races when I see Saint's father. His green eyes search the room as if he's looking for his son. When he sees I'm alone, his cold stare meets mine. "Your presence is required."

The hairs on the back of my neck rise at his words. "For-for what?"

"A session," he responds.

I let out a sigh of annoyance. I thought I was done with those. "Yeah, okay. Just, uh...I need to get dressed." I stumble, trying to explain that I'm naked and in his son's bed. It's not like he doesn't know we fuck. He saw him take my virginity.

He nods. "She's expecting you in the basement." Shutting the door, I frown.

Why the fuck would I need to go to the basement? It would be easier if she just came to me.

Throwing off the covers, I use the restroom and grab a piece of toast that Jessie brought me earlier with my breakfast. I haven't touched it until now. Might as well eat something. Who knows how long she'll force me to listen to her annoying voice?

I get dressed, throwing a T-shirt on with a pair of Saint's sweatpants. It'll rub the least on my brand. After I put on some socks and tennis shoes and throw my hair up in a messy bun, I leave Saint's room.

You know that feeling when you stand up too fast and get dizzy? That's how I feel. I don't know if it's because of my lack of food or the fact that Saint gave me a pain pill at three this morning, but either way, I feel weak and tired. I'm going to crawl back into bed after the session.

Making my way down in the elevator, I reach the basement level.

It's quiet down here and always cold. It smells of rotten eggs—demons. The stories of Carnage that I heard when I was little were that they torture until they finally get tired of playing with you and let you rot. The souls stay trapped to haunt the new ones brought in while they await their same fate. Torture at its finest.

"Ashtyn. Hello, dear." My mother's therapist walks toward me. The way she's smiling makes me think that maybe she doesn't know my mom was killed.

"What are we doing down here?" I ask. Carnage is a massive place with multiple buildings scattered over the land. It's a maze that one could get lost and never be found in. So why here?

I've been told that it was once a college that was started in the late 1800's that was eventually abandoned. Now that's just hearsay, considering if you google it, there is absolutely nothing to find on said college. But I'm not surprised. To the world, Carnage doesn't exist. Therefore, neither would the college that the Lords acquired.

"How are you feeling, Ashtyn?" She ignores my question and asks her own. Her eyes scan over me once as if assessing me and her lips frown.

Did she expect me to be runway ready for her? "I'd rather be in bed." I cross my arms over my chest.

"We'll make this quick." She assures me and turns her back walking back down the hall where she came from.

I follow her slowly, not liking the way she said *we* as in I won't be alone with her. Maybe Saint is with her? He has to be here somewhere, right? The sound of her heels clapping on the concrete floor echoes off the walls as she sways her hips back and forth in her tight pencil skirt. She's got a silk blouse on that's tucked into it. Her hair is up and in a tight, perfected bun. I wonder if she comes here often? I know she's friends with my mother, but I don't remember her ever being close to my father. So why would she be here at Carnage?

She comes to a stop in front of a room, and I stumble over my feet when I see it's the observation room. The same one I stood in when I watched the Lord drop off his wife to be sentenced to a long life of torture. Also, the room that their fathers watched me get branded from.

"Come on in, hun. It's okay." She smiles at me.

"Why are we here?" I take a step back. "Why are you here?"

She frowns, tilting her head to the side. "I'm here for you, Ashtyn. I know the past few days have been...difficult, and I want to make sure you're okay."

"I'm fine." I go to turn around and head back to Saint's room, but I stop when I see his dad standing at the opposite end. Swallowing, I try to slow my racing heart and not panic. I don't know what they'll do to me without Saint. I should have never left his room. But I didn't really have a choice either.

"If you're going to stay here, you'll have one session a week," he informs me. "It's part of Saint's and my...understanding."

I don't know what he means or why my mental health would matter to him. They don't want you levelheaded here. Maybe that's the plan, to make me think I'm going insane. The Lords are masters at manipulation. But I don't want to make Saint mad. He's the only one really on my side. The one who has taken care of me even if it's in his own twisted way. *It could be much worse.* "Yes, sir," I say, and he nods, turning his back and walking off.

Doing so myself, I turn back and enter the room. The first thing I notice is the two-way mirror. I'm unable to see through it because it looks to be blacked out somehow. Like they're hiding what's on the other side of it. The second thing is there is a metal table in the center. A chair on either side facing one another.

"Have a seat, Ashtyn." She offers me a chair with my back to the glass and sits across from me.

I fold my hands on the cold table and shiver, wishing I had grabbed one of Saint's hoodies out of his closet before coming down here. "Do you know?" I ask her vaguely, seeing if she needs an explanation.

"I do." She nods.

A silence lingers in the room at her acknowledging my mother has been killed. She doesn't even bother with giving me her condolences. Instead, she asks her own question. "Which Spade brother are you the closest with?"

I frown. What kind of question is that? "Why?"

"I'm just curious."

"I'm Saint's chosen." She knows this. She and my mother were so worried about me not bleeding at the vow ceremony.

"Yes but they all three fuck you, no?"

I stiffen in my chair. My pulse thrums in my neck. "A Lord is allowed to share his chosen with whoever he wants," I add softly. Everyone knows this. It's not a secret. It's another way for the Lords to throw their power around. But I actually love Haidyn and Kashton. They'll always hold a special place in my heart.

"Are you being cautious?"

My frown deepens. Why the fuck does she care about this shit? But her question has me thinking…I haven't been on birth control since I've been here.

"I doubt Saint would be happy if one of the others knocks you up." She goes on.

"Oh, no that wouldn't happen." I shake my head.

She tilts her to the side. "And why is that?"

"They…" I trail off not wanting to finish that sentence.

"I see." She writes something down in her notebook. "They don't fuck you vaginally."

Why does that sound more vulgar than anything Saint has ever said to me? I bow my head, refusing to say anything to that and avoid eye contact. If my mother knew what I allowed the Spade brothers to do to me she'd be so ashamed.

"Would you say that you care about Kashton and Haidyn the same as you do for Saint?"

"What kind of session is this?" I ask defensively.

"It just seems that they are willing to risk their lives for you, and I'm trying to figure out why." She places her manicured nail on her chin. "It can't be sex. Kashton and Haidyn have their own chosens. I'm wondering what you offer them that they can't get elsewhere."

I glare at her, trying to decide her angle. Is she questioning me or them? She knows that they won't tell her shit. So I'm guessing she thinks I'm the weakest link. Family recently dead, me freshly branded. The newest victim to Carnage. She thinks I'll spill information on them. It's probably their fathers wanting to know, and I refuse to give it to them. I'm not a snitch. And no matter what they've done to me, they're all I have left. I know if something were to happen to Saint today, Haidyn and Kashton would never abandon me.

I cross my arms over my chest and sit back in my seat. The cold metal is making me shiver even through my shirt.

"Show her." She calls out.

I frown, looking around. "Show me what?" Who is she talking to? Getting to my feet, I turn and stare at the two-way mirror.

Just then I realize it looks black because the light is off in the other room. It comes on, lighting up the space, and I see a man hanging from the ceiling. His arms are cuffed above his head, secured to a chain. He's shirtless, but his jeans sit low on his hips, showcasing his abs and deep V. His body stretched while he gently sways back and forth, shoes dragging across the concrete floor.

His muscular body is taut. Blood runs down his arms from his cuffed wrists, his bare chest is covered in sweat, and white sticky pads on his abdomen have wires running to a machine that sits on a roller cart next to him. He's got a black hood over his head, hiding his face, but the Lords crest branded on his right pec is clearly visible.

The door opens to the opposite room, and someone new enters with a black cloak and Lords mask on. I place my hands on the glass. "Who is that?" I ask, licking my lips nervously.

She doesn't answer.

My breathing picks up when the man in the mask comes to a stop by the machine and flips on a switch. "Ready for your session?" I hear him speak to the man in the hood.

He doesn't move or answer. He's either passed out or gagged.

"Let's turn it up this time. I think your last session was too easy." He turns a knob, and the lights dim as the man hanging starts to shake, his legs kicking, muscles straining, and I realize that the patches on his body are electrocuting him.

"Stop!" I say, slamming my hands on the glass. "What the fuck is he doing?" I turn to look at the woman. "Why is he doing that?"

"Actions have consequences, Ashtyn."

What the fuck is she talking about? I turn back to look through the two-way mirror, and he turns the knob off. The man sags in the cuffs. His chest is now rising and falling quickly as he breathes heavily into the hood. His abs contract as he continues to sway back and forth.

The man in the Lord's mask turns it on again—higher this time—and the man's body spasms. I bang my fists on the glass. "Stop. Stop. You're going to kill him."

The man in the Lord's mask laughs, and I know he can hear me. Haidyn said that they could hear me just not see me when he found me in here.

"How do you not know that man doesn't deserve his punishment?" she asks me, reminding me I'm not alone.

I didn't answer her. The Lords never ask questions. They decide you don't deserve what they give you and they take it away. You're never innocent until proven guilty.

The Lord slaps the man hanging on the back, and it causes him to spin around in the chains. I see there are more of those white sticky pads on his back as well, but that's not all. There are also red marks that cover his tan skin. He's been whipped.

"Why?" I face her once more and demand. "Why are you making me watch this? Why did you want to even see me?"

She gives me a soft smile. "This is a reminder, Ashtyn, from the Spade brothers." She means the fathers. "That you are a guest here, and it will be best to remember that."

I look at the glass, and the guy in the Lords mask turns off the white patches, and the shirtless man hangs in the cuffs connected to the chains. "Until next session," he states before walking over to the door. He shuts off the light, bathing the room in darkness before he exits.

I RETURN TO SAINT'S ROOM, GET UNDRESSED, AND CRAWL INTO bed, whimpering at the sting of my brand. The last pain pill Saint gave me has officially worn off. Or maybe it's because of what I just saw. I hate knowing the man still hangs in the dark, probably terrified.

How long will they play with him before they kill him?

It makes me think of my brother. What he's seen or had to do to people here. Is that why he ran? Was he really set up by the Lords? Or did he do what he was accused of?

I'm not saying that Saint, Haidyn, or Kashton are innocent. I've seen what they do here, and it's terrifying. But they have no choice, right?

Their fathers wanted to give me a message today. One that I can't ignore. I get it. I'm only safe because of Saint, Haidyn and Kashton. They think I have something with all three of them. Don't I? I love all three of them but in different ways.

The sound of the door opening has me sitting up. I flinch at the sudden movement, the bandage pulling on the edges of my branding.

"Hey, you okay?"

I look up to see it was Saint who entered. I'm on edge. Afraid now that his father will come and get me for another "session." "Where have you been?" I ask, tears starting to sting my eyes.

"House of Lords. We had a meeting this morning." He comes to sit down next to me. "I'm sorry, you were sound asleep. I didn't want to wake you."

"It's fine." I wave him off. A part of me thought he was hanging in the basement. The man looked familiar even though I couldn't see his face, and the mind likes to play tricks on you.

"Here." He gets up and walks over to his nightstand. Opening up the top drawer, he pulls out the pills and pops the top. "Take one of these and get some rest."

I greedily take them when he offers me the bottle of water that sits on my breakfast cart. I hope it makes me pass out.

"Good girl." He leans in and gently kisses my forehead. "I'm going to take a quick shower."

"Then you'll lie down with me?" I ask, needing him right now. Even after everything he's done to me, I feel safe with him.

"Of course," he assures me.

I lie down and snuggle into his pillow when his cell rings. "Hey, man...yeah, I've tried calling him twice. He hasn't called me back yet...yeah, probably."

"What was that about?" I ask.

Saint plugs his cell phone on his nightstand and looks at me while pulling his shirt up and over his head, exposing his chiseled abs. "That was Kashton. He wanted to know if I've heard from Haidyn."

I yawn. "Why?"

"He was the only one who missed the meeting this morning." With that, he turns and walks into the bathroom.

I yawn again and close my eyes. But they spring open the moment what he said registers in my brain. I sit back up, my heart racing, when I hear his shower start. Was that Haidyn hanging in the room? Surely not? Why would they torture Haidyn? Why would his father allow that?

Snorting, I remind myself that it's common for fathers not to care about their children. "Saint?" I call out. "Saint?" I do it again.

I have to tell him what I saw. If it's Haidyn, I can't leave him down there hanging in the dark. All alone. Saint can help him, right?

"What's wrong?" He comes running into his room, no towel and dripping wet. He had already gotten in the shower. His cell beeps, signaling a text.

"I..."

"One sec." He interrupts me picking it up. After typing out a message, he sets it back down. "I'm sorry, sweetheart. It was Haidyn. What do you need?"

It was Haidyn? I look at his phone and then back up at him. "Nothing." I breathe a sigh of relief. My mind is playing tricks on me. Of course it wasn't Haidyn. I'm paranoid.

"You sure?" he asks, water dripping onto his floor.

"Yeah." I lie back down.

He turns and walks back into the bathroom, leaving the door open in case I need him. When I hear the shower door open and shut, I lean over and pick up his cell. I check current messages and see Haidyn's text. I open it up.

Sorry slept in. What'd I miss at the meeting?

SAINT

I LEFT ASHTYN IN MY BED, NEEDING TO TALK TO MY FATHER. She's been here two weeks, and I can see her going stir-crazy. She's always been one to get out and go places. She's not a homebody, and there has to be something that can be done.

Just yesterday, she asked me about finishing her classes online for Barrington. I hated to tell her that she will no longer get to graduate. To the world, she's dead. I can't change that. No matter how much I want to.

After she fell asleep last night in my arms, I thought about it. And I wouldn't change it even if I could. If whoever is after her thinks she's dead, then they can't hurt her.

Stepping off the elevator, I come up to his office door but pause when I hear his voice on the other side of it. "What do you suggest I do?" He sounds irritated.

I don't blame him. One of his brothers is missing. Our fathers are as close as me, Kash, Haidyn, and Adam. Although I'm pissed off at

Adam right now because he left the love of my life behind to die for his sins. There's still no word on her father or Adam. At this point, I don't expect either one to show up at the gates of Carnage in one piece.

"I have connections." I hear a woman's voice answer, and my hand tightens on the doorknob, recognizing it. "There's a facility..."

"No," he growls, interrupting her. "Saint will never agree to that." I almost smile that he thought of me. He doesn't give a fuck about her. But he doesn't want to piss me off. Last time I spoke with him in his office after he found I was hiding her in my room, he told me I could have her. Of course I didn't give him much of an option.

She snorts. "You're in charge here. Not Saint."

"It's complicated," he states.

"Look..." She sighs. "I'm not trying to harm her."

My jaw clenches at the lie. I know what she's done and what the bitch is capable of. I put nothing past her.

"I can prescribe her medication. Place orders to keep her so high that she won't even realize where she's at...what's going on. She will be in a safe place under twenty-four-hour supervision. You'll have full access to her. And if Altus shows up..."

"I don't know," he says conflicted.

"Abso-fucking-lutely not!" I shove the door open, and it slams against the interior wall.

My father jumps up from his seat, and she spins around to face me. Face tight. "Saint—"

"You touch her, and I'll slit your fucking throat." I interrupt whatever bullshit she was about to spew.

She gasps and looks at my father. "You're going to let him speak to me like that?"

"Leave us."

"What—?"

"Get the fuck out," he barks at her.

She lifts her chin and stomps out of the room, slamming the door behind her.

I walk over to his desk, slapping my hands down on it. "She's not going anywhere," I say through gritted teeth. Ashtyn's life may never be what she wanted, but she will have one here. With me. I can make her happy. I can give her everything she wants except freedom. I won't risk her life. Someone wants her dead; I refuse to let anyone get that close to her. "We have a deal," I remind him.

"Saint..."

"I mean it, Father." I don't give a shit what her excuse or concern she has regarding Ashtyn. She's here under my protection. "If anything happens to her—"

"She's safe." He raises his hand, cutting me off. "I gave you my word." At least he remembers our last conversation.

Ending this current one, I turn to leave when he calls out my name. "Saint?"

"Yeah?" I ask, my hand on the doorknob to leave.

"We gave her to you, but she only gets one chance. If you can't control her, she goes down to the basement where she's free game."

"But—"

"That's all I can promise you, son. One chance."

Coldness rushes through my veins at the threat, but I nod. "Understood." Yanking the door open, I exit, shutting it. Free game? Means anyone will get a piece of her. They will rip Ashtyn to pieces down there. I can agree to whatever the fuck he says, but I'll never let it happen. Even if I have to keep her tied to my bed or locked in my closet, I will not let it get to that point.

"She's unstable."

I come to a stop at the woman's voice behind me. I turn to face her.

"She's unpredictable. Her entire family was. I've been seeing her mother for years. Ashtyn too. I have a long list of reasons as to why she should be medicated and locked in a padded room." She steps closer to me. "Remember that the next time you threaten me." She goes to walk by me, but I reach out grab her dark hair with one hand while the other slaps over her mouth before she can scream. I slam her back into thc wall, placing myself in front of her and pinning her to it.

Wide eyes stare up into mine. "If you're going to threaten someone, you better make sure they don't have something they can use against you." She sucks in a breath through her flared nostrils. "I know what you did." She tries to shake her head, but my hand on her face tightens, making her whimper into it. "I have a video of it." Her body sags against the wall. "Touch her, and I'll make sure it's released." Removing my hand from her face, she gasps in a breath.

"You wouldn't..." She doesn't even try to deny it. "You'd implicate yourself."

She's right. I've gone to extremes to ensure that I get what I want. Knowing that there would be consequences if anyone ever found out. The risk is worth the reward.

I smile. "That's the thing about a man with everything to lose. I'm willing to sink the ship. And I'll make sure you drown with me." With that, I push off her and step into the elevator. I make my way back to my room to find Ashtyn still lying in my bed, sound asleep and naked.

I'm on the clock. Either she goes crazy and my father locks her up downstairs or I watch her slowly die inside.

I have to get her out of here. Even if it's just for a few hours. Take her mind off this hell.

Getting an idea, I smile and pull out my cell, sending a text to Haidyn and Kashton.

Want to go for a ride?

They both respond immediately.

TWENTY-SIX

ASHTYN

I wake up to Saint yanking the covers off me. "Saint," I groan, rolling over and giving him my back while he stands next to the bed. "I'm tired." He kept me up most of last night. I'm so sore and want to just be lazy today. Not like I have anywhere to go or anything to do.

He waited a week after he branded me to even touch me sexually. It was the longest week of my life. I've begged him every day since to fuck me. My mom was right, I've become addicted to sex. To him fucking me into his mattress with his hands wrapped around my neck. It stops my mind from running wild with the what-ifs.

When he makes me his good girl, I'm important because I'm his. My purpose is to serve him. His lips touch mine, and I'm breathless. His hands touch me, and I burn. He ties me up and fucks me like a worthless whore and then he holds me while I cry. I've never been so high and so low within a matter of seconds in my life. My head hurts just thinking about it.

"Get up." He slaps my tender ass. "We're going out."

I sit up, my heart racing, and I'm instantly awake. "Going out?" He smiles at me. "As in leaving Carnage?" No. I must have heard him wrong. I can't leave here. At least, that's what they've been telling me. My brother is still MIA along with my father. I'm not even sure what happened to my mother's body. No one will tell me anything when I ask. I keep having this reoccurring dream that they burn her body in the middle of the woods, and my father is the one who lights it on fire.

"Yep." He opens his nightstand. "But first we've got to get you ready."

I frown at his choice of words.

He grabs my arm, yanking me off the bed and spins me around to face it. "Bend over, chest on the bed," he commands.

I don't question him. I'm too excited to get out of here. I love being here with him, but I just wish it was our place and under different circumstances. Although I'm grateful he saved me, I don't feel safe here. But thankfully, I haven't had to watch anyone be tortured, and my therapy session this week was like it used to be—I sat there and refused to answer any of her questions about my sex life.

I've tried changing my mindset to Saint and I are on vacation in the middle of nowhere, and no one can find us.

Stretching my arms out above my head, I lie across the edge of the bed smelling the clean linen sheets. My brand has healed nicely, and it no longer hurts. Every now and then, I'll move a certain way and be reminded it's there, but for the most part, it's okay.

He spreads my legs wide as he stands between them. I jump when I feel his fingers on my pussy. "Saint, I'm so sore." I remind him.

"I know, sweetheart." His fingers run along my swollen lips to my ass, smearing what I recognize as lube. "Just relax. Can you do that for me?"

"Yeah." I breathe, letting out a deep breath.

"Good girl," he praises, pushing a finger into my ass. I moan, my hands gripping the sheets. He thrusts it in and out of me until I'm rocking back and forth on it.

"That's it." His free hand gently rubs my back. "Feels good, doesn't it, sweetheart?"

"Mm-hmm." I moan. My heavy eyes closing.

He adds a second finger, and I whimper. He doesn't give me time to adjust to them before he enters a third.

I cry out rising on my tiptoes. "Saint." I go to stand, but his hand on my back shoves me down, holding me in place.

"Almost there, Ash. So close."

I bury my face into the mattress, arching my ass for him, and he removes them just as I think I can't hold my breath anymore. Letting it out, I relax, but it's short lived as I feel something hard and cold being pressed into my ass. I cry out once again, and he slides the butt plug in place, filling my ass, and it reminds me of the vow ceremony.

"Good girl." I feel the head of his dick at my pussy.

"Saint, I need to pee..."

"You can hold it," he argues, and tears sting my eyes at the burning sensation of him stretching me. I'm so sensitive. He grabs my arms and brings them behind my back. Pinning them in place, he fucks me into the side of the mattress. Hard and fast. His body slamming against mine.

I can tell it's about him. I won't get to come.

"I can feel the balls from the butt plug in your ass." He groans. "Fuck, sweetheart." His knees spread mine wider, and he readjusts my arms into one of his hands while the other grips my hair and shoves me face-first into the sheets.

I try to breathe but get nothing. My arms fight his hold, but it does no good. And honestly, I don't want him to stop or let up. I like the fight. My sheer helplessness to his power and strength. I'm a slut for him.

The sound of him moaning makes me weak. I clench my soaked pussy, and he slams forward, holding his body into mine when I feel his cock throb inside me.

After a second, he yanks my head up, and I'm gasping for air as my vision goes in and out. He lets go of my arms and they fall to the side when he leans over and kisses my tear-streaked cheek.

I tremble when he grabs my arm and pulls me to stand. Turning me to face him, he wraps his hand around my throat, forcing me to arch my neck to look up at him. His green eyes search mine as he speaks. "How do you feel?"

"Unsatisfied," I answer honestly while my knees shake.

A smirk graces his perfect lips before he leans down, pressing them to mine. I open for him, wanting him to devour me. Swallow my fucking soul and make me his servant. Saint is all I have left. In a matter of one night, I lost everyone I've ever loved. Not like any of them ever loved me. Not like Saint does. I regret ever running from him after what I saw him do to that woman here at Carnage. I made a mistake, and he's right. He'd never hurt me. Not like that.

Slowing the kiss down, he pulls away, and my heavy eyes open to look up at him. His hand lowers from my neck to my chest, and he plays with my hard nipples.

I press my body into him, moaning and feel his cum leak from my desperate pussy. "Please, Saint?" I whimper when the pain takes my breath away.

"You're going to have to work for that, sweetheart." He taunts me, and I groan.

"Anything," I say, ready to fall to my knees, and he chuckles at my expense.

"I know." He lets go and pulls away. I want to scream. "Let's get you dressed."

He leaves me standing and goes to his closet. A couple of days ago, he went to my house and grabbed some of my clothes. But honestly, I haven't needed any. I've spent all of my time locked away in his room. After what I saw last time I was here, I don't argue or venture out when he tells me to stay put. I don't trust anyone here other than him, Haidyn, and Kashton.

Saint returns a second later and helps me into the tight-fitting bodysuit. It's black and has a high neckline with long sleeves. He turns me around and zips it up. I've never worn it because it doesn't have snaps for easy restroom use. And let's face it, when you go out and drink, you need something with easy access.

"Go braid your hair." He slaps my ass. "While I grab a couple more things."

I go to the bathroom, very aware of the plug in my ass and his cum leaking into the bodysuit. He didn't even let me put underwear on.

I run a brush through my hair and then pull it to the side and throw a quick braid in it. It's not perfect but good enough. Once done, I walk back into his room once again. His right hand is down by his side, and he's holding something black and leather in it. I see a buckle and holes punched into the straps.

"Come here, sweetheart," he orders softly. The tenderness in his voice has me shaking with need. I would let this man do anything to me. I trust him with my life. He's saved me. My life hasn't always been the greatest, but now it's shit. I have no one and nothing to live for...other than him. Saint is my savior, and I'm his dirty little whore who will obey without thought.

Stepping forward, I meet his eyes. He reaches up with his free hand and runs his thumb over my trembling lips. "Open up," he commands.

I part my lips as wide as I can, and he places a gag in my mouth. I know enough about gags to know it's an open mouth ring gag by the feel of the unforgiving leather that rests behind my top and bottom teeth. It pries my mouth wide open, making me whimper.

It's a harness type by the straps that frame my nose, going over the top of my head, and another under my chin. Clear plastic covers the bottom half of my face and circles my open mouth as he pulls it tightly at the back and buckles it in place. I inhale sharply through my nose, and he tightens the second strap under my chin. It squishes my face, and I blink rapidly, trying to calm my racing heart.

"You're going to wear this while we're out."

My eyes widen in understanding, and I shake my head. I can't go out in public like this. What is he thinking? I begin to mumble unintelligible words and reach up to try to pull it free.

He grabs my wrists and shoves my hands down. "Don't worry, Ash. No one will see you."

How can he say that? He said we were leaving Carnage.

Picking up something on the bed, he places it inside my open mouth, and I go to step back, to pull away, but he places a hand on the back of my head to hold me in place. "Breathe through your nose for me, sweetheart," he says as I feel the object in my mouth grow larger.

Panic grips my chest as I taste rubber. It feels like it's getting bigger by the second, filling my mouth and pinning my tongue down.

"You're doing great, Ash." He assures me and both of his hands cup my face. "Once we get to where we're going. I'll deflate the gag."

I blink, tears stinging my eyes while I remind myself to breathe through my nose.

"You look gorgeous, sweetheart." He smiles, and I feel butterflies in my stomach. I lean into him, and my eyes grow heavy as I moan around the gag that fills my mouth. I wish it was him. "Such a pretty whore." He praises me, and I try to swallow the saliva that pools at the back of my throat.

The plastic around my mouth already feels slippery from the drool I'm unable to swallow down. The inflatable gag is too big inside my mouth that when I try to push it out of the way, it won't fit through the ring gag that rests behind my teeth. I'm powerless. All I can do is drool all over myself.

"Sit down," he commands, and I fall back onto the side of the bed. "You'll be okay. No one will see you. The gag will obviously keep you from talking." He smirks, placing my legs into a pair of jeans. Thankfully, I already had a bandage on my brand from last night so my jeans won't irritate it. Once they're on, he grabs a helmet, and my heart beats wildly as I realize we're going for a ride.

My ass clenches the plug that's buried deep inside it. He slides the helmet onto my head and fastens the chin strap in place, locking me in.

He looks at me and smiles before he pushes the visor down. The sound of my heavy breathing fills my ears and slobber begins to leak from the corner of my lips. The leather from the straps are shoved into my cheeks and head due to how tight the helmet is. "Let's go, sweetheart."

SAINT

I GET HER RIDING BOOTS AND GLOVES AND USHER HER downstairs. Ashtyn and I have been staying here since Tyson messaged me about her, but the guys have been staying at the house of Lords. As much as I want them here to have the extra help to protect her, we have to go on as if nothing happened. We have to complete our senior year. Although we never go to classes, we still have to act like nothing has changed.

Entering the garage, I see the guys already on their bikes. Laughing at one another.

They turn to face us and Kash smirks. "Look who's getting out," he says to Ashtyn and smiles when she has nothing to say.

She didn't need to be gagged for this ride, but I have a plan for her. And I bet her cunt is dripping wet right now. And I don't just mean from my cum. Ashtyn is the type of woman you've got to have an imagination with. She doesn't like missionary or a quickie in the morning. She enjoys the foreplay, the degradation, the praise. You've got to surprise her. Keep her on her toes. She needs to be dominated. I like that she lets me do whatever I want with her. I have an endless number of ideas on how to get her worked up and begging to be fucked.

I grab my helmet, fasten it, and straddle the bike. I pull up the kickstand and look over my shoulder. Kashton and Haidyn are putting their helmets on and getting ready to go.

She places her hand on my shoulder and taps it twice. It's her silent request if I'm ready for her to get on, so I nod. She hops on the bike, and I swear I hear her moan in my ear. All of our helmets have earpieces in them so we can hear each other. Even the one I put on her.

I turn the bike on and feel her bend over, leaning onto my back, placing her hands on the black tank.

I imagine her ass clenching the plug and her mouth drooling. Fuck, I'm so goddamn hard right now.

"Let's roll," I call out into the helmet and put it in gear, revving the engine. Kashton pulls out first, then Haidyn. I follow. Once we're out of the garage, they slow down to let me take the lead. Just in case something were to happen to us, I want them behind me so they can see it. They know to get her first. We take off down the road, and a whimper fills my ears, making me chuckle.

"Feel good, sweet cheeks?" Kashton asks, and Haidyn laughs when she doesn't respond.

I reach back, placing my hand on her thigh and giving it a little squeeze. She adjusts her body on my back, and I know she's pushing her ass back just like she did when she rode my thigh that night in her room. She wants to feel the vibration of the bike on her cunt. Her tits press into my back, and I hear a sharp intake of breath.

"Fuck, Ash. You about to come on that bike?" Haidyn asks.

She sniffs, and I know her nose has started to run. I want her mind occupied with the possibilities of what I'm going to do to her. No matter what she can come up with, it won't even come close.

"She's not going to respond to you guys." I finally speak, and I feel her tense against me.

"She pissed at you?" Kash asks.

"No. She's gagged," I answer.

Their laughter fills my ears.

"If you wanted to suck on something, all you had to do was tell me," Haidyn jokes. "You know I'm always willing to let you drool on my cock, baby girl."

TWENTY-SEVEN

ASHTYN

My body vibrates as much as the bike I straddle. I'm trembling. My legs shake against Saint's as he rests his hand on my thigh. We've been riding for thirty minutes, and I'm so fucking needy right now.

My pussy is drenched, and so is my face from tears, drool, and snot.

Saint slams on the brake, and my chest pushes into his back. I bite down on the leather that sits behind my teeth. Fresh drool runs down the plastic part of the gag, making it slippery.

I rock my hips back and forth, rubbing my pussy on the seat to get some kind of friction, but it's not enough. Just leaves me frustrated. My hands grip the tank, wishing I could desperately touch myself. Even my breasts are sensitive, nipples hard. I would beg Saint to stop right now, bend me over the bike and fuck me on the side of the road as cars pass by. I think that's why he gagged me.

"Cover me," Haidyn speaks into the helmet. Kashton slows down, puts one knee out to adjust himself on the bike, and looks back over his shoulder.

"You're good," he tells Haidyn.

He revs his bike, brings up the front wheel, and rides a wheelie away from us. He holds it quite a ways before I see him put it down and slows so we can catch up.

Kashton reaches out, and they fist-bump like fucking teenagers.

Slowing down, we pull into a gas station, and my heart races that someone might see me. I don't know what's more embarrassing, the guys listening to me getting off on this bike or a stranger seeing me gagged.

Coming to a stop, I sit up, stretching my back, and stifle a moan. I will crawl to Saint when he gets me back home to fuck me. Use me. Every hole begs to be taken right now.

The guys remove their helmets, but thankfully, Saint makes no move to remove mine.

"Hey"—Haidyn slaps Kashton's chest—"got any more gum?"

"No. Last piece." Kashton points at his mouth. "But you can have it..." He spits it out and hands it to Haidyn.

He tosses it into his mouth, and I roll my eyes. "Thanks."

They share everything. Always have. I've seen them share their chosens with one another and others as well. Kashton fills up his tank, and Saint turns to face me. "Doing okay, sweetheart?"

"Mm-hmm," I say because that's all I can fucking get out, and they all laugh. It makes my nipples harden.

Saint smirks, placing his hands on my thighs. I stiffen as he rubs them up and down over my jeans, fucking playing with me. He knows exactly what he's doing.

They finish filling up their tanks and get back on their bikes. I'm biting into the gag that has my mouth drooling like Niagara Falls as Saint's cum continues to soak my bodysuit. My plugged ass vibrates on the seat, and I grind back and forth.

I know Saint can feel me moving back here, but I can't help it. If I wasn't gagged, I'd be begging him to fuck me. Not caring what the others hear.

He pulls off onto a backroad, and I look over my shoulder to see them following us. We ride down a gravel road until it comes to a clearing. It's a dead end, and my heart starts to race as to why we're stopping.

Nothing but a lake surrounds us, and we're the only ones here. He gets off the bike and removes his helmet before he helps me off. Saint removes my riding jacket and undoes my helmet. When he pulls it off, I can't help the whine that leaves my gagged lips.

The helmet already fit snug but then add the straps and buckles on my face and head, and it's given me a headache. My entire body aches from not only last night but how tense it's been this entire ride.

He runs his knuckles along my tear-streaked cheek. "Are you a needy little slut for me?" he asks.

I nod, sniffling, and he reaches up to my gag. He does something because I feel it deflating and he removes the rubber, leaving my mouth wide open. I suck in a breath, and he smiles, looking over the drool that covers my chin and cheeks.

Tossing the deflated gag to the ground, he turns to face his bike. He grabs the key and goes to his seat. He lifts it and reaches into it, removing a roll of duct tape.

My pulse quickens when he walks back toward me. I turn around and see Haidyn and Kashton both grabbing something out from underneath their seats. But they both hold rope. They had this planned—get me worked up, bring me out, and tie me up.

I turn back to face Saint, and he's already right in front of me. Reaching down, he undoes my jeans, jerking on them. Then he unzips them before yanking the rough material down my already shaking legs.

I whimper when he removes my riding boots. Haidyn comes up behind me and wraps his arm around my upper waist, lifting me up off the ground so Saint can get me undressed except for my bodysuit. As if I can't do it myself.

Saint nods to Haidyn. "Put her on the table."

He turns me around, and I see a picnic table over where Haidyn and Kashton parked their bikes. It looks old. After sitting out in the weather for years, pieces have chipped off the sides.

Haidyn carries me over to it and sets me down on the edge. "Lie down," he orders, and I place my back down onto the hard surface. It's warped from the heat and cold, making the wood uneven and poking into my back. The buckles dig into the back of my head.

Kashton comes over, and I try to calm my breathing as the excess saliva pools at the back of my throat. I swallow it as they each grab an ankle. "Bend your knees," Kashton commands. "Heels to your ass."

I put my bare feet on the edge of the table, bending my knees. I squint up at the bright sky as they each start to tie my legs with the rope. Haidyn wraps the rope around my right ankle and then ties it to my right upper thigh while Kashton does the same to my left leg, securing them so I can't straighten either one out.

"Sit up, sweetheart," Saint says, and Haidyn helps me up since I can't use my legs. "Arms behind your back."

I do so, and Saint brings them parallel across my back. I cry out when he pulls on my arms, stretching my shoulders, pinching my spine. He has Haidyn hold them in place while he begins to wrap the duct tape around them from elbow to elbow, leaving no wiggle room whatsoever.

When I lower my head, drool runs from my mouth and drops onto my bent knees. "Let's get you in position," Saint speaks.

He and Haidyn pick me up and move me to lie on my back once more, my arms now taped underneath me. It's uncomfortable, and I try to move to ease the pain, but nothing helps. They're too tight. The tape offers no give.

Saint kneels in the middle of the table at my bent legs. He places his hands on my knees and shoves them open. I arch my back and cry through the hole in the gag, spit flying from my open mouth as the position stretches my inner thighs.

"I know, Ash," Saint says, and my body trembles as my legs try to fight his hands holding them wide open. "But I want to see how wet your cunt gets while they fuck your mouth."

Tears burn my eyes before they leak down the side of my face. I try to rock back and forth, arch my back. Anything to try to relieve the pain, but Saint doesn't let up.

Haidyn comes to stand to my right at the table while Kashton stands at the left. They each take the excess rope connected to each leg and then bend down on either side of the benches. Moments later, they stand, and Saint removes his hands from my knees and jumps off the picnic table.

I try to close my legs now that he is no longer holding them down, but they remain wide open. I try harder but the rope just tightens on my sensitive skin. Spit flies from the gag and hits my face as I try to calm my racing heart. They've got my legs bent, ankles tied to my thighs, and spread wide open so the heels of my feet touch my ass. Then tied the remaining rope to the benches, keeping them open.

Saint walks around to where my head is and pulls me toward him enough so that my head hangs off the sharp edge. I blink, and fresh tears run down my face. He takes a new piece of rope and begins to wrap it around my slick neck, then he bends down and secures it underneath the bench.

He's made it impossible for me to lift my head. The table's edge smashes my tightly secured arms, and I struggle to breathe through my runny nose.

"Be a good girl for me, sweetheart, and show them how good you've gotten at swallowing dick."

SAINT

I STAND NEXT TO THE PICNIC TABLE WATCHING HER SQUIRM. I have her tied in a Frog tie position with a single tie: double column tie —each ankle to thigh. Then I had the guys tie the remainder of the rope down to the benches. It keeps her cunt and ass wide open for me to see and her completely immobile.

"Your bodysuit is soaked, Ash," I say, looking at the wet spot between her legs. "Is that from you or me?"

Reaching out, I pull the material to the side exposing her to the world. Cum covers her swollen cunt, and I smile. "A little bit of both." I observe, and the sight of the butt plug gets my attention. I grab the base and turn it counterclockwise, making her squirm and moan through the open-mouth gag.

Kashton steps up to the edge of the table and smiles down at her tear-streaked face as he undoes his jeans. He pulls out his hard dick and doesn't waste a second thrusting it into her mouth. He takes it slow, fucking her pretty face. He shoves his hand down the high collar of her bodysuit and squeezes her nipples, playing with them while he rocks his hips back and forth.

I push two fingers into her cunt, and she clenches down on them as I add a third.

"Look at you, sweet cheeks." He praises her. "You are getting so much better at taking a dick. You're not even gagging." He removes his hand from her bodysuit and places it under her tied neck, arching her more so he can go deeper.

"You like to spend time on your knees, don't you, sweetheart?" I force a fourth into her soaked pussy, and my dick strains against my zipper.

Her tied legs shake, and her stomach caves, outlining her ribs through the thin material while she tries to breathe between his thrusts.

"I love a whore on her knees." He groans, watching his cock slide in and out of her drool-covered face. She's a mess. Just how I like her. "What about you, Haidyn?"

He's standing over by his bike, watching intently. The outline of his hard dick on full display. "I prefer an ass." He shrugs. "But a mouth can be good too when it's not filled with a gag."

"Goddamn, Ash..." Kash trails off, both hands reaching across her tied body and grip her inner thighs, digging his fingers into her flesh. She arches her back the best she can as he pounds into her mouth harder, the sound of him fucking intensifies with each gurgle of saliva.

He slams forward, holding his cock down her throat, his zipper pressing into her face, and she fights the ropes harder, begging to breathe before he groans and comes down her throat.

Pulling out, she's gasping as drool and cum leak down the sides of her face.

Her body shakes as tears run from her blue eyes. "Such a pretty little whore, sweetheart," I say, continuing to finger her soaked cunt. I can see her hard nipples through the thin material of the bodysuit. I want to rip it off her and suck on them, but I won't. She needs something to wear on the way home. I just wanted to get her out of Carnage for a good time. When we return, I'll tie her naked ass to my bed and use her for my own pleasure.

Haidyn steps up, staring down at her. "I won't go as easy on you, baby girl." He smirks, making her whimper while she tries to catch her breath.

Removing my fingers from her pussy, I return to the butt plug. I pull it out a little, only to push it back in. She cries out, fresh drool running from the corners of her open lips. I do it again, fucking her ass with it as Haidyn steps into her with his now hard cock fisted in his hand.

"Take a deep breath," he orders, and she inhales, her stomach sinking in before he pushes into her.

I watch her throat work as she tries to adjust to his length. Her cheeks fill out, pushing against the leather straps holding the gag. What I love most about an open-mouth gag is that she can't suck. All she can do is lie there and take it. It's literally a throat fuck, and when she tries to swallow...goddamn, it feels so good.

He pulls all the way out and slaps her wet face, making her whimper and body tremble.

She's so fucking gorgeous. I love seeing them use her. Her body was made for me, but that doesn't mean I won't share the wealth. She belongs to me; she goes home with me. She lives for me.

"Relax your throat for me." He groans, pushing his hips forward, and I watch her neck bulge as his cock forces its way down it. The rope pulls tight as he fills her throat.

Her body jerks as she fights the restraints. I continue to fuck her ass with the plug, loving the way it opens up and sucks it back in and knowing she enjoys the different size balls it has.

Haidyn pulls out, and she's crying before he pushes back in, silencing her. "Fuck, swallow it, baby girl. All the way down. You can take it." He reaches across her body with his hand and places his palm over the bandage on her pelvic bone, pushing two fingers into her smooth pussy.

Haidyn has always been on the rougher side. He likes to hear them scream and watch them cry. That's why he prefers an ass. Any woman can spread her legs or kneel. But anal? That narrows your options unless you don't give them a choice.

He pushes a third finger into her pussy, and I continue to fuck her with the butt plug with the juices that run from her cunt. Her ass and thighs are soaked from earlier. He takes both of his hands and spreads her wide open to allow me a visual. *Fuck, it's a gorgeous sight.*

I have the urge to see how many fingers I can fit inside her. The thought of fisting enters my mind, but I quickly squash that idea. She's not ready for that. Not today anyway. But soon.

"That's it." He lets go and watches his cock fuck her mouth like Kashton did as her body rocks back and forth on the picnic table she's tied to. His free hand grabs her nipple over her bodysuit and pulls on it, making her tremble as his fingers go back to her pussy. "I can feel your cunt clenching, baby girl. How much you like it."

Pulling out, she sucks in a breath before he shoves it back into her mouth. He removes his fingers and slaps her pussy, making her jump. He does it again. Harder. It's swollen and bright red.

I can't wait to bury my face into it when we get back to Carnage.

He pulls out and lowers his hands to her mouth, shoving his fingers into it. "Taste that, Ash? Only a whore gets this turned on from sucking dick."

She blinks, her wet lashes clumping together, and her throat works as she tries to suck on his fingers.

Kashton stands by them, his phone in one hand while he records it. She arches her back, once more trying to fight the tight position we've got her tied in.

He pulls his fingers out and a line of fresh drool covers her face before he slaps it again. "Make me come, baby girl," he orders, guiding his hard cock back into her mouth. "Make me come down your throat like the good whore we know you to be."

He fucks her face, ignoring every whimper, cry, and moan that manages to escape her full mouth while I play with her ass and the plug. Her cunt looks so pretty as it glistens from my cum and her arousal. It's begging for me to fuck it. But not yet. I'm going to make her wait.

It doesn't take him long before he's holding his length down her throat and coming as well. When he pulls out, he's gasping for breath, and she sobs, her body trembling as we start to untie my good little whore.

TWENTY-EIGHT

ASHTYN

I haven't left Saint's bed in three days. After we returned from our bike ride, he fucked my ass before he had me ride his face. I sobbed when I finally got to come. It was so euphoric that I swear I lost my vision. I hate but also love when he makes me wait to get off.

It's torture at its finest.

As much as I love being with Saint, I'm losing myself. I can feel a part of me dying each day. My old life is becoming more of a memory than a reality.

I need to feel like me again. So I got up, showered, dressed, and put a little bit of makeup on. I wandered down to the cafeteria instead of waiting for Jessie to bring me food. Saint's gone today at the house of Lords. He said he had a meeting he couldn't miss.

A part of me wanted him to make the decision for me, tie me up, and leave me waiting. When he didn't, I realized just how pathetic I've become. My mother's words still haunt me in her death.

He won't love you, Ashtyn. No matter what I do or what I give him, this is just temporary. He'll get tired of me and eventually toss me to the side. Carnage will swallow me up. I know that he told me he loved me, but he also told me he'd never hurt me. The brand on my skin proves differently. I understand why he did it, but it doesn't change how it got there.

Plus, all Lords are expected to reproduce, even the Spade brothers. I'm no longer alive, just existing. I can't give him the family he must have since the Lords assume I'm dead.

It's something I must come to accept.

Exiting the cafeteria, I get into the elevator. I ride it up in silence, watching the floors pass until it comes to a stop and opens. I step off and stop when I hear "M.I.N.E." by Five Finger Death Punch filling the hallway.

Slowly stepping over to a cracked door, I stop when curiosity gets the best of me. Haidyn and Kashton usually stay at the house of Lords, so it's just me and Saint here. I push it open and see a man working out in a room resembling a small gym. He wears black basketball shorts and a white muscle T-shirt with the sleeves missing and half the sides cut out. He's doing pull-ups on a bar with his knees bent and ankles crossed.

I lean against the doorframe, watching with wandering eyes. It's Haidyn. His dark hair is wet from sweat and the T-shirt sticks to his back as well. His arms bulge as he grunts over the music, pulling himself up over and over at a quick pace.

He does it several more times, then straightens his legs before dropping to his feet. He reaches up and grips the back of the T-shirt, rips it over the top of his head, and uses it to wipe his face off before throwing it to the side.

He turns, and his blue eyes meet mine, paralyzing me where I stand. But it's not because he caught me staring. It's because, without his T-shirt, I got a view of his back. He stalks over to me, and my wide eyes lift to meet his when he stands in front of me.

"What are you doing, Ash?" he demands.

I'm shaking and breathing heavily, my heart hammering in my

chest. He reaches out, grips my arm, and yanks me into the room. Slamming the door shut, he shoves my back into it. I don't even fight him when he grips my neck with his large hand and forces my head back against the door as he lowers his face to mine. "Ashtyn?" he barks over the song.

"It...it was you." I manage to say even though I'm having trouble breathing.

His eyes harden on mine, and he tightens his hand, growling, "Baby girl..."

"They punished you...because of me." I'm not sure if he understands what I'm trying to say because even I couldn't understand my mumbled words since he's cut off my air. Tears sting my eyes, and his face blurs.

Letting go of my throat, he steps away, and I blink, letting the tears fall to clear my vision while coughing. He gives me his back, and I step forward. "I don't understand," I say, roughly licking my lips. "You texted Saint." He walks away, and I see the fine lines of the whip all over his muscular skin. It's healing and faded, but they're still visible.

Haidyn was the man I saw hanging in the room in the basement when Saint's father made me see my mom's therapist. "You..." My lips tremble. "You were still hanging." I take another step toward him when he picks his cell up and turns off the music. I can hear my heavy breathing fill the room now. "How did you text Saint...?"

He says nothing. He picks up a barbell and sits down on a bench. He places his elbow on his knee and starts working out again. "Haidyn—"

"Leave, Ash. I'm busy." He interrupts me flatly.

I sniff and wipe the tears from my face with trembling hands. "Why did they hurt you?" He continues to ignore me. "Because of me?" I point at myself. Swallowing, I try to think back... "She said actions have consequences. What did you do that they would punish you for?" The moment I ask, my chest tightens. "The branding..." A lump forms in my throat. "You sedated me." He gets to his feet and drops the barbell, letting out an aggravated sigh. "Haidyn, I'm so sorry," I cry.

He storms back over, and he reaches out to me, both hands cupping my face. He forces my eyes to meet his. "Don't fucking apologize to me, baby girl. I did what I did because I wanted to." Letting go of my face, he runs his hand gently through my hair.

"But why would you do that?" My watery eyes search his, and he gives me a soft smile.

"I told you that you deserved a better life. And I meant that."

I frown, trying to understand what that has to do with him and that night. He leans in and gently kisses my forehead. "Run along, Ash. Saint will be home soon." With that, he walks over to his phone and presses play. The song comes back on, and I slowly walk back to the door.

Saint? Why not punish him? He was the one who told Haidyn to give me the adrenaline. How do they know that Haidyn didn't give me the wrong thing?

Then the text. Haidyn was hanging in that room so that means someone else had his phone and pretended to be him when they responded to Saint so he wouldn't be suspicious as to where he was.

How long did they keep him in there, all alone and hanging in the dark with the hood over his head and gag in his mouth?

Does Saint and Kashton know what happened to him? That one I can answer myself. No. He wouldn't tell them, and I'm not going to either. I'll keep his secret. The Lords like to humiliate their own. And Haidyn is too big of a man to let his brothers know that he was electrocuted and whipped. That makes me wonder how they got him? Did they trick him into that room? Did he willingly let them string him up by chains? The thought makes my chest hurt.

Exiting the room, I pull the door back where it was and numbly make my way to Saint's room. I get undressed and crawl into bed under the covers and close my eyes. I hate that they punished him because of me. I don't want the guys to get hurt. Or hate me. I love all three of them.

That also means that Haidyn overheard the conversation that the therapist and I had about how the guys treat me sexually. She asked who I'm closest to. Do they think that I'm going behind Saint's back to be with Haidyn? Are they trying to use me to get between the guys?

I don't like that thought. It makes my stomach knot because nothing good could come from that situation. I'd never cheat on Saint. I've never been with Haidyn or Kashton without Saint right beside me. He's the one who offers me to them. Not the other way around.

Numbly, I stare up at the ceiling trying to clear my mind and figure out what the fuck this all means knowing I'm not going to get an answer.

I KNEW IT WAS TOO GOOD TO BE TRUE. IT'S SUNDAY, AND I GOT called in for my therapist's appointment. I thought...no hoped she had forgotten about me this week, but no. She had Jessie come and get me, which I found odd, but I couldn't say no, no matter who she sent to get me. Especially now that I know she's going to use the guys when I don't do what she says. I'll follow the rules the fathers have set just to keep their attention off my friends.

I see the open door and enter the room.

"Close the door, Ashtyn," she orders, not even looking up at me.

I slam it shut, and she looks up, removing her glasses from her face, and her eyes narrow on mine.

Plopping down in the chair across from the desk, I cross my arms over my chest. "I'm doing fine." I get to the point.

Saint isn't at Carnage at the moment, but I want to be naked and in his bed when he returns. I wish I had some sleeping pills. I'd love to knock myself out and leave him a note on the bed to have his way with me when he gets back. But since I no longer have any pain from the brand, I no longer get any pain pills of any kind.

She leans forward and sets something on her desk.

"What is that?" I ask.

"A pregnancy test," she answers.

My wide eyes meet hers. "I don't need that."

"You've been here for what, two, three weeks now...A month?" She looks at the calendar on her desk. "You haven't seen Devin or requested any type of birth control prevention. And I highly doubt that Saint wears condoms."

"I'm on the shot," I lie. It's none of their business what I'm on.

She sits back in her seat, letting out an annoyed sigh. "Use my restroom, Ashtyn. I'll wait with you for your results."

"I'm not taking that." I jump to my feet. "It's impossible." Okay, so that's another lie. Any time you're fucking someone, pregnancy is always a possibility, and she's not wrong. Saint has never used a condom.

She leans forward, and her pointed red nail hovers over a black button on the edge of her desk. When her eyes meet mine, she pushes it. "You either pee on this stick, or Devin comes in here, ties you down, and draws your blood. Which one is it going to be?"

My stomach sinks, and my chest tightens at her threat. "But... I'm not...No." I'd know that, right? Aren't there symptoms?

Standing, she walks around her desk. "Contrary to what you think, I'm not trying to make things harder for you, Ashtyn. I promised your mother I'd look after you if anything ever happened to her. And I want to help you. Just take the test, honey." I flinch at the endearment. My mother used to call me that, and I thought I'd never hear it again. "I can't help you if you don't let me."

I try to calm my breathing, but all I can think about is that I'm pregnant, trapped in this hell by a man who will never let me leave. Saint told me...*Carnage is no place for a child.* And that husband had told our fathers to *terminate the pregnancy if she is and then perform a hysterectomy.* What will happen to me if I'm pregnant?

Will it be okay since Saint is a Spade brother? Will it be worse for him?

My eyes drop to my left hand, and I fist it, a feeling of dread coming over me as I think of what we did, and the visual reminder I have on my skin.

The sound of the door opening behind me has me spinning around to see Devin enter the room with two other men. "You need me?" he asks the woman who I want to punch in the fucking face.

My watery eyes go to her, and she addresses me. "That question is for Ashtyn."

Swallowing the knot in my throat, I shake my head. "N-o." My voice cracks on the single word.

She picks up the pregnancy test and holds it out to me. I take it and walk over to the door to the adjoining bathroom. Opening up the pregnancy test, I undo my shorts as the first tear falls down my cheek. Sitting down, I close my eyes and take a calming breath, praying to a God that I don't even think exists that I'm not pregnant.

I finish up and wash my hands. Exiting the bathroom and returning to her office, I see it's just her and me again. I place the test on her desk. I haven't even looked at it. I put it back in the package the moment I was done.

Sitting down in the chair across from her, I feel numb and sick to my stomach. She pulls out the test and sits it on her desk. With a smile on her face, her eyes meet mine. "Congratulations, Ashtyn. You're pregnant."

I stare at her, my breath getting caught in my lungs. It can't be. I don't believe her.

She tosses the test into the trash can next to her and places her forearms on top of her desk. "What are you going to do if Saint finds out it's not his?"

"It's his." I manage to whisper. That I'm a hundred percent sure of that.

She arches a brow at me.

A fresh tear runs down my cheek, and I sniff. "I haven't been with anyone else." I pull on my shirt, my skin flushed and clammy. "I told you...Haidyn and Kashton don't fuck—"

"Your pussy." She interrupts me with a nod.

The room goes blurry, and my body trembles. "I'm not pregnant." My tongue feels swollen, and I feel lightheaded.

"Ashtyn..." She sighs. "We need to talk."

TWENTY-NINE

ASHTYN

I run out of her office, not caring that she's calling out to me. I can't hear anymore. So many lies. So much betrayal. And now a baby?

Sucking in breath after breath, I round a corner and run into someone. I scream as hands grab at me and lift me off my feet. I kick and fight, but they drag me into a room. It's one of the fathers. She called them to come get me and take me downstairs. They're going to kill my baby, force me to have a hysterectomy, and then throw me in a cell.

Saint won't protect me, not after what he finds out. A hand slaps over my mouth, muffling my screams, and I buck wildly since my nose is so stuffed up I can't breathe through it.

"Shh, Ashtyn, calm down." A familiar voice growls.

My body instantly goes limp, and he releases my mouth. I sob as he sits me in a chair and kneels in front of me. "What the fuck is going on?" He places his hands on my shaking thighs and rubs them over my legs.

"I'm...pregnant," I cry, knowing I can trust him.

"Shit." He sighs, running his hand through his hair. "Does Saint know?"

I shake my head, tears spilling from my eyes, and I run my hand under my runny nose.

"I'll call him." He stands and removes his cell from his pocket, and I slap it out of his hand. "Ash—"

"No, you can't," I cry out, and he grabs my trembling shoulders.

"It's okay," he assures me softly.

He's so wrong. "No." I shake my head quickly. "He cheated."

His brows pull together. "What? No. He'd never—"

"He cheated." I gasp, trying to breathe, but my throat is closing on me. "You...can't."

"Ashtyn."

"Tell him." I grip his T-shirt and bury my face into it. He wraps his arms around me, and I begin to sob, repeating over and over that he cheated, hoping that he'll understand what I mean because I can't form a fucking sentence right now.

"I know what to do," he assures me. "Trust me."

SAINT

I pull up to Carnage on my bike. I don't even bother putting it in the garage. Instead, I leave it parked out front and rush up the stairs inside. I've been gone all day at the house of Lords. Mandatory meeting for some bullshit assignment. I'm not even sure why they care that I attended. I get my orders from Carnage.

Entering the building, I make my way to my room and rush inside to see Ashtyn sound asleep in my bed under the covers. "Hey, sweetheart." I grab the back of my shirt and rip it up and over my head just as my bedroom door opens. "What the fuck?" I spin around to see my father enter. "You could knock first." I throw my shirt to the floor. What if I was balls deep inside Ashtyn? I'm not a fan of my father seeing her at all, let alone naked.

He looks over me and then her asleep in my bed. "She had a session today."

I frown. "And?"

"She got upset and needed to be medicated."

"She what?" I snap, stepping toward him. "What the fuck do you mean medicated?" I turn back to look at her. Ashtyn is on her stomach, head facing away from me with the covers up and over her. I rip them back and place my hands on her bare back. "Ashtyn?" I shake her but get nothing. "Ash, sweetheart? Wake up." I roll her over onto her back, and her body remains limp. I yank the covers up to her neck, and her head rolls to the side. I grip her cold cheek before forcing her eyes open. They're dilated. "What the fuck did you give her?" I shout, standing up I turn back to face my father, but *she* is there now as well. I swear my father is fucking her, and that's the only reason he keeps her around Carnage.

"It was just a sleeping pill," she answers.

"I fucking doubt it," I grind out and look at my father. "We had a deal."

"Son..."

She raises her hand to stop him and steps toward me. "She's okay, Saint. Just getting a good night's rest. We spoke about her mother, and she got very upset. Found her inconsolable. She willingly took them with her dinner and went to bed. She's been in here alone ever since."

"Get the fuck out of my room." I point at the door in case she doesn't understand what I said.

"Saint—"

"I said get the fuck out!" I shout in her face, my heart pounding in my chest. Who the fuck does she think she is? And why the fuck did Ashtyn agree to take something? Without me here? How long has she been passed out? And who knows who the fuck has been in and out of my room?

Glaring at the bitch, she lifts her chin and lets out a huff as she turns around and exits my room. My father follows her. I slam my door shut and lock it behind them. Then I finish getting undressed and crawl into my bed with her. Pulling her body into mine, I push her dark hair from her face. Her eyes look puffy like she had been crying and her nose is red.

I don't believe it. Her mother? I mean, yeah, she was upset that her mother was killed. But they weren't overly close. She hasn't even mentioned her mother since that night.

Reaching over, I grab my cell off my nightstand and pull up the group chat with the guys.

Did anyone see Ashtyn while I was gone?

Kashton: Nope. I'm still out with Melony.

Haidyn: I haven't been at Carnage all day.

Sighing, I place my phone back on the nightstand and lie down with her. My hand gently strokes her soft hair, giving her cold cheek a kiss. I settle in and close my eyes ready to get some sleep as well.

THIRTY

ASHTYN

I haven't been trapped in Carnage long, and I'm already getting depressed, and I think Saint can tell. He's been extra sweet. Trying to keep me busy and my mind off my dead mother because he thinks that's why I was so upset last week when he came home to find me passed out. It couldn't have been further from the truth.

I'm in a constant state of panic. Him finding out I'm pregnant and that I'm hiding it from him. There is no good outcome. I'm just biding my time, trying to come up with a solution to save me and the baby. He thinks fucking me is a distraction, and in a way, it is. I never have to think when I give him my body. But I'm exhausted, mentally and physically drained.

Having to keep this secret from him is making me sick. Or I guess it could be the pregnancy. Either way, it's getting worse.

It's almost three in the morning, and I find myself wandering aimlessly inside the main building of Carnage. I couldn't sleep. My mind runs a hundred miles an hour trying to figure out where my future goes from here. I used to think I didn't have one, but now I realize it's true.

I was digging last night asking him when I get to leave here. Or just live a normal life. His response was I have to hide out here until my father returns and everything settles down. I call bullshit. He's just telling me things he thinks I want to hear. Those who are sent here don't escape. I've seen more evil here in the past month than I ever knew possible. I always thought the Lords were sick, but what the Spade fathers do is just pure disgusting. I wish Saint and I could run away, start a family, and live happily ever after. But like my mother once told me, Lords don't love the women in their lives. My time here has proven she was right.

I'm not sure how much more time I have before I start showing. But once I do, it'll all be over. I can't lie to him forever.

I walk down a hallway and turn a corner to see a door cracked open. Looking back over my shoulder, I make sure I'm not being followed. So many people have been killed within these walls that a cold chill always follows you—as if their souls are left behind.

Pushing the door open, I step inside and come to a stop. My body stiffens at what I see. Four men lie facedown and blood covers the floor. The sound of it dripping through the drains in the floor echoes throughout the cold room.

I've seen bodies before, but these seem...different. They all have black hoods over their heads, and their arms are cuffed behind their backs. Of course, they've been killed—execution style.

Walking over to one of them, I bend down and carefully pull on the top of the hood. The blood covering it makes it sticky, but I manage to remove it. I drop it to the floor and look over the hole that's in the center. Bile begins to rise, and my breathing catches.

Leaning over, I look at his cuffed wrists, pulling on his sleeves, and the sight of a wedding ring catches my attention. It's a simple silver band. I remove it and bring it up to my face. I squint to see the words engraved on the inside.

"Hey?" a voice snaps at me, causing me to drop it while taking a quick step back when I see two men standing there. "What the fuck did you do?"

They both wear a Lords mask and cloak covering a hundred percent of their bodies. They even have gloves on. "I…uh…"

"Call the guards," one snaps to the other.

The voice is altered so I can't tell who they are. I lift my hands. "I didn't do this. I found them…"

"Bullshit!" he shouts, cutting me off.

The other walks to the opposite side of the room and pushes the intercom button. "Code 26," he snaps into it, and I take another shaky step back.

"I swear." Tears fill my eyes. How could I kill four men? I would never. Let alone tie them up. And a gun? I don't have one of those.

"Contain her," the one by the intercom shouts, and I turn and run.

I turn a corner as a hand fists my hair. I go to scream out but another slaps over my face. I'm pulled into a room and pressed into a wall. It's pitch black. I blink rapidly, trying to focus on anything as I wait for my vision to adjust to the darkness.

A hard body presses into mine while I hear the two men running down the hall outside of the door looking for me. "Don't make a sound," a voice whispers in my ear, making me whimper. "Or you're dead."

SAINT

I WAKE UP TO MY CELL BLARING IN MY EAR. IT SOUNDS LIKE A horn going off on a car. Without even bothering to look at it, I ignore it and roll over, throwing my arm over Ashtyn. My eyes spring open when all I feel is the cool sheets.

"Ashtyn?" I sit up, looking to my left. Yanking the covers back, I see no one is there.

My phone goes off again, and I pick it up to see it says code 26. "Fuck!" I hiss, jumping out of bed just as it rings.

"What the fuck is going on?" I demand when I see it's Kashton.

"I heard the code is for Ashtyn," he rushes out.

"No." My stomach drops. "It can't be."

"Is she with you?" he demands.

I stand naked and stare at my messy bed.

"Fuck." He curses at my silence. "I'll help you look for her. I'll be there in two minutes." He hangs up, and I immediately dial Haidyn's phone.

"Hello?" he asks, voice rough.

"Where the fuck are you?" I snap out of it and start pulling on a pair of jeans.

"In bed. Where the fuck are you?" He yawns. I swear he can sleep through anything.

"Ashtyn is missing, and we've got a code 26." I yank on a T-shirt.

"Fuck." He sighs, sounding more awake now. "What do you need me to do?"

"Get up, get dressed, and help find her before the guards do." They don't send an alert out for no reason. But if they get to her before me, it could be days before I'm allowed to talk to her. She would never do anything that would warrant a code.

You get one chance to control her. If she fucks up, she's going to the basement.

"I'm up," he assures me, and then I tell him we'll split up and to call me if he finds her first.

THIRTY-ONE

ASHTYN

I run down the dimly lit hallway, looking over my shoulder. My hair sticks to my tear-streaked face. Sucking in air, I hold my side, trying to ignore the sharp pain.

"ASH!"

My breath hitches, and I stumble over my own feet but manage not to fall flat on my face. I sidestep into a dark room and yank the door open to shield me as I push my back into the interior wall, allowing the door to cover me. Maybe if they see it's open, they won't think to look in here. My bloody hands come up to cover my face to quiet my sobs.

Don't let them hear you.

"Ash," Kashton calls out, making me jump. "Where the fuck did she go, man?" he growls.

"I don't know. But we better find her. You go that way; I'll go this way," Saint suggests and just the sound of his voice makes my chest tighten.

"Where the fuck is Haidyn?" Kashton asks.

"I told him we needed to split up. He's covering the hospital. If he finds her first, he'll call me," Saint answers.

I close my eyes after they go quiet, pressing my back into the cold wall, praying it'll swallow me up and I won't be seen.

Footsteps grow heavy as someone approaches, and I bite my tongue to keep from whimpering. Prying my watery lashes open, I turn my head to peek through the slit in the door and see Kashton walk by while typing away on his cell.

I knew I'd never survive here, but now I have no choice. The Spade brothers are free to come and go as they please. They're not prisoners here like I am. As much as they mean to me, they'll never understand my need to leave. To escape. Especially Saint. No matter how much it physically hurts me to know I won't have him in my life. That once I'm gone, he'll move on and be with another woman. That's part of being a Lord—marriage, kids. They have to provide the world with more of them. That way, when they die one day, they'll have an heir to carry on their name.

Once Kashton's out of sight, I push my back into the wall once again and inhale a deep breath before pushing off it. My shaky hand wraps around the edge of the door, and I slowly push it away from me so I can get out from behind it. It squeaks, and I hold my breath for a second as my heart races. After a moment of silence, I go to step out of the room, but a hand hits my chest, shoving me back inside.

"We've been looking for you, sweet cheeks." Kashton's chuckle fills the concrete room, making my heart skip a beat. "Playing hide-and-seek, huh? What do I get for finding you first?"

I look up into a set of blue eyes through my watery lashes. His narrow on me when he realizes I'm covered in blood. "What the fuck happened, Ashtyn?" Kashton snaps, his playful banter now gone.

"Shh." I yank on his black T-shirt, pulling him farther into the room to keep from being seen and heard. "Keep your voice down," I whisper harshly, panic starting to set in. I can't let them stop me.

"I'm not going to be quiet. What the fuck happened? Is that your blood?" He yanks my shirt up, but I shove him away, pushing the material down. "You're in some deep shit, Ash. Everyone is looking for you. Come on." He grabs my hand and goes to remove me from the room.

I yank back, and he spins around to face me once again, but I slam my fist into his nose.

"Fuck." He stumbles back, grabbing it. "What the fuck, Ash?" When he removes his hand from his face, blood gushes down his chin to fall on his T-shirt.

I knee him in the balls, and he falls to the floor groaning. I rush into the hallway and run the opposite direction that I came from. Coming to the end of the hall, I slowly peek around the corner and immediately slam my back to the wall when I see Saint approaching. My eyes dart back the other way to make sure Kashton isn't chasing me.

"Ash—what the fuck? Where are you?" Saint adds, calling out. "We're going to find you, sweetheart. But we can't protect you if you don't surrender."

He's right. If I hand myself over to them, they can protect me, but it still won't be enough. Three guys can't save me from an army of men. They'll destroy me. Rip me apart. All I have are the Spade brothers. My mother is dead, my brother left me here, and my father...who knows where the fuck that bastard is. And the baby...I can't leave its life to chance like that. It deserves a better life than I was ever offered. It won't survive in this hell. And even if it did, they'd never let me see it or be a part of its life. And I refuse to let them be punished for my actions. If they tried to protect me, they'd be in trouble. I'm not worth that.

I place my hand in my front pocket and feel the keys as fresh tears run down my face. At least I had one person on my side. That's all I needed. A chance.

"Don't make a sound," a voice whispers in my ear, making me whimper. "Or you're dead."

I inhale sharply through my runny nose. "Can you do that?"

After I nod quickly, he removes his hand from my mouth, and I suck in a deep breath. He takes my hand, and I feel something placed in it. I close my fist around the keys and let out a sob, my shoulders shaking.

"Good luck," he whispers, and I swallow the lump in my throat.

I can do this. It just means leaving everything I love behind. But nothing lasts forever. My world teaches you that at a young age. You can't sell sweet dreams to those who constantly live in nightmares.

Taking in a deep breath, I hold my hair back and slowly peek around the corner again just as Saint walks into one of the rooms. I push off the wall and keep running, needing to get as far away from them as possible. I expect to hear his cell ringing any second with Kashton giving him my location away.

Shoving open a door at the end of the hall, I ignore the loud bang it gives off from hitting the interior wall of the stairwell and run down three flights of stairs to the first floor. No one is down here this time of night. The morgue is the last place anyone wants to be. It smells of death and reeks of formaldehyde. I have avoided it at all costs the past few weeks but desperate times call for desperate measures and all that.

Carnage is a city of terror. A prison that you cannot escape, not even in death. It collects your soul and demands your mind. Trap a person for long enough, and they begin to believe their only purpose is to serve. It's like a hamster running on a wheel—you never get anywhere.

I swallow down the vomit that rises and wipe the tears from my face with my bloody hands. Making my way down the hall, I see an **EXIT** sign hanging from the ceiling, and I let out a cry of relief.

So close.

I turn the corner and come to a stop. My tennis shoes squeak on the floor. My stomach sinks, and my body begins to shake when a set of green eyes land on me.

"Noooo." How did he beat me down here? He must have taken the elevator.

Just seeing him is making this harder than it already was. I wanted my last memory of him to be of us in his bed earlier this evening. His lips on mine and his hands in my hair while he called me his good little whore. Afterward, he passed out with me in his arms and his cum running out of my pussy. I'm still wet from it.

I whimper, taking a step back.

Saint's steps match mine, stepping toward me. His six-foot-five frame towers over my five-five. "What in the fuck are you doing, Ash?" he snaps, making me flinch. "What—?" His eyes drop to my bloody clothes. "Jesus!" He hisses, raising his hands to run through his disheveled dark hair. I did that to him when his head was between my legs before he fucked me.

I left him two hours ago. It's now three in the morning. No doubt he was woken up to *collect* me. "Who the fuck did this to you?" His voice echoes down the hall.

"Shh." My lips tremble.

"Are you fucking serious?" he demands. Reaching out for me, he grabs my upper arm and yanks me to him. His clothes now covered in the blood from mine. "Everyone is fucking looking for you. You're lucky I'm the one who found you." He drags me back down the hall, letting me know that he has no clue Kashton had found me first upstairs.

"No, please ... Saint—"

He spins me around, shoving my back into the concrete wall and steps into me once more, pinning me in place. His large, muscular body vibrates with his anger that I'm not doing as I've been told. "Where do you think you're going to go? You can't escape—"

"I have to try." I interrupt him.

He lets go of me and takes a step back. "You're serious?" His dark brows crease. "You're going to risk your life to leave here?" His voice softens. "To leave me?"

I swallow the knot in my throat but don't respond. I can't. I hate this. Our life. Deciding to leave here was the hardest decision I've ever had to make, but I have no choice. The Lords always make sure you're backed into a corner. They live to test you, and if you fail, you're dead anyway.

I could tell him the truth, but I know what he's hiding from me. It's a lose-lose situation. I won't be the one who gets him in trouble, so I'll just remove myself from the situation.

He quickly looks me up and down. "I'm going to kill whoever the fuck touched you, Ash. But you've lost your goddamn mind if you think I'm letting you leave me."

Come with me. Those words come to mind, but I can't make my lips work. Saint will never leave Carnage. This is his home. His world. His future. I'm just a girl he's fucked. A Lord never picks pussy over his title. No matter that we haven't already made promises to one another. I knew I'd break mine one day.

I wrap my arms around myself. Not sure why I suddenly need to protect myself. Not from him. Saint is one that I know would never hurt me. Not to inflict harm. Do I allow him to do some fucked-up shit to my body? Yes. But I love it. He'd never torture me for his own pleasure. He's protected me and saved me from the worst. But I'm no longer safe. He's no longer my biggest threat in this hell.

He reaches out, his knuckles running down my tear-streaked face. I must look awful because I feel like shit. The action so simple, delicate. It makes me rethink my entire plan to leave him behind. "Sweetheart—"

"They're down here." A guard speaks, coming from the stairwell I just came from. I'm guessing into the radio that they have attached to their bulletproof vests. "Morgue."

And just like that, I'm reminded why I have to get the fuck out of here. I push off the wall and run the opposite direction, and Saint pulls me back. Yanking on my shirt, he practically chokes me. "Ash..."

"Ple—ase?" My legs give out, and he releases me, letting me fall to the cold floor. I start to scoot backward on my hands and ass. My legs kicking out so he can't grab me again.

"There you are, you little bitch!" The guard runs past Saint and grips my hair. He yanks me to my feet before shoving me face-first into the wall, making me cry out. His forearm presses into the back of my neck, smashing my face and the front of my body into the wall.

His beer belly squishes me, and I can feel his dick against my ass. It makes me want to vomit.

"Stop," Saint barks, pulling the man off me. I take a step back from the wall, sucking in a deep breath. "You don't have to be so rough with her. She didn't do anything wrong," he defends me. That's one thing about Saint, he's always got my back. That's what makes this decision so hard.

The guard pushes Saint's hand away. "This is your fault." He points a finger in Saint's face. "You allow her too much freedom."

What? Why would he say that? Saint has no control over what I'm allowed to do. Freedom? No one here at Carnage has freedom. Not unless you're a Spade brother. But even they are called to serve the Lords. They wear the brand on their chest, so they must pay their dues.

Saint, Kashton, and Haidyn are a product of Carnage. One day, the next generation of Spade brothers will take over this hell, and I can't be here when that happens. The truth is, I'll be dead before they even get the chance. That's why I have to get out now. The only person who can save me and the baby is myself.

I can't hold back the whimper that escapes my shaking lips, and the guard's eyes slam to me. He reaches up, pushing the button on his radio, and speaks into it. "Bring the jacket."

My chest squeezes. *Please, no.* I can't let them put me in that. They could leave me for days. Forget about me. I've seen others pee and shit all over themselves when in that. Not to mention starve. When Saint and Haidyn strapped me in it, it was only for about an hour, and the time I was awake to experience it was torture.

My watery eyes shoot to Saint, and his sharp jaw flexes at the guard's order, knowing exactly what it means. "That's not necessary," he snaps.

"Shut the fuck up, boy. I don't take orders from you." The guard dismisses Saint.

"You're not fucking putting her in it!" Saint informs him.

"I'll do whatever the fuck I want to the whore."

While they argue, I decide this is my best chance. I push to my feet and start to run. The back of my hair is pulled, pin pricks like a thousand needles penetrate my scalp, and I'm yanked up off my feet before I'm slammed down onto the floor on my back. My breath is taken from me, and dots dance across my vision. I roll onto my side, hugging my stomach, coughing as pain explodes behind my eyes and runs down the back of my neck along my spine. My fingers and toes start to tingle from the blow.

"Don't fucking touch her," Saint shouts, followed by the two of them struggling.

As I get to my hands and knees, a loud bang rings through the hallway, momentarily deafening me. My hands cover my ears to subside the ringing, but it doesn't work.

Looking up, I see the guard fall to his knees and then flat on his face. The sound of the ringing in my ears intensifies as I watch Saint lower the gun that he must have taken from the guard. He tucks it into the back of his waistband of his jeans, glaring down at the dead guard.

I jump to my shaking legs and slide my back against the wall to get around the pool of blood that grows under the guy. I have enough blood on me already.

"Saint," I breathe, running up behind him.

"Let's go." He grabs my arm and drags me down the hall back in the direction I came from. I can't do it. I won't go back. I'm too close.

Yanking his T-shirt up, I grip the handle of the gun tucked into the back of his jeans and pull it out. We both come to a stop, and time slows as I press it into his back, knowing there's no going back after this.

He stiffens, the thin material of his T-shirt straining against his taut muscles, hands down by his side. Slowly, he turns around to face me. His eyes narrow when he stares down the barrel. "Jesus Christ, Ash. You really have lost your goddamn mind." He sighs, and his eyes soften with empathy as if I'm that pathetic that he actually feels sorry for me.

I am, but I refuse to become my mother. I will do anything and everything I can for my child. I will put them first and make sure they have a safe and healthy place to grow up. If I don't break the cycle, then who will?

Tears run down my face while the gun shakes in my hands, but my legs are spread wide, anchored to the floor as if I'm a ship bracing for a storm.

Lifting his arms out to his side, he takes a step toward me, the gun now pressing into his chest, and I take a stumbling step back.

"Sweetheart." He calls me by my nickname, and it makes me whimper. "We both know that you won't shoot me. Come on." He motions with his raised hands to give him the gun. "I'll be right here with you. Nothing is going to happen to you. I'll make sure of it." He's referring to being punished by their fathers. But he doesn't know what I know. Not yet, anyway.

No one leaves Carnage. Ever. And those who have tried were caught and never saw the light of day again. The world already thinks I'm dead; no one would miss me if they killed me in here.

Saint adds, "Whatever happened is over, and whoever touched you will pay." His eyes drop to the bleeding corpse behind me before meeting mine again.

I've never doubted what Saint would do for me because I've seen firsthand how he protects those he loves. But even I know some things are beyond his limits. I'm not meant to be his wife or the mother of his children. I'm just the whore he uses until she comes along. And that is the hardest pill to swallow. The vows we took will mean nothing to the Lords when they find out he betrayed his oath

A laugh escapes my lips. I feel manic, like a ticking time bomb. The littlest thing will set me off. "Over? It'll never be over," I choke out, hating how careless he is. But he grew up in this life. He's a Lord. His bloodline guarantees he'll never have to go through what I'll have to endure. He's a man. I'm just a whore for them all to use until I rot in this place.

I hear faint sounds of voices, followed by the sound of shuffling feet. They're coming to take me. And I know one of them has the jacket in their hands. They'll secure me in it and drag me down the hall by my hair...if I'm lucky. Or like the woman who had the rope wrapped around her neck that they dragged her by.

"Come on, sweetheart. Be a good girl and hand me the gun."

Good girl? My knees almost buckle at his choice of words. I've always been that to him. I've given this man everything I had to offer. His friends too. But my life? At some point, a woman has to stand up for herself and draw a line. This is where I make a stand. I either escape or let them kill me trying. I'd gladly let him kill me than me kill him. But nothing about my life has ever been easy. Especially our love. "Would you kill me, Saint?" I ask, fresh tears running down my cheeks. Maybe they would keep me alive long enough to give birth, but after that? They'd just torture me. "Would you end my life if it was the only way to save me?"

He told me he'd hurt me if it meant he could keep me. But would he kill me to save me?

His head tilts to the side, his features showing his confusion. "No," he answers softly. "I never want to exist in a world without you in it, sweetheart."

I don't know if I should laugh or cry at his answer. But he told me what I already knew—he'll never let me go.

He reaches for the gun, and I shove it into his chest. He raises his hands, softly chuckling. I suck in a deep breath. "I'll do it," I warn, my body trembling but knowing this is my only way out of this hell.

"No, you won't." He sighs heavily as if I've lost my mind.

That's what this place does to you. People weren't meant to be caged. Do you know what it feels like not to exist? To know that no one is looking for you? It's crippling. Mentally and physically. And then you find out that you have a life inside you? That there is something good to come out of something so awful? I want better for my child.

There is a life outside of this place, far past the Lords, and I'm going to get it. By shooting him, it gives me an out. I'll be free. It'll only cost my soul and the love of my life. But freedom always comes with a price.

"I'm... sorry," I choke out, my throat so tight all I can do is whisper the next sentence. "I love you." He's said those three words to me several times. This is the first time I've said them to him.

His green eyes narrow on mine, and he takes a step toward me. "Ash—"

I pull the trigger.

I STAND, SHAKING WITH THE GUN DOWN BY MY SIDE. HIS BODY lies on the floor, blood pooling underneath him. He's coughing, body jerking at the movement.

"Saint?" Kashton calls out. His shoes echo off the concrete walls as he stomps his way down the stairwell. He heard the gun go off. Everyone had to.

I take a shaking step back as his body continues to convulse. Tears fall from my cheeks as my throat closes. "I'm so sorry," I whisper. "I—"

"Ash-tyn." He coughs my name, blood splattering across his face.

"Saint?" Kashton yells once more, and he's getting closer.

I lick my wet lips and turn my back to him, needing to leave. I didn't shoot him for nothing. I rush out the hallway and down the corner. I scream when I hit a hard body. Looking up into a set of hard eyes, they drop to my gun.

My shaking hand tightens on it, ready to shoot anyone to get out of this place. "Get the fuck out of here. As far as I'm concerned, you're dead. Do you understand me?" he growls, not making a move to take it from me or step back.

"I...understand." I manage to say through a sob with a nod.

"Saint! Fuck!" Kashton shouts from around the corner. He just found his brother bleeding out in the hallway.

The man steps into me and lowers his lips to my ear. "We all pay for our sins, Ashtyn. You are no different. You can run from them all you want, but they will catch up with you no matter where you go." Pulling back, he turns and walks back in the direction he came from, going away from the hallway I ran from.

Taking a deep breath, I run toward the **EXIT** and shove it open, entering the black night and run deep into the woods. I'm sucking in breath after breath, and my lungs burn. I try not to trip over the uneven ground as I come up to the door that's hidden inside a hill.

I sniff, my shaking hands unlock it, and yank it open. Bending down, I pick up the flashlight left for me and turn it on, closing the door behind me.

The sound of dripping water and rats scatter away from the light. I feel the bile rising, and I can't stop it. The smell, the fear, the blood...

Bending over, I hold my hair back as I vomit. My head pounds from the guard tossing me around, and my ears ring. I try to take a calming breath and get myself together. I can't stop now. We've come too far.

SAINT

The gunshot echoes through the hall. One second, I'm staring at a blood-covered Ashtyn, and the next, I'm blinking up at the ceiling as it fades in and out.

"Christ," a familiar voice hisses, and then Kashton hovers over me. His bloody face in mine.

"What ... happened?" I'm having a hard time talking. I can't seem to get the words out. Why is he bleeding? Did he hurt Ashtyn? Is that why they were both covered in blood?

"The bitch shot you," he shouts before placing his hands on me and presses down.

"Nooo." He can't be talking about my sweetheart. She wouldn't do that. She'd never hurt me. She loves me. The pain that shoots through my body makes me arch my back off the floor. I go to scream, but nothing comes out as my breath is taken away.

"You're okay," he rushes out. "Hang on."

My body relaxes into the cold concrete floor, and I blink, my eyes heavy. The fluorescent lights that run along the ceiling fade in and out.

"Saint!" he screams as he looks up from me and down the end of the hall. "Haidyn, call the medics," he orders.

"Ash-tyn?" I choke out. The guards were coming for her. Maybe they shot us both? Is she lying next to me bleeding out? If so, he needs to save her before they get to her. They'll save me and leave her to die. She's no one to them, but everything to me. That's why I couldn't let her leave me. I almost lost her once. I won't let it happen again.

"She's gone, Saint." Kashton growls.

They killed her? "No." I cough, and I taste blood. "Save her—"

"She ran," Kashton snaps at me. "Haidyn, he's been shot. She fucking shot him! He needs Devin! Now!"

"I—" My tongue won't work. My lips are no longer able to move. I try to reach out for her, to hold her hand, but they don't move either. She has to be next to me. Why isn't he helping her?

"Fuck," Kash curses, ripping my shirt open, and I feel like I'm floating. The lights dim, and the floor gets colder as he fades into nothing. The last thing on my mind is if they killed Ashtyn, I hope I die too.

I'M PUTTING ON MY BELT THAT JESSIE HAD BROUGHT ME THIS morning, finally getting out of my hospital stay here at Carnage.

They've kept me drugged up in here for two weeks, and I'm losing my goddamn mind. Ashtyn got away, and that's two weeks that she's had the opportunity to run. Every time I woke up and went to leave, they'd give me something to knock my ass out. Said I wasn't ready and that I needed to take time.

She shot me in the chest. She was either a really good shot and knew it wouldn't kill me. Or she was a bad shot and missed my heart. Either way, I'm still alive, and I'm going to find her and bring her back.

We still don't know who was after Adam, and I'm still not clear if they wanted her dead or to use her as bait. So, the Lords need to assume she's dead. She won't be able to survive out in the real world without me.

The sound of my hospital room door opens, and I keep my back to it as I pick up my shirt and gently pull it over my head. I'm still sore as fuck. "Where are Haidyn and Kashton?" I ask, knowing it's Devin. He came in this morning, and I told him I was done putting up with this shit. He said he'd be back to give me some meds in case I needed them. *Fuck the drugs.*

"Hello, Saint."

I spin around at the sound of a woman's voice, knowing that was not Devin. She stands in my room in a tight-fitting white pencil skirt that hits her knees with a pair of black high heels and blood-red top. It's tucked into her high-waisted skirt with a deep V-cut neckline showing off her enlarged breasts. Her dark hair is up in a tight bun, showing off her neck, and she wears a pair of red-rimmed glasses that showcase a set of dark green eyes. They drop to my combat boots and run up over my jeans and T-shirt.

"Can I help you?" I give her my back and pick up my watch off the hospital bed and place it on, clasping it.

"Actually, I'm here to help you," she says cheerfully.

I snort; no one can help me. Not right now. Not with this. I don't know how long I'll be gone or how I'll find her, but I'm not coming back until I have Ashtyn in my arms. Whatever she did, whatever happened, I can fix it. I can protect her.

Locking my cell, I put it in my pocket, zip up my bag, and toss it over my good shoulder and turn around to leave. "Move," I bark when she stands in my way. I'm really not in the mood to hit a woman. I don't give a fuck who she is.

"I'm sorry, but I can't do that." Just then, the door behind her opens, and four men step into the room, all coming to line up behind her on either side, and the door shuts once more.

I take a deep breath, about to lose my shit. "Dad, what the fuck are you doing?" I bark, looking over their cloaks and masks. If they think this changes our agreement, it doesn't. "I don't have time..."

"Your father is dead, Saint," she speaks.

My eyes scan the four men once more before I look back down at her. "Listen." I fist my hand. "I don't know who the fuck you are or why the fuck you're here, but you need to get out of my way before I body-slam you into the fucking wall." If my dad were dead, I'd know.

A smile graces her done-up face as if the idea of being tossed around like a rag doll turns her on. "Things have changed, Saint," she says cryptically.

"Get the fuck—"

"Show him, boys." She interrupts me.

One of the men move out from behind her and picks up the remote to the TV that hangs on the wall to my right. Pushing in a code, it goes to the surveillance system here at Carnage. It's of the pits.

The view is from the corner of the room, pointed down at the concrete floor. Both pits on the outsides look dry and empty but the one in the middle is full of water. My chest tightens remembering what it was like to be in there, suffocating, cold and mind fucking. "What am I looking at?" I growl through gritted teeth.

"You asked where Haidyn and Kashton were. I'm giving you an answer."

My head snaps to look at her, my heart racing. She remains smiling. "You've been out for two weeks, Saint. A lot has happened since then."

"What the fuck are you talking about?" I look back at the TV. Stepping closer, I watch the water spill over the top of the bars onto the concrete floor. The five vertical bars recede three inches into the pit and lock in place. That's why I couldn't breathe when I lifted my nose through them when it filled to the top.

The water is dark, and given the angle, I can't see down into it, but there is a tube of some sort popping out of the top where the head would be if someone were lying down. It's black and rubber, maybe four inches past the water with a valve on the end. My eyes shoot to the wall across from the pit looking for a timer but I don't see one.

"Your fathers are dead, and you and your brothers are to blame—"

"They're not dead! And Haidyn and Kashton would never do that!" I shout, a sickening feeling in my stomach. "Who the fuck is in there?" I point to the TV, glaring at her.

She ignores my question. "They're dead because of Ashtyn."

I shake my head. "No."

"You let her escape, Saint. The Lords didn't like that." She steps closer to me and I take one back trying to figure out what the fuck is going on. I've been in and out for two weeks but I haven't been in a fucking coma.

"The Lords *think* she's dead," I grind out. I can't lie and say she's dead. This woman obviously knows she isn't.

Her laugh makes my teeth clench. "If they wanted her dead, she'd be dead," she says cryptically.

My eyes go back to the TV. "Who the fuck is in there?" I demand once more, a throbbing pain in my right arm. The last pain pill they force-fed me last night starting to wear off. Dropping my bag, I clench and unclench my right fist. My hand numbing.

"That is Haidyn," she answers. "Sensory deprivation..."

I wrap my hand around her neck and slam her back into the wall below the TV. I hear the guys shuffling behind me and she raises her hand to stop them before her dark green eyes look up to meet mine.

"You better be fucking lying." My body vibrates against hers. "Where is Haidyn?" I bark in her face.

Her eyes grow hard, and she lifts her chin. "He's where he belongs." They search mine, and she adds, "Go ahead, show him."

My eyes look up at the TV that we stand underneath. The screen still shows the pits, but the middle one is empty and all three have the bars off.

The double doors open to the room and two men enter pushing a stretcher. Haidyn lies on it. He's dressed in an all-black dry suit that divers wear. It's unzipped down the front though exposing a cut and bruised chest. He's also unconscious. His face looks swollen, lip busted. Whatever happened, he put up a fight that he ended up not winning. Something tells me it wasn't a fair one.

I let go of her neck and step back, watching as the blood rushes in my ears. They bring him to a stop and lift up his head and shoulders, pulling a hood up from underneath him that's connected to the suit. Lying him flat once again, one of them begins putting stickers on his chest. Four of them in various places before zipping it up to his neck.

The other man pulls out two small plugs and shoves them up his nose, taking away his chance to breathe through them. Then they both maneuver the tight hood over his head, covering every inch of his face except for his mouth. There's already some sort of mouthpiece in and they connect a tube to it that has a ball valve on the end.

My eyes shoot to the pit as it starts to fill with water. So high to the point it slowly flows over the top and onto the floor. Their shoes splash the water as they step in it and pick him up before lowering him into the watery pit. One holds onto the tube to make sure the bars don't knock it off while the other closes the hinged bars down into the pit and locks them in place.

The one holding the tube, twists the valve while the other guy pulls out his cell. He looks at it and nods a few times mouthing words that the video doesn't allow me to hear.

Then they turn and walk away, pushing the stretcher with them, while locking my brother inside.

"He's been in there for—"

"Fucking bitch!" I slap her across the face so hard it throws her to the side. I reach out to grab her by her bun, but the back of my legs are hit, knocking me to my knees and my arms are yanked up and behind my head, held by my wrists. The position has pain shooting up my chest momentarily taking away my breath.

"You've pissed off the Lords, Saint." She rubs her cheek, coming to stand in front of me. "And I've been sent to train the next generation of the Spade brothers before you're allowed to step up and take your position here. For the next six months, I will put the three of you through hell." She kneels in front of me. So close I can smell her expensive perfume. Her smile makes my stomach drop, "I'm going to teach you not to let pussy get in the way of your oath." Reaching out, she takes a red-painted nail and pushes on my chest where Ashtyn shot me.

I clench my teeth to keep from screaming while holding my breath.

"Haidyn and Kashton already have two weeks of training done, so you're going to have to catch up." Her eyes drop to my lips. "I have a feeling that you're a quick study."

I take the opportunity of her closeness and ram my head into hers, knocking her back off her heels and onto her ass as her back hits the wall. My arms are freed as they go to help her, but before I can get to the bitch, I'm pushed down onto my stomach, and they're yanked behind my back. This time, they place me in handcuffs.

Breathing heavily, I try to roll over so I'm not lying on my burning chest but someone steps on the back of my neck, pinning me down.

She snaps her fingers, "Let him see."

I'm yanked to sit up, and I glare up at her. If I wasn't so enraged, I'd enjoy the blood running down her face as she shoves a phone into mine. "I control everything. The water is forty degrees, but he's burning up inside of the dry suit. The stickers on his chest...those are wireless chest monitors and they show me his vitals." She points to the screen with the tip of her nail. "See that? His core body temperature is up to a 103. 107 is brain dead, by the way."

I can't speak, I can barely breathe from the weight on my chest.

"He woke up some time ago." She goes on. "His current blood oxygen content is around fifty percent. Probably experiencing problems with circulation, possible hallucinations, body spasms…" She pauses. "And this one here, it controls the valve on the end of the tube—his only access to air. I can give him more or take it away…"

"I'm going to fucking kill you." I manage to say through gritted teeth, cutting her off. If it's the last thing I do, I'm going to hang this bitch by her fucking neck on the gates of Carnage for all to see as they drive by.

She laughs and signals for them to get me to my feet. I bite down on my tongue as they lift me by my arms and try to ignore the pain that shoots down my side. The cuffs are undone and I take a step toward her, ready to knock her fucking teeth out when she speaks.

"You have a choice here, Saint. Stay and willingly give yourself over to me. Or go and chase your whore while I play with your brothers."

My hands clench. "She's my …" I refuse to finish that sentence. She arches a brow. A very select few know what Ash and I did that first week she was here. And right now, both of them need me.

Fuck Ashtyn for doing this. For making me choose. For making me let her go! And fuck this bitch for thinking she can give me an ultimatum.

I'll do what must be done now, but I won't forget Ashtyn. She can't run forever.

"Pull him out," I demand. "Right now." My eyes go to the screen and my already tight chest seizes when I see the black tube and valve. How many times has she taken it away? Who knows how long he's been in there and it's such a tight space it gives little movement to begin with. I had barely any and Haidyn is taller than me.

"And you'll stay?" she asks, and my eyes drop to her as she arches her brow. "Because I could really use your help. The other two have not been cooperative, Saint. I've had to force my power—"

"LET HIM OUT!" I shout, my throat burning, tired of her fucking voice. I want to shove that black tube down her throat and slowly fill it with water and watch her drown.

She smiles and dials up a number on her phone. Placing it to her ear, she speaks one word. "Enough."

My eyes shoot to the screen and two men enter the double doors once again pushing the stretcher. They go to the center pit and unlock the bars, pulling them up. The water remains as they reach down and grip his shoulders first sitting him up, then drag him out. They lie him on the floor, and he doesn't move.

"If he's dead..."

"Take him to Devin," she says into the phone. "I want a full checkup." When she hangs up her phone, my eyes shoot back to the surveillance.

They remove the hood, and his eyes are closed, but I can see his chest moving in the tightly fitting suit. His body is shaking and his hair and face are soaked from sweat. They remove the plugs in his nose and the tube with the mouthpiece. Then they place him on the stretcher and push him out of the room.

My breathing is erratic, muscles tight, and my blood is boiling. Someone will pay for this. Even if it takes years to get my revenge, it will happen. That's what I've been taught to do, and I let Ashtyn fool me into forgetting who the fuck I am.

Lowering my eyes from the TV, I look at the unknown woman. She smiles at me while addressing her four men. "Take him down to the observation room, strip him naked, and get him ready for his initiation." Stepping into me, she places her palm on my heaving chest. Her eyes light up when she feels my racing heart. "I'm looking forward to making you a good boy, Saint."

Part Two

FOUR YEARS LATER...

THIRTY-TWO

SAINT

Four Years Ago

I enter my bedroom to find Ashtyn still in my bed lying on her stomach. The fresh tattoo down her spine gets my attention.

I vow. You vow. We vow.

The three numbers I branded on her body weren't enough for me. That's a reminder she belongs to Carnage. I wanted something on her that was mine and something that she actually wanted. We settled on the vows we took last week.

"Good evening, sweetheart." Reaching up, I grip the back of my shirt and rip it off my head.

"Sa-int." She moans, her ass shakes back and forth trying to lift her hips off the bed. "Please…" She trails off.

"How many times have you come since I left you with that vibrator in your cunt?" I ask.

Before I left to go have a meeting with our fathers, I stripped the duvet and top sheet off the bed and tied her face down and spread eagled. I put a vibrator in her pussy and a butt plug in her ass.

"I haven't." She rubs her face into the fitted sheet while her body fights the ropes that keep her in place.

I smile. That's because I've been controlling it from my phone while I was gone. I kept it on the lowest setting to drive her nuts. I wanted her soaking and begging by the time I returned. I've only been gone for an hour.

Walking over to my nightstand, I pull out what I want and finish getting undressed. Then I crawl onto the bed between her tied legs. I pull the butt plug out, and she whimpers as I toss it to the floor. Taking my hard cock in my hand, I pour the lube all over my length.

Her voice rings out as my cock pushes its way into her tight ass. It's much bigger in size than the plug I had put into her, but my girl doesn't mind. She enjoys the pain.

"Saint." She pants, her arms yanking on the ropes while she buries her face into the bed.

I grab her hair and yank her head back. The sound of her scream makes my cock twitch inside her ass. My free hand picks up my cell next to me and turns up the vibrator, and the scream turns to moans and whimpers. With my knees, I spread her legs as wide as the ropes will allow, readjusting myself, then start to fuck her ass while she gets off.

"Such a good whore." I praise her, leaning over her and wrapping my hand around her face from behind.

She may not have a choice at how her life turned out, but she chose me. And I'm going to spend the rest of my life reminding her that no other man could ever come close to what she needs. Even if that means I have to keep her tied to my bed twenty-four seven.

My hand rests on the marble wall as I stand in the shower. My eyes close as the water hits my face, remembering that day with Ashtyn.

Four years she's been gone. And I still hate her as much as I did the day I was forced to choose—chase a ghost or give my life over to Carnage to save my brothers.

When she shot me, I was in denial. When I snapped out of that, I went feral. Filled with nothing but hatred and revenge. I've spent all that time trying to find her with no luck. No trace whatsoever.

Someone helped her.

Ashtyn is smart, but able to escape Carnage without help smart? No. I refuse to give her that much credit. Or maybe I just refuse to look that stupid.

Shutting off the shower, I get out and dry off. Looking at myself in the mirror, I wonder if she'd even recognize me if she saw me today. Four years is a long time.

Wrapping the towel around my hips, I tuck it into itself as my cell beeps, I have an incoming message from Kashton.

She's ready.

I walk into my closet and get dressed before exiting my bedroom. We've been running Carnage for three and a half years now. And things are different than what they once were. Our fathers thought they taught us how to torture unlucky souls. They had nothing on Ashtyn. Her leaving us changed us all, and I can't say it was for the better.

Exiting the elevator, I walk down the quiet hallway and shove open the door. Wide eyes meet mine, and she starts thrashing in the straitjacket Haidyn and Kashton placed her in. She mumbles nonsense through the gag in her mouth as spit flies out from around the black rubber ball. The stretcher she's secured to rattles as she tries to loosen the straps that tie her down to it.

"Where's Haidyn?" I ask Kashton who is over by the counter getting everything ready for our newest addition to Carnage.

"He got a phone call. Said he had to take it," he answers.

I turn and look over at the two-way mirror. Every time I'm in here, I think someone is watching me.

The woman thrashes around, continuing to scream as loud as she can through the gag.

"Adrenaline?" Kashton asks.

"Nah," I say, walking over to her. I place my hands on the stretcher and look down at her. Tears and snot cover the familiar face I haven't seen in a long time. "How's it feel?" I ask, yanking on the jacket. "Itches, huh?"

She closes her eyes as a sob racks her petite body. My eyes drop to her shaking legs and watch her pull on the straps that hold them open. The sound of the stretcher rattling echoes in the concrete room.

"I think a good twenty-four hours should be a good starting point. Kash?" I look up at him.

He nods. "At least."

A lot has happened in the past four years. Any time the Lords have a chance to fuck up someone's life, they take it. One of our good friends Tyson was one of those Lords. And a few weeks ago, his misfortune was our gain.

WE SIT IN THE CATHEDRAL IN THE MIDDLE OF NOWHERE. THE ONE where the Lords come to perform their rituals. A friend needed our help tonight, and we were more than willing to do so. A woman lies hogtied on the Lord's altar in front of us, and she said the one word I never expected to hear.

"Ashtyn," she calls out.

I'm instantly on my feet, not even thinking about it. I haven't heard anyone say that name in so long that there are times I think she's dead. Buried in the graveyard behind the cathedral. Long forgotten.

Tyson steps back, and I yank the knife from his hand. Shoving her onto her back, she screams as the hog-tied position smashes her folded body underneath her. I wrap my hand around her throat and squeeze, pinning her down.

I press the knife to the side of her face. "What the fuck did you just say?" I'm shaking with fucking rage. If she's lying...

"Ashtyn..." She tries to catch her breath. "I know where she is."

I squeeze harder, not believing her, and she thrashes around. "Bullshit," I spit out, pushing the tip of the knife deeper into her face, breaking the skin.

She's turning blue, her lips white. Her body softens as her struggle lessens.

A hand touches my arm, and my eyes snap to see Tyson standing next to me. "I want her dead, but just in case she knows something useful, she's better alive for now."

I release her neck and remove the knife, stepping back. She rolls onto her side and gasps for breath. "If you're lying..."

"I'm not," she cries, choking out sobs. "I promise."

My heart hammers in my chest. For four years, I've wondered where the fuck Ashtyn would be. Who she's with. If I'd ever see her again.

Now is my chance.

THE WOMAN'S SOBBING BRINGS ME BACK FROM THAT MEMORY. It was just a few weeks ago. We've let her sit, naked and chained in her cell while Tyson was able to get the answers he deserved.

Honestly, I wasn't sure if I wanted to know where Ashtyn was just yet. I've waited so long for her. There were times I just hoped she'd come back on her own. That she'd miss me so badly she couldn't stand to be without me. But now that the answers are so close...?

My mind is filled with the what-ifs. Is she even still alive? If so, how has she survived so long on her own? Is she with someone? Does she have children? Am I prepared to take her away from any one of those things?

Abso-fucking-lutely. I will drag her back here kicking and screaming, removing her from anything she has accomplished while away from me. I'm going to strip her naked and remind her who the fuck owns her.

"Here you go." Kashton hands me the branding iron.

I twirl the handle around in my hand as the woman's cries grow louder. I lower it to her leg, just hovering over her skin letting her feel the heat but not burning her just yet, and it trembles in the restraints. I make my way up her body and across the straitjacket before hovering it over her face.

She cowers away, trying to look to the side, but the strap around her neck is too tight for that kind of movement. I take my free hand and dig my fingers into the leather strap of the ball gag and her cheek, yanking the rubber from her mouth, and her sobs immediately fill the room. "Pl-ease..."

I grip her chin, squeezing it so hard she whimpers, and shove her head back. She blinks rapidly while fresh tears roll down her dirty face. I hold the 666 branding iron right over her left cheek as I speak. "Where is my wife, Whitney?"

ASHTYN

I sit in the dressing room of the strip club. Tonight is particularly busy for a Thursday because it's a themed mask night. Everyone, even the customers, come in dressed up with masks. Some are even dressed in full costumes.

My cell lights up, sitting on the counter in front of me, and I pick it up to see it's an incoming call from **BOSS LADY**.

"Hello?" I sit back in my seat.

"Question." The woman on the other end greets me.

"Shoot."

"Monica called in tonight with the flu. Maggie is picking up her shift, but she can't tomorrow..."

"I'll take it." I sit up straight, not even letting her finish asking me to work tomorrow night.

"Perfect. I'll put you down. Thanks so much, girl."

"Anytime," I tell her, and she knows it. She's changed my life for the best. When I didn't think anyone would take a chance on a woman who was on the run, she did. She isn't aware of what I'm running from. Never asked. When I tried to explain, she said I didn't have to. The fact that I wanted a fresh start was all she needed to know. Something tells me she's done the same thing.

"Damn, woman. You Daddy's little girl tonight?" Destiny asks as she walks by me.

I lock my cell and set it down to look up at her in the mirror in front of me when she comes to stand behind my chair. I did my makeup like Harley Quinn.

My red-painted lips smile, and I say, "I'll be whatever Daddy wants me to be." Cliché, I know. But it's fun to get to dress up every night of the week. I get to be someone else. It helps me forget who I once was. Ever since I ran from Carnage, I wear a mask that can never be removed. It's a hard pill to swallow sometimes.

Bending over, I grab one of the fishnet thigh-highs and pull it up my freshly spray-tanned leg, getting it in place without tearing it before repeating the other. Then I slide on red six-inch fuck-me heels. Picking up the collar off the counter, I look over at Cherry. "Hey, will you put this on me, please?" I ask her.

"Of course." She gets up, walks over to me, and I grab my dark hair in one hand while she steps behind me, fastening it in place. "Feel okay?" she asks, tugging on it to ensure enough room for me to breathe.

"No," I answer honestly. It's bulky and uncomfortable, but I paid a hundred and fifty dollars for it. "I'll remove it after Benny leaves," I tell her.

I considered buying a blond wig with pigtails but thought better of it. You already get so hot dancing under the lights that it would just drive me nuts. So, tonight I am a brunette Harley Quinn. I decide to keep it down because when you're on stage, shaking your ass for cash, men like to see your hair.

I've always kept mine really long. It's naturally dark, but years ago, I dyed it black. It's so dark that when the light hits it just right, it glows blue.

A bleach-blond enters the dressing room and stops by my chair. "Jake dropped by."

"Oh." I sit up straighter, my hands clapping excitedly. "Did he bring gifts?"

Her black-painted lips widen into an evil grin. "He did." She places her fist out, and I open mine underneath it. She drops two pills into mine before I close it, concealing what's in it.

"Tell him I said thank you."

Sadie laughs softly. "You can thank him later. He'll be back with his friends." Pushing off the wall, she plops down next to me.

She's my best friend here at the club. Sometimes I feel guilty about how much I've lied to her. I feel like I'm pretending every day. She doesn't know the real me; if she did, she probably wouldn't be my friend.

I pop both pills into my mouth and sip on my Red Bull. I'm going to need both to get me through tonight. I worked last night and was up early this morning, running errands all day. I barely got three hours of sleep last night. I'm going to crash hard when I get home later tonight.

"Hey, Sadie, those two guys from last weekend are here talking to Bones," Cherry tells her when she enters the room.

I look over at Sadie and ask, "The two who each gave you five grand?"

"Yep," Cherry answers for her.

"God, they were so fucking fine." Sadie sighs, slumping back in her chair.

I took last weekend off because of James. We live together but are currently in the middle of a breakup. I can't get the bastard to move out of my place. I told him to pack his shit and go. He cried. Begged me to let him stay. Said he had nowhere else to go after he lost his job.

That was six months ago. He prefers to live off me instead of going out and getting one on his own.

"They're getting the room again. I just saw them walk to the back." Cherry winks at Sadie.

"Hey, Luna, Benny is here," Bentley calls out, entering with her G-string and garter belt overflowing with bills from just getting off the main stage.

"Thanks." Sucking down what's left of my Red Bull, I give Sadie a wink and walk out into the club. The music is loud, and the lights flash. I'm used to it by now. I've been working here for the past two years. I was working at another club here in Vegas when Glass opened. This one was just better all around—bigger and classier and my bosses are amazing.

You have to audition to be an entertainer in Nevada and get a license. Thankfully, when I ran from Carnage, I had help. I was given a new name and identity. Without that, I'm not sure where I'd be.

When I decided to start a new life, a stripper was the only option. You get to be someone else. Stage name, dress-up, and it's like a girls' night every night while you take money from men as you drink. If there's anything better, let me know.

Plus, when you're running from the Lords, you have to be assumed dead. If not, they will find you. I might have killed Saint, but the others will still be looking for me. And a Lord believes in blood for blood.

I started taking drugs to help me forget...what I gave up. What I ended up losing. And him. It didn't work. But I realized that it did help me sleep, and in my dreams, I was able to live a different life. One where he wasn't a Lord, and I wasn't the coward who shot him. We were able to live happily ever after like you hear in fairy tales.

I walk up the three stairs and over to the round table where the guy sits. Benny always sits in the same section, same table, and orders the same thing to drink. He looks up from his phone to see me, and he swallows.

"Hey, handsome." I plop down next to him.

Reaching over, he slides his hand between my legs and pulls mine to rest over his jean-clad thighs, across his lap. His lips near my ear, his voice rumbles. "Fuck, you look hot tonight, sweetheart."

I still cringe whenever someone calls me that. It reminds me of Saint. I don't know if I killed him, but he still has so much power over me it's pathetic. At times, I think killing myself would have been easier than living a life without him. I wish he would have just killed me when I asked him. I ended up losing everything anyway.

I muster up a fake smile. "You look pretty good yourself."

He didn't dress up, but I didn't expect him to. He's a regular. He's been coming into Glass to see me since opening night. I slept with him three months later for the first time. We've never been a couple or anything like that. He comes in regularly and sees me. Every now and then, he rents a suite in one of the hotels on the Strip, and I spend the night with him.

"How long before you go on stage?" he asks, his hand softly running up and over my upper thigh at the top of my thigh-highs.

"Thirty minutes," I say.

He gives me a kind smile just as a server comes over to us. He orders himself a glass of scotch and me a Red Bull and vodka. I need another energy drink and for this ecstasy to kick in.

Technically, in the state of Nevada, if a strip club serves alcohol, the dancers aren't allowed to be nude. But if you can serve alcohol, the club is more lucrative. So Glass doesn't follow the law. But when you have two bosses like I do, they're bound to bend the rules to their benefit. They've either paid someone off or just don't give a fuck.

THIRTY-THREE

ASHTYN

Forty-five minutes later, I walk off the third stage, pulling the bills from my G-string, and head down the steps off the end and back into the locker room.

"How is it out there?" Cherry asks.

"Good." I walk over to my locker, pop it open, and shove all the cash into my backpack before locking it. I won't count my money until closing when I go through it and cash it all in for larger bills.

Making my way over to my chair, I stand in front of the mirror, getting a good look at myself. Reaching up, I scrape my nails over my scalp, messing up my already tangled hair, and my eyes practically roll into the back of my head at how good it feels. Then I reapply my red lipstick and pucker my lips, looking over my eyes. They're dilated. The pills started to kick in about fifteen minutes ago. My skin tingles, and I feel hot—flushed. Of course, that could be from the neon lights that I was just dancing under.

"Luna?" One of our bosses enters the room. Pretty sure they're both involved with the Mafia. Bones is a King. Well, that's what everyone calls him anyway. He owns Kingdom—a hotel and casino—

with three other Kings here in Las Vegas. Titan, Grave, Cross, and Bones own this city.

"Yeah?" I ask, looking up into his dark-blue eyes.

"You've been requested to join the Fountain room." He arches a brow, waiting for my response.

"Yeah." I smile and quickly look around for Sadie, but don't see her. She's probably already in there and waiting for me. "Be right there."

He taps the side of the doorframe before he exits the room.

"Man," Cherry sighs. "He's so fucking hot."

"He's been claimed," Mercedes reminds her.

It was all over the news. Of course, she's some Mafia princess—that's what the media calls her anyway. Just furthers my point of who he really is.

"I'd gladly be his side bitch. Like no lie. He could ruin my life, and I'd thank him." She fans herself, making all of us laugh.

I put my outfit back on since I took it off while on stage, then exit the locker room. I make my way to the bar and grab a new drink before I head toward the Fountain room. It's the most expensive room a customer can purchase here, and I couldn't be more excited to spend my night in it.

When your presence is requested in the Fountain room, you're automatically skipped over when it's your turn to make your rounds on the stages because you're making a substantial amount more than you could make on a three-minute song.

I make my way up the stairs and down the hallway to see one of our security guards standing in front of the black double doors to the room. Joe has been here since they opened. He's your typical man who works in a strip club and tries to fuck all the exotic dancers. And he always wants free dances.

"Who all is in here?" I ask. Usually when two or more rent this room, you've got multiple dancers going in and out until the club closes. They're paying for the room and bottle service, not the girl specifically. We're extra.

"Sadie is already in there. They saw you on stage and requested you to join them," he says with a big smile, reaching for the doors. "Let me know if you ladies need anything." He winks, pulling them open for me.

I take a deep breath, stepping into the room and the atmosphere changes. The Fountain room is meant to feel more secluded and personal. Even the songs played in this room are different from what the dancer requests to play on the main stage when it's her turn.

It's a large room, meant for a bachelor or birthday party. The lights are just as bright, but they're not as flashy. They're more subtle. Red rope lights line the ceiling and black walls, giving off a seductive feel. The carpet is black with what looks like gray-and-blue confetti. The stages—there are two—are both matte black with chrome poles.

"Hey, girl." Sadie stands on the main stage with her hand around the neck of a bottle of champagne.

"Where are they?" I ask, noticing she's alone.

"Stepped out. They'll be right back." She crouches, holding out the bottle to me, and I take it, throwing it back. "How are you feeling?"

"They've started to kick in," I answer, knowing what she's asking.

"Good." She smiles at me. "Just so you know, they're dressed up."

I frown and take another drink from the bottle. "Dressed up?"

"Wearing masks." She bites her black-painted bottom lip. "Fuck, it's so hot. Like *chase me through the woods and make me scream for my life* hot. I'd let them both have their way with me."

I laugh, handing her back the bottle. She holds out her free hand, and I take it, letting her help pull me up on the side of the stage. I step on the chair and push off it a little too hard, and I crash into her. We both fall to the cold stage, laughing.

"How much have you had to drink?" I ask, looking up at her while she moves to straddle my hips.

"Not enough." She tosses her head back and gulps down the champagne. Some spills over her chin and onto her chest.

I look over her Red Riding Hood outfit. My hands grip her hips and feel the soft material between my fingers. She gasps, bringing the tip from her lips and sucking in a deep breath. "Open wide." She smiles down at me.

I part my lips, letting go of her waist and run my hands over my chest and up into my hair, loving the feel. The pills doing their job. She brings the tip of the bottle to my lips and tips it back.

The cold, sweet bubbly fills my mouth, and I open my throat, swallowing it. She tilts it a little more, and I cough, spitting it out all over her making her laugh. She gets off me and helps me up. I walk over to the back of the stage and face the floor-to-ceiling mirror, looking at myself.

I run my hands over the booty shorts and decide to go ahead and remove them, leaving myself in nothing but my white thong that reads *Daddy's* in red. I have my Harley Quinn top on that says *Daddy's little monster*. It's so short that my under boob can be seen. Benny paid for my boobs last year. It was my Christmas present. I'm all for body modifications. I don't care if you're tucked, sucked, or flipped. If you're happy with yourself, that's all that matters.

The light hits my wedding ring on my left hand, and it makes my already racing heart pound in my chest. Most dancers wear them when they work. Some really are married, and others do it to make the guys think they're not actually available outside of the club. If the men think they can date you, they quit paying you. If they think we're unavailable, they offer us more for our time. Plus, the married men don't want anyone knowing what they do with us. They just want you to give them what their wives won't.

It's a simple concept. One that I'm more than willing to play along with.

THIRTY-FOUR

ASHTYN

I'm bent down over by the mirror once again, sucking down what's left of my drink that I had picked up at the bar when I see the doors open. I quickly set it down and grab my lipstick out of my clutch that I brought back here with me for this very reason. I reapply the red to my already numbing lips so it's fresh. Some of it had rubbed off on the bottle of champagne that me and Sadie finished off. I toss it by my now empty drink and walk back toward the pole, looking down at my heels. Slowly dragging the toe of them on the stage as I take my time.

"I can Tell" by 504 Boyz begins to fill the large room, and I smile, letting the pole swing me around, giving my audience my back as they get seated to enjoy the show, knowing Sadie is on the opposite stage.

This is what I love about my job. So many women look down on us and will talk shit about what we choose to do with our bodies. Saint made me comfortable with my body. And why not make money off it while I'm young? I know this type of job has an expiration date, so I'm going to use it to my advantage while I can. *You only live once.*

And when you were once as close to death as me, you learn to take that saying seriously.

Turning around, I spread my legs wide open and slide my back down the pole, eyes closed. Once my ass hits my heels, I open my eyes, and I gasp at what I see sitting at the front of the stage.

A guy leans back in his chair—center stage—legs spread wide. His hands rested on his jeans-clad thighs and a black hoodie on. It's the mask he wears that throws me off. *They dressed up.* Sadie had said.

It's a devil mask. But unlike any one I've ever seen. It's mainly white, faded to gray and black in places. The eyes are red and so are the horns that curve up out of the top where eyebrows would be. The jaw comes to a point, the lips are black, and there's an upside-down cross between the eyes. It looks ridiculously sexy under the neon lights.

My heart races when he leans forward, placing his forearms on the edge of the stage. The mask tilts to the side, and my body heat rises while my breathing picks up. I can't see his eyes, but I can feel them on me. Scorching hot and unashamed. I lick my already numbing lips.

I've always had a mask kink. It's one of the reasons I love Halloween so much. Give me a group of men with nothing but masks and jeans on, and I will drool all over myself like a fucking idiot while begging them to fuck me. I blame Saint, Haidyn, and Kashton for that. The Lords in general always wore masks.

Some women want roses and diamonds, candlelit dinners and I love yous. Not me. I want to be choked and told I look pretty with your cum covering my face.

I get to my shaking legs, and he sits back in his seat, slouching, getting comfortable once more. I notice a hundred-dollar bill lying on the stage, and I walk toward the edge, turn around and bend over. Grabbing my ankles, I balance on the balls of my heels so I don't fall over on my face. I watch him upside down as he leans forward once again.

I right myself only to fall gracefully. Lowering my right knee first, then my left. I place my chest and the side of my face on the cool stage and lift my ass in the air. Pulling my knees toward my face, I arch my back even more. I spread them wide giving him a view of my glowing white G-string before I raise my chest and face up off the floor and start bouncing my ass while pushing myself backward, closer to him.

I sit up on my knees, looking at him over my shoulder, my hands in my dark hair as he stands. Fuck, he's tall. Something about a man who could overpower me just makes me want to fight them. *Force me to submit to you.*

My pulse races when he leans over the stage and places his hands on my thighs. They're allowed to touch at Glass. How far they can go is up to us. But the Fountain room? You don't reserve and not touch whatever you want. If you're an entertainer and don't want to be groped, then you decline any invite to this room. It's always your decision how far you want to go.

I release my hair, reach down and grip his wrists and guide his hands up and over my waist. I let go and his hands slowly continue upward to run over my ribs.

I'm panting, my skin tingling in his wake, making goose bumps cover my sensitive skin.

His right hand wraps around my throat, forcing me to arch my neck and stare up at the blinking fluorescent lights while his other travels downward to my thigh.

My heavy eyes fall closed, and I let out a moan as he squeezes my throat, and his other hand slaps my thigh before he lets go of me.

Biting my red-painted lip, I lean forward, placing my chest on the stage again, pushing my ass up in the air for him to look at. His fingertips graze my spine—I shiver at the contact as he touches my tattoo—before trailing over my bare ass and down the back of my exposed thighs. His fingers dig into my fishnets, and he pulls on them, tearing them in the process.

I moan at the tenderness of his fingertips yet the power of his grip. The pills makes me feel better and better every second.

Opening my eyes, they land on the second guy who I hadn't noticed until now. He's perched on the white leather couch, his hands on Sadie's ass while she straddles his hips, giving him a dance. He's dressed the same—ripped blue jeans with a black hoodie and a mask on. The shape of the skull and horns are identical except it's white and gray. No red. The eyes as black as night and the two holes for the nostrils in the nose match.

His fingers pull down her G-string and her hands go to her hair as she begins to bounce up and down on his lap.

The man standing behind me slaps my ass, and I rock back and forth. A moan escapes my parted lips when he digs his fingers deeper into my thighs. My legs spread wider, begging for another slap to my sensitive skin.

My body tenses, and I hold my breath when I feel his fingers slide into my G-string and ever so slowly down inside the material. He pulls it from my pussy just the slightest to where I can feel his knuckles graze my cunt.

I want to beg him to touch me, but I refrain. Instead, I bite my lip to keep in the whimper that wants to escape. You can do whatever you want in these private rooms. As much as they want to pay for. I can tell you right now, I've fucked worse for free. My body tingles, all hot and bothered. Whether he pays me or not, it'll be worth it.

If Sadie and I become uncomfortable or worried at any time, all we have to do is press the red button on the wall by the stage. It alerts the security guard standing outside the door. He will kick down the door if he has to and break fucking bones to get to us. Armed guards are always on the property. That's one thing about the owners, our safety is important to them.

It's happened before. Once, there were over fifteen guys in here with ten dancers. Things got out of hand, and one of the girls pressed the emergency button. All fifteen men were escorted out by the police and taken straight to jail. Broken noses and all.

He lets go of my G-string, and I wonder if he felt the wet spot I know is there. The song changes to "cult leader" by KiNG MALA, and I lower my hips to the stage before turning around onto my ass. I spread my legs wide and lie my back on the stage. My hand goes between my legs, and I run my fingers over the G-string that glows under the black light, silently telling him I want more.

I keep my eyes trained on the man standing at the edge of the stage. His tatted knuckles are on full display while his fingers wrap around the edge as he leans over. The flashing lights make it too hard to see the details of the tattoos. I rise up, grab the back of his mask, and bring his face down to my pussy as I lift my hips off the stage at the same time.

He surprises me by grabbing my hips and yanking me to the edge. I scream in surprise, but you don't hear it over the music. My heart hammers in my chest when he guides my legs to wrap around his waist. The material of his hoodie and jeans seems so rough against my skin. When I tighten my legs, his belt digs into my skin. I like pain. It turns me on.

Running my hands up my ribs and over my breasts, I push the crop top up, exposing my chest to him.

Fuck, I'm so horny. The subtle red lights have my vision going in and out, and the room spins. My hands move to my hard nipples, but they're grabbed and pinned down to the stage by my side.

I lift my hips, moaning and the guy standing between my legs thrusts his hips into me, letting me feel how hard he is. "Fffuuuccccck-kkk," I groan, my eyes rolling back into my head.

My mother's worst fear has come true—I'm an addict when it comes to sex. She believed sex was a duty, not something we should enjoy. Saint taught me that it's okay to enjoy it. Want it. Crave it. I honestly thought I'd be with him the rest of my life, but ever since I left him, I've been chasing that high that only he was able to give.

The man pulls on my wrists, yanking me to sit up. His hands drop to my ass and fingers dig into it painfully as he carries me over to the other end of the white leather couch that runs the length of the back wall.

My hands go between our bodies to his belt, and I undo the black studded leather. Once done, he grabs it and yanks it from the loops. He pushes my arms behind my back and ties them together with the belt. The metal studs dig into my skin in the most delightful way.

I push my breasts into his mask now that my arms are behind my back. His hand comes up and wraps around my throat, and my pussy clenches. I stare into the black circles where his eyes should be as his free hand pulls my G-string to the side. This time, he runs his fingers over my cunt, feeling my wetness, and I groan, rocking my hips back and forth, wanting him to fuck me.

His fingers are rough, making me whimper, and his hand tightens around my throat, restricting my air. It's as if he can read my mind and knows what I need.

He fucks me—two fingers, three fingers—in and out while I ride them as if it's his cock. My head falls back, and I close my eyes. My chest heaves as I try to breathe, and my nipples are hard aching to be pinched.

I have no shame when it comes to what my body likes. I love to be degraded and praised at the same time. Make me a wet, sobbing mess while you tell me how pretty I look with my face covered in your cum. I'm a slut for that.

I'm convulsing, my lungs burning, and I can feel my heartbeat in my face from lack of oxygen when the wave hits me like a hurricane. If I was standing, the force would knock me to my knees. He releases my throat, and I suck in a deep breath as he removes his fingers from inside me. The loss makes me cold, and a shiver runs through my body.

My eyes are heavy, and my heart races as he picks me up off his lap and lays me flat on the couch. The studded belt digs into my lower back and wrists in the new position, but I don't even care.

His hands fall to my G-string, and he pulls it down my shaking legs and then pushes them wide open as he kneels between them on the couch. The white leather dips with his weight. He runs his tatted knuckles over my pelvic bone as if he can see the brand that's been covered for the night. If I wasn't so fucked up, I'd flinch from the contact.

He unzips his jeans and removes his cock. It's darkly lit under the couch, but I see the silver balls that run up and down under his shaft —Jacob's ladder. Four more silver balls show in the head—a magic cross piercing—it's two barbell piercings that go straight through the center of the head, making it look like a cross.

I arch my back, swallowing as he rubs the head of his pierced dick along my swollen and soaking cunt. When he slides into me, my breath catches at the burning sensation of him stretching me so wide for his size.

He tosses my shaking legs over his shoulders, leans over, and grips my throat once again. My body rocks back and forth on the leather couch as he starts to fuck me. The studded spikes rip into my back. I arch my neck, trying to relieve the pressure on my shoulders, but he tightens his hand, choking me once more.

My skin is on fire, I'm sweating, and my body fights his. But I love it. Need it. I'm one of those women whose will to be fucked is greater than my will to live. Fuck me, leave bruises, and remind me who I am. A fucking slut for cock. I'll heal, eventually.

He pulls out and slams into me. My pussy clenches down on his pierced dick, and if I could breathe, I'd beg him to fuck me harder. Faster. Make me bleed for him.

He leans over my body, and his mask stares down at me. It's what nightmares are made of, but it turns me on so much. The thought of fucking a stranger I'll never see again. That I don't even know his name. I could pass him on the streets and have no clue. The mystery turns me on.

I feel his eyes looking down at me, watching my face turn blue at the lack of air. My numb lips are probably turning white. They're numb, along with most of my body. All I feel is his dick pounding in and out of my pussy as I clench down on him. My body begs to breathe, but my mind says I don't need it.

He slams forward, his free hand slapping the side of my face and that wave washes over me once again. My skin grows hot and sweaty. Then a cooling sensation followed by a tingling all over. My eyes grow heavy, blinking. His mask blurs in and out before my vision goes black. My body softens into the leather couch and tears run out of the corner of my eyes and into my hair.

The last thing I see is his mask lowering to my face as he slams into me one last time before his dick pulses inside me.

THIRTY-FIVE

ASHTYN

I enter my house, tossing my backpack and work bag onto the floor in the entryway. I make my way down the hall into the kitchen. I grab a bottle of Pedialyte out of the fridge and throw it back, some running out of the corner of my mouth and down my chin to soak my shirt.

I'm dying of thirst.

It's the ecstasy. It's a little after three in the morning, and I'm starting to come down. The fuck session I had with the stranger took everything out of me when I was fucked like a cheap whore in the Fountain room. He didn't pay me like I was cheap, though.

After he came inside me, he got up, zipped his cum-covered jeans, and tossed some money on my shaking body. He and his friend walked out, leaving us satisfied and five thousand dollars richer. I still have his belt; he left my arms tied behind my back. Sadie had to untie me while I lay there waiting for my body to come down from the high. I offered for her to take it. Give it to her boyfriend. I sure as fuck wasn't going to give it to James. She told me to keep it. That it was a clear sign he was going to come back and see me again to get it. Like when a woman leaves her underwear at a guy's house so she has a reason to contact him again. I couldn't disagree with her, so I stuffed it into my bag. I just pray that if he does come back to Glass, he wears his mask again.

I walk toward the primary suite and come to a stop when I see the back sliding glass door wide open. Sighing, I walk over to it and pull it closed, locking it. James must have left it open. I won't let him smoke his weed in my house. And he always has to have one before he goes to bed. When he pays the bills, he can make the rules. Until then, he has to follow mine.

Entering the primary suite, I see him sitting up in bed, watching TV. His eyes meet mine, and he smiles. "Hey, how was work?"

"Good," I answer, heading to the bathroom. I need a shower.

Just as I shut the door, it opens. I pick up my toothbrush and cover it with toothpaste, and he comes to stand behind me. His hands go to my hips, and I stiffen. "I've been waiting up for you."

"Why?" I ask, running my toothbrush under the water and begin to brush my teeth.

He gently pulls my hair off my shoulders and twists it around his fist, tugging on it. I go to pull away, trying to brush my teeth, but he yanks it back. "James." Spit and toothpaste flies from my mouth and covers the mirror in front of me. The toothbrush falls from my hand, hitting the countertop before dropping to the floor.

He reaches around and slides his hand into my cotton shorts. "Your pussy is soaked, Brittany. Did grinding your cunt on men who pretend to want you get you all worked up?"

I'd never tell him that the reason I'm so wet is because a man came in me a few hours ago. I don't answer. Instead, my eyes hold his in the mirror. He smiles, thinking my silence means he's correct.

He shoves my cotton shorts and underwear down my legs, pushing my chest and face down onto the counter and kicks my legs farther apart with his. He grips his cock, sliding into me, and my eyes fall closed on their own. We may be broken up, but sex was never our problem. He doesn't have a useless cock; he knows how to use it. It's the rest of him that needs work.

He pounds into me, my hips hitting the edge of the counter, and I hate how unsatisfied I feel. My body is drained; the guy from earlier fucked me so close to death that I don't have any energy left. Plus, the drugs have started to wear off. I'm crashing hard.

"Come on, Brittany, come all over my cock, baby," he groans.

Four years I've gone by my new name, and I'm still not used to hearing it. A part of me died when I shot Saint. And Ashtyn was one of those things. I'll never be who I once was again, and I've come to terms with that.

I close my eyes as if I'm close, but I'm just exhausted. I'm going to have to sleep in tomorrow and most of the day to be ready to work the extra shift at my second job tomorrow night.

"That's it," he speaks, his cock slamming into me. "Get ready..." he warns.

I know the drill. I'm on birth control, but he refuses to use a condom, and I've never let him come inside me. The last thing we need is a child. He'd probably use my job against me, get the kid, and make me pay him child support.

Just my luck, he'd win.

He pulls out, yanks me up off the counter, and spins me around, where he pushes me to my knees. I look up at him, mouth already open, and he places the tip of his cock between my lips while he jacks himself off onto my tongue.

I look up at him through heavy eyes as he closes his, and his warm cum fills my mouth. I swallow the best I can, and he pulls out. "Leave it open," he orders, and I do as I'm told. He runs his hand along his shaft once more, squeezing what's left out of the tip and onto my tongue. I wait until he pulls away before I close my mouth and swallow.

I can taste the stranger's cum from earlier. It was all over James's cock. It makes me wonder how many times James has fucked another woman before he fucked me, and I wasn't aware. I've never been the jealous type with James. I'd actually be glad to catch him cheating. I'd make a big deal out of it and use it as an excuse to kick him out.

Maybe I'll pay someone to come on to him, here in my house, and fuck him in my bed. I'd plan it so I walk in on him and kick them both out. I'd pay her of course. An actress deserves money for her time and performance.

But Saint? I'll kill a bitch just for thinking she could have him. That man made me a psychotic fool. A sick and twisted part of me hopes I killed him because I couldn't imagine him with anyone else other than me. The thought still makes me sick to my stomach. Most Lords don't have social media accounts, and I sure as fuck don't have one. When I do get on, I use another account from a girl at work. So there is no way for me to know if he survived or what he's doing today. But whatever it is, I'm sure he's got a wife. Lords aren't expected to stay single for long. They have to reproduce. They are all required to produce an heir sooner rather than later.

"Fuck, babe." James sighs, taking a step back. Reaching down, he grabs my hand and helps me to stand. He gently kisses my lips, and I don't pull away although I want to.

He exits the bathroom to crawl into my bed and pass the fuck out. I finish getting undressed and start the shower, needing to wash the night off, ignoring the toothbrush on the floor.

I dig my cell out of my pocket, connect it to the Bluetooth speaker that I had installed in my shower, and pull up my Spotify playlist. "I hope ur miserable until ur dead" by Nessa Barrett fills the bathroom, and I remove the wedding ring on my finger. I place it in the glass dish on the counter before I step in the shower. Getting under the sprayer, I hiss in a breath at the sting of the hot water burning my cool skin. It feels so good. I close my eyes, reach up, and run my hands over my hair, pushing it back from my face.

My mind wanders to *him*. Saint is always on my mind. He has been ever since I left him lying in the hallway down in the morgue covered in his own blood. It haunts me more than any nightmare ever could.

Did I sell my soul for freedom? Of course, I did. Isn't that how it works? In order to be free, a sacrifice must be made. I gave up my one true love and my only chance at happiness. I might have been his whore, but I never doubted that he loved me. Not many would ever understand what we had. How badly I burned for him and how much he loved me. Saint taught me that love is a sickness with no cure. It slowly kills you, but the only thing is that you don't die. Not really. You can numb the pain, try to erase the memories, but no matter what, your body never forgets the way he touched you. The way he kissed you. The way he looked at you.

That guy tonight reminded me of Saint in the best way. He just knew what I wanted and took it. Do I put too much trust in men sexually? Yes. My mother's therapist once told me that if I wasn't careful, I'd find myself dead in a ditch in the middle of nowhere. That possibility didn't stop me.

Tonight just proves how far I allow myself to go. Maybe I have a death wish. I don't believe we live on in the afterlife. That doesn't exist where I come from. There's a living hell and an actual hell. Sins in our world aren't forgiven, no matter how much time you spend on your knees.

The song comes to an end, and before it can switch to the next on my playlist, I hear glass breaking. "James?" I call out, staring at the white tiled wall ahead of me. Nothing. "James? You okay?" Silence. Sighing, I shut off the water and step out. Grabbing the towel, I turn off the music on my phone and put it back down so I can wrap the towel around myself.

I open the bathroom door and see he's not in the bedroom. "What the fuck are you doing, James?" I bark, starting to get pissy. It's almost four in the morning. I'm not in the mood for his shit. It wouldn't be the first time he's invited friends over at a late hour and got so fucked up, they broke shit in my house.

I exit the bedroom and march down the hallway to the living room. I gasp when I find him lying on the floor, covered in blood. "James?" I fall to my knees beside him. The glass coffee table is shattered as if he fell on top of it.

He groans, but his eyes remain closed.

"Hang on," I tell him. "I'll call 911." Getting to my feet, I spin around to get my cell out of the bathroom but halt when I see a figure step out of the dimly lit corner. My pulse races, and my eyes widen when he steps closer to me.

I take a step back but scream in surprise when I hit a body. An arm comes out and wraps around my neck, holding my back to his front. I kick out my legs, trying to twist out of his grip, but the arm just tightens its hold, restricting my air.

The man comes to a stop as he steps into me. Reaching into his pocket, he removes a syringe. I try to scream for help, but nothing comes out. My fingers dig into the skin of the arm wrapped around my neck, but it does no good because he's wearing something thick that covers his arms. I'm unable to get a good grip. My towel falls to the floor during my struggle, and I don't even care that I'm still wet and naked.

The arm around my neck releases me, and I gasp in a breath. I try to run away, but his hands grip my arms, bringing them behind my back and holding me in place while the other one grabs my chin, holding my face as he shoves a needle into my neck.

The last thing I see are those red eyes on the devil mask before mine fall closed, and my body goes limp.

THIRTY-SIX

ASHTYN

My heavy eyes open to fall shut quickly. I try again, but all I see are my lashes with my blurry vision. I close them once more. An ache fills the back of my head, and my body is sore, muscles tight.

My head falls from side to side, unable to control it. I go to roll over, but I can't. Something rough and thick rubs against my skin. I lick my numbing lips, noticing my mouth is dry.

A shiver runs through my body, goose bumps covering my skin, and I realize I'm naked and freezing.

I begin to shake, my teeth chattering. "He-llo?" I call out, heavy eyes opening once more and my voice cracks. "Hello?" I ask again, trying to get up, but I can't move. That dull ache in the back of my head intensifies into a pounding sensation. My breathing comes quicker, making my chest tight.

I start to pull on my limbs, trying to figure out why I can't move. How much did I take? I should have slept off the pills by now. How long have I been asleep?

Turning my head to the left, I blink rapidly until my sight clears, and I see a concrete wall with black cabinets running along the bottom of a metal-looking countertop. A few boxes on top of the counter are taped closed.

My heavy eyes blink once more as I turn back to look up at the ceiling, and I feel something on my neck? It's rough and rubs tightly against my skin. I try to lift my hands to feel what it is, but I still have no control over my body.

Lifting my heavy head, I suck in a deep breath, as the thing around my neck chokes me. Looking down over my naked body as my chest heaves, I see straps pinning me down to a black table. One is high across my chest. I feel another one across my waist as I twist side to side and another over my hips. More on my legs. My wrists are also secured by my sides. They look like thick belts, buckled tightly in place with small locks that require a key to remove.

Blood rushes in my ears. "HELLO?" I scream, my body thrashing on the table in the cold and silent room. My breathing is so heavy that it feels like the restraints tighten, making it harder to get in a breath. "He-llo?" My voice cracks. "Anyone...?" Tears sting my eyes. "What the fuck?" I grind out, yanking on the leather. But it's useless. Even if they weren't buckled, I'm still too weak to get out of them.

A lock sounds over to my left, and I try to see, but I don't have a clear view from where I'm at. The door creaking open makes my pulse race, and I'm hyperventilating. "Who...are you?" I demand, trying to yank free. "What do you want?" I scream so loud my throat burns when no one answers. "Where's James?" Was he dead? Had they killed him? My memory is foggy, but I remember him lying on my living room floor covered in glass and blood. Had he fucked someone over for drugs? It wouldn't be the first time he owed someone money for the shit he put in his body, and I had to bail him out.

Why can't I remember anything after that? Is it the pills I took? Or something they gave me? How long have I been like this? There's no window in here, so it could have been days since I found James on the living room floor.

Cold air blows on my shaking and naked body. My hands fist, and I arch my neck, trying to swallow the lump in my throat.

Sagging in the restraints, the tears start to fall from the corner of my eyes while I try to calm my racing heart. It's about to leap out of my chest. My breathing comes in short, rapid pants, and the room seems to spin. I think I'm going to be sick.

A bright light is turned on above me as if I'm strapped to an operating table and they're about to perform surgery on me. It makes me flinch. It's so blinding, and my body trembles at that thought.

My eyes are tightly closed, trying to block out the light when it's moved to no longer shine down on my face. A hand grips my cheeks, and I start thrashing around to try to knock it off, but my arms are tied down by my sides, and the one around my neck makes it hard to move my head. The fingers dig into my cheeks, prying a whimper out of me, and my eyes spring open.

I look up into a set of red eyes, framed with a devil mask and two red horns. Fresh tears run down the sides of my face, and I sniff. "Pl-ease."

Trying to catch my breath, I arch my neck, but his grip just tightens, smashing my cheeks into my teeth. He lets go, and I sag into the sticky leather. He reaches out and a clear mask is placed into his hand that has a long tube attached to it. He places the rubber mask over my mouth and nose. His tatted hand holds it in place, pressed into my face. I try to lift my hips off the table, but all it does is dig the straps into my skin.

My eyes go to the guy who had handed it to him, but all I see is the back of him. Jeans, black hoodie, and mask...the same as him.

"Please—" I sob. "Let me go." My voice is muffled by the mask. Cold air covers my face, and I hold my breath, afraid to breathe it in. His free hand comes up, and I flinch when he touches my forehead, running it down over my hair. His touch is soft, almost lovingly compared to the way he gripped my cheeks.

My lungs start to burn, and my chest heaves as I continue to hold my breath. Tears fall from my eyes as I open my mouth and gasp in a deep breath, unable to hold it in any longer. Crying, I take another deep breath, and a calmness comes over me. A tingling sensation runs through my body to the tips of my fingers and toes. My body relaxes on the table. It's as close to a high as I've ever experienced.

His hand continues to brush through my hair while I breathe in whatever is coming from the mask. My eyes grow heavy, my mind foggy. My vision goes in and out, and I blink several times before the devil mask becomes nothing more than a blur of white and black with red eyes and horns.

Is this what hell looks like?

I swear I hear a voice say *"That's my good girl"* as everything fades away, and my tightly fisted hands unclench. But that's just my mind playing tricks on me. I haven't heard that in years. And the man who used to call me that is dead.

THIRTY-SEVEN

ASHTYN

I wake up, a moan escaping my lips. Rolling over onto my side, my hands come up to my face, and I cover my sensitive eyes to block out the bright light. When it doesn't work, I grab the soft fluffy blanket, pull it up and over my face, and relax into the comfortable mattress.

My eyes instantly spring open, and I sit up gasping, shoving the covers off when everything comes rushing back to me.

I was awake, tied to a table, and the mask...he placed something over my face. My hands come up to my face once more, and my fingers quickly run over my skin, feeling for cuts or pain of any kind that will tell me if anything is broken.

My hands drop to my sides, and I let out a deep breath, but my ease quickly turns to panic when I feel something on my stomach.

I shove off the covers to see I'm naked. My 666 brand covering my pelvic bone is on full display. I always keep it covered with makeup when at work and washed it off when I take a shower back at home.

But that's not the part that makes my heart skip a beat. No, it's a small white bandage over my right hip. It's got tape over it. The way I'm sitting, it's pinching my skin.

I almost trip out of bed—my legs are shaky, my head a little foggy, and the room spins, making me feel light-headed.

What the fuck? They drugged me, and it's still in my system.

I manage to make my way to a set of double doors to the right and shove them open to see it's a bathroom just like I hoped.

Rushing to the long mirror that runs the length of his-and-her sinks, I look over my body to see that's the only thing that looks different from what I remember. Other than a bandage wrapped around my right arm in the crease of my elbow. I rip it off to see a poke hole and a small bruise already forming. *What the fuck happened?*

I have bruises across my upper chest, hips, wrists, and legs where I was tied down with the leather restraints. My knees are scraped and covered in dried blood from when I kneeled next to James.

With shaky hands, I reach down and pick at the corner of the tape, trying to get it off. I whimper when the tape pulls on my skin. My nose is running, and tears sting my eyes when I finally get it started. My shaky hands tear it across the top and then both sides before ripping off the bottom.

Closing my eyes, I take in a shaky breath before I remove the bandage. My skin is red and irritated. It's got several stitches. It's a tracking device. I've seen them done before. At Carnage.

My heart stops at what I see. I choke out a sob, my knees threatening to buckle at the numbers. I've spent the past four years running from a life I knew would kill me.

This can't be. It's a nightmare, and I need to wake up from it.

My shaking hands go to touch it, but I stop myself, unable to accept what I see. "No—" Doors opening have my head snapping up. I turn to face the doorway, and all the air leaves my lungs when I see the white and black mask from Glass now standing in the bathroom.

I shake my head, fresh tears burning my eyes.

It can't be. I'm hallucinating. The drugs that Sadie gave me have fucked me up. I'm having a nightmare. A bad trip. Maybe I'm dead, dragged to hell, and this is how you live out eternity.

The masked man steps forward, slowly making his way to me as if he has all day. I stay cemented where I'm at, unable to breathe, let alone run.

I see the next guy standing behind him in the doorway of the bedroom. It's them. Haidyn and Kashton found me. They dragged me back here to make me pay for killing their brother. I didn't mean to. I just wanted to wound him to give me a head start. They have to know that I never meant to hurt Saint. It was my only option. He told me he would never let me go.

The one closest to me comes to a stop. He reaches up and grips the bottom of his mask. He slowly removes it, and fresh tears fill my eyes as a set of green eyes glare down into mine.

"N-o." The broken word is barely a whisper on my shaking lips.

It's worse than I could have ever imagined.

The ghost of a man stays silent as his hand comes out and runs his knuckles down my wet cheek. The single touch makes me whimper. My shaking legs give out, and I stumble back into the counter. My hands grip the edges to hold myself up. I allowed him to fuck me in the club.

I'm gasping for breath, my body practically convulsing as I stand naked in front of the devil himself. This has to be a mistake. I spent months mourning him. Years trying to forget him and accept what I did.

"It's been a long time, sweetheart." His voice knocks what little wind is left out of me, and all I can do is stare up at him through watery eyes. Gently, he cups my tear-streaked face, leans into me, and whispers, "Welcome home."

SAINT

She stares at me with her wide, tear-filled eyes as she stands before me naked. Fuck, have we come a long way since that day she shot me. She thought she could run from me and get away with killing me.

"I..." Her eyes run up and down my body. She swallows when they meet mine again and whispers, "I thought I killed you."

When I reach out to cup her face, she trembles but doesn't pull away. She's too stunned for that. *Oh, Ashtyn, the things I'm going to do to you will make you beg the devil himself to come and take you from me.* "You can't kill what isn't alive, sweetheart," I tell her.

It's true. After she left us, we were never the same. The six months we spent "training" rewired anything we ever felt for anybody, and I can't wait to spend the rest of my life doing the same to her.

Her breath catches, and my eyes drop to her heaving chest, unable to stop myself from looking at her hard nipples. Her erratic breathing fills the bathroom just like when I fucked her at Glass, and my cock is hard. It proved to me that my girl is still the same as she used to be. A woman who needs to be fucked like the whore she is.

I made her that way. Taught her everything she knows she likes. I can't wait to show her all the new things she'll experience. My tastes have gotten a little...darker since she left me.

My gaze lifts back up to meet hers, and her eyes fall to my neck. They trace my tattoos, and she takes a step back, my hand falling from her face. I'm not who she loved. I'm a different man now. I've seen what hell looks like, and I've embraced it, become it. Now, I will drag her down into the depths of it with me by the chains that I lock her up in, and we will burn together.

THIRTY-EIGHT

ASHTYN

I push him out of the way and run out of the bathroom into the bedroom where I come to another stop when I see the white and black mask still standing in the doorway. Arms crossed over his chest and legs spread wide, he takes up the entire space.

His laughter fills the large room, making heat run up my spine. He pushes the mask up and over his head, and his eyes meet mine. "Hello, sweet cheeks. It's been far too long."

Kashton Landon Pierce stands before me, and I watch with watery eyes as he raises his arms and grips the top of the doorframe, blocking my only exit. His T-shirt rises in the process, showing me more ink on his defined V underneath the hem.

My heart is in my throat, my breathing erratic. I feel like I'm having a heart attack, my chest is so tight. He leans forward and his eyes drop to my bare feet and run up over my body. It doesn't matter. They've seen me naked. I've allowed all three of them to fuck me, use me.

"I must say, you look good, Ash." He laughs as if it's some inside joke that only he and Saint know.

His eyes meet mine briefly before he looks over my head and smirks, reminding me that Saint is still in the bathroom.

I turn to run in the opposite direction, but Saint is already at my back. My very naked body runs into his, and he wraps his hand around my throat before I can even make a sound. The action lifts me off my feet. My hands come up and grip his wrists, twisting the skin the best I can, trying to get in a breath.

"How's it feel to be the devil's newest toy?" Kashton asks in my ear. "To know he's going to rip you to pieces with his bare hands?"

I kick out my feet, and they hit Saint's shins, but he doesn't release me. Instead, he yanks my face into his and drool runs out the corner of my lips because I can't swallow. His eyes search mine before he pulls his lips back with disgust.

He shoves me backward, letting me go, and I fall on my ass. Rolling over, I get up onto my hands and knees, coughing. My body convulses as I suck in a breath. Fuck, I've still got the sedative they gave me in my system. I'm useless right now.

Kashton grabs my hair and yanks my head up as Saint crouches down in front of me. His hand cups my face, thumb running over my parted lips. "Just like old times," he says with the slightest smirk on his lips.

"No—"

"This is your hell now, Ashtyn, and your life sentence starts today."

My teeth grind, and I lift my chin. Opening my mouth, I'm about to tell him to go fuck himself, but I pause when he reaches out and cups my face. "The next time you leave me, it'll be in a body bag because I put you there." His words are spoken softly, lovingly, but they make my blood run cold.

With that, he stands. Kashton lets go of my hair, and I watch through watery lashes as they exit my room, slamming my door shut.

SAINT

I WATCH HER HEAVY EYES FALL CLOSED, AND HER BODY RELAXES into the leather table. I softly run my tatted knuckles through the tears that have fallen down the side of her once flawless face.

She's out. Once again. When she wakes up this time, the world she's known will no longer exist. I've waited so long for this day. Honestly, I should be more excited than I am.

My wife is back where she belongs. In my hands.

She looks the same as I remember. Her hair is a little darker, but that doesn't change her appearance much. My eyes drop to scan her naked body. The one I used to own. The brand is still clear as day. I hated giving it to her the way I did, but I'm glad she's had a reminder of me all these years every time she looks at it.

My fingers run over her hard nipples. I dropped the temperature in this room just for her arrival. I wanted it as cold as my heart is for her. I have to admit, I like that she got them done. They look good.

Walking to the end of the table, I grab the edge and shove her legs apart—the table opening up for me. From the waist up, it's one piece, but her legs are strapped down individually for this very reason.

The door opens, and I smile at the doctor who is here to help me out with what I'm about to do to her. Devin goes to work with starting her IV. She needs to remain unconscious for quite some time. What I have planned for her will take most of the night.

I remove my devil mask, placing it on the counter and grabbing the rolling chair. I plop down on it, making my way over to the table and slide between her parted legs. Her pussy is wide open for me.

She let that piece of shit fuck her when she got home. I watched it on my phone. I would have been there sooner and stopped it, but I didn't think she'd actually let him touch her. They've been broken up for months. Stupid on my part for thinking that. She allowed a complete stranger to fuck her, so of course she was going to give up her pussy to the guy she lives with.

From here on out for the rest of her pathetic miserable life, I'll choose which cock fucks her and how they use her. She's mine and will belong to me until the day she dies.

"She's ready, sir," Devin tells me as he tapes the IV in place and looks at me.

I roll closer and reach out grabbing what I need from the cart that sits next to me and smile to myself. When you wake up, sweetheart, you will know where you're at and who the fuck owns you.

Kashton and I exit her bedroom and walk down the hall as Haidyn's door flies open. A petite redhead rushes out into the hall, not even bothering to shut his door. She's carrying a pair of high heels and a bra in one hand, and a cell phone in the other. Her wide tear-filled eyes meet mine before going to Kashton's.

"Your friend is fucking crazy," she cries.

"You should be more careful who you go home with," Kash informs her.

My eyes drop to her white club dress. The cuts on her neck have blood running down and soaking up into the fabric. She's shaking like a leaf on a tree. Her knees are bruised, and she has rope burns on her wrists and ankles.

"You told him you could handle it," I remind her. The woman has been trying to get into Haidyn's bed for months now. He finally caved, and well, it doesn't look like it was up to par with what she wanted him to be.

We've all got our demons, and we each let them play in different ways.

"Fuck you!" she hisses, running past and knocking her shoulders into both of us.

Kashton turns to watch her skip the elevator and rush down the stairs while I enter Haidyn's bedroom. It looks like a tornado hit it with the sheets ripped off the bedding and broken glass on the floor. A couple of empty bottles of vodka and it smells like weed. The rope is still wrapped around each bedpost and puddled on the carpet. There's a knife on the nightstand, and the curtains have been ripped from the floor-to-ceiling windows showcasing the woods.

I sigh, running a hand through my hair.

Kashton enters and grunts at the scene. "You did the right thing," he reassures me.

Haidyn isn't ready for Ashtyn to return. Her leaving left us all with very bad tastes in our mouths. We each paid for her freedom. But Haidyn was dished out the worst when it came to our "training."

No one leaves Carnage. Ever. Doesn't matter why or how you got here. Once you're brought in, you die here. We had to be taught a lesson. One we'll never forget and one we'll pass on to her as well.

Kashton slaps me on the back. "I'll call David." He pulls out his cell, and I make my way out of Haidyn's room and down the hall to the elevator.

Making my way to the seventh floor, I walk toward the open door, hearing a feminine voice.

"Talk to me, Haidyn," the therapist says to my brother as I approach the door.

It's open so I peek into it, leaning against the doorframe to see him standing at the floor-to-ceiling windows, hands shoved into the pockets of his jeans. She faces the back of him while sitting in the white leather highback chair. They're clueless I'm present.

"What are you thinking?" She goes on.

He snorts, turns, and walks over to her. His stride is confident and slow. She straightens, her legs crossing as she looks up at him. If she wasn't already fidgety, her eyes would give her away.

Haidyn is the biggest one out of the three of us. Six-foot-seven and two fifty. Covered in ink and usually blood that isn't his. Men fear him, and women beg him to fuck them.

He places his hands on both armrests and leans over to where his face is in front of hers. "You don't want to know what I'm thinking." His eyes drop to her tits that her fitted button-up white silk blouse shows off.

"I'm...I'm here to help you," she whispers, rubbing her sweaty palms softly down her black pencil skirt. Poor girl didn't know what she was getting into when she recently took the job. She's the sixth one over the last three years.

"Help me?" he asks as if that's a foreign idea. Unreachable. "Do you really mean that, Charlotte?" Haidyn plays with her.

She swallows nervously, her eyes dropping to stare out the window. Unable to make eye contact, she softly answers, "Of course."

"I know what you can do." The corners of his lips pull back, showing a shadow of a smirk.

Her eyes move to his, widening as her breathing accelerates. "W-what?"

"Let me rip off your clothes."

She gasps.

"I'll tie you up in a tight little ball, suspend you from the ceiling so that your cunt, mouth, and ass are easily on display for me to fuck."

Her pretty face pales at the thought of him touching her in such a way. If she were wearing pearls, she'd clutch them.

He goes on, feeding off her fear like a fire does oxygen. "Once I'm done violating you, I'll sit down, have a smoke while I let you hang there, and watch my cum leak from your stretched-out and overused holes like the worthless whore you're meant to be."

She's trembling. Her back pressed into the chair, praying it swallows her up from the big bad man who wants to use her like a sex doll.

"I can't promise you'll like it, but it'll make me feel better," he adds. "Still want to help me, doll face?" He releases the armrest with his right hand and places it on her knee, making her jump, and a whimper escapes her nude-painted lips.

"Haidyn," I say, announcing my presence.

He gives a rough laugh, pushing off her chair, and she stands to run out of the room, pushing me out of the way.

Haidyn goes back to the windows. There's nothing around for miles—just woods, more woods, and mountains. The Spade brothers—our fathers—once thought that was enough to keep the prisoners contained. But Ashtyn proved them wrong, so we added extra precautions to make sure no one ever escapes again, including us. Not like we'd ever walk away from Carnage. No matter how much we want to.

"We brought her in to help you," I remind him.

"She can't," he growls.

"You don't even let her try," I argue. I think a part of her wants to fix him even though she understands he's not broken. He's just a man with demons.

"Unless she's on her knees, she's useless," he mumbles.

"Kash called David."

David is a pimp, and the women he loans out are as close to therapy as Haidyn's ever going to get. At least they seem to help for a little bit. When you're willing to pay for sex, you get to do whatever you want. Case in point—I was balls deep inside Ashtyn not even forty-eight hours ago, and she had no idea who I was. Just a man willing to pay to use her body. She'll be giving it to me for free from now on.

"Is *she* here?" Haidyn asks, ignoring my previous statement.

"Yeah." Kashton and I arrived with Ashtyn yesterday morning, but we hadn't seen Haidyn until now. I kept her sedated for quite some time. I wanted her to heal somewhat before she awoke and realized her life has forever changed. I have plans for her, and I can't start fulfilling them until she's ready.

His hands fist as he whispers, "You shouldn't have brought her back."

I run mine through my hair. "She's here for us to use. You...we all deserve our revenge." I once loved Ashtyn, but I let her cloud my judgement. It made me soft and almost got my brothers killed. I won't make that mistake again.

He turns around to face me. "I'm going to kill her," he growls. "Don't you get that? If I touch her, she's dead." He takes in a deep, calming breath. "And the worst part of that is she doesn't deserve it." He hangs his head and shakes it. "She's not responsible for what happened once she was gone."

"She left us," I grind out. Just thinking about her running from me and getting away with it makes me want to kill some unlucky bastard. We got lucky, or I probably would have never found her. I hate to admit it, but my wife hid well.

"No. She left you. She never belonged to Kashton or me. She was yours, and you let us borrow her. Big difference."

I did. I got off on watching my brothers get off. She loved it. And that's what turned me on the most. She was mine to use, but she was also mine to loan out. Now she's under our roof and the three of us will make sure she's always on her knees. "Well, she's ours now," I say just as Kashton enters.

"I sent a car for the girls. They'll be here soon," he announces.

Haidyn gives us his back once more and stares out the windows, watching the clouds roll in. It's supposed to storm its ass off for the next few days. The thought makes me smile. I love to watch the world go dark.

I WALK INTO OUR OFFICE AND SIT BEHIND MY DESK. THE FIRST thing I do is pull up the camera footage on my computer. Ashtyn stands in her bathroom, hands on her stomach, while she stares at herself in the mirror. Tears run down her cheeks while her fingers lower to her brand. Even though she's had it for years, it was more of a reminder of where she came from. Now it's a reality.

I placed a tracking device in her while she was out this time. She'll never get away from me now.

Sedation at the time was the best option because I didn't want her to know just yet who had her or what was happening. Seeing the look on her face in the bathroom when her eyes met mine was worth the wait.

She takes a few steps back, her naked body shaking with the sobs as tears run down her face like the rain that hits the windows at my back. She's a sobbing mess, and it makes me smile.

Cry for me, sweetheart.

The door opens to the office, and I look up to see Kashton enter. He plops down at his desk to my left and looks at me. "The girls arrived. At least they'll keep Haidyn busy for the day."

I snort. "Maybe." *If he doesn't kill them.*

"We can only hope." He picks up the remote to the TV on his desk and turns on the seventy-inch screen that's anchored on the far wall.

A friend of ours appears, standing outside of his business. **BLACKOUT** is written in black letters behind him and his wife who stands next to him. Her hand on her belly. It's not noticeable yet, but she's expecting.

She's got the biggest smile on her face when he reaches down and grabs her right hand as he addresses the large gathering of reporters. He wants the world to know that she is his everything. I get it. He gave up his life for her. And almost ended up losing everything he loves.

Sitting back in my seat, the news goes to a commercial, and I pick up my cell, dialing his number.

"Saint? What's going on?" Tyson Crawford answers on the second ring.

"Just saw you on the news. Thought I'd call and check in." My Spade brothers and I don't have many *friends*, but Tyson is about as close as they come.

He chuckles. "That's like the fifth time they've played that clip. I knew I could count on them to get my point across."

I almost laugh at his choice of words. I knew there was a reason he allowed his wife to be seen. "How's the build going?" I ask about Blackout.

"Faster than I expected. Opened last week." Before I can say anything, he asks, "Find what you were looking for?"

My eyes drop to my computer screen that still has Ashtyn pulled up in the bathroom. She's got the water running in the tub. "I did.

Thanks for that by the way." If he hadn't handed over Whitney, I'd still be looking for her.

He snorts. "Whatever I can do to help."

"Tyson—?"

I hear his wife in the background entering the room. "I'll let you go. Just wanted to call and see how things were going," I add, not wanting to keep him.

"Come by the club. Bring the guys. Drinks are on me."

I nod to myself, watching Ashtyn step into the bathtub. "Yeah. We'll take you up on that."

We hang up, and I see Kashton staring at me. "What was that about?" he asks.

"Tyson." I stand, pocketing my cell. "He invited us out to Blackout."

He types away on his computer. "I'm always up for a night out."

That night Tyson messaged me a picture of Ashtyn on her stomach with her hands tied behind her back and tears running down her face saved her life. At the time, I was grateful for that. But a month later, I was lying on the floor bleeding because she shot me. Like her brother, she chose herself.

I should have seen it coming, but I was blinded. The Lords assumed she might have been dead, and in a sense, she was. Still is. She had to live a life as someone else after she escaped Carnage. But not here. Not this time. She'll be Ashtyn—my little whore who will beg me. And I'll be the man I should have been all along—a ruthless Lord with a pet to play with.

Standing from my seat, I exit the office and take the elevator up to the birdcage where all of our rooms are. We have houses on the property, but we stay here most of the time. It's just easier that way. Carnage never sleeps, so neither do we.

Getting off the elevator, I pass my room, along with Kashton's and Haidyn's. All the walls are soundproof so he could be stabbing someone to death in there and I wouldn't hear a fucking thing. Not like I'd stop him if he was. When he's in a mood, you step back and let him do whatever the fuck he wants.

I walk up to her door and turn the knob, entering because I own the fucking place. Coming to a stop, I look over the room. An odd feeling falls over me knowing that she's on the other side of the closed bathroom door, naked in the bathtub with my brand on her body and tracking device in her skin. She'll never be able to leave me again.

I've dreamed of this day ever since I woke up and was told she shot me and ran, leaving me for dead. I hate that I still have feelings for her. Don't get me wrong, I hate the bitch, but I also love her in that *I'm going to rip your heart out and hang it on my wall so no one else can have it* kind of way.

Walking across the bedroom, I enter the bathroom to find her sitting in the tub just like she was on my computer screen. She's got her legs pulled up to her chest, and her forehead rests on her bent knees. Her wet hair sticks to her hunched-over back and shoulders.

She's crying, and the sound makes me smile. Leaning my ass against the countertop, I cross my tatted arms over my chest and wait for her to realize I've entered the room. If she wants to survive here, she needs to start paying attention to her surroundings at all times.

Our fathers no longer run this place. We do. And we'll make sure that she endures every sick and twisted thing that any other prisoner would.

THIRTY-NINE

ASHTYN

I'm shaking, my entire body throbs and aches.

Just like everything else. The drugs—the ones I took—plus the ones they gave me no longer linger in my system. I just feel ashamed now. Pathetic. I thought for years that I killed him, and I grieved the loss of him.

I've feared a lot over the years. But leaving here made me realize how much I fear myself. I willingly shot the man I wanted to spend the rest of my life with. I would have done anything for him until I was put in a position where it was him or me, and like a coward, I chose myself.

But he pulled me back to his hell, and now I'm his prisoner. His chance at revenge. His whore. Is it bad that I'm glad he's still alive? He'll most likely make me regret what I did. I should have run farther, for longer. But I only had enough help to get out of Carnage. After that, I was on my own, and starting a new life was harder than I thought it'd be.

I sniff, trying to calm myself and stop the tears. *Crying won't save you, Ash.* That's what my mother used to tell me whenever life wouldn't go her way. She'd straighten her shoulders, lift her chin, and face the fucking day like she was unstoppable. Obviously, she wasn't. Watching her get stabbed to death proved that she wasn't.

Lifting my forehead from my knees, I jump to my feet when I see a set of green eyes watching me. "Sa-int?" My voice cracks just saying his name as I stare at him. They used to be so bright, but now they're a darker shade of green.

How long has he been in here watching me? This is what he'll do. Have eyes on me at all times. There are probably cameras all over my room and bathroom.

He pushes off the counter, and I swallow nervously as I watch him pick up my towel. He holds it open for me, standing next to the tub, hinting that it's time for me to get out.

Slowly, I step out on shaky legs and stand before him dripping wet and naked. I feel nervous. I've let this man violate my body, yet it feels like it's about to be our first time. I wasn't even this nervous then.

He brings the towel to wrap around my shoulders. He runs the soft material up and down my arms, over my chest, and over my lower abdomen where my brand is. He pulls it from my shoulders and crouches down in front of me, taking his time to wipe off my shaking legs.

When he stands, he tosses it to the side, and I wrap my arms around myself. Goose bumps cover my skin, and I can still feel water run down my back from my hair. I shiver when his eyes meet mine, and it's not because I'm wet and cold.

He's changed. I've never stopped to think what he would look like now if he had lived. I saw him bleeding, lying there in the hallway, coughing up blood. And it changed me. I'll never be the same.

But here he is, standing before me looking like the god I remembered him to be. Have you ever seen a Lord go after someone who wronged him? I have, and it's bloody. Lots of screams and torture. I have no doubt he once loved me, but he doesn't anymore. I ruined any chance I ever had of a future with him.

We were going to have a family and grow old together, but it was all bullshit. I was kidding myself, making up a world that would never exist for me. Him making me his pet is the closest I'll ever get to him loving me again. And I'll take it. I'd rather believe the beautiful lie than a sour truth.

He's lost the black hoodie and mask. He now wears a black T-shirt that pulls tight across his broad shoulders and muscular chest. It shows off the ink that covers his neck and arms. I can't help but wonder where the bullet hit him and if you can even tell. Has he covered it up with ink?

I reach out, my hand going to his T-shirt, but his shoots out and grips my wrist, making me jump in surprise.

He steps into me, grabbing my other wrist as well and shoves them behind my back. He pushes my arms behind my back and wraps one large hand around my wrists to hold them in place. The position forces my chest to push into his.

His free hand comes up and cups my chin. My breathing accelerates. "I'm sorry," I whisper, needing to say the words before he kills me. I need him to understand that I never meant to hurt him. I loved him.

"For what, sweetheart?" he asks, tilting his head to the side.

The sound of his voice...that nickname...my thighs clench. "Saint..." My lips tremble. "I—"

"Shh," he says softly, running the pad of his fingers over my lips. "It's okay, Ash."

Tears prick my eyes at his lie, and my throat closes, making it hard to swallow the sob I don't want him to hear. I did this. This is because of me. I didn't trust him, made a choice, and now I have to live with the consequences. Well, until he kills me. Is it bad that I hope he draws out my punishment? A part of me feels like this is my second chance at love. At what I wanted us to have from the moment I decided to be his. But I'm not stupid—love will no longer exist between us. Not on his side anyway.

"I knew I'd find you in here."

I jump at Kashton's voice.

"Join us," Saint offers, his eyes watching the first tear run down my cheek.

Kashton comes to stand behind me, and I sniff when both of his hands grip my wrists to hold me in place as Saint lets go and steps back from me. He reaches into his back pocket and pulls out a pair of handcuffs. My knees buckle.

"Whoa." Kashton chuckles, holding me up by my arms. It pinches my skin, making me cry out. "No need to get on your knees yet, sweet cheeks." His laughter grows.

"Here." Saint holds out the handcuffs. "Make her more comfortable."

Kashton grips both of my wrists in one of his hands while he takes the cuffs from Saint. I don't fight. It's useless. He places the first one on, tightening it, and then the other. It's the kind with the hinge in the middle so there's no give. My hands lie across the top of my ass, and I jump when Kashton's arm wraps around my neck from behind.

I rise up on my tiptoes and swallow as his muscles flex, holding me in place. I can breathe, but barely.

Saint reaches up, rubbing his chin while his eyes look me up and down. "How?" I ask breathlessly.

"How what, sweetheart?" he asks, meeting my stare again.

"How did you know where I was?" I have to know. He could have just taken me at any time. I know Saint. If he knew I was living in Las Vegas, then he would have known for some time. He does his research. He stalks his prey. That was not the first night he had been into Glass to see me. Although that was my first time seeing him.

He ignores my question. "You look...stunning, Ashtyn."

I whimper at his words, and Kashton presses his body into my back, smashing my already cuffed arms between us. His large muscular arm is still wrapped around my neck, and it makes me arch at an uncomfortable position. My wet hair sticks to my exposed skin, making me shiver.

"These tits." Saint's hands come out and grip both of my breasts, massaging them before pinching my hard nipples. "They look good."

Stepping back into me, he finds my eyes. "They will look even better with my cum all over them."

A moan escapes my lips, and Kashton laughs. "I think they need some jewelry," he suggests. His free hand comes around and grabs my left breast.

"No—"

Kashton's hand releases my breast and slaps over my mouth before I can finish my protest.

My fight or flight kicks in, and I start thrashing in his hold. His arm around my throat flexes again, tightening, taking away what little air I could still breathe in. I try to kick out my legs, but Saint steps into me, sandwiching me between them. They're both six-five. Towering over my five-five. I'm barefoot, and they're wearing combat boots.

I'm fucked. Forget the fact I'm handcuffed, soaking wet, and naked.

Saint's eyes narrow on mine. "You need to understand one thing, Ashtyn. You're here because I want you here. You have no say in what I do to you. You're mine to use, to play with. When I'm done with you, I'll be sure to return the favor."

My eyes widen, knowing what he means—shoot me. But it won't kill me. No, Saint will make sure I suffer for a long time for my betrayal.

"That's if Haidyn doesn't get to her first." Kashton laughs, and the blood rushes in my ears at the sound of the name.

My lungs burn, tears fall down my face, and my chest heaves as I try to breathe. Saint's figure fades in and out, and my eyes grow heavy.

I'm not dying, just passing out. They won't kill me this soon. I know how they work. They like to play with their food before they eat it. I think that's the worst part. I know who they really are. And how fucked I truly am.

My body jerks involuntarily, fighting to breathe before everything grows bright and almost euphoric-like. Saint has choked me out before during sex, and I loved it. I've even come waking up with him still fucking me. It was hot as hell.

Kashton's hand leaves my mouth, and he removes the arm around my neck. He steps back from my body, and I fall to my knees, unable to hold myself up. A cry rips from my lips as I hit the marble floor. I'm coughing, lungs burning as I lean forward with my hands cuffed behind my back, sucking in a deep breath. Spit flies from my mouth along with the tears that fall from my watery eyes.

A hand grips my wet hair and yanks my head up. I look through watery lashes to see Saint crouch down in front of me while Kashton holds my head in place.

"I always loved you on your knees," he says. Reaching out, he cups my tear-streaked face and runs his thumb over my trembling lips. I take a shaky breath, and he slides it between my lips.

They automatically wrap around his thumb, sucking on it. It's like muscle memory.

He smiles. "That's it, sweetheart. Such a good girl." He pulls it out, and I take another quick breath before he shoves two fingers into my mouth this time, making me gag. I try to pull away, but Kashton's hand in my hair prevents that.

Saint removes them, and Kashton laughs. "Looks like you've been a lazy whore, sweet cheeks. Spent too much time on your back rather than on your knees."

I lick my wet lips and taste my tears. Saint frowns at me. "You'll work on that first. We know how much I love fucking that pretty face of yours." His eyes travel down my body before he slaps my outer thigh. "Spread your legs."

My back is arched at an extreme angle from Kashton's hand in my hair. My knees hurt, legs shake, and my feet are already going numb while I try to catch my breath from being choked. I no longer feel my hands, other than the cuffs digging into my wrists and lower back.

I adjust myself to spread my legs the best I can in my position. Saint's hands slide up my inner thighs, and he digs his tatted fingers into my skin, making me hiss in a breath. He wears several rings, and each one leaves a fire as they slowly make their way to my pussy. "You're wet, sweetheart." He slides two fingers all the way inside, curling them inward, and I moan. His laughter follows. "Still the same whore that I loved to fuck."

"Sa-int?" I gasp as he pushes a third into me. My mind flashes back to the way he fucked me at Glass, and my knees slide on the wet marble, opening up more for him. The floor digs into my sensitive skin. "Please?" What am I asking for? I'm not sure. Kill me? Fuck me? Knowing Saint, he'll make them both feel equally as good.

"Begging already?" He chuckles. "You always were an addict, Ashtyn," he adds. "You want to be seen, need to be loved, and beg to be fucked."

His thumb plays with my clit, gently rubbing over it, and I push my hips forward, wanting him to pinch it, slap it, anything to make it hurt.

I like pain.

But he removes his fingers and Kashton releases my hair. My head falls forward, and the wet strands cover my face to help hide my embarrassment. The handcuffs are removed from my wrists, and my hands come up to cover my face as I begin to cry.

"You get one day, Ashtyn."

I look up at Saint to see him leaning up against the counter like he was when he was watching me in the bathtub. His body tenses, and his eyes narrow. Just a preview of what's to come between us. Sex, fight, and crazy madness. It's comforting to know not much has changed between us.

I loved him, but even I can admit we were toxic to one another. I always challenged him in a way that forced him to prove who he was. This time will be no different.

Hurt me, fuck me, love me comes to mind. I guess two out of three isn't bad.

"One day to relax, regain your strength. After today..." He pushes off the counter to stand in front of me. He doesn't bother crouching down his time. Instead, I lean my head back to look up at him as he glares down at me. "Your body is mine; your mind is mine, and your will is mine." With that, he exits the room, and I uncurl my legs out from underneath me. I rest my back against the side of the bathtub and close my eyes, trying to hold the tears back.

SAINT

I FIND MYSELF SITTING BACK AT MY DESK, WATCHING HER ON MY screen. She's lying under the covers on her bed, crying while in the fetal position.

My cell rings as it sits on my desk, and I pick it up seeing the name flash across it. I answer and place it on speakerphone. "Hello?"

"You have a problem," the man says in greeting.

Kashton snorts, getting up from his desk to come over to mine. "That's nothing new."

"Seriously. Ashtyn was supposed to have worked last night, and she never showed."

I frown and remind him, "You knew we were coming to collect her." Once we found out where she was, we made some phone calls to get our plan in motion.

"Not at Glass. Her *other* job."

I sit back in my chair and look up at Kashton, who runs his hand down his face and asks, "And?"

"And I'm calling to warn you that *she's* looking for Ashtyn."

"She'll never find her." I shake my head.

I'm aware that Ashtyn had two jobs. I watched her for three weeks before I made my move. I wanted to see what kind of life she lived. I wasn't surprised to see that all she did was work. She always needed to stay busy. And as far as I know, when she left Carnage, she had no money, and my girl fights to survive.

"Look..." Bones sighs heavily into the phone. "I didn't get in your way because you and Ashtyn have a past. You came to us and gave us a heads-up of your plans, and we appreciate that courtesy. But I'm telling you right now, Jasmine will find her. I've known her all of my life. She's fucking stubborn and will not give up until she's standing at your doorstep demanding to take her home."

"I'll take care of it." Kashton chuckles, running his tatted hand down his unshaven face.

"By *take care of it*, I expect you to send Jasmine back untouched when she shows up at your door," Bones adds tightly to Kash. "She isn't part of your *world*," he growls, referring to the Lords. "She's one of us, and we don't tolerate anyone fucking with what's ours."

Click.

"Fuck," Kashton hisses, his joking attitude now long gone.

"Well, that could have gone better," I state the obvious.

"I can handle it." Kashton nods to himself.

"How? You're here at Carnage, and she's there in Las Vegas. It's not like you can fuck her from two thousand miles away."

The Lords have always done business with the Kings. Just like our fathers, their fathers handed them a legacy they didn't want. But just because our worlds intertwine doesn't mean that Bones knows everything.

The Lords have been paying for Queens—the Kings escort service—for years. Jasmine used to be a queen for a short while, and Kashton was one of her best-paying customers. Still is as far as I know, although she no longer works for the Kings. She started her own business. One that we know of well. But I guarantee you the Kings and Jasmine have no clue just how intertwined our worlds are. And I'm sure as fuck not going to be the one to tell them.

"I'll call her." Kashton finally speaks.

"And tell her what?" I question. "If Bones is right, it'll lead her to our front door sooner rather than later." I would prefer to avoid a scene. I'd really hate for us to piss the Kings off, but Jasmine is crazy if she thinks she'll walk out of here with Ashtyn. I'll throw her in a cage in the basement and call Bones to come and fetch her before I allow Jasmine to take what's mine.

"What do you want me to do?" He throws his arms up in the air.

"Drop it," I answer. "She has no clue that you even know Ashtyn. Let's keep it that way."

It's pure coincidence that a woman Kashton has been fucking also knows Ashtyn. It really is a small world. But it also worked in our favor. When we found out that Ashtyn was in Vegas, it was the best outcome we could have hoped for. Because like Bones said, we gave the Kings a heads-up that we were coming, and they didn't stand in our way. It also just pissed me off how close we had been to her and never fucking knew it.

Kashton gives me his back before stomping out of the office and slamming the door shut. I know Kash, and he won't drop it. I just have to be prepared for what's to come.

Opening my top desk drawer, I remove Ashtyn's cell that I took from the bathroom back at her house in Las Vegas. I unlock it and see she's got over fifty missed calls and countless texts. I've had her phone on silent, not wanting to be bothered by it. It's almost dead.

Skimming the calls, I see they're all from **BOSS LADY** a.k.a. Jasmine.

No surprise that 90 percent of the texts are from her as well. They're all the same.

Where are you?

Are you okay?

I'm worried. You never go MIA.

Just then, the screen lights up flashing **BOSS LADY,** and I grind my teeth. I wait for it to stop and turn the cell off completely, toss it back into the drawer, and slam it shut.

Fuck! This will complicate things.

FORTY

ASHTYN

I finally crawled out of my bed and made it to the other set of double doors that I found leading to a balcony. I was surprised to find they were actually unlocked. It's nice to have a little freedom, no matter how false it is.

There's nothing but woods as far as the eye can see. Just as I remember it. I've always loved Pennsylvania. I grew up here. I hated the desert, but it was one of those things I had no control over.

Curling my fingers around the iron railing, I look down at the ground below. Good thing I'm not afraid of heights.

The thought of jumping to my death crosses my mind, but I quickly dismiss it. I've never been suicidal. I won't give Saint the satisfaction of thinking I couldn't live with myself. I did what I did and now I must pay for that decision. Being his prisoner sounds better than being without him.

The sound of my bedroom door opening has me pushing off the rail and rushing back into my room, expecting to see Saint enter. I hate the way my shoulders slump when it's not him.

"Good evening, miss."

"Jessie." I give him a kind smile.

Of course, he's still here. Just like the Spade brothers, Jessie is tied to this place for life. He still wears his all-black tux and looks just like I remember him. A set of kind eyes I always thought was too soft for this place. He has a few more wrinkles around them than I remember, but at least one thing hasn't changed. I wonder if he hates his life here since he has to serve. He's not allowed to marry or have children and has to devote his life to the Spades.

He wheels a cart into my bedroom that has three silver plates with dome lids over the top. "You need to eat," he says, looking me up and down and frowning. All I wear is an oversized T-shirt that hits mid thigh. "Help with your strength."

I want to laugh at his choice of words. No amount of strength will win me a fight against Saint.

Bringing the cart to a stop, he removes the lid, and my mouth salivates at my favorite meal, baked pineapple salmon. "You remembered."

"Of course." Then surprising me once more, he steps into me and pulls me in for a hug.

My arms come up and wrap around his waist. Closing my eyes, I inhale deeply. A part of me really did miss this place. This was my home until it wasn't. But isn't that how life goes? It's always good until it's not.

Pulling away, he takes my hand and balls my fingers into a fist. "For the pain," he whispers, dropping his eyes to my waist before they meet mine again. "It should help you through the night." With that, he turns and exits my room, closing the door behind him.

I don't have to open my hand to know that there are two pills in it. He understands how much my body has endured and that I'm not only exhausted but sore.

Plus, the throbbing reminder of the tracker that's inside me.

Honestly, it's the least of my worries. Does it hurt? Like a bitch! But Saint knows how I feel about pain. He wants me to have a constant reminder that I'm his. The bastard also knows that I'm a slut for ownership. *Carve your name into my neck and show me off.* I'll be a drooling mess for you.

Nothing is sexier than a man who knows what he wants and shows the world he has it.

Picking up the bottle of water he left me, I turn and step out onto the balcony. With my back facing my room, I toss the pills into my mouth and take a greedy sip. I know there are cameras all inside. I'm hoping that there isn't one out here. I'd hate to get Jessie in trouble. He always was a kind soul. Too good for this hell.

Making my way back into my room, I pick up the plates and set them down on the round glass table that sits by the double doors that lead out to the balcony and eat my food. Jessie wasn't wrong about the fact that I need to eat. I won't give the Spade brothers the satisfaction of starving myself.

SAINT

I PUSH OPEN THE DOOR TO HER ROOM TO FIND HER LYING IN THE center of the bed. The covers are pulled up to her neck, and she's hiding herself. The double doors to her balcony are open, and the smell of rain fills the large space as thunder rumbles the walls. Lightning flashes, and my eyes catch the sight of the cart that holds the empty plates. I smile. She ate her food. Good girl. I made sure the kitchen fixed her something she couldn't turn down.

Walking over to the bed, I pull the covers and shove them down to the backs of her knees, exposing her body to me. She's naked. Not surprised. She hated wearing clothes to bed, and I never wanted anything between us when she slept beside me. My girl always let me have a piece whenever I wanted it. At any time of the night.

I climb in next to her, lean up against the headboard and reach out, my fingers gently running up and down the curve of her spine. Over the vows that she let me tattoo on her. I have them on me as well. She just doesn't know it. I got them after she left me.

I meant what I said. She needed to take it easy. Needed a day to recover from the drugs she willingly took and what I gave her. I had Jessie slip her some medication hours ago when he brought her dinner. Something to take the edge off. As much as I want my sweetheart to suffer, I want her to think at least one person here cares for her, even if it's a lie.

A false sense of hope is exactly what she needs.

Everyone at Carnage is either a prisoner or works for us. We make the rules, and they follow.

She stirs, a soft snore coming from her parted lips as she rolls onto her back. My eyes fall to her brand. I've dreamed of her with it for four years now. Wondering how she explained it to other men who wanted to fuck her. I realized at Glass that she covered it up with makeup the best she could when I removed her underwear. I should have placed it on her neck. Made sure it was noticeable no matter what she wore.

Reaching out, I gently rub her hip bones with my fingertips before sliding them between her legs. I can't help myself. Never have been able to with her. She was always my weakness. She's like fucking crack. One hit is never enough.

I slide my fingers along her lips and watch her face to see if she notices. She doesn't move.

My free hand unzips my jeans, and I lift my hips to pull out my hard dick. I stroke it, debating if I want to fuck her right now.

I'll never forget the first time she asked for me to fuck her while she sleeps.

Senior year at Barrington University

I'm at Barrington when my cell rings. "Hello, sweetheart," I answer, walking toward my car.

"I want to try something new," she rushes out as if nervous.

I smile, loving that she still worries about such little things. She knows I never tell her no. "Whatever it is, I'm down."

A giggle fills my ear as I pop my trunk to toss my bag inside. "As you know, my mother is away for the weekend."

"I'm aware." I have plans to tie her to her bed and fuck her senseless for the next two days, starting tonight. I removed the cameras her father put in her house. And although I don't mind her staying with me at the house of Lords, sometimes I prefer the privacy of just the two of us.

"Well..." She takes a deep breath. "I found a bottle of her sleeping pills."

I open my car door and fall into it. Her mother takes pills for everything, so no surprise there. "What about them?"

"I was thinking..." She pauses, and I give her the second she needs to tell me what she wants. "What if I take some and you meet me at my house?"

I know exactly what she's talking about, but I want her to tell me. "How am I going to fuck you, sweetheart, if you plan on sleeping?"

"Well, that's the point."

I sit back into my seat and look down at my hard cock inside my jeans. "You want me to fuck you in your sleep?"

"Yeah," she answers softly.

"What exactly do you want me to do to you?" I pull on my jeans, lifting my ass up off the seat, trying to get comfortable.

"Whatever you want." Her voice is no longer unsure, and her breathing has picked up. Her nervousness is replaced with excitement.

"So if I tie your unconscious body to your bed, fuck your cunt and ass, you won't mind?" I inquire.

"No."

"And what if you wake up still tied up?"

"Even better." She all but moans.

I finally start my car and order, "Head home and go ahead and take them when you get there." I have to go to the house of Lords for a meeting and grab a few things before I can head that way. It'll give her plenty of time to get ready for my arrival.

"Okay—"

"Ashtyn, don't take more than you're supposed to." I want this to be something we both enjoy, not something we regret. She's smaller than her mother and also doesn't take them on a regular basis, meaning she doesn't have a tolerance for them and needs to take less than what is suggested for her size.

"Of course."

As my finger pushes inside her, she lifts her hips and moans.

Fuck, I've missed that sound so much. It was so hard to keep my identity a secret when I fucked her in the Fountain room. I wanted to rip off my mask and have her eyes on mine as she came. My sweetheart has no control over her body. Never has. She loves to be used and left with my cum dripping out of her.

Removing my finger, I get up and shove what's left of the covers off the end of the bed. Then I crawl onto it, spreading her legs in the process. Her head is tilted to the right, and her dark hair fans the white pillow, but she doesn't stir. She's been through a lot the past few days. It's just the beginning.

Settling between her spread thighs, I lean over her upper body, reach between the bed, and pull the leather straps up. I proceed to fasten one around each wrist, securing them above her head.

She's out, but I know my girl likes being dominated. Sitting back, I reach out and rub her breasts and squeeze them. Then slap the outer side of both.

That gets a response. Her heavy eyes open, her long and dark lashes fluttering as she looks around aimlessly trying to make sense of her surroundings.

I slap them again, and a whimper comes from her parted lips. "There she is."

Her chest rises with a deep intake of breath, her arms gently pulling on the restraints. "Wh-hat?" she stutters, arching her neck to see why she's lost the function of her arms. The sound of her yanking harder on them makes me smile.

I run my hand over her smooth cunt, and her breath hitches as her heavy eyes find mine. She's drugged but not entirely out of it. Two of my fingers slip inside her, and she arches her back, groaning.

Removing them, I grab the head of my pierced dick and push into her, loving the way her cunt clenches. Her legs push against me, and I grab the back of her knees, shove them up and out, opening her up wide, and her voice rings out over the thunder as I slam into her. Burying my cock inside her pussy. She's not wet, but she's also not dry. I love it when she's dripping for me, but I also like it when I have to work at it.

Everything with Ashtyn has always been complicated. I love her. I hate her. It's always been black or white. Never any gray areas.

"Fuck, sweetheart." I moan, my eyes dropping to watch my cock go in and out as she continues her useless fight with the leather restraints around her wrists. I should tell her to save her strength, but I won't. She'll figure it out.

"Saint," she gasps, her body arching, her legs shaking in my arms. "Oh...God."

I pull out and slam forward, the headboard banging against the wall, forcing a cry from her lips. Her cunt clenches down on me, and I slowly watch my wet dick slide out. She slumps into the mattress, trying to catch her breath.

I release her legs, grip her hips, and turn her over onto her stomach. She tries to fight me, but I easily shove her legs open, forcing her ass up in the air, arching her back in a high position.

Grabbing my wet cock, I slide back into her. My free hand reaches out, grips her dark hair, and yanks her head up off the bed. She cries out while lightning flashes from behind me, illuminating the room.

My knees hold hers open, and I lean over her back, my elbows digging into the bed on either side of her head. I gently pull her hair from her face and twist it before lying it to the side. "I want to see your face, beautiful," I inform her before my left hand clamps over her mouth.

She goes wild, bucking her hips and rocking her body. It just forces her cunt to fuck my dick, and it makes me chuckle. Her arms are crossed at the wrists due to her new position. "I'm sorry, sweetheart." Lie. "You were just lying here...naked and begging to be fucked." I've been fucking dying for her all day. I tried to be patient but told myself that I don't have to be. She's here, so I might as well get what's mine.

I push my body down on top of hers and slam my cock into her. "Your tight cunt is soaking wet for me now." She sucks in a deep breath through her nose, rambling unintelligible shit from her mouth that my hand covers. I reposition my hand so that my pointer finger and thumb pinch her nose closed, taking away her air. The action makes her pussy contract. "It's like old times." I go on, pulling out and slamming forward. Fuck, she's so tight, and the thought of all the men she's fucked over the past few years makes me want to beat her fucking ass with my belt to the point she can't sit for a week. "You tied to my bed while I make you my dirty little whore."

Tears run down her face as she tries to look at me out of the corner of her eye. I lean in, unable to stop myself, and kiss the side of her face, tasting the salt from them. I moan, "Have you missed me?"

She nods her head the best she can, blinking. I give a rough laugh, knowing we're both lying to one another just about different things.

I push into her, and her head shakes, trying to dislodge my hand from her face. It's not happening. I continue my hard thrusts, the headboard hitting the wall each time followed by her muffled screams and cries. Her hands fist as she pulls on the chains that are connected to the leather cuffs, needing to escape.

Her eyes are getting heavy though due to the pain pills she took and the lack of oxygen from my hand. "You're about to pass out, sweetheart." She blinks, and this time it takes her wet lashes longer to flutter open. "You were out when I started fucking you, and you'll be out when I'm done with you."

I slam forward, burying my dick into her soaked cunt, and hold it there. One hand on her face, the other on the opposite side of her head, and I watch her fight to breathe. "You're so goddamn gorgeous, sweetheart," I say in awe. My hand is slick from tears, snot, and drool.

Her body softens under me. "That's it," I coo, watching her hands unclench. "Such a good girl."

She's always been the girl of my dreams—the one I wanted and needed. "Get some rest, sweetheart," I say as her eyes fall closed. This time, they don't open, and her body goes slack beneath me.

I wait another second and release my hand from her mouth and nose. I gently lay the side of her face down onto the bed, sit up, grab her hips, and finish what I came in here to do.

FORTY-ONE

ASHTYN

I wake up, a groan escaping my lips as I roll over and bury my face into the soft cool pillow. I'm so tired. It's the pills. They linger in my system, making my head foggy and body sluggish.

What the fuck had Jessie given me? I hallucinated last night. Or dreamed it. Either way, it felt so real. Saint was there, hovering over my restrained body. His hand over my mouth and nose while he fucked me in the most delicious way.

My hands instinctively go to my lips, and I wipe the drool off. Looking up from the pillow, I catch sight of two leather cuffs on the bed, and my pulse begins to race. Sitting up, I pull my knees up and under me as I face the headboard. I shove the multiple pillows to the floor. I pick up the chains that connect to the leather restraints and yank on them, but there's no give. I lean over, feeling down between the bed and headboard, and find the chains connected to the bedframe.

It was real. Of course, it was. I should have known. The pills I swallowed wouldn't have made me sore between my legs. Only Saint has that effect on my body.

He left them here. Saint wanted me to see them. A reminder that it wasn't a dream. That I'm in his hell and that he has control of me. I used to love that, and he knows it. We tried it one weekend when my mom was out of town, and I was obsessed. I loved the feeling of waking up and knowing he had used me. I submitted to him in any way that I could. It was even better when I woke up with my ass red from his hand and my body sore from how rough he'd gotten.

I fall onto the bed, my head now by the footboard, and I realize something is between my legs. Propping myself up on my elbows, I look, and it's a white-crusted substance—cum—all over my pelvic bone and inner thighs.

"Fuck him..." My hands go to my face and push the wild hair back. I blink rapidly, my eyes sensitive to the harsh light that filters in through the double doors that lead out to the balcony. I never closed them last night after I had dinner.

"Fuck." What time is it? I have no cell phone. Shocker. Only a clock in my room hangs on the wall. It's large and loud as it slowly ticks by the seconds. Time doesn't matter when you're a prisoner. At least I get conjugal visits. *Silver lining.*

I TOOK MY TIME GETTING READY, MAINLY BECAUSE I DIDN'T have the strength to move any faster. The bathroom was fully stocked with all of my things. I highly doubt they packed up my stuff and had everything moved. I'm sure they've been watching me for weeks, months even, and they've been in my house. They just bought all new and had everything prepared for my arrival. None of it had been used before. That sounds better than the voice in the back of my head that was shouting *Saint knows you. What you like and choose to use.*

I won't lie; I am pretty predictable. The only thing that changed in my life was him no longer being in it and the hole in my chest that was left behind from losing everything.

Once finished in the bathroom, I walk back into the bedroom to find a robe on the end of my now made bed. Someone was in here while I was in the shower. I'm not surprised. You're never alone here at Carnage. Someone is always watching. I know that from experience. I bet there are cameras all over this room and the bathroom. Hell, they probably have them in the closet.

They're probably watching me right now.

I can't help but notice the leather cuffs are gone. They were connected to the bed, so I'm sure they just shoved them back down between the headboard and the wall.

I walk over to the robe, and my tongue feels heavy. This is what they want me to wear? Again, no surprise. Saint wasn't wrong. Carnage is hell, a place where people come to die. They don't allow privacy in a place like that, and I hate how excited I am at the thought of him wanting to chain me up and make me his.

I've been dead for years. So no one will be looking for me here. Or anywhere. Other than the dancers at Glass. But let's face it, the two years I've worked there, girls have come and gone quicker than the weather can change.

No one will ever think of me again. I have no cell, no dignity. Just my body and the three numbers branded on my skin to remind me that I'm a slave to the Spade brothers until the day I die. Saint will own me.

Wrapping the thick black robe around me, I tighten the sash high on my waist as if it can save me from them. I open the bedroom door to find a man standing outside it. They've given me a guard. Afraid I'll try to escape again. I could never get as lucky as I was last time. I had help then, and my freedom was short-lived. I won't try again, mainly because I won't kill them. I may hate them now, but they were once all I had. I was a coward, and I'm no longer that person.

The man grabs my robe, yanking on it to pull me forward. Once I pass him, he hits my back, shoving me once again, and I stumble but manage to stay standing. "Quit touching me," I turn and yell at him.

He slaps me across the face. I've been hit harder before, but it knocks me into the wall, and I fall to my knees in the hallway. The lingering drugs make me sluggish and weaker than I'd normally be. I catch sight of a Lords ring on his right finger, and I reach up to touch my cheek to make sure it didn't cut me.

"Fuck you, bitch." He laughs. "No one here gives a shit about you. You're here to be nothing more than a fuck-toy for the brothers. And believe me when I say anyone is allowed to have their piece."

A part of me doesn't want to believe him. Saint sharing me with Kashton and Haidyn? Now that I believe, but just anyone...? I refuse to think that's a possibility. But I also know that I no longer mean to him what I once did. I can't blame him. He loved me, and I shot him, then left him for dead.

I swallow the knot in my throat and get to my knees, my vision a little blurry from his hand to my cheek. I get to my wobbly legs, and he grips my hair, yanking me forward, and I cry out at the sting of my head and the jerk of my neck.

A door to my left opens, and I'm yanked back off my feet and shoved to the floor once again. "Fuck..." I groan, sitting up.

"What in the fuck do you think you're doing?" a voice snaps.

"I was told to deliver her to your office," the man assigned to be my babysitter answers in a rush.

I look up, rubbing the back of my neck just in time to see Haidyn grab the guy's hand in one of his and squeezes it. The man falls to his knees, and I hear bones snap like twigs. "Deliver her, not beat her," he growls.

My breathing accelerates as a set of blue eyes meets mine. Haidyn Jamison Reeves is by far the biggest of the three Spade brothers. He stands six-foot-seven and is built like a fucking house. He's always had anger issues and chose to take them out on other men. He used to spend all of his time in the gym.

But I've seen him be the softest teddy bear out of the bunch. He's a complicated man. Of course, that was the old him. I have a feeling the Spade brothers have all changed just as much as I have over the past few years.

The fact he's covered in ink like the other two and has a nose ring proves my point. He's got a pair of black sweatpants on, and that's it.

They rest low on his narrow hips, and he's just as chiseled as I remember with his defined V and abs.

The guy on his knees continues to scream into the hall, and I cover my ears, pushing my back into the wall.

Haidyn's eyes drop to my robe, and I realize it's open. I quickly grab it and pull it closed. He looks away to glare at my babysitter. "Take her to the office and don't fucking touch her, or I'll break both of your fucking hands. It'll be hard to jack yourself off without them." With that, he releases his hand and steps into the room, slamming the door shut so hard it makes me flinch.

The man gets to his feet, cradling his now broken hand. A bone sticks out of his pinky, and his finger is already turning colors. "Get the fuck up," he growls through gritted teeth.

I get to my feet, and this time, the guy walks in front of me. We enter the elevator at the end of the hall, and he turns to face me when the doors slide shut. I push my back into the mirrored wall as he glares down at me, but I don't miss the sheen in his eyes. He's trying everything he can not to cry.

I wrap my arms around myself, and he gives a rough laugh. "Once my hand heals, I'm going to fucking break your neck with it."

I step into him, my chest hitting his. "Good luck with that." I give him a sweet, fuck-you smile. After what Haidyn just did, I know that no one at Carnage will touch me. Because if Haidyn protects me, all of the brothers will protect me, and they run this bitch.

"You won't be smiling when you're trying to breathe while I'm raping you, you piece of shit trash. Don't worry, I won't kill you until *after* I come all over your fake tits."

My stomach drops at his words, and he sees it because the smile he gives me raises the hairs on the back of my neck.

The elevator dings as it comes to a stop, and he spins around to walk off. I follow him slowly, my feet heavy. His words getting to me more than they should. Carnage is a big place, a city of its own, and I have to remind myself that the Carnage I left behind might not be the

Carnage that it is today. It was evil then, and I'm sure it's even more so now.

He stops in front of a door and pushes it open, glaring at me. I walk into the room, and my pulse begins to race as I see Saint sitting behind a large black wooden desk. He doesn't even bother looking up. He's bent over, a pen in one hand, his cell to his ear.

The man who delivered me clears his throat, and I turn around to see him walk out, shutting the door. I don't miss the fact that he's got his broken hand behind his back. He obviously doesn't want Saint or Kashton asking any questions. Then he'd have to explain what he did to me.

I hope he runs to his room and cries like a baby.

When I turn back to face the office, my breath catches when I see Saint standing in front of me. He holds out his right fist, and I stare at it. His left hand reaches out, grabs mine, and holds open my hand as he opens his to drop a ponytail into it.

"Put your hair up. And none of that messy, half-ass shit. I want it all out of your face," he commands, giving me his back. He's clearly not going to acknowledge that he fucked me last night and left me unsatisfied. It's just another way to throw around his power. He wants me crawling on my hands and knees, begging for release. We both know that I have no shame when it comes to getting off.

Licking my lips nervously, I lean over, running my hands through my thick hair to gather it into a high pony and then tie it up tight. When I return upright to my full height, Saint now stands by his desk at the other end of the office. He nods his head once as if I asked if it was good enough.

"Strip," he commands, and my heart leaps with excitement and fear. Why am I here? What is he going to make me do?

My eyes dart around to take in the room. A set of floor-to-ceiling windows runs the length of the wall behind his desk. The white curtains are pulled open and tied back to show off the woods that surround the city. It's a gloomy day here in Pennsylvania. I've missed the trees, the rain, the cold winters. Everything in Las Vegas was always hot.

"Ashtyn," he snaps, making me jump.

My fingers fumble to undo the sash, but I get it done. I shrug the soft material off my shoulders, and it falls to the floor at my feet. My hands go to my side, refusing to hide myself but also not knowing what to do with them. I won't go back in time and be that innocent woman in her room who hid herself from him.

Saint moves to stand in front of a large mirror framed in black wood. He turns and opens a drawer in his desk and tosses some rope on top of the surface.

My heart races as I try to slow my breathing because the office is silent.

"Come over here." Just the sound of his voice makes me whimper, and I hear Kashton chuckle from his desk. He hasn't even looked up once. He's too busy reading something on his cell, leaning back in his chair, combat boots propped up on his desk.

My feet are heavy, but I manage to get over to him without tripping. Once I stop, he grabs my upper arm and pulls me to stand in front of the mirror. He stands behind me, and I watch him in the glass. He picks up the rope, and my breathing accelerates.

He doubles the rope and then reaches over my head, bringing it around my upper chest and arms. The rough material sits on top of my breasts. He brings it behind me, and the rope pulls against my skin as he tightens it. I can't see what he's doing with it, but I know he's tying it off when I feel the knot on my upper back.

"Hands behind your back and interlock your fingers," he orders.

His commands, his words, the voice...I've dreamed of him every night since I escaped this place. Careful what you wish for, ladies. Sometimes the devil hears you and delivers exactly what you want, knowing it will be the last thing you ever get.

I do as I'm told, and the rope wraps around my upper arms. He pulls on it hard, forcing my chest out, and pinching my shoulder blades together.

My head drops to stare at the floor, and a moan escapes my parted lips. My breathing can now be heard throughout the room. There's no hiding it. At this point, it'd be better if I just passed the fuck out.

Once my upper arms are secured, I feel the rope drop to my wrists, tying them as well. The remainder of the rope falls between my feet, and he walks around to stand in front of me. I look up and stare directly at his chest. He blocks my view of the mirror, but I can't bring myself to look him in the eye due to how wet I am.

Kneeling, he picks up the rope with one hand while the other goes to my pussy. I gasp when he spreads my lips and slides the rope between them.

"Saint?" His name is spoken softly, but my heart races.

He smirks but doesn't say anything. He yanks on the rope, and I cry out as it rubs between my legs.

My head falls forward to look down at my chest to see he's taken the excess rope between my legs and then through the two pieces around my upper chest.

Once satisfied he's tied it tightly, he yanks my ponytail, forcing me to look up. "Eyes on me."

The blood rushes in my ears, and I'm panting. My hips thrust forward to rub the rope on my pussy, and he notices because he smirks.

Fuck me!

He lets the access rope hang as he reaches into his back pocket. Before I can see what he's grabbed, he places something rough around my neck, and I hear the familiar click of a lock.

Then he picks the rope back up and ties it off to what he just put around my neck. He steps back, admiring his work.

I try to move, but the slightest wiggle pulls on the rope where it sits between my legs and my neck. I swallow nervously.

"I never forgot how beautiful you are, Ash," he says softly, and my eyes rise to meet his. Reaching out, he cups my face. His thumb runs over my parted lips. "Today, you're going to work on this mouth of yours."

I whimper, knowing exactly what he means.

"Your jaw will be sore and your throat raw by the time you're done. Do you understand me?"

"Yes," I whisper.

He reaches into his jeans pocket and pulls out what looks like a small container of Vaseline. He places his finger in it and then rubs a generous amount onto my shaking lips.

He leaves me to go over to his desk and opens up the top drawer. I get a look at myself in the mirror, and as I suspected, he placed a collar on me. It's black leather and has a silver ring in the center. The rope is looped through it and then tied to the piece that sits high on my chest.

Saint returns to stand in front of me, stating, "Open wide." I do so, and he sprays something that resembles a sample size of a perfume bottle into my mouth, making me flinch. But I keep it open like the good girl I am. And he sprays it again. The taste of cinnamon overtakes my senses, and I cough a few times.

"On your knees."

He tosses the spray onto his desk, and I fall to my knees in front of the mirror, whimpering as the new position pulls the rope even tighter, making it only harder to swallow as the collar pulls on my neck, but the tightness of the rope squeezes my clit.

"Kash." He looks over at him. "I need your belt."

Kashton stands up from his desk, removes his belt, and tosses it over to Saint without even looking away from his phone that sits on his desk. Saint then removes his own and leans down. He places his between my leg and the floor, he wraps it around my right thigh and shin, pulling it tightly, buckling it in place, and then does the same with my other.

I'm immobile, and that has my pulse racing. He knows how much I love this. Goddamn him. He's going to use everything my body likes against me in the worst torturous way.

He goes over to his desk, opens the top drawer once more and pulls out a dildo. My heavy breathing grows louder, and I can feel my pulse throbbing against the inside of the collar.

Coming back to me, he kneels and suctions it to the mirror. Then he grips the back of my head and shoves it forward until my Vaseline-covered lips are just inches from it. I'm breathing so heavily that it fogs the mirror.

I stare at the clear dildo that faces me, my mouth already watering excessively. It has a small silver ring that resembles a piercing at the bottom of the shaft, right above the balls. There is a short chain that hangs from it. It softly clanks against the mirror as it swings back and forth.

"You will fuck your mouth with this. I sprayed numbing spray down your throat. You should feel it already starting to work."

I swallow nervously and realize there's a tingling feeling at the back of my throat. I blink, staring up into his narrowed eyes in the mirror unable to respond.

"It'll last for a good fifteen minutes." He goes on. "But as it begins to wear off, you will start to gag. Your throat is like anything else, Ash. It needs to be trained. Conditioned. So you're going to sit here and suck this fake dick until you can swallow the whole thing. Do you understand?"

I can barely breathe from the rope and collar around my throat let alone speak so when a cracked "y-yes" comes out of my slick lips, he seems satisfied.

SAINT

I STAND BEHIND HER, ARMS CROSSED OVER MY CHEST. SHE stares at herself in the mirror and licks her trembling lips. Slowly, they part, and she leans forward, closing them around the head of the dildo.

It's got lines indicating one inch, two inches, three inches, and so on to ten. Do I think she'll be able to take the entire thing today? No. Like I told her, it takes practice, and then you have to continue to work on it to train that gag reflex. Honestly, I like the sound she makes when she gags. This is just a way to humiliate my girl. Because I know she's into that shit. Plus, it keeps her on her knees in the office by my desk while I work. Because if I moved my desk to her room, it'd be too obvious how much I missed her. The last time she was out of my sight, she managed to disappear for years. I won't make that same mistake again.

She pulls her head back and takes a deep breath before going back to it. Her head bobs as she takes a little bit more, and I smile. "That's a good girl," I praise her, and her body shakes as her eyes fall closed. "Watch yourself, Ashtyn. I want you to see how pretty you look while you suck a dick."

Her eyes open, and they're already filled with tears. I can't wait to see her crying and drool running down her naked body. I tied her so she'd feel every little movement. Her pussy will be soaked by the time I allow her to stop.

I bend down, and she pulls back, the head falling from her mouth. *That won't do.* I grab the back of her head. "Open wide." And push it forward. Not enough to hurt her, just enough to take the head once more, and I reach out to grab the chain connected to the ring in the dildo. I open the clasp on the end of the chain and connect it to the ring around her collar.

Her wide eyes meet mine, and she mumbles nonsense around the tip of the dildo. "This will make sure you keep sucking, sweetheart," I inform her, and her eyes close as her shoulders shake. "Don't want you to stop too soon." There's plenty of give in the chain. It's not like I shortened it to where she's deep throating the dildo. That'll come once she gets better at it. This is the beginner's class.

Standing, I turn and walk over to my desk. She's to the left of my back, but I don't need to see her to know she's being good. I can hear her sucking on the dildo.

I pick up my cell to see that Haidyn had texted me five minutes ago. Opening it up, I read.

HAIDYN: Check the hallway cameras in the birdcage.

I pull them up on my computer. Nothing looks off to me. There are four bedrooms and an elevator along with access to the stairs. Nothing more. I'm about to exit when I see the elevator door slide open.

A woman steps out in a pair of black thigh-high boots, black booty shorts, and a white crop top that shows off her large tits. She walks over to Haidyn's door and knocks on it. Spreading her legs, she places her hands on the doorframe while she waits for him to answer.

The door swings open, his hand reaches out and wraps around her neck, forcing her chin up. Her arms fall to her sides, and he yanks her into the room, slamming it shut behind him.

I frown, knowing that's not what he meant for me to see.

The sound of Ashtyn slobbering all over the dildo gets my attention, and I rewind the cameras back to when she would have been up there.

Once I get the clock on where I want, I push play. I see Ashtyn walking out of her room, and Emerson already waiting for her. He yanks on her, then shoves her forward. I pause it, place my earbuds in, and push play once more. I don't want her to know that I'm watching the video by hearing the audio.

What follows makes my blood boil. Why didn't she tell me what he did? Why didn't I pay attention to him when he entered the office with her? My body tenses when he speaks to her in the elevator. My brothers and I don't really give a fuck what happens to those that are here, but Ashtyn? I fucking care who speaks to her, touches her, and threatens her.

I wait until he exits and shuts the office door before I stop the video, yank the earbuds from my ears, and turn to look at her. She's got her eyes closed, her body pressed forward, and she's now up to three inches on the dildo. Drool runs down her mouth. The fact that she can't feel her throat will cause her to produce more saliva than usual.

Going over to Kashton's desk, I lean over, and he looks up at me. "Keep an eye on her. I'll be back."

He nods and goes back to whoever the fuck he's texting on his cell. I can't take him with me because I won't leave her here alone tied up and vulnerable. Especially after what I just saw and heard.

Shoving the door open, I exit the office and take the elevator up to the birdcage. Once I get off, I march down the hall and don't even bother knocking. I shove the door open to find Haidyn sitting in the chair by the double doors to his balcony. The woman I saw on the camera is on her knees before him. Her arms handcuffed behind her back. She's naked, and he's fucking her mouth.

"I need your help," I inform him.

He nods but doesn't pay me any attention. I lean against the door as she gags and slurps on his dick like it's a straw. It reminds me of Ashtyn, and the thought pisses me off. I should be listening to her do this right now instead of what I'm about to do.

His hands tangle in her short, bleach-blond hair, and he arches his back, forcing his cock farther down her throat. She shifts on her knees, trying her best to fight him. It's useless. He holds her head down as his muscles stiffen, and he forces her to swallow.

When he pulls out, she's gasping as cum and drool fall from the corner of her mouth. I get sight of her eyes, and they're solid black—blackout lenses. They're like blindfolding someone without putting something over one's face. It allows them to see nothing but darkness, but he can still see her expressions. Haidyn loves using them on whoever he fucks.

Standing, he yanks her up from her shaky knees by her hair, making her cry out. He walks her over to the far wall and turns her to face it. "Don't move," he orders, slapping her bare ass, making her jump.

He then picks up a collar, fastens it around her neck, and pulls on the end of the chain that hangs from the ceiling, connecting it to the front. The position forces her to arch her neck and rise up on her tiptoes. She struggles between moaning and gasping, still trying to catch her breath.

He picks up his jeans off the floor and pulls them on along with his shirt. Then he walks toward me. "I'll be back." She fights harder in her restraints as we exit the room, and he slams it shut, locking the door from the outside. All of our doors have keyless access. They each require a fingerprint. It keeps others from getting in and killing us in the middle of the night. I wouldn't say anyone would, but you can never be too sure.

Lots of measures have been taken since my sweetheart got away.

Haidyn doesn't even ask what I need help with. He never does. He's always down to fuck some shit up. And I'm about to do just that.

I remove my cell from my pocket and pull up the location that I need. Everyone here at Carnage has a tracking device—even us brothers. Everyone else's is so no one can hide from us. Ours is for our protection.

We're Lords, but we're not untouchable. We're what you would consider the outcasts of our secret society. The only reason they haven't killed us off is because they need us. No one else would want to run Carnage. That's why they invented the Spade brothers centuries ago. The Lords are known for killing those who wrong them or go against their oath. But death is too easy and sometimes a Lord goes too far. He deserves more than a knife in his neck with a shallow grave. And that's where we come in.

"Morgue," I say, and my teeth grind. Every time I'm down there, I'm reminded that Ashtyn almost succeeded in getting away from me. I mean, I can overlook her shooting me. A part of me gets hard just thinking about the fact she had the balls to do it. But leaving me? She'll pay for that. And no matter how much I love her, I can't overlook or forget what we went through after she escaped.

Haidyn doesn't speak. He just shoves his hands into the front pockets of his jeans and leans back against the wall, staring straight ahead. I'm not even sure he's breathing.

I send a quick text and pocket my cell.

The elevator comes to a stop, and we step off. I don't even feel the coldness down here anymore. I'm used to it. Haidyn follows me, and I round the corner. Voices echo from down the hall.

"Yeah, man. A fight broke out," a familiar voice lies.

"What the fuck did you do?" another asks.

"I taught him a fucking lesson."

Haidyn grunts, letting me know what I already do. We round the corner, and I come up behind a man who has his back toward us. The one standing across from him spots us. Swallowing nervously, he takes a step back. "I need to go..." He turns and runs.

"What the hell, man?" the guy in front of us calls out. "I need your help. I can't wrap this myself."

"We can help," I say.

The man spins around, and his eyes widen. I punch him in the side of the face, knocking his ass out before he can even speak.

FORTY-TWO

ASHTYN

My throat is numb, my body aches, and I'm crying as I watch myself in the mirror with heavy eyes and drool running from my lips. I'm a very competitive person, and the fucker knows that. I know Saint. He thinks I can't do this. And I'm going to suck this dick like I'm a man on center stage for a fucking hot dog eating contest on the Fourth of July, dammit. I'm determined to win no matter what it takes. Even if I can't swallow after this damn numbing spray wears off.

The mirror is covered in spit, and my nipples are hard. I'm so wet between my thighs, and not just because I'm drooling all over myself.

I'm horny as fuck. I've always had a thing for sucking dick. I loved the way Saint would moan and groan. How he'd grab the back of my head and fuck my face. It turned me on. I craved that sort of attention. I especially loved it when he had me do it in front of an audience. As if he was proud to show off what I could do...how I could please him.

I've slept with countless guys since I escaped Carnage, but none were like Saint. They never even came close. They say you never get over your first love, and I can't argue with that.

Closing my eyes, I part my lips as wide as I can and push my face forward. Not only is my tongue and throat numb but so are my lips. The spray had been on my tongue when I licked them. My nose runs, and my eyes are bloodshot and watering.

And since he connected the short chain, I can't remove my lips from the dildo, so my mouth is always open. My hips rock the best they can to create friction on my pussy from the rope wrapped around me. He tied my thighs with the belts on purpose. They restrict the movement of my legs for this very reason. He wants me to torture myself. It prevents me from being able to move around.

I'm dripping wet and need to come so bad. I love pleasuring Saint. And the fact I'm pretending to suck his cock makes it unbearable. A part of me hopes that he comes back here and tests me. Makes me show him just how good I can be.

I try to see just how far I can go and push my face forward. I can't feel it, but there's pressure as I breathe through my runny nose. I unlace my fingers only to lace them again. That's the slight amount of movement the rope allows. They're sweaty, and so are my tied legs. My lashes are stuck together, and I pull back as much as I can only to shove my face forward, watching myself. It just turns me on more. I want Saint to tell me how pretty I look. He loved it when I'd get all ready for him only to let him smear my makeup.

SAINT

I LEAN BACK AGAINST THE COUNTER, AND HAIDYN STANDS NEXT to me, watching the cameras in his room, checking on the woman he's got tied up and waiting for him.

The door opens and in walks Devin. "Just in time," I say.

He pushes in his cart and nods to me. Devin doesn't say much. He doesn't have to as long as he does his job.

The man sitting in the middle of the room stirs, and Haidyn locks his cell, putting it away. We've got him strapped in what we call the high chair. It looks exactly how it sounds. Just an adult version. His ankles are secured to the metal bars that run horizontal across the bottom. There's a tabletop to it that is latched on each side, securing him into it. And his arms are strapped down to the top of it.

"W-what…?" The guy opens his swollen eye. "What the fuck?" He tries to move, but the metal collar I've secured around his neck has a short chain connected to the chair's high back.

"I heard you were in a fight," I speak.

His eyes snap up to look at mine before they go to Haidyn. "Saint…I didn't…"

"Hit my wife?" I arch a brow, and he swallows. "I guess the footage I saw of you and her in the elevator must have been fake as well?" I look at Haidyn who snorts.

"I…uh, no…I didn't—" he rambles unable to lie but refusing to tell me the truth.

"Threaten to rape and kill her." I finish for him. Not caring what else he has to say, I push off the counter and step forward, and he starts screaming, trying to pull away, but he's not going anywhere.

Devin pushes the cart over to Emerson and removes the syringe as Emerson begins to scream. He knows what's coming. He's been through it before. It's routine for brandings. But this one will be a little different. The Spade brothers pride themselves on being creative. It's not as if there is a rule book on how to torture and kill people. But if there ever was, we would be the ones to write it.

"Small pinch," Devin says, placing his left hand on Emerson's bare chest while he shoves the needle between his ribs, injecting the shot of adrenaline straight to his heart. I don't want the fucker to pass out and miss the fun.

Blood begins to run from his mouth, and I look at Haidyn. "He bit his tongue."

"Pity," he says dryly.

Devin finishes and removes the needle, nodding to me before dismissing himself.

"Haidyn," I say, and he walks behind Emerson as he wails. His body thrashes uncontrollably in the chair. He's strapped down as tight as can be, but his body runs on adrenaline now. For the next fifteen minutes, he's going to fight as hard as he can before he passes the fuck out.

I pick up the old, rusted, and stained blood meat cleaver off the counter and walk over to the front of the chair.

He manages to find his voice as spit and blood fly from his mouth. "No. No. No. Please..."

I bring the sharp blade down right at his wrist, slamming it down into the metal table, cutting it clean off.

His shrill scream follows, making my ears ring, and blood squirts all over it and to the floor. The fact that he no longer has a wrist means his arm is free from the restraint. So Haidyn grips his forearm and holds it down on the table. His broken hand rolls off the edge of the tabletop and onto the floor. I kick it out of the way into the far corner as it leaves a trail of blood along the way.

"Don't worry, I have something for that," I assure him, picking up the brand I had sitting in the bucket with hot coals. Haidyn holds his arm down while I push the 666-branding iron onto the end of his arm where his hand once was.

His scream ricochets off the concrete walls as I heat it up once again and repeat the process. "I'm going to do it as many times as it takes to stop the bleeding," I tell him while he sobs like the motherfucker he is.

After two more times, I'm satisfied that it's covered enough. Haidyn lets go, and he cradles it to his chest. "Just one last thing, and then you're free to go," I tell Emerson.

"Why'd you do it?" I ask Haidyn over Emerson's cries, watching him go over to the counter. He removes the key from his back pocket and unlocks one of the upper cabinets.

Haidyn doesn't turn to face me as he says. "I've done lots of questionable things in my life. I'm going to need you to be more specific, Saint." His voice is flat, but I can see how tense he is. Usually, this shit gets him off. He's still in a mood and just needs some pussy.

I smirk at his way of avoiding what he knows I'm asking. "Ashtyn. Why did you tell me what happened?" For someone who just told me two days ago that he'd kill her if he saw her, he sure as hell protected her when the time came.

Placing what he wanted from the cabinet onto the counter, he turns to face me and crosses his tatted arms over his chest. Emerson's sobbing fills the room, and he speaks over it. "Did she tell you what happened?"

I frown, not expecting that as an answer. "No..." I trail off, realizing what he meant. He wants her to be in trouble. He's telling me she's still the same conniving little cunt who shot and left me for dead all those years ago.

I can't argue with him. Did I think dragging her back here would change what happened? No. But I'm just a selfish piece of shit. All Lords are. That's what we're taught to be. You want it? It's yours. It doesn't belong to you? You take it. That kind of thinking can mean anything in our world. Doesn't matter. Lords are, above all, unstoppable.

Ashtyn was always mine before, and I wasn't going to let that change. She'll live here with me until I decide I no longer want her, and then if she's lucky, I'll kill her. If not, I'll pass her on to someone else. After all, a Lord can share his Lady with whoever he wants.

AN HOUR LATER, I'VE CLEANED MYSELF UP AND AM WALKING back into the office. Haidyn chose to return to his room. I'm betting it has more to do with Ashtyn in here than the naked girl chained in his room.

Ashtyn still kneels in front of the mirror; her eyes are closed, and her head moves ever so slowly as she sucks on the dick. Tears and drool run down her pretty face. I'm sure the numbing spray has worn off by now.

I'm no longer in the mood to sit at my desk and listen to her suck on a fake dick.

I'm pissy and horny as fuck. She's pissed me off once more. I expected it. Nothing about her being back here was going to be easy. That's too much to ask for. Plus, I know who I am, and when it comes to the naked brunette sucking on the dildo, I can reach fucking blackout rage level.

I walk over to her and lean down, undoing both belts that wrap around her thighs. Then I undo the latch to her collar, and it clinks when it hits the mirror, still attached to the shaft. Pulling on her ponytail, I remove her swollen lips from the dildo. She sucks in a deep breath and starts to softly cry.

"Lie down. On your stomach." I order, placing my hands on her shoulders to help her do so. I'm not untying her just yet, and with how I have her arms tied behind her back, there's no easy way for me to carry her. So she needs to lie flat facing down so her legs can stretch out and get the blood they need before we walk out of this office.

She whimpers, her body shakes, and her crying grows louder. I know my girl. She's begging to come.

I stand over her, looking down at her naked body. Admiring the way the rope wraps around her arms and wrists, then disappears between her legs. I don't miss the way she gently rocks from side to side, trying to relieve whatever frustration she feels.

Fuck, she's a sight to see—bound and crying. She doesn't even have to ask me, and I already want to give her what she wants. Well, with limits of course. I wasn't lying when I told her the only way she'll leave here is in a body bag. But it's only a half-truth because she won't actually leave Carnage. She'll be buried here in the cemetery next to me, where we'll remain together forever just like we said that day in the cathedral when she became mine. We took vows, and I took them very seriously, even if she thought they were a joke.

I'm going to take everything she has from her. I've already taken her freedom. Next will be her body. That will eventually bleed into her mind. I'm not a fan of breaking her soul so quickly. That's no fun. If I wanted to fuck a soulless corpse, I'd buy a sex doll.

Me. Mine. Yours. That'll be her thought process. Kashton and Haidyn may never love her like I do, but if I were to die tomorrow, they'd keep her here just like I was going to. They've been given instructions, and I know they will do everything in their power to see them through.

A cell phone rings, and I look over my shoulder to see Kashton stand from his desk, phone in hand. "Hey?" he answers before stepping out.

I place my attention back on Ashtyn and lean down, grabbing both of her upper arms. "Stand," I command harsher than I meant to, but I don't apologize or make her think otherwise.

Her small body shakes as she gets to her feet. She keeps her head down, and I release her arms, hooking my finger into her collar and yank her into my body. She more falls into it than anything but stays upright.

I cup her tear-streaked face and force her bloodshot eyes to meet mine. "How did you do?" I ask her.

Licking her swollen lips, she whispers brokenly, "Go-od."

I release her face and run my knuckles down her heaving chest, hooking two fingers into the rope, I pull on it. She stands on her tiptoes, gasping as the rope between her legs pulls on her pussy. "We'll see," I say and walk over to my chair and turn it to face her. "Come here," I order, unzipping my jeans.

She takes a deep breath and slowly walks over to me, whimpering with each step. Being the good girl she is, she drops to her knees in front of me.

"Open wide and stick out your tongue," I tell her.

Her swollen lips part for me, and her pink tongue darts out. I place one hand under her chin, tilting her head back while the other enters two fingers into her mouth. I push them to the back of her throat not wasting any time, and she gags, pulling away.

I sit down in the chair and sigh as if I'm disappointed. I knew it'd take more than one time. Dropping her head, she breathes heavily.

I reach out, grab her ponytail and pull her forward, making her cry out. "Open wide, sweetheart. Practice isn't over."

Sucking in a deep breath, she opens up for me, and I slide the tip of my pierced cock into her mouth. I push her head down, sliding my dick along her tongue. I reach the back of her throat, and she gags. She hasn't even taken half my dick yet. "Relax your throat," I command and push a little farther.

Her body fights the rope that binds her arms behind her back, and her watery eyes shoot open to look up at me. I smile down at her. "Feel that?" I hold her in place, and she blinks rapidly. "The way my cock fills your mouth?" I groan, pushing deeper. The farther I go, the tighter it gets.

She gags, her body involuntarily jerking.

"Breathe through your nose, Ash," I say, watching tears spill over her bottom lashes. I pull her head back just enough to keep the head inside her mouth. Then push it down again. "Tongue out," I remind her. "I want that throat open for me." I push just as far as last time and watch her pretty eyes go wide with panic. I love that other men haven't been this deep in her mouth. I used to be. But it's something we had to work on. I don't mind doing it again. Training my sweetheart was always fun. This time won't be any different.

Pulling out, I leave the tip in, and again she gasps, drool running down her chin. That's one of the things I love about face fucking, all the drool. I always loved seeing her pretty, messy face.

I lower her head and push it farther in this time, feeling her throat constrict on the tip of my cock. My head falls back, and I groan, holding it in place as the sound of her gagging fills the room. "Fuck, Ashtyn." My fingers tighten in her hair, pulling pieces from her ponytail loose. "That's it." Lowering my head, I meet her bloodshot eyes.

I pull out all the way this time, and she takes in a quick breath while I slap the side of her wet face. She cries out before I lower her face once more to my hard cock that stands at attention, begging to fuck her pretty face.

"You're such a good whore on your knees for me. Aren't you, sweetheart?"

She tries to nod but fails as she adjusts herself on her knees before me.

"I'm going to fuck this pretty face now, sweetheart," I warn her, and she closes her eyes, body trembling.

Face fucking and throat fucking are two different things. One is just a mouth; the other is a throat. And although I want to watch my entire cock disappear down her throat, she's not ready for that just yet.

I take both hands, place them on the back of her head and start fucking her face. I go too deep, making her gag once more, but it just makes my cock swell even more in her mouth. Her slurping, gasping, and gagging fills the office as I watch my cock go in and out of her drool-covered face.

"Such a pretty slut," I say, making her whimper around my dick, and I like the way it feels. So I go on. "That's a good girl. Swallow my cock, Ash. You'll be able to take all of me in no time."

Her eyes are closed, and I look up at the mirror behind her that allows me to see the show. "Fuck, you're so pretty on your knees. Drooling all over yourself. I bet that pussy of yours is just as wet as your mouth."

Her hands fist tightly together, her legs tucked underneath her, and I can only imagine how the rope feels rubbing against her pussy every time I force her head to move since I have it tied to her collar.

The sound of the office door opening has her trying to pull away, but I press her head down, my cock hitting the back of her throat, and she gags, lifting her hips off the floor. "You're doing so good, sweetheart," I encourage her. "But you're not done until I'm coming all over that pretty face."

She fights me, gagging again, and the action has her throat constricting around my cock like a vise. I groan, pushing her head down even more and feel my dick force its way farther. "Goddamn..." I push it even more. I watch amazed as the tip of her nose almost touches my jeans. She's got a little more to take, but that's good enough for today's training session.

I hold her there as I feel my balls tighten, and just when I think she can't take anymore and is about to puke, I pull out, grip my pierced dick, and come on her face just like I said I was going to.

FORTY-THREE

ASHTYN

I'm on my knees, gasping to breathe. My stomach muscles are tight, my body shaking and pussy throbbing.

He fucked my face. I tried to prove to him how good I could be. That it was like old times, but I failed. My body wasn't prepared no matter how hard I tried to tell myself it was okay. Kashton was right. I've spent more time on my back than my knees.

My head hangs forward, my eyes shut because there's cum all over my face. I feel his hand on my drool-covered chin, and he pushes my head back. "Look at me," Saint speaks.

I shake my head, and his fingers grip my sore cheeks painfully hard. "Open your fucking eyes, Ashtyn," he orders this time. His voice is deeper, rougher, and it sends a shock to my swollen cunt.

I slowly pry my cum-covered lashes open and blink rapidly. It burns.

I realize he's now out of his chair and standing in front of me. "That's a good girl." He softens his voice, and I whimper. "Stand. Let's get you dressed."

He helps me to my shaking legs, and I stare at the keyboard on his desk, unable to look around the room. I know we're not alone. I heard someone enter before he came on my face.

Wrapping the robe around my trembling shoulders, he then ties the sash tightly high on my waist. Grabbing what's left of my once tight pony, he ushers me out of the office and to the elevator. We both stay silent as we ride it up. I can feel my skin tightening on my face as his cum dries and hardens. It's itchy. I swallow, and it makes me flinch. My throat is so tender that I leave my mouth open. If I drool, I drool. Not like I haven't already.

We step off the elevator, and I see the hallway where my room is. I almost cry in relief. He's going to fuck me. My body is begging for a release. My pussy needs to be used like my face was.

He places his thumb on the outside of the door, and I realize his thumbprint unlocks the door. It pops open, and he pulls me inside.

We pass the bed and go straight to the bathroom. He turns me to face the mirror, and I try to pull away, but he yanks my head back. His free hand undoes the sash, so the robe falls to the floor. "Saint—"

He shoves me forward, my hips hitting the edge of the counter, and it bends me at the waist. I cry out as it pulls the rope and the collar.

"Look at yourself, sweetheart," he says much more gently than his hands are being. He pushes the side of my face, smashing my cheek into the cold mirror. "Go ahead. Look at my cum all over that pretty face of yours."

My face slides against the cool glass, and I can't hold in the tears that stream from my eyes like waterfalls, smearing the dried cum. At least they've washed out my eyes. They still burn, though. He pulls me back and forces me to look at myself in the mirror. My eyes are bloodshot like I spent all weekend drinking and getting high.

His meet mine in the mirror as he stands behind me, holding me in place. "I want you to shower and wash up. Once done, I'll have Jessie bring you some food."

I hate that my stomach drops. He's not going to fuck me. It's about him.

He smirks, noticing the look on my face. He yanks me to stand, spins me around, and grabs my chin. Shoving my back into a wall, he smashes my tied arms in the process. His body presses into mine as he speaks. "This should be a given, but I'm going to tell you anyway. You do not touch yourself in any way. Do you understand?'

He can't expect me not to give my body what it wants. He never had a problem with watching me get myself off before. "Saint—"

"It's a yes or no answer, Ash." He interrupts me before I even get the chance to beg him.

"Yes," I whisper, licking my swollen lips and tasting his dried cum. It makes me gag, and he chuckles.

"If I find out you've done so, you'll be punished, sweetheart."

This is a trick. He knows I love punishments. "How?" I can't help but ask.

He smirks. "You will be placed in restraints at all times when out of my sight."

My throbbing clit reminds me that we like being tied up. Case in point: my pussy is as soaked as my drool-covered face.

His face grows serious, smirk fading away as his eyes harden on mine. "If you make me punish you, Ashtyn, I will make sure you don't enjoy it."

My breath hitches, and he reaches up to cup my face in his hands. He tilts my head back; the movement pulls the rope tied to my collar, and I know he does it on purpose when a moan escapes my lips after it pulls on my pussy. Lowering his lips to mine, he kisses me. I open up, needing to feel some kind of physical touch from him. It's been years since I've felt them. He always had power over me that made me a stupid bitch. This time will be no different. Like a tsunami hitting a city, it knocks me down and washes me away with nothing left.

I moan, leaning into him, wishing I could touch him. Feel him and pull him into me. His lips are soft, his kiss tender, whereas my lips are desperate. My tongue enters his mouth, and I lean forward, opening up more and wanting him to devour me.

But he lowers his hands from my face to my chin and holds my head into the wall while he pulls away. My heavy eyes open to see him glaring at me. He's panting, and I'm still trying to catch my breath. His eyes look over my face, and I hope I made him proud today. I'm going to change, do better for him. Be the woman he deserves. He wants to make me his little slut, so I'll be the most devoted, dick-crazed whore he's ever seen.

I lick my lips, silently begging him to kiss me again, but instead, he pulls me from the wall and steps behind me and begins to untie the knot that's wrapped around the ring to my collar. I feel his eyes on mine as I look up and meet his stare as he grabs the rope where it's tied at my wrists behind my back, and he slowly pulls on it.

My thighs tighten on their own, feeling the rope slide along my pussy. A moan escapes my cracked lips as the rope burns the sensitive skin between my legs. I feel frustrated when it pops free, and he finishes untying me. My arms fall to my sides like dead weights once they're free, and my eyes drop to the counter as I feel them tingle. I suddenly feel lost and cold. A shiver runs through my body.

The piece of rope is removed from around my upper arms and chest before he drops it onto the bathroom counter. Then he unclasps my collar. I've never felt so naked in all my life. His cum on my face, my body shaking, and my knees buckling while my pussy throbs with need.

He doesn't say anything, just turns and exits the bathroom. When I hear the sound of the bedroom door shutting, I fall to my already sore knees in the middle of the bathroom and cry it out.

FORTY-FOUR

ASHTYN

Saint and Kashton may have dragged me back here, but that doesn't mean I'll spend my life locked in my room. I'll go crazy. Literally. Maybe that's their plan. Let me drive myself nuts. It wouldn't be hard to do in Carnage. Look at my track record.

I wasn't even here a month last time, and I shot Saint and escaped.

I've been wandering the halls for an hour now. Not really going anywhere specific. I just needed to get out of my room. There's not even a TV in there, and listening to my own thoughts was giving me a headache. And that damn annoying clock...was driving me mad.

Coming to a stop in the hallway, I hear voices down at the end and make my way toward them.

No one is ever alone here. The place was always full of those that the Lords no longer wanted to deal with. The justice system puts criminals away in the real world but here, Carnage is where you go when death is too good for you. Carnage is a punishment for the ones who the Lords can't control. They get the taste of power and wealth. They think that they can pull a fast one over on the Lords and the

Lords prove them wrong. An overpopulated prison isn't enough. Here, you are tortured and wish for death.

Eventually, I know I'll feel the same way. I might not be a prisoner locked in a cell in the basement, but I'm also not free.

I'll die here.

Saint was right. He'll keep me alive and use me until he gets bored. Then he'll bury me in the woods with all the others. The world will never know the difference. To them, I've been dead for years.

Coming to a stop, I peek into a room and see two guys and a woman. None of whom I know. I bite my bottom lip, watching the man separate the large batch of coke out onto a coffee table while he sits on a leather couch. Both men are wearing faded blue jeans and black T-shirts, and each has a gun on their hip attached to their belts. Security of some kind, I'm sure.

"Can I have some?"

He pauses, the razor blade in the center, and he looks up at the woman. "What will you do for it?" he asks. His dark eyes lazily run over her body. She's dressed in a pair of cotton shorts and a tank top. Her dark hair is matted, and her clothes are too big. They're starving her. They do that to you here. It's harder to run and fight when you're weak. They love to see you beg for the essentials.

"Anything," she says desperately, licking her cracked lips. Her vacant eyes focus on the drugs she's craving. Another way to keep you compliant—get you addicted to drugs.

She reaches up and moves her hair to lay over one shoulder, and my breath catches when I see the 666 brand on the back of her neck. It's her! The one I watched get dragged into the room and was placed in the straitjacket and then tortured.

She changed my life that night. I've wondered more than once if Tyson and Miles showed up at my mother's to get rid of me for what I saw here at Carnage while trying to blame it on my brother and whatever he was going through. I hate that I'll never know the truth.

After that night, I had fallen for Saint more than I already was. I still wish things would have been different. I never blamed Saint, Haidyn, or Kashton for the life they were going to live one day. They hated their fathers, but they were Lords, and a Lord never questions when he's asked to serve. I actually wanted to be his and love this life with him. I would have run hell with him, no questions asked. But I was an idiotic little girl who didn't understand what lay ahead.

"Hey. I bought it. I get a piece too," the other guy whines.

"Sure. To show you our good faith, we'll let you take a hit before payment," the guy on the couch says as he finishes separating five lines. He removes his wallet, rolls up a hundred-dollar bill, and hands it to her.

She bends over and takes her hit before throwing her head back, sniffing. The muscles in her neck tighten at the motion.

"Go ahead. Have another," the guy offers with a smile.

She doesn't need to be told twice and greedily takes another.

"How's that feel?" he asks, standing from the couch.

"Good." She nods softly. "So...good." She stumbles, probably already on something else, and he gets up to help steady her.

Who knows what the fuck is actually in that. It could be laced with anything.

"Time for payment." He chuckles, grabbing her matted hair and throwing her down onto the coffee table. She moans, her back arching. The first guy walks over to a drawer and removes some rope. He brings her arms around her legs, tying them in place, practically putting her in a ball. He walks to the edge of the coffee table and wastes no time, ripping her shorts and underwear off her and starts to fuck her pussy while the other fucks her mouth that hangs off the opposite end.

A third guy I hadn't noticed before stands in the far corner jacking off. This is exactly how I remember Carnage to be when I was hiding out here. What else is there to do other than get fucked up, drink, and have sex? Absolutely nothing!

Honestly, it was the perfect place for me until it wasn't. I spent most of my time naked and tied to Saint's bed, and he used me whenever he wanted. I have a feeling history will repeat itself, and I hate how wet my pussy gets at that thought.

I shouldn't want him. He's going to hurt me. *You like pain.*

He'll kill me eventually. *What's there to live for?*

I have no one and haven't for years. I've been walking the earth pretending to be someone I'm not. It was lonely. Even when I met James and moved him in with me, it wasn't the same as it was with Saint. If I'm going to die, it might as well be death by sex at the hands of the only man I've ever loved. I guess I owe him that. I did shoot and leave him for dead. Lords always get their revenge.

The woman takes the guys cock down her throat like a pro. I'm guessing she's had plenty of practice. I can see from here the way her body gets off on them fucking her. The guy who is balls deep in her cunt laughs. "Who said you could come?" He pulls out, looking down at his cum-covered cock.

He goes to plunge into her once more when the one in the corner steps out. "I want a taste."

The guy fucking her pussy runs two fingers between her shaking legs to wet his fingers. He holds them up, and the third guy opens his mouth, but instead, he slaps him and orders, "Then get on your fucking knees."

The third guy drops to his knees and opens his mouth, begging like a baby bird needing to be fed. The man standing takes his wet cock and pushes it into the mouth of the man on his knees and starts to fuck him. "How's she taste?" He smiles down at the guy.

The man moans.

"Such a good boy." He grips a hold of his head, pounding into his mouth. His sucking fills the room in rhythm while the other continues to fuck the tied woman's mouth as well. "You take cock better than some cunts," the man jokes.

I take a step back, seeing enough. Carnage doesn't care who you are. You're treated all the same—like a piece of meat everyone gets a taste of. I was just used to belonging to Saint. I'm not sure of the rules anymore or where I fit in. And as much as I love sex, I don't want anyone but him.

Turning around, I go to run but hit a wall, squealing in surprise.

"Fuck!" A hand grips my hair and drags me into the room. "Someone likes to watch." He shoves me forward, and I fall to the floor on my hands and knees.

Silence fills the room as I stare at the floor, my hair shielding my face while trying to calm my breathing.

"Someone call Saint," one orders.

"Why?" the guy who shoved me into the room asks, and I hear him unclasping his belt. I begin to tremble. "She wants a show? Let's give her one, but she can be the main event."

"No," one of them snaps. "You know the rules."

I want to ask what the rules are, but instead, I keep my mouth shut.

The door opens, and one of them steps out. I stay on my hands and knees, eyes on the floor as if I'm paralyzed as they slowly filter out of the room, one by one, until I'm the only one in here. Slowly, I get to my shaky legs and turn to face the door as it opens. Saint and Kashton enter together.

"Heard you've been sneaking around and watching women get fucked." Kashton speaks first.

I'm unable to speak, my mouth dry and tongue heavy.

"What am I going to do with you?" Saint asks, his eyes falling to my heaving chest. I'm still trying to catch my breath.

"A few things come to mind," Kash jokes, walking to the minibar in the corner. It was where the guy was watching the others. Kashton lights up a joint and brings it to his lips. His eyes are on mine.

"So curious," Saint adds. "Like a cat."

"Fucking hate cats." Kash growls. "They're disobedient and always fucking shit up. Now dogs." He nods to himself. "Dogs are where it's at. They're loyal and easy to train."

"You'd make a good pet," Saint says, running his free hand down my face. And all I can think about is what he did to me earlier this morning in his office. My throat still isn't a hundred percent.

"Well then you better put a collar and leash on her. Pets are known to be taken around here." Kash laughs at some inside joke I'm unaware of.

"That's a great idea." Saint smiles. He grabs my hair and yanks me to my feet.

I grind my teeth at the sting, but my thighs clench. Fuck, I'm so dead. He forces me to stand on tiptoes, and my eyes lift to meet his hard stare. "I liked the one you wore earlier, but I think you need something a little...different." He refers to the collar I wore while deep-throat training. I used to wear a collar for him, so if he's trying to scare me, it's not working. "Something more permanent."

"You should ask Tyson where he got his." Kashton laughs, and I stiffen at the sound of the name.

I haven't seen Tyson Crawford since the night he killed my mother. He was going to kill me, but he called Saint to come and get me. I know it wasn't because of me. Lords don't give a fuck about women. He did it because he didn't want Saint, Haidyn, and Kashton after him. I was Saint's chosen at that time. And killing another Lord's chosen is something you don't want to do unless you have a death wish.

The corners of Saint's lips twitch when he notices my unease at the mention of his name. "I think that's a great idea."

SAINT

She's trembling although her small body is pressed into mine. Ashtyn isn't stupid. She knows I'm her biggest threat here, but she also knows I won't allow anyone else to touch her.

I saw the smug look on her face when she was in the elevator, and Emerson got in her face, threatening her. She may be a whore, but she's my little whore. Usually, I'm the type of guy to do whatever it takes to prove a point, but I'm not going to let her get herself in a sticky situation just to prove her wrong.

She can call this a win.

I run my tatted knuckles down the side of her cheek, and her eyes remain on mine. "What are you doing out of your room?" I question.

She takes a step back from me. I allow it and drop my hands to my sides. "I didn't know that I couldn't leave my room," she answers softly, her eyes dropping to the floor.

Kashton snorts and takes another hit.

"Guess I'll have to shackle you to the bed from now on after your training sessions," I offer.

She licks her lips, her arms coming up to wrap around herself, but I can see her thighs clench. My sweetheart has been denied to orgasm. I'm just waiting for her to get herself off so I can punish her.

"I think that's a great idea." Her eyes lift to meet mine, and I step forward, pushing her hair back from her face. "You always looked so pretty when you were desperate."

"Please," she whispers.

"That's a good start." I smile at her as her wide eyes go to Kashton. He just snorts, hitting his joint. No one here at Carnage will save her. There is no one but me. "Go to your room," I order, and she swallows nervously.

Bowing her head, she rushes out of the room and slams the door shut on her way out. Silence fills the room, but I can feel Kash's eyes on me. "Don't," I mumble.

He raises his hands and shakes his head but doesn't speak.

FORTY-FIVE

SAINT

Haidyn, Kashton, and I pull up into the parking lot and get off our bikes. I needed to ride tonight. Clear my mind.

The time that I spent without Ashtyn was excruciating. Knowing she was out in the world without me drove me fucking crazy. But now that she's back, it's still got me on edge. For many reasons.

I wanted to tie her to the bed and fucking leave her there all night with my cum dripping out of her freshly fucked ass, but I didn't. I pride myself on my patience, so I decided to do the exact opposite of what I told her I'd do. Let her wonder what the fuck I'm up to.

"This place is packed," Kashton states the obvious, bringing me out of my thoughts as he looks over the parking lot littered with cars.

We park our bikes right up to the back private entrance and walk inside.

Blackout was closed for several months due to the rebuild. But I think it's safe to say it's better than ever. We make our way to the elevator and up to the second floor where the office is. We don't even knock, just walk right on in, and Tyson looks up from his seat behind his desk.

"Brothers." He comes around his desk and gives us each a man hug-shake. "Glad you all could make it out tonight."

If I had stayed at Carnage, I'd be balls deep in Ashtyn's mouth right now. I had to get out and get some fresh air. She's everywhere there. I figured she would be, but I have to constantly fight the battle of choking her out and fucking her. It's the hardest love-hate relationship I've ever had with anyone in my life.

"How are things?" Kashton asks him.

"Good," he answers. "How about you guys?"

Haidyn just snorts. He's in a mood like always. The guy just wants to fuck and kill. I get it. I feel like my hands have been tied ever since that bitch showed up in my hospital room and took any option I had to find Ashtyn away from me.

I was a fucking wildfire ready to destroy everything that came near me, knowing I was locked there and she was out in the world without me. I needed her in a way that I couldn't even explain. It was more of a you belong to me than anything else.

Now that I have her again? I'm not sure what to do. My mind is a fucking mess, my cock constantly hard. She wandered out of her room today, but it didn't take long for her to go running back. The place isn't the same. She thought it was bad before, but it's way worse now. She only has herself to thank for that. After we took over, we changed everything.

The door opens, getting my attention, and I turn around to see two other Lords enter the room. Sin and Ryat. We didn't know them while attending Barrington because they're younger than us. But we've become close to them over the past few months. They've spent quite a bit of their time up at Carnage lately. Sin more so than Ryat but for different reasons.

We've got something that Sin wants, and well, Ryat is close with Tyson—we have something he wants so he's always there as well. It's a cycle, really. Lords always scratch another Lord's back. That is, until one wants you dead.

If you've got something I want, I'm more than willing to give you something in return. And I would have paid anything to get my wife back.

"What are you guys doing out tonight?" Ryat asks, plopping down on the couch.

"Came out to see the new place," Kashton answers. "What about you two?"

"The wives are having a girls' night at Tyson and Lake's, so we thought we'd get out for a bit." Sin is the one who responds, typing away on his cell.

Tyson gets my attention as he looks up at me. "I called in a favor."

I arch a brow. The Lords owe him a lot for what they put him through. "What kind of favor?"

Pulling out his top desk drawer, he pulls out a manila envelope. "It's for you."

Picking it up, I open the envelope and see that it's a report of some kind. I quickly scan it over and slam it down once I've seen enough.

"What is it?" Kashton asks, walking over to me.

I don't answer, so he picks it up and reads over it. "Wait." He frowns. "Are you saying that Luke is the one who called the hit on Adam?" he asks, looking up at Tyson for verification.

"Seems so." He nods, falling into his seat. "Makes sense." Tyson goes on. "He was the one working with Adam and Ashtyn's mother."

"Brenda was the only one killed that night..." Kashton trails off. "The only person who could have ratted him out was dead. He thought he was safe. Adam kept saying that he was being set up. Who else to do it other than your mother's bastard child?"

"Maybe he thought Adam knew about him?" Sin offers.

He and Ryat don't know everything about the Spade brothers, but they've had a pretty good crash course over the past few months. Especially Sin. We almost killed him. I'm sure he knows it was nothing personal. As a Lord, we all do what needs to be done. But I was setting him up. He's just lucky it worked out as I wanted it to.

Kashton runs a hand down his face. "I just don't see Adam running. Even if he did, where the fuck is he now?"

Adam did nothing wrong. He could walk into Carnage now, and his place would be ready for him.

"Does Ashtyn know about Luke?" Tyson asks.

I shake my head. "Doubtful. She never mentioned him back then. And we didn't find out they were even related until recently."

"Adam never mentioned it either. I'd say it was another secret that Brenda kept from everyone. If they can't connect them, then they can't both be blamed for raping and killing women," Kashton adds.

Luke put Tyson through hell. And when Tyson was finally able to get ahold of him, he asked if he could keep him at Carnage. I was more than willing to do so. Considering if I knew where he was, then I knew where he wasn't. My biggest fear when all of this came to light a few months ago, was that Luke had taken Ashtyn and sold her into sex trafficking. That was his MO. If he didn't rape and ditch their bodies, he sold them for money. He had done it back when we attended Barrington but then the cops got onto him and after Brenda was killed, it stopped. For a little bit.

"I think Adam knew something was going on," I say. "Maybe not specifically with Luke. But he knew his mother was involved in something."

"Are you talking about the detective who came to the house of Lords to see us?" Kashton asks.

"What about it?" Tyson sits up straighter in his chair.

"Lincoln called us to the house of Lords." Kashton starts.

My eyes are on Sin, and I notice the way his hand tightens on his phone at the mention of Lincoln.

"When we met with this man. He wasn't related to the Lords at all but he had a picture of a girl found dead, throat slashed and wrapped in barbed wire. It was his sister, and he was trying to find out who killed her."

"Why did he contact you guys?" Ryat questions.

"Because all he had to go off was a picture of his sister last seen at the mall. And Brenda was in the picture with her."

The door opens, and four guys enter who work for Tyson. I would call them his bitches because they do all his dirty work, but I actually like them.

"Hey, man." Ryat stands and shakes Finn's hand, while Sin stands and does the one arm handshake hug with Colton. The other two—Alex and Jenks plop down on the couch.

I turn to face Jenks. "I need a favor."

He smirks. "Name it."

Reaching into my pocket, I pull out a cell phone. "Can you get me a detailed list of all contacts that are in this phone?" I ask.

He nods, taking it from me. "Yeah. What all are you wanting?"

"Addresses, legal names, work information. Whatever you can find."

"On each contact?" He makes sure he understands.

"Yep. There aren't many." I want to know every person she ever spoke to. Who the phone was under, where all she lived. What she ever googled. It's amazing how much a phone can store that you never even think about. Or are even aware of.

"Consider it done."

WE STAND INSIDE THE CLUB BY THE MAIN BAR ON THE FIRST level. The lights flash, and the music blares. I'm not much of a club person. I honestly don't know how Tyson does it day in and day out. I need silence. Time to think to myself. It's too hard to do with all of this noise.

Someone bumps my elbow, and I look up to see Kash standing next to me. He gestures to Haidyn, who focuses all his attention on a woman on the dance floor. You can't miss her. She looks out of place compared to the rest of the people dancing. She also looks familiar.

All the other women are dressed in dresses and high heels, but she's wearing a pair of jean shorts that are low on her hips and cut high up on her legs. She has a white T-shirt tied into a knot right underneath her large breasts. Her dark hair is up in a messy bun, and she's dancing by herself.

Haidyn sees her when she comes into Carnage.

Kashton laughs, watching Haidyn take a sip of his drink, eyes glued to her ass as she moves it back and forth to the beat.

"You can't be serious, man. She's what? Maybe five-foot-two and a hundred pounds. You're six-seven and like two fifty. You'd destroy her," he jokes. "Not to mention, I'm pretty sure she's a virgin. You'd scare that poor girl to death."

"Isn't that the best part? Seeing how much they can take before they break?" Haidyn speaks before throwing back what's left of his drink.

We don't answer him. He wasn't expecting one. Kashton just shakes his head, and I pull my phone from my pocket to check the time. Almost one in the morning. I see I have a message from Jessie and open it up.

> Your package has arrived. Also, she took
> the meds, sir.

With a smile, I lock my cell and place it back in my pocket. Of course, she did. On top of being sore, I've got her scared. She's questioning my motives. I never make fake threats that I don't follow through with, but this is part of my plan. I wanted her to explore Carnage and see what it has to offer her.

How do you make someone feel safe with you? You put them in an environment that they fear. One that you can control. You become their hero, their shelter. You show them just how cruel the world can be without you. And then you step in and save them. All the while, you're their worst nightmare.

FORTY-SIX

SAINT

Once we return to Carnage, I find myself going down the hallway to enter her room. She's asleep in bed, face down, arms spread out wide, hair still a little damp from a shower earlier.

Last time she lived here, we shared a room in the east wing. That was when our fathers occupied the birdcage. I never went a day without her, let alone slept alone. It was something that I had dreamed of. But men like me don't get to live out their dreams. Not for long anyway.

Walking over to her bed, I sit down next to her. She doesn't move as I lower the covers to her ass so I can see she's naked.

I should tie her down and fuck what's mine just like I did last night. But I won't. I want her to know it's me. I want her to be conscious and aware that she's my dirty whore who I'm going to use.

I get a look at the package I ordered earlier that Jessie left for me. Walking over to it, I open the box and smile. It's perfect. Once I put it on her, I kiss the side of her cheek. "Sleep tight, sweetheart. Tomorrow is a new day for your training." With that, I get up and leave her room to go to mine. We both need our rest.

. . .

ASHTYN

I WOKE UP THIS MORNING DISAPPOINTED BUT ALSO SURPRISED. My body wasn't sore so that meant that Saint didn't fuck me last night while I slept. But he did come and see me at some point because I woke up with a gift wrapped around my neck.

The thin black leather collar has a black silk bow in the center with a bell. He's made me a cat. It's so he can hear me when I'm out walking around. He thinks it's going to stop me, keep me locked in my room.

Fuck that!

If he wants me confined to my room, then he should shackle me to that bed. The collar also has a small lock on the back so I can't take it off.

I like it. Just another way for him to claim me.

Jessie brought me some breakfast, which I refused to eat. I wasn't hungry. My mind's a mess, my body on fire. He's toying with me. What's the point of making me his pet if he won't play with me? I was always needy. That hasn't changed. My pussy is wet and begging to be touched.

Have you ever craved something so much that you'll do anything for it? That's where I'm at. I've paced my room, sat on the bed, stood on the balcony. I've even called out Saint's name a few times, hoping he'd hear me on the cameras that I know are in here even if I can't see them. Nothing. I'm being ignored. It's him proving his point that I'm to be used, not rewarded.

I can't take it much longer.

I've dressed in a pair of yoga pants and a white crop-top sans bra. Those are some things I know I won't need. I never used to wear one, so I'm not sure why he'd let me now.

Walking over to the bedroom door, I twist the knob, half

expecting it to be locked, but to my surprise, it opens. Maybe I'm not a prisoner after all.

The thought of staying in my room crosses my mind, especially after the way that man hit me, but I square my shoulders and refuse to let him stop me. Besides, a part of me wants to get Saint's attention. He used to love coming to my rescue. We'd go out to a club or bar, and I'd start a fight with some random man and then Saint would come in, beat the fuck out of him, and save the day.

We'd end up fucking in the back seat of the car while one of the others drove us all back to the house of Lords. I love a man willing to fight for what is his.

Entering the hallway, I see three other doors. The one to my left has to be Haidyn's. That's the one he popped out of the other day. The one directly to the right of it is propped open.

Placing my hand on it, I gently push it open to see it matches the one I'm in size-wise. Large open space, double doors that lead out onto a balcony. A four-post bed sits in the center with deep-purple bedding and matching pillows. The walls are matte black with intricate gloss black designs.

I walk over to the bed when something catches my attention. It's a metal collar and a chain for a leash. A large and bulky lock sits beside them. Kind of like what I wear but bigger, heavier, sturdier. I imagine the bruises it'll leave and lack of movement it'll provide once in place.

"Interested?"

I jump at the voice behind me and spin around to see Kashton leaning against the doorframe, arms crossed over his chest.

"In being someone's pet? No thanks," I lie, giving a rough laugh to avoid how nervous I am that he just caught me in his room.

He arches a brow, his eyes dropping to my bell collar. Saint might as well write *Saint's bitch* across my forehead. Kashton pushes off the doorframe and steps into his room, and I step back.

"Imagine..." He gestures to the items on his bed. "You lie down after a long day at work. You're exhausted. When you wake up the next day, you're naked, wearing a collar with a chain connected to it and anchored to a wall."

"Every woman's dream." I roll my eyes even though my pussy clenches at the thought. I've wished to wake up bound and gagged, left to wait for Saint to come and fuck me.

"Isn't it, though?" He calls my bluff. "Diamonds and pearls are offered in a world where if a man doesn't give them, he's broke or not interested. But..." He reaches next to me and picks up the collar in one hand and the leash in the other. The chain clanks as it drops to the floor at his feet. "This shows a committed man. He feeds her, bathes her, fucks her." His eyes meet mine. "He gives her everything she needs to survive and then some."

"She's a slave," I argue, but it's breathless.

The corner of his lips twitch. "She's his to do as he pleases. She's taken care of."

"Locked in a basement."

He shrugs. "If she wants to scream her lungs out until she's got no voice left in order to feel better about her situation, she's more than welcome to do so."

I snort. "Yeah, because no one can hear her."

He sets down the collar and leash, the weight of them making the bed dip, then he steps into me, pinning me between the foot of the bed and him. "Women want to be desired, cherished, owned." His eyes drop to my lips, and I suck in a shaky breath before they return to mine. "I'd be more than glad to strip her naked, walk her around the block, and show her off to the world."

"Kashton..." His name trembles on my lips. He's so close if I puckered them, he'd kiss me.

He reaches up, cupping my face and my pulse races. "Women love a man who is proud to call her his."

"You're degrading her." I manage to get out.

"You of all women know that some are into that." He turns to leave, but I stop him.

"How many women do you have chained in the basement,

Kash?"

He turns and smirks at me. "None right now. But one day there will be one. I'm a patient man."

The way he says it tells me he already knows exactly who it will be. He turns and exits his room.

I LEFT KASHTON'S ROOM AND WENT BACK TO MINE. I PACED FOR another two hours, waiting for Saint to barge into my room and get onto me for wandering around in Kashton's. But I was still ignored.

So I left my prison again to explore some more. This time, I go to the elevator. I used to spend a lot of time roaming the halls of Carnage, but no one was allowed up here on this floor. I'm not sure if these rooms have always been here or if this is something the guys did after they took over.

Stepping inside the elevator, I take it down to the basement. I know that no matter where Saint is, he's watching me on the cameras. Maybe he'll show up and drag me back to my room, tie me down, and fuck me.

A girl can hope.

Stepping off the elevator, I shiver. It was always so cold down here—something I never got used to. A song filters down the long and cold hallway. "Hallelujah" by No Resolve.

It makes the hairs on my neck rise. It's such an odd song to be played down here. I find myself walking toward it with my arms out wide, running my fingertips along the concrete walls.

I come up to pieces of plastic strip door curtains that hang in the doorway. You know the kind I'm talking about? They're in every scary movie usually covered in blood. I push them out of my way and step through them. The music has grown louder, but I realize the song has started over. Whoever it is has it on repeat.

I slowly come to a stop outside of an open door, finding the source. Taking in a shaky breath, I look inside. A man has his back to me, but I'd recognize him no matter what. Haidyn stands in the center of a room, his right hand is down by his side, holding a knife as blood drips from it onto his black combat boots. A line of it flows down into the drain next to him.

A man hangs from the ceiling. His arms are tied above his head with chains, and he's naked. He softly rocks back and forth because his toes cannot touch the floor. He's bleeding from his chest. It appears his brand has been removed. Pieces of skin cover the metal table to the left.

It looks like Haidyn has used the man's body as target practice. Different sizes of knives are sticking out of the man's legs, arms, and stomach. Blood runs down his sweaty body and onto the floor as well.

My hand comes up to my mouth and nose to try to lessen the smell of blood, sweat, and piss. A knot forms in my throat. I almost forgot how sick this place is. It's made of nightmares.

The man lifts his head, a strangled moan escaping his busted lips. His dead eyes meet mine when he speaks. "He-lp...me."

I take a step back just as Haidyn turns to see me. I freeze, my body stiffening.

Haidyn has always had the power to tear a man's head off with his bare hands. I once watched him gut a guy without blinking. So the fact he's smiling at me right now with a bloody knife in his hand scares the shit out of me.

Without even looking back, he stabs the knife into the man's stomach as he hangs from the ceiling. His head falls back, and he begins to sob. His voice is hoarse. There's no telling how long Haidyn has had him down here.

Haidyn walks over to me, and I tremble as he reaches for me. "Haidyn—" He yanks me forward and wraps his arm around my neck from behind. I start kicking and screaming over the music as he lowers his lips to my ear.

"Shh, calm down, baby girl. I'm not going to hurt you," he says softly.

Tears spill over my bottom lashes as my fingers dig into his bloody forearm. My throat is still sore from Saint yesterday, then the added pressure of his muscles makes it even worse. "Haidyn, please—"

"Watch him." He interrupts me. "Watch him suffer, Ash. Like the piece of shit he is."

The guy's head hangs forward, and snot and drool fall from his face. He's sobbing uncontrollably, and every breath he takes makes the knives move.

"Do you want him to suffer, baby girl?" Haidyn asks.

It's a trick question. Suffering is what Carnage was built on, what the Spade brothers do. The man coughs up blood, and it lands on me, making me flinch. "No," I say roughly.

"Go ahead." Haidyn removes the arm around my neck, gently placing my feet on the floor and instead grabs the back of mine. His fingers pinch into my sensitive skin. "Go ahead, Ash." He repeats. "Help him out. Show him the mercy that you think he deserves."

"Pl...ease," the man cries, his voice barely audible over the song that plays on repeat. It's almost as terrifying as the bleeding man hanging naked before me. "Help me."

I sniff, my nose running. But I reach out with a shaky hand and wrap my fingers around the bloody handle. When I yank it out, he screams. I pull another one out of his side, and he starts to thrash around. Blood gushes from both wounds, and his body begins to spasm, making the chains rattle. Blood pours from his mouth and down his naked torso before his head falls back and his body goes limp.

He's dead.

I release the last knife as if it just burned me, and it clanks to the floor. I'm grabbed from behind, and I scream out in surprise. My back is slammed into a wall. So hard that the air is knocked out of me, and my watery eyes look up to meet Haidyn's hard ones. His large hand wraps around my throat and he gives it a firm squeeze, crushing my collar into my skin as he holds me captive to the cold wall.

"If you don't want to get hurt, I suggest you stay in your room, Ash. There are no cameras down here. Saint can't save you if he can't see who is hurting you." His words aren't menace in any way. They're actually spoken softly.

I always loved Haidyn. Something about him terrified yet excited me at the same time. I wonder if he still keeps my secret.

Four Years Ago

I run out of her office, not caring that my mom's therapist is calling out to me. I can't hear anymore. So many lies. So much betrayal. And now a baby?

Sucking in breath after breath, I round a corner and run into someone. I scream as hands grab at me and lift me off my feet. I kick and fight, but they drag me into a room. It's one of the fathers. She called them to come get me and take me downstairs. They're going to kill my baby, force me to have a hysterectomy, and then throw me in a cell.

Saint won't protect me. Not after what he finds out. A hand slaps over my mouth, muffling my screams, and I buck wildly since my nose is so stuffed up I can't breathe through it.

"Shh, Ashtyn, calm down," a familiar voice growls.

My body instantly goes limp, and he releases my mouth. I sob as he sits me in a chair and kneels in front of me. "What the fuck is going on?" He places his hands on my shaking thighs and rubs them over my jeans.

"I'm...pregnant," I cry, knowing I can trust him.

"Shit." He sighs, running his hand through his hair. "Does Saint know?"

I shake my head, tears spilling from my eyes, and I run my hand under my runny nose.

"I'll call him." He stands and removes his cell from his pocket, and I slap it out of his hand. "Ash—"

"No, You can't," I cry out, and he grabs my trembling shoulders.

"It's okay," he assures me softly.

He's so wrong. "No." I shake my head quickly. "He cheated."

His brows pull together. "What? No. He'd never—"

"He cheated." I gasp, trying to breathe, but my throat is closing. "You...can't."

"Ashtyn,"

"Tell him." I grip his T-shirt and bury my face into it. He wraps his arms around me, and I begin to sob, repeating that he cheated, hoping he'll understand what I mean because I can't form a fucking sentence right now.

"Ashtyn...I can't keep this from him." Haidyn rubs my back.

I pull away and wrap my arms around myself, bowing my head. "If you do this, it'll get him in trouble." I lift my watery eyes to his, hoping I can get through to him.

He frowns. "Saint loves you, Ashtyn. He would do anything..."

"I know." Sniff. "That's the problem."

His eyes search mine before he lets out a long breath and runs a hand down his face. "What do you want me to do?"

"I need a doctor." I have to know. What if Laura somehow made the test have a positive result? I don't put that past her to try and scare me. I need more tests done. Blood work? Ultrasound? Something that can confirm it other than her.

"I'll call Devin..."

"No." I shake my head. "Someone else. Someone...not here." Devin is devoted to the Spade brothers, not me. I need someone on my side.

"Gavin." He nods to himself, pulling out his cell. "I'll call Gavin."

I rock back and forth as he steps away, giving me his back, and I close my eyes, trying to stop the tears. I'm shaking, having a hard time catching my breath.

"He can see you now," he says, getting my attention.

Licking my wet lips, I taste my tears and whisper, "How?"

"I'll take you. No one will even know we left. But Ashtyn..." He pins me with a stare. "Who all knows about this?"

I give him a quick rundown of what was supposed to have been my therapy session, and he curses. "We'll have to come up with a story. When we get back, you'll have to go back and see her. You need to confide in her. Let her think she's helping you, okay?"

I nod, hating that thought but knowing he's not wrong.

"I mean it, baby girl." He kneels back down in front of me, taking my shaking hands in his. "I'm going to help you, but it won't be easy."

Things changed after I saw Gavin. I knew right then and there when I saw the baby on the monitor that I had to stop thinking about me and Saint. But like everything else in my life, it just wasn't meant to be.

My lips tremble as I look up at Haidyn. I can only imagine what he's going through after that day as well. I've wanted to say it for a long time, but that would have required me to return, which I never planned on doing. "I'm sorry...."

"Don't fucking apologize!" he yells in my face, making me whimper. Closing my eyes, I try to turn my head away from him, but he's got a death grip on me. "Look at me," he commands.

I pry my watery eyes open and meet his and take in a shaky breath. My hands dig into his bloody T-shirt, trying to push him away, but he's got his large body pressed into mine.

"Accept your punishment, Ashtyn. We all had to." He steps back, yanks me from the wall, and shoves me toward the door. "Get the fuck out of here before I make you skin what's left of him."

I don't have to be told twice. I run out of the room, through the plastic doorway as "NUMB" by Ryan Oakes blares from the room I just vacated.

I look over my shoulder, making sure he's not chasing me down, my hair slapping me in the face. I'm gasping for breath, my heart in my throat. I look back to see where I'm going just in time to see I need to turn a corner.

I run toward the opposite end of the hall, needing to get the fuck out of here and back to my room. Coming up to the elevator, I pound on the button and rush in when the door opens. I continue to hit the button on the inside for the floor that my room is on.

FORTY-SEVEN

SAINT

I'm sitting in my office watching Ashtyn on my computer. I do it all the time. It's consuming to the point I want to punch myself in the fucking face. She scared herself today. I'm not surprised. She can't sit still. I knew she wouldn't stay confined to her room unless I tied her to her bed and locked her door from the outside.

My cell rings, and I look down to see a familiar number. "Hello?" I answer.

"Hey, man. I have an assignment," the Lord says in greeting.

I sit back in my seat. "Okay. How can I help?" I'm assuming he called me for a reason.

"It's to deliver a Lord to you."

"Are you on your way now?" I ask, already getting to my feet.

"No. That's the thing. I have to go get him first."

I smile. "Need help?" It's been a long time since I've gone hunting. Nowadays, they're dropped off at our front doors. Honestly, there's no rush anymore. It's the same old shit. Now that Ashtyn's back, I need more. I'm bored. I need blood and something bigger than her to keep my mind busy.

He chuckles. "Sure."

"How far out is he?"

"His last known location he was held up in a run-down motel two hours out of town."

I'm already headed to the office door to leave. "Meet me here at Carnage. I'll drive."

THIRTY MINUTES LATER, I'M STANDING OUTSIDE OF CARNAGE IN the circle drive when I see the headlights of the W Motors Lykan Hypersport coming down the drive. It pulls right up front, and the engine shuts off. The Lord gets out and smirks at me, leaning up against the car I pulled from the garage.

"A hearse, really?" Ryat smirks, removing a duffel bag.

I push off the front. "It has the room we need."

Locking his car, he climbs into the passenger seat and looks at the back. "Jesus. Are we dropping off a dead body on the way?"

I start it up, smirking. My eyes go to the casket that is in the back. "No. It's to transport him back."

He laughs, and his phone rings. Pulling it out of his front pocket, he answers it while I drive away from Carnage. I inhale the fresh air, knowing that I can breathe better without Ashtyn so close. My skin already tingles with what I'm about to go do.

"Hello, little one," he answers softly. "Yeah...I'll be a while." Pause. "Have fun with Lake. Call Tyson or Sin if you need anything. I won't be able to answer once I get there." He nods to himself. "I spoke to Sin a minute ago, and they were about to head that way once Elli was ready." Another pause. "Once I'm done, I'll head over to Tyson's." He chuckles. "Yes, I'll wake you up. I love you." He hangs up and pockets his cell once more.

Silence fills the car, and when I realize he's not going to talk, I reach over and turn on the radio, and Five Finger Death Punch "Welcome To The Circus" fills the speakers of the hearse. I can't take a two-hour drive in silence. I need to drown out my thoughts and clear my head.

FORTY-EIGHT

SAINT

Ryat was pretty spot-on when he said the guy was two hours away. The GPS brought us to a run-down piece-of-shit motel out in the middle of nowhere. It's five miles off the main road.

Shutting off the vehicle, we get out and make our way to the tiny office. Walking inside, we find a young kid standing behind the desk. He looks from me to Ryat and then back at me.

"We're looking for someone," Ryat speaks first, pulling out his cell. He holds it up to show the picture he has of the man we're here to collect. "Is he here?"

The kid smirks. "Who are you two? The police?" He then laughs. We don't.

"Yes or no?" I go on. We don't have time for this. If he's not here, then that means we may be spending the rest of our night looking for him. I know how assignments work. You're given an order and a time-frame for completion. I'm not going to hold Ryat up from making sure he gets his done.

The kid's face grows serious, and he straightens his shoulders.

My eyes slide to Ryat's, and he nods. *The kid is going to be an issue.* "I'm not allowed to give that information out."

Ryat walks over to the single window that looks out on the parking lot. He pulls back the dingy curtains that look like they've been up since the place opened. They're discolored from use and cigarette smoke. "There are only two cars in the parking lot. Is one of them yours?" Ryat asks.

"My girlfriend dropped me off," he answers nervously, confused by the question.

Ryat lets the curtains close and comes back to me. "How many rooms are currently occupied?" he asks the kid.

"Look, man." He places his arms out. "I need to see some kind of identification...or a badge—"

Ryat reaches across the desk, grips his shirt, and pulls him over it. Then slams his back into the front of it. "Every question you choose to avoid, I'm going to cut a fucking finger off starting now," he growls, having no patience. "How many rooms are currently occupied?"

"One," he shrieks. "Only one. A man came in...the one in the picture. With a woman..."

"Let's go." Ryat pulls the kid toward the door, and I hold it open for them as he drags him outside. "Which room?" Ryat barks, shoving the kid forward, and he trips, falling onto his knees in the gravel parking lot.

"Five," he rushes out, pointing at it. "They're in room five."

Ryat looks at me, and I nod. Walking over to the hearse, I open the back, grab a few things that I had packed, and walk toward the front door of number five. I place what I wanted on the ground in front of it, and the kid gets to his feet and starts to run away.

"No, you don't. You watch. From your knees." Ryat kicks the back of his legs, and the kid falls to the gravel parking lot once more.

I go around the back and pour the gasoline in front of each back door, leaving a trail from room to room so there are no gaps. Then I take the boxes of matches and light several of them, tossing them into the gasoline.

Making my way back to the front, I cross my arms over my chest, spread my legs, and wait. The smell of fire grows stronger, and the kid on his knees sniffs the air.

"What is that? Is the building on fire?" he rushes out.

"Not yet," I answer.

"Fuck," he whimpers. Leaning forward, he grips his sandy blond hair with his hands. "My dad is going to kill me."

Crackling wood fills the air, and I smile when I hear screams from inside the motel. We could have stormed in and dragged him out, but this is better. More exciting.

The door to number five is ripped open, and a woman rushes out first. Her shrill scream follows as she steps into the center of the bear trap I planted. It was meant for him, but anything to slow them down is a win in my book.

He runs out after her, tripping over her body that thrashes around on the ground while she tries to open the bear trap—as if they work that way.

"Hello, Timothy," Ryat speaks, stepping forward.

The guy's head snaps up, and wide eyes meet Ryat's before they go to mine. "What the fuck?" He shuffles back toward the building.

"Tim?" The woman sobs. "Help me..."

Timothy gets to his feet and goes to run back into the motel, trying to run from us but realizes the fire is growing bigger by the second, consuming the old wooden building. I can feel the heat taking over the night.

"Fuck," he hisses.

"Two ways, Timothy," Ryat announces. "One, you get in the car willingly. Two, I make you."

He looks at Ryat and then turns to run. Ryat sighs, pulls out his gun from the back waistband of his jeans, and fires, making the woman cry out as Timothy falls to his face by the hearse. He hit him in the back of the leg. Nothing life-threatening. Just to slow him down.

I walk over and open the back of the hearse, pulling out the casket on the rollers. Ryat grabs Timothy's shirt and drags him to where I am.

He's screaming for the bitch he was fucking that is still stuck in the bear trap as Ryat picks him up. I open the top of the casket and help throw him inside. "Lie down. I don't want to kill you too soon," I inform him as I start to close it.

"Nice." Ryat nods, admiring the inside. "Did you make that?"

"Haidyn did," I say, looking over the spikes he placed on the inside of the lid. So when it's closed, it keeps whoever is on the inside lying flat. He said he didn't want them lying directly on it because it'd impale them and they'd bleed out too soon.

Shutting the lid, I take the latch and lock the man inside. Then we shove it forward and shut the back door.

"What do you want to do with them?" I nod to the woman crawling away from the burning building and the man kneeling in front of it while he cries, thinking of all the ways his father will kill him.

I go over to her and undo the bear trap. She pulls her leg to her chest while lying on her back, sobbing.

Ryat goes to the Porsche parked on the side, opens the door, and digs around in it. Finding the set of keys, he tosses them to the kid. "Take her to the hospital. And enjoy the new car. Timothy won't need it where he's going."

ASHTYN

THE FOLLOWING MORNING, I GET OUT OF THE SHOWER TO SEE A note on the counter between the two sinks right in front of where Saint pressed my face into the bathroom mirror. You can still see the print of tears and cum on it. Picking up the piece of paper, I read.

Do your makeup. Red lipstick, black mascara, and eyeliner to match. Make yourself look pretty for me.

Rushing over to the bathroom door, I yank it open. "Hello?" I ask, searching the bedroom, but I'm alone. No one else is in here. But I catch sight of the large mirror from their office. The same one I kneeled in front of and fucked a dildo. It's sitting up against the wall next to the open double doors to the balcony. Next to the table and high-back chairs.

Swallowing, I go back to the bathroom and do as I'm told. I find all of my things underneath one of the sinks. Of course, it's my bag that I took to the club for work. My everyday makeup that was in my house is nowhere to be seen.

I take the time to do my makeup as if I'm still Luna, about to go out on stage and bat my eyelashes at men who want to fuck me.

Once satisfied, I decide to get dressed and wait for further instructions. But you can only access the closet from the bedroom.

I exit the bathroom this time and come to a stop when I see Saint has joined me at some point. He stands on the balcony. He's bent over, forearms resting on the railing. He's dressed in black jeans, combat boots, and a white T-shirt. I shuffle on my bare feet as he turns around to face me, and my heart races because I'm already naked. I left my towel in the bathroom.

Leaning back against the railing, he crosses his tattooed arms over his chest and looks over my face and hair. The silence that lingers makes me nervous, so I tuck a few strands behind my ear, worried. I hate to admit that I put a little more effort than I would usually do to look my best for him.

Pushing off the railing, he enters my room and walks up to me. I lift my chin in order to meet his stare.

FORTY-NINE

SAINT

She did a good job at getting all done up for me. She looks gorgeous. I used to love taking her out and showing her off. I won't say that I don't get jealous, but I was always proud to call her mine. If a man tried to touch her, I'd cut off his hands. If he hurt her, I'd slit his fucking throat. But allowing a man to see how beautiful she is when she comes for me—fuck, I'd let any man see that.

I never did mind letting Haidyn and Kashton have a piece. It was always about them. They never fucked her cunt, and she was never allowed to come for them. I loved that control I had over her. Lending her out but being able to control her pleasure. It's a power that only she could give me.

Her breathing is erratic, and her pretty pink nipples are hard. I couldn't pass up an opportunity to see her. To touch her. To fuck her. "How's your throat?" I ask.

She swallows and gives me a soft nod. "Better."

Grabbing her hand, I turn her to face the mirror that I had Jessie place in here from the office. "Arms behind your back," I command.

She drops her head to stare at her bare feet and places her hands behind her back. I pull them to where they are parallel and begin to tie them in place with the rope.

"On your knees," I tell her, and she drops to them. Her ass rests on the heels of her feet. "No." I grab her hair and pull, making her cry out while lifting her body at the same time. "I want your ass up off the floor. Back straight."

She sniffs but does as she's ordered.

"Move forward. I want the front of your body touching the mirror."

Once she's in place, I pick up the dildo and hold it down in front of her face. "Lick it." I hold the suction cup at her lips, and they part. She lifts her eyes to meet mine as her tongue darts out, and she runs it along the suction cup. The action makes my cock twitch in my pants.

I stick it to the mirror and then grab what I want out of my pocket. "Open wide, sweetheart, and stick out your tongue." I give her two sprays, then toss it to the side. "Made these just for you," I say, pulling the last thing out that I want and squatting down next to her. I spit on the mirror and place the tiny clear suction cups on it. Then I stretch out the short chains just as far as they'll go and attach the sharp teeth to her hard nipples.

She whimpers, her shoulders now shaking. I gather her pretty hair in my hand as I continue to squat next to her. "You're going to suck on this dildo for five minutes. Deep throat it. Don't swallow. I want all your drool running out of the corners of your pretty lips while you watch yourself be the best slut you can be. Understand?"

Nodding, she sniffs, and I push her head forward as she parts her shaking lips. I lift my right hand, eyeing my watch as my hand helps her fuck the dildo. There's not much sucking involved when you can't feel your mouth. I hold her head, forcing her to take more and more of it with each push.

Once the drool runs down the corners of her mouth and her makeup smears, I push her head farther, and her large eyes meet mine in the mirror. "Look how good you're doing. You'll be swallowing it whole in no time."

I pull her head back just enough to push it back down her throat. She tries to pull away, but the nipple clamps stop her, and fresh tears fall from her bottom lashes.

"Halfway there," I tell her, and she looks up at me in the mirror. My free hand comes up and grips her chin. "Watch, sweetheart. Look at yourself." Her eyes go to hers in the mirror as I hold her chin and the back of her head, forcing her to swallow the fake dick.

Her legs shake, and she tries to adjust herself, but it does no good because the nipple clamps keep her in place.

This is part of her punishment. I know she ventured out yesterday, and although I'm not mad about it, I feel she needs to remember why she's here.

Pushing her head more, I watch as the dick disappears into her drooling mouth, and she tries to breathe out, spit flying from her lips. "Fuck, I love it messy," I tell her.

She blinks rapidly, and streaks of black mascara run down her cheeks.

I pull her mouth free and squeeze the suction cups from the mirror to release them, leaving the clamps attached to her nipples. Standing, I bend down and pick her up and lay her on her back on the table.

She arches her body, trying to relieve the pressure of her tied arms underneath her. Unzipping my jeans, I pull out my hard cock. "I'm going to fuck your throat, Ash, and then I'm going to come down it."

I slide my cock into her mouth, having to adjust her more so her head hangs off, giving me a better position of her mouth. She bends her knees up, and they fall open as if I'm going to play with her soaking wet pussy. I don't. None of this is about her.

Looking up, I see how wet her cunt is in the mirror, and I smile. She always enjoyed being used. I loved showing off how wet I could make her without even touching her. How much she craved me.

I don't give her time to work up to it. The point is to fuck her throat before the numbing spray wears off. So I wrap my free hand underneath the back of her neck, arching it more, and watch my cock bulge her throat. My balls hit her wet face, and I groan as she takes me whole. "That's a good girl." I slap the side of her breast with my free hand. Then I grab the clamps and pull on them. She lifts her hips off the table before slamming them down, making it rattle.

"Like that, sweetheart?" I do it again, pulling on them harder, and her bent knees shift from side to side. Pulling my cock from her mouth, she gasps, and I slide it back in. I watch it move in and out, covered in her drool. Seeing her once painted lips wrapped around my dick has my heart racing.

I've imagined this a million times since she left me, and nothing compares to seeing it right now.

ASHTYN

He pulls out of my mouth, and I gasp, finally able to breathe. I'm shaking, eyes burning, and my pussy throbs with need. My mind screams to hate him. My body wants to beg him to get me off.

"Good girl," he groans, stuffing his wet dick into his jeans and zipping them up.

I'm still on the table. My head hangs off the edge, and I'm crushing my numb arms underneath me. My nipples throb, and my inner thighs are soaked.

Reaching out, he removes the clamps, and a strangled cry comes from my parted lips at the pain. I've always liked the rougher side of sex with Saint. After I ran from Carnage, the sex I experienced with other men just wasn't the same. If a man slapped me, I'd knock his teeth out. But Saint? I want to smile and say hit me harder. Leave your handprint on my face. Let all the other men know I like to be your fuck toy.

He grabs my shoulders and sits me up. I bite my wet lip to keep from whimpering at how sore I am. He already ruined me for other men, and now he's on a mission to slowly kill me with his dick. I have feeling in my mouth back, and now it's just sore. My tongue feels swollen.

I bow my head, still trying to calm my racing heart when he steps away, and I close my eyes. My lashes are wet and stuck together from the makeup he had me put on first.

A moan escapes my mouth when I feel his hand in my hair. He gently pulls my head up, and my heavy eyes open to see him now standing between my shaking legs.

"You've earned this, sweetheart." He runs his tatted knuckles down the side of my tear-streaked face while he stares at my collar.

I swallow against the restricting leather and flinch. It feels tighter than it did before, for some reason.

"You'll get used to it," he assures me, and then flicks the tip, making the bell ring.

I suck in a deep breath. "Sa-int—"

"Now you won't be able to hide, Ash." He interrupts what I was about to say. His thumb runs over my parted lips. "You make such a pretty pet."

Fresh tears sting my eyes, and I pull on my restrained arms. Is he going to leave me like this? A part of me hopes he does. It means he'll come back and visit me soon. I hate being in this room all alone with my thoughts.

"All you're missing is a leash and a gag." He smiles down at me. "And of course, cum dripping out of your swollen cunt."

My hard nipples ache at his words. They beg to be touched, and I find myself leaning forward, silently begging for him to put the clamps back on. To pinch them, pull on them, slap them. Something... "Please?" I beg, and I don't even recognize my own voice it's so rough from his cock just fucking it.

"What, sweetheart?" he asks, his pretty green eyes on mine, and I hate that I can't touch him.

"Please, may I get off?" I ask softly.

"You know the rules."

"Saint....please, I need..."

"A whore gets fucked, Ash. She gets used when she's needed. Not the other way around." He steps back from me, and it gives me a clear view of myself in the mirror.

I look awful. Makeup smeared across my face, and black streaks run down the sides as if I was crying black tears. The smeared red lipstick makes me look like the female version of the Joker. My hair is a mess, and my watery eyes fall to the black leather collar.

Saint walks behind me and undoes my wrists. Gripping my hair, he yanks my head back to meet his stare in the mirror. "Touch yourself, and those go back on, understand?"

"I understand," I whisper, and he lets go of me. Satisfied, he exits my room, closing me inside this hell while I count down the minutes until he visits me again and makes me his good little whore.

FIFTY

SAINT

I exit her room just as Kashton's door opens, and he steps out. He looks from me to her closed door before they meet mine again.

"I'm headed to the basement," I inform him before he can say anything about what I was just doing.

"You think he'll tell us anything?" he asks, knowing I'm referring to visiting Luke.

I shrug. "We're about to find out." Passing Haidyn's room, I ask Kash, "Seen him this morning?"

"Not since the other night at Blackout," he answers as we get into the elevator at the end of the hallway.

Me either. He's either downstairs playing or out fucking shit up. Either way, he'll come around when he wants to.

"I caught Ashtyn in my room yesterday," Kash tells me.

"What the fuck was she doing?" I ask. But I like the idea she's being nosy. It means I get to punish her for not staying in her room.

"Just being curious. Like I said...fucking cat."

I smirk. I didn't get back until late last night with Ryat. We unloaded our newest member, and I offered to let him stay and help me initiate the man. By the time we finished, it was almost six this morning. I was exhausted by then and went to bed. I knew I had an early morning with Ashtyn coming.

My cell rings, and I pull it out of my pocket. I show it to Kashton before I hit answer, and he smirks, knowing exactly what it's about. "Hello?" We step off the elevator on the basement level. The concrete ceilings are low in this section of the building. We keep this room open for many reasons. I push through the double doors when the Lord speaks into my ear.

"Saint. What's been going on?"

"Same thing, just a different day. You?" Kashton and I enter the room. It's currently empty, but this is where we like to leave the ones to "hang" while we wait for them to offer up information.

"Pretty much." He grunts. "Just wanted to extend an invitation to the Spade brothers for the show."

Kashton holds the door at the other end of the room open for me, and I step inside it. "We'll be there," I inform him, and we hang up.

"Who's the new guy?" Kashton asks when I pocket my cell while walking past the pits.

The pit in the center is currently occupied by the guy who I went to pick up last night with Ryat. We stripped him naked, removed his Lord's crest, and rebranded him with the 666 Carnage brand. Then threw him in the pit to cool off. He's currently sitting in cold water. It won't kill him, but by the lack of color in his face and the way his head shakes, he's pretty fucking cold. "Collected him last night," I answer.

I've been in there quite a bit since that first initiation. How do you get over your fear? You do it over and over until it becomes part of your routine, your life. And then you do it for fun. That's what the bitch said to me when we were "training" anyway. At the time, I wanted to drown her. I still would like to if ever given the chance.

We walk through the next set of double doors and enter the hallway where the cells are located. They're on either side.

I unlock the cell, and the guy in the corner looks up as we enter. "Hey, Luke," I say, coming to stand in front of him.

He lifts his right hand to shield what little light comes in from the hallway with the door open because he's normally in darkness.

"I've been given some information lately." I crouch down in front of him. "Why did you call the hit on Adam?" No need to beat around the bush or waste my time.

His sunken eyes widen, and he sucks in a deep breath. I arch a brow when he says nothing. "Maybe we should remove his tongue." I look over at Kashton. Tyson already removed all of his teeth, but you can still talk without them.

Luke shakes his head quickly, and I reach out and grip his hair. I yank him to his feet and slam his face into the wall. "You've got three seconds to talk, or I rip it out."

"I...I placed the hit on Brenda—"

"Bullshit!" I snap. "Tyson was there for Adam."

"I swear. It was on Brenda. She was threatening to tell the police. She got spooked. Said a cop was asking around and that she wanted to talk to them."

I yank him from the wall and spin him around. "Does Ashtyn know about you?"

He shakes his head. "No. There was one time I was at her parents' house, and she was there but asleep."

ASHTYN

Four days, I've stayed in my room. I haven't left once. I eat, I sleep, and I cry mostly. I also spend a lot of time in the bathtub or shower. There's just something so therapeutic about crying in there.

Saint visits me once a day for training. I'm getting better, or so he says. I suck a rubber dick, and then he fucks my mouth with his, leaves me crying, and then I scream into my pillow because I'm dying to fucking come so bad. I can't even explain how raw, swollen, and wet my pussy stays. It's a constant reminder that I'm his whore. This has to be his plan. I feel like I'm going through withdrawal. It could be the lack of alcohol, drugs, or the need to get off. It's an itch that I can't scratch because my hands are tied. My body has no clue what the fuck is going on anymore. I used to drink every night at work. More often than not, I'd pop some pills to get through my night. Then I'd go home and fuck James. Even if the sex wasn't amazing, I still made sure I was getting myself off. Now none of that is happening.

Thoughts of my encounter the other day with Haidyn keep running through my mind. What did he mean by *we all take our punishment*? What were they punished for?

I haven't seen him since. I know he's avoiding me, and I'm fine with that. The less I have to see him and Kashton, the better. It's hard enough to handle Saint. I'm just waiting for all three of them to enter my room and for Saint to tell me it's part of my "training."

I lie in bed, staring up at the ceiling. What else am I supposed to do? So I just lie in bed, eat when Jessie brings me food, and try my best to ignore the need to be fucked. My deep throat training is still daily, but I haven't been granted a release.

Typical Lord. It's all about them. It's how they show their power. Their dominance. I've always been the submissive one in our relationship, so my body doesn't understand what my mind knows.

I'm a toy now. He used to love me. But not anymore.

My throat is raw, my lips cracked, and my pussy is so swollen it aches. I find myself waking up in the middle of the night rubbing my thighs together praying it helps. It doesn't. I've cried myself back to sleep and find myself having dreams that I get off.

Saint hasn't come in and visited me yet today, so I'm not surprised when I look over to see my door open. My heart begins to race in anticipation to show him how much progress I'm making. Maybe this time he'll let me come.

The bed dips at my side, and a hand caresses my cheek. It feels ... wet. Am I crying? Possibly, I'm not sure.

My head tilts to the side, and I meet a set of green eyes. Saint stares at me with an emotionless look. I wish I could turn mine off. I've never been one to hide how I feel, and since I've returned, my emotions are tenfold.

"Get up and get ready. We're leaving in two hours," he states.

My heart leaps in my chest. "Where...where are we going?" I ask roughly. There's no one for me to talk to so I never use my voice. The only thing my mouth is good for is for his cock to fuck. At least I've made progress in that department. Drooling all over myself like an infant while he calls me a "good girl" is the highlight of my day.

"An art show," he answers, running his tatted knuckles down my jawline and chest. My nipples harden, and my breathing picks up.

"So...we're going out?" I whisper. "Leaving Carnage?"

"You can stay here if you want."

"No." I sit up, and he arches a brow at my quick movement. "I want to go." I clear my throat.

He doesn't say anything. Instead, his hand makes its way back up over my breast and chin. He cups my cheek and leans in. I think he's going to kiss me, but instead, he places his lips to my ear. "If you're good for me, sweetheart, I'll let you come tonight."

I bite back a groan. Finally! My pussy throbs.

FIFTY-ONE

ASHTYN

Less than three hours later, we're boarding a private jet in the middle of the woods. Nothing but a runway. Just like anything else the Lords have, it's over the top. Black carpet with white leather seats with black stitching. And several tables around the aircraft are black marble.

Haidyn sits on a couch, texting away on his cell. He looks up, and his cold stare meets mine for a brief second before he goes back to what he was doing.

I tuck a piece of hair behind my ear as Saint guides me to a seat. I sit down, and he buckles my seat belt as if I'm incapable of doing it myself. Kashton walks onto the jet a moment later, his cell to his ear. He walks right past all of us, and I watch him enter a door in the back.

A flight attendant walks over to us, and he gives me a kind smile. "Anything I can get you, miss?"

"We'll take a bottle of Moet Imperial Brut." Saint answers for me.

"Of course, sir." He turns and walks away.

"Maybe I didn't want champagne," I say.

Saint snorts, and I cross my arms over my chest.

I rub my sweaty hands down my bare thighs, and I readjust myself in the seat. The flight attendant returns with our bottle and pours us both glasses. I greedily take a sip, trying to calm my nerves. I feel like this is a setup of some kind.

Saint hasn't even let me leave my room in days, and all of a sudden, he's got me going to an art show with them? I'm horny, not stupid.

I sit silently beside him while he does the same as Haidyn and goes through his phone. At some point, Kashton joins us. He sits down next to Haidyn on the couch, and they hold a quiet conversation. I look out the window, trying to figure out where we're going, but it's too cloudy to see anything. Not like I'd know anyway. I'm not an expert at landmarks.

I jump when Saint taps my leg. "Come on," he orders, standing up from his seat.

"What—?"

He takes my drink from my hand and places it on the table. Then he undoes my seat belt and pulls me up by my hand and drags me down the aisle.

Coming to a stop at the door that Kashton had entered earlier, he ushers me inside and shuts it behind us. "Strip," he commands.

My wide eyes look up at him, waiting for him to say more, but when he just stares at me, I reach down and grab the hem of my shirt, pulling it up and over my head. Then I remove my bra, undo my shorts, and shove them down my legs along with my thong. I kick off my shoes and stand before him naked.

If you're a good girl, I'll let you come later.

I need that. So I'll do whatever he wants me to do right now.

"Turn around."

I give him my back and place my hands behind me, expecting him to tie me up in some way, but his dark laughter makes me question what the fuck I'm supposed to do.

He walks over to the bed and opens a box. Removing something, he says. "Hold your arms straight out."

Like a zombie, I lift my arms out in front of me, and he slides both of my arms into what looks like bra straps. He pulls it up to my chest and moves to stand behind me. Once they cover my breasts, I hiss in a breath, my shoulders instinctively rounding in at the sting on my chest. "What the—"

"This bra is made especially for you." He interrupts me as I feel him fasten it. "It's got spikes on the inside that will dig into your breasts." Grabbing my shaking shoulders, he spins me around to face him. "Don't worry, they're not going to pierce your skin or anything, but they will poke you."

I whimper as my nipples harden, and the spikes dig into my sensitive skin. "Oh God." I reach up to adjust it, but he grabs my hands and holds them down to my side.

"No touching," he warns, and I want to scream in frustration.

Letting go of my wrists, he cups my face, and I lean into it. His thumb runs over my lips, and my tongue darts out. He takes the hint and pushes it into my mouth, and I suck on it.

My body craves to suck on him. My training is working. I feel him empty when he's not inside of me. He pulls it free from my lips, and I inhale sharply. "Saint?"

"Yeah, sweetheart?" He gives me a proud smile.

"Kiss me." I lean into him, his hard chest pressing my spiked bra into mine, and wetness pools between my naked legs.

The smile drops off his face, and his cold green eyes meet mine. "You don't kiss a whore, Ashtyn."

My stomach drops at his words, but they also make me mad. He made me this way. Yes, I wanted to be his slut before I even knew I'd belong to him, but he made me want more. His friends. Did he expect me to never have sex again? How is that fair? How many women has he fucked since I left? I'm sure the number is high.

I slap him across the face.

He wraps his hand around my neck, shoving me backward onto the bed. He straddles me, pinning me down. His hand tightens, taking away my breath, and he lowers his face inches from mine.

"You know what you do to a whore, Ash? You strip her naked, put a collar on her, and parade her around for all his friends to see."

I try to push him off me, but it doesn't do me any good. Instead, it just makes the spikes dig more into my chest, and it has my hips lifting to grind into him.

"You put her on display, let everyone see how much she begs for it. Then you fuck her ass to remind her who the fuck she belongs to." His eyes search my watery ones, and my hands grip his wrist that is wrapped around my neck. It digs the collar into my already sensitive skin. "That's what you do to a whore, sweetheart." Letting go, he gets up off me, and I roll onto my side, coughing and sucking in a deep breath.

"Fuck...you...Saint." I manage to get out through gasps.

His laughter fills the small room, and my hands fist the white comforter, messing up the bed. Grabbing my hair, he yanks me to stand, and I cry out. "Now, let's finish getting you ready for the show."

SAINT

WE STEP OFF OUR PRIVATE JET AND GET INTO THE WAITING limo. She hasn't even looked at me since I refused to kiss her. Honestly, I'm dying to kiss her lips both on her face and the ones between her legs. I used to love going down on her. The way she'd call out my name and grab my hair. Pleasing her made me happy. Now I have to deny myself because I refuse to give her what she wants.

I know it sounds childish. But it's not the first thing I've done that seems stupid.

She sits beside me in the limo, legs crossed over one another. Refusing to pay me any attention, she stares out the window as New York passes by. We're here to support a friend. A fellow Lord who started his own business right out of Barrington.

He owns twenty-five locations in the world, but the very first one was here. He's turned it into a franchise. I look up at Kash, and he's staring at his cell. He swore to us that *she* wouldn't be here tonight. Otherwise, Ashtyn wouldn't be joining us.

I didn't want to leave her back at Carnage, though, not with all three of us gone. Even if it is just for the night. So here we are.

We turn down into an alleyway, and the car comes to a stop. I get out first, then reach my hand inside to help her. Her hard eyes look up at me while ignoring my help, and my lips twitch, holding back a smile. I always win. And I will make sure to remind her that later tonight when I get her all alone.

A man stands at a black metal door with a clipboard in one hand and wearing an earpiece, dressed in an all-black suit. His eyes go straight to Ashtyn. I reach out and take her hand, tightening my grip when she tries to pull away.

"Name?" he asks.

"Spade," Haidyn answers before I can.

The guy finds the name, and you can see him counting in his head to make sure it says times four on the piece of paper he's been given. After a second, he nods and steps to the side. Kashton opens the door, and I usher Ashtyn in first.

We walk down a dimly lit hallway. Ashtyn's heels are the only sound. I pull her behind me, still holding her hand captive in mine. We come to a new set of doors, and we enter the main building.

FIFTY-TWO

ASHTYN

"What is this place?" I whisper, looking around with wide eyes, no longer caring about giving Saint the silent treatment.

There's a woman on all fours and a piece of glass that sits on top of her flat back. People are sitting on a couch surrounding her using the glass as a coffee table while her back supports it.

Another naked woman is on her knees and elbows in the middle of the room. Her legs spread wide open for everyone to see her ass and pussy. Cum leaks from it as if she was just fucked. Her wrists are tied together and behind her head, secured with the rest of the rope wrapped around her neck, forcing her forehead down onto the marble floor.

A set of hands land on my hips, and I jump. Saint leans his lips down to my ear. "This is an art show, sweetheart. An exhibit of sorts."

"Of sex?" I question, mouth open.

He chuckles in my ear and then slaps my ass. "Come on. We've got a show to catch." Grabbing my hand, I allow him to pull me down a hallway to a set of double doors at the end. He pushes one open, and we enter a room.

We walk down the aisle with rows of chairs on either side. A chill runs up my spine of how much it reminds me of the vow ceremony day when I gave myself over to him in front of the Lords. But I'm not the one on center stage this time.

We make our way to the front, and I sit next to Kashton on my right. Saint sits to my left in the aisle seat, and Haidyn is on the other side of Kash.

I look over the set that is center stage. There's a red leather couch with a black curtain backdrop. That's it. Nothing and no one are present. The lights are dimmer in here than out in the hallway.

I lean into Saint and ask, "What are they going to do?"

He places his right hand on my left thigh, and my eyes drop to look at it. My inkless skin looks out of place against his tatted knuckles. He squeezes my thigh before he slides his hand up my leg. I tense when it reaches the hem of my black shorts. Saint notices and looks over at me. The cocky smirk he gives me makes me nervous as if he knows what's to come.

"You parade them around in front of their friends." I pray this isn't some sort of show where they take volunteers from the audience.

A man walks out onto the stage, and all chatter ceases.

"Hello, gentlemen." He claps his hands once, and I notice that he makes no attempt to acknowledge the women in the room. Giving a quick look around, I count several. But I get a sickening feeling in my stomach once more, reminding me that it's like the night of the vow ceremony at the cathedral where we willingly gave ourselves to our Lords. The women here are to be put on display, not respected.

He continues to address the men in the room, and I tune him out as I look him over. He's attractive—dark hair, clean cut, and shaven face. He wears black slacks and a matching button-down with his sleeves rolled up his tan and muscular arms. I see no wedding ring—just a watch on his right wrist.

He looks familiar, though. Something about him...

A woman gets my attention sitting on the red leather couch. *When did she get there?* She wears a black silk robe with a matching sash secured high on her stomach. Her dark brown hair is slicked back into a perfect bun. I never can figure out how to get mine to look so flawless. She has one leg crossed over the other and has topped off her look with red heels that match the couch.

She sits perfectly still like a doll. The only thing that shows she's real is her eyes. They follow the man on stage like a hawk. Wherever he stands, her eyes follow.

Two men walk onto the stage, and she gets to her feet. The main guy turns to face her. "Remove your clothes," he orders her.

With her eyes on his, she reaches down and unties the sash, then she slowly pushes the robe off her shoulders, and it pools on the stage at her heels. She's naked underneath like I expected.

I'm as bad as the men I sit with because my eyes shamelessly look over her naked body. She's gorgeous. Her boobs are fake, larger than mine, so at least a double D. She's got a thin waist and long, lean legs. Not a single blemish to be seen. No tattoos, no scars, not even a scratch on her freshly spray-tanned skin. She has a Barbie-doll-shaped face with big pouty lips that I envy. Long, dark lashes fan her cheeks when she blinks. I can't look away. She's what any guy would drool all over.

"Hailey is a BDSM model," the familiar-looking man announces to the crowd as the other two begin to tie her up. "She has experience and knows her limits. What we're about to do is not something I'd recommend for a beginner."

The two men walk off the stage, leaving her standing naked with her arms now secured behind her back. The way they tied her up reminds me of how Saint tied me up on the day I sucked the dildo in his office. It's not identical, but it's similar.

"This particular form of Shibari is known as a box tie," the guy states, running the tips of his fingers along the rope wrapped around her large breasts. "Turn around," he tells her, and she places her back to the crowd to show how her arms are secured behind her back. "This should be comfortable enough that your partner can spend a long time restrained in this position. If done correctly, it should feel like a snug hug."

The rope is wrapped around each breast and cinched tight in the middle. It wraps around her upper shoulders to where her arms are tied parallel to her back. He walks over to her and grips her neck. Her eyes go heavy as he yanks her into him. Nothing but devotion in them. Pure lust and the need to please him.

I get it.

Some of us are just wired differently than others.

His free hand drops between her legs, and she begins to pant, her nipples hardening.

"My whore is soaked," he states, and a few men in the audience laugh. Letting go of her neck, he slaps her pretty face, making her whimper. His hand goes back to her throat, and he squeezes. Her pouty lips fall open, but nothing comes out. His hand between her legs picks up, the sound of him fingering her fills the room as her watery eyes remain on his. Her hips buck as she rocks on her high heels, riding them.

He pulls them free and places his fingers into her mouth, pushing them down her throat. She doesn't even gag. Instead, you see her relax her jaw as his fingers disappear down to his knuckles, spreading her mouth wide open.

"You're such a good girl, princess," he praises her, and she blinks. The tears spilling down her mascara-covered lashes leave a trail on her once flawless face. She has a full face of makeup on with black shadow, thick winged liner, and red lipstick. I've never understood the appeal when Saint would have me get all dolled up just to mess it up. But I do now. She looks even prettier with the black running down her cheeks.

He removes his hand from her mouth, and she takes a deep breath before swallowing. "Let's get started." He walks over to the far corner and grabs a box and pulls a rolling cart that I hadn't seen before to the center of the stage.

One of the guys from earlier rushes onto the stage and places a set of carpeted stairs in front of the cart. He then undoes a few locks on the clear box. The top and each end are removed, leaving both sides remaining upright. He steps aside, placing them at his feet, and waits.

The man in the black button-down takes the woman's upper arm and helps guide her to center stage. He assists her up the stairs, and when she gets to the top one, she comes to a stop.

"On your knees," he commands. "Spread them wide. I want everyone to be able to see how wet you are."

She slowly gets to her knees and positions her ass and heels to hang off the back edge of the box. His hands go to her tied arms, and he helps her get into position with her legs spread wide as he instructed so her chest is flat on the bottom of the box. I realize there are also two holes, and part of her boobs hang out of the bottom.

The main guy, with his hand on her back, looks at the other guy and motions for him to bring the other glass pieces. He helps him put the top on, fastening it to the two standing sides. The height is so short that it smashes her tied arms to the glass, keeping her chest pushed down to the floor of the box.

I shift in my seat, the panic gripping my chest of being confined in such a tight space. The feel of Saint's fingers digging into my thigh makes me whimper. I can feel his eyes on me, so I avoid him by watching the woman on stage. She wiggles her body, but she has no luck in moving whatsoever. Even the sides of her legs are pressed against the sides of the glass.

The man takes one of the end pieces and places it on. There are two half holes on the bottom for her ankles to hang out and a hole in the center to allow him access to her ass and pussy. The sound of the locks has her breathing picking up. He walks to the front, and the man hands him the other piece of glass.

He places it on the opposite end, where a hole at the bottom allows her head to hang out over the edge. He locks it, securing her naked and inside the box.

The man holding the glass pieces holds out his hand, and the guy takes what he offers. "Open wide," he orders to the woman, and she obliges greedily.

He shoves a large black rubber ball gag into her mouth and then proceeds to place the harness over her head. When I see it has a blindfold connected that he slips over her eyes, my heart races.

She can't move, see, or speak. It makes me feel like I'm suffocating. It's my worst fear, yet my hard nipples press against the spikes on the inside of my bra.

He fastens the two buckles at the back of her head, then reaches into his pocket and removes something. He slides it into the silver ring where it buckled and then pulls it up. Her gagged moan fills the large room as he connects it to the top of the box, forcing her to arch her head back.

Going over to the couch, he picks up a box and opens it. He removes the contents and walks back over to her. Bending down, he plays with her breasts that hang through the two holes on the bottom. He pulls on her nipples, more of her breasts coming through the tight hole before he twists them. He's not gentle in any way, and it has my pulse racing.

When satisfied, he places nipple clamps on each one and then stands. I watch them dangle back and forth and notice that they each have weights on the end of them, pulling on her breasts.

Her hands clench and unclench behind her back as her body wiggles the little amount it's allowed. He turns to face the crowd and begins to speak. "There are many different kinks that go along with this scene," he begins. "One is breeding." Walking to the end of the box, he reaches out and runs his hand over her pussy that is on full display for all to see. "Women are strapped in, and men line up to wait their turn. The point is to fill them with their cum. To force pregnancy. Another is for humiliation or degradation. It can also be for punishment ..."

I tune him out as I watch him finger her pussy as if he's not talking to the crowd. Again, he's rough as he thrusts two fingers. But even I can see from here that she's wet. He removes them and slaps her pussy a couple of times, and it makes mine pulse. Then he's shoving three into her this time. She's breathing heavily through her nose, mumbled moans and whimpers come from her gagged mouth, and a line of drool has started to drop from the ball. Her red heels shake as she tries to move the best she can.

When he removes them this time, her body sags in the box.

He walks over to a table and picks up a syringe that is already full of clear liquid. Then something that resembles a butt plug. When he's standing behind her once more, he presses the tip of the syringe into her ass and her body jerks, forcing the box to move just a tad. He slaps her ass cheek, making a popping sound and leaving his handprint on her porcelain skin. He plunges it into her and then places the now empty syringe on top of the box before pushing the butt plug into her now lubed ass.

A black tube hangs out with a ball on the end. He reaches down and squeezes it a few times. "This is an inflatable butt plug," he informs the audience. "I'm going to leave it in fifteen minutes. Pumping it every five."

I don't know which is worse. The fifteen minutes she has to stay locked in the box or the fact he's stretching her ass in front of an audience. I remember when we were at the house of Lords a few weeks after the vow ceremony, and Saint punished me by giving me an enema in front of the guys in his room. He then took me to the bathroom. Afterward, he tied me to his bed, and he let Haidyn and Kashton fuck my ass. It was humiliating and the most amazing night of my life. I wasn't allowed to come unless it was with Saint's tongue, dick, or fingers. Haidyn and Kashton were allowed to fuck me, but it was always for their pleasure, not mine. Once they finished with me, Saint would reward me for being a good girl.

But right here, right now? In front of strangers? I'm not so sure. I knew all the guys at the house of Lords. As stupid as that sounds, they had their chosens naked all the time. People were always fucking on any surface they could find. It wasn't uncommon.

I wouldn't mind if I was blindfolded from the beginning and

hadn't seen all the people sitting in the crowd. I'm breathing heavily, and my heart races just thinking about it, so I can only imagine what she feels like. The butt plug, the nipple clamps that rock back and forth, pulling on them painfully, the fingering...fuck, my clit pulses, and I shift in my seat. The room grows hot at the thought of being restricted so tight in a box. But the way he has her on display in front of everyone as he brings her to orgasm with his fingers makes me jealous. I want Saint to show me off. Be proud and show everyone what a whore I am for him.

Isn't that what he said you do with a whore?

Why does his wanting to be proud of me make me the whore? He's the one fucking me. He's the one getting off on parading me around.

"Ash..."

Saint's voice in my ear makes me jump to my feet and rush up the aisle and out of the double doors. I breathe in deeply, and it's like the air is polluted. My lungs burn, and my legs shake. I'm all worked up now, and I'm not sure what to do. Goose bumps cover my heated flesh, and my mind races to what it would feel like to be her right now. Locked up tight and waiting for Saint to fuck my ass.

I rush over to a door that reads women on it and practically run into the bathroom. A cry of surprise leaves my lips when I run into a woman. "I'm so, so—"

"Brittany?" she squeals. "Oh my God, girl. It's been too long."

"Hey," I say, trying to calm my racing heart. "What are you doing here?" I ask the woman. She worked with me at Kink back in Vegas. She was only there for a few weeks before I heard she quit.

"I got a job here at Kink in New York," she answers, and I frown.

"There's one here too?" I didn't know that.

She nods. "Oh yeah, Hooke started it."

Hooke? Can't be...

"He's in the performance room right now." She rolls her eyes. "With his protégé." Scoffing, she adds, "She was a ballerina for like fifteen years. Flexible and gorgeous." Turning to face the mirror, she replaces her lipstick, and the puzzle pieces start to fall together. "Anyway, I've missed you. You should come visit sometime."

"Yeah," I say, knowing that'll never happen. I have a tracker inside me. I won't be going anywhere without supervision for the rest of my life.

"Here." She reaches into her purse and pulls out two pills. "Just like old times." Winking, she hands them to me and then zips her purse. "I have to go. I'm on stage in ten minutes and have to stretch."

SAINT

I EXIT THE ROOM AND SEE HER STANDING BY HERSELF IN THE hallway. Rushing over to her, I grab her upper arm, and it makes her jump. "Saint," she gasps.

I push her back into the wall and grip her chin, forcing her to look up at me. I can feel her pulse racing under my fingers. Her lips are parted as she pants. My eyes drop to watch the rise and fall of her breasts, and I smile at the thought of the spikes digging into them.

"Did you enjoy the show?" I ask.

Her eyes narrow at mine, and she takes a deep breath but doesn't answer.

"Let's see." I drop my hand to her shorts, and I unbutton them.

"Saint," she squeals, trying to pull away, but I have her back pinned between me and the wall. "Stop." Her hands slap at mine.

I grab hers and pin them above her head, crossing her wrists with one of my hands. She softly whimpers, and I use my free hand to cup her chin. "Look at me, Ashtyn."

Slowly, she lifts her lashes, and her eyes meet mine. "Are you wet?"

She pulls her bottom lip between her teeth and nibbles on it nervously.

Reaching down, I squeeze her breasts, and she cries out as I growl, "I asked you a question."

"Y-yes," she answers, shoulders shaking.

"Yes, what?" I arch a brow.

Her wrists fight me as I easily hold them in place, and I know she's doing it on purpose loving the way the spikes dig into her sensitive breasts. "Yes...I'm wet." She blinks, and tears fill her eyes.

Satisfied, I release her and step back. I wasn't going to fuck her right here and now. Way too many eyes are watching. I don't mind Haidyn and Kashton watching, but they know she belongs with me. Other men won't understand that, and the last thing I want to do is piss Hooke off at his show because I kill some rich bastard for watching her come. But I wanted her to think that it wasn't out of the question. I want her to think that I will fuck her anytime and anywhere I want.

The doors to the room open, and I look up to see Kash and Haidyn exit along with others. "You missed the best part, sweet cheeks." Kash winks at her.

She drops her head and wraps her arms around herself.

"How about we put her in a box when we get home?" Haidyn offers, and her breath hitches.

I could hear in the room while we watched the show. The way her breathing picked up. The way her body tensed as I had my hand on her leg. She got hot and bothered and also scared. Fear is good. She's always liked to be scared. Chased down and taken by force.

But there was also more than that. I know her greatest fear is being buried alive. And the fact that Hooke's sub couldn't see and was secured in a box brought that fear to the surface.

I want to see that fear in her eyes, knowing that I can do whatever I want to her. That if I want to secure her in a box with her ass, cunt, and mouth out, I can. And I'll keep her there as long as I want.

We've all been there. Haidyn, Kashton, and I know what that kind of hell feels like, and I want to hear her desperate voice beg for freedom.

FIFTY-THREE

ASHTYN

"I need to use the restroom," I say, cursing myself for not using it when I was in there a moment ago.

Saint looks down at me and steps to the side. His silent way of telling me I can go without supervision. *That's nice of him.* I have no cell and no money. They're not worried about me running away. What would I even tell the cops when they ask why I have a harness locked to my chest? *Yeah, well, it's to keep me from removing the spiked bra I have on underneath.* Yeah, they'd lock me right up.

"Hurry back," he orders before turning away from me to speak to Haidyn. Kashton no longer stands with us, but I don't know where he went.

Pushing off the wall, I walk off down the hallway through the crowd of people and make my way to the restroom that I know we passed earlier.

I turn the corner to find myself at the end of another hallway. A sign for the women's and men's restrooms is on the opposite wall. A man stands with his back facing me below the signs. He's got both hands on the wall on either side of his head and he's looking down.

Dropping my eyes, I see a pair of black peep toes high heels. He's blocking my view of her. But I know exactly who *he* is.

It's Kashton. The dark ink on his knuckles against the pristine white wall gives him away. His sleeves to the black button-up are rolled up, and I can make out the bottom half of his nun tattoo. He steps back, giving the woman he's got cornered some space, and she goes to enter the bathroom, but he reaches out, grabs her arm, and pushes her into the wall next to the women's restroom.

Pushing into her once again, he drops his face to the right side of her neck. I have a profile view of both of them now but still can't see her face.

His hand drops to her leg, and he lifts it to wrap around his hip as his hand slides along her toned and tanned thigh before disappearing into her dress. Her soft moan travels to where I stand.

Her hands are in his hair, red nails scratching his scalp while he sucks on her neck. She arches her back off the wall as her breath hitches. Her hips push into him. It's not hard to figure out that he's fingering her, and I'm a jealous bitch.

I was ashamed to tell Saint I was turned on by what I saw. And too embarrassed to tell him I'd like to try it. I know Saint would never judge me, but it's more of the fact that if I try it, what if we have to stop because I can't take it? I hate feeling weak.

He moves his head, trailing his lips across her throat to the other side, causing her head to fall toward me. I gasp, my hands coming up to cover my mouth when her eyes open and land on mine.

She lets out a scream, shoving him off her.

"What the fuck—?"

"Oh my God," she shouts, cutting him off, and runs toward me.

I stand, my heels cemented to the floor as she throws her body into mine. Her arms come up and wrap around my shoulders and squeeze. The action makes the spikes dig into my breasts, and the pain and pleasure it brings takes my breath away.

If she notices, she ignores it. Grabbing my shoulders, she pulls back but keeps ahold of me. "Girl. Where the fuck have you been?

I've been calling you. Texting you. I even went to your house and broke the sliding glass door. The neighbors called the cops." She rolls her pretty eyes dramatically. "I got out of being arrested but filed a missing person's report on you. Of course, the broken glass on the living room floor helped my case. James wasn't there. Motherfucker. I thought he killed you. God..." She sighs as a wide smile spreads across her face. Her eyes fill with tears of relief, and mine start to sting as well. I've never had someone care this much about me. "It's so good to see you. What the fuck are you doing in New York City?"

I don't answer, unable to form a sentence. What's she doing here? Kissing Kashton? How is my friend connected to the Lords? I have a thought and get a sickening feeling in my stomach. Did she tell them where to find me? Did she tell Hooke about me? Surely not. I didn't know they were connected.

No. She's too excited to see me. And she didn't know about my past. But I just watched Kash finger her.

"Fuck, I can't tell you how glad I am to see you." She yanks me in for another hug. My arms stay down to my sides, and she squeezes me once more, the spikes making my pussy clench.

I look over her shoulder to see Kashton still standing against the wall, arms crossed over his chest, and his hard blue eyes on mine. He's mad at me. What the fuck did I do?

"Time to go."

I stiffen at the sound of Saint's voice behind me.

"Who the fuck are you?" Jasmine barks, pulling away and taking my hand. She spins me around to face Saint and Haidyn.

He reaches out for me, and she wraps her arm around my shoulders. "She's not going anywhere with you."

Saint steps forward, and Kashton speaks. "Jasmine—"

But he stops the moment someone joins us. Dark blue eyes find mine. "Brothers." The man acknowledges them. Then nods to me. "Ashtyn."

"Her name is Brittany, Bones. Gah, she worked for you, for Christ's sake. You think you'd know her name." Jasmine sighs, grabs my shoulder, and turns me to face her. She rubs my exposed arms, giving me that warm smile as if she'll fix whatever the problem is. "Let's get you home."

"She's going home with us," Saint announces.

Jasmine straightens her back, glaring at him. "I'm not leaving here without her," she states.

Saint's eyes lift over her head to Kashton. His silent order to take care of the woman he was just finger-fucking in this hallway.

My eyes go to Bones, and he's already staring at me. My heart begins to race as my mind starts connecting the dots. "You set me up." I manage to find my voice.

"What? Who?" Jasmine demands.

Bones sighs.

"You set me up." I repeat. How do the Kings know the Lords? I don't know why I'm surprised. The Lords aren't the only secret society that hides in plain sight. But I'm sure all of them communicate. Scratch each other's backs sort of thing.

"What the fuck did you do, Bones? What is Brittany talking about?" Jasmine snaps at him.

"Her name is Ashtyn." Kashton finally speaks.

She turns to face him. "You know her?"

A laugh bubbles up. *Know me?* I always liked Jasmine. If she knew what me and Kashton have done, would she hate me?

"Yes," he says tightly. "And as Saint already stated, she's leaving with us."

"No. She's fucking not," she shouts, pointing at Saint. "I don't know who the fuck..."

"Jasmine..." Kashton growls, stepping into her. "Don't make a scene."

It just pisses her off more. Her eyes narrow up at him, and she goes to slap him, but he catches her wrist midair and yanks her back. She falls off the side of her high heel, and he pulls her back to his front, places a hand over her mouth as she goes to scream, and carries her off to the women's bathroom. The sound of the door locking behind them fills the hallway.

Bones goes to step forward, but Haidyn steps in front of him. "I warned you—"

"He's not going to hurt her." Saint interrupts Bones before he can finish his sentence.

The door to the women's bathroom opens behind us, and I spin around, my hair slapping me in the face to see Kashton exit alone. His button-down shirt ripped open, and he's got a cut on his face that is bleeding. He comes over to us, and Haidyn steps back from Bones.

"She's waiting for you." Kashton growls at Bones, then storms out of the glass doors.

"Let me give you a little piece of advice," Haidyn says to Bones. "You have no clue just how far the Lords are willing to go." Then he looks back at the women's bathroom door before he too follows Kashton.

Saint grabs my upper arm and yanks me forward and out the door as well. Our limo waits in the valet circle. Saint opens the back door for me before he shoves me inside. Haidyn is already there, but there's no Kash.

"Where is he?" Saint questions after noticing.

"Took a cab. Said he'd meet us there," Haidyn answers. His hard eyes are on mine like I did something wrong.

Saint huffs. I can feel the air shift from comfortable to hot. Both of them are mad. I don't know what I just saw, but I know I wasn't supposed to see it. What do they expect me to do about it? Who the fuck am I going to tell?

At least I know now that Bones was the one who gave me up. I've been racking my brain for weeks about how they found me. Of course, a King was the answer.

"What does this mean for Jasmine?" I ask softly, breaking the silence.

"What about her?" Haidyn asks carelessly.

I lift my eyes to look at him, and he's typing away on his cell. I'm guessing to Kashton. "You mentioned the Lords...is she in trouble?"

Haidyn snorts but doesn't answer, so I look over at Saint. He's already looking at me when he answers. "Don't worry about her."

I wish someone would have worried about me at one point. Then maybe things would be different.

SAINT

We waited for an hour for Kashton to board our private jet before we took off. I refused to leave him, and his cell was turned off. Haidyn spent the entire time in the back room, and Kash didn't speak one word when he finally boarded. It was a long ride home, considering Ashtyn didn't say anything to anyone either.

I didn't think about Bones being at the show tonight. We know Hooke, and he owns Kink—an exclusive BDSM club in New York. He puts on the *art show* once a year. It's a way to bring in big clients, many of whom are Lords. Kashton promised us that Jasmine wouldn't be there. Obviously, she changed her mind since he spoke to her last.

We landed, and Haidyn jumped in his car and left. He didn't bother telling us where he was going.

Once we enter the building, Kashton goes straight to his room, and I follow Ashtyn to hers. She tries to slam the door in my face, but I stop it with my foot and storm in behind her. "I don't take kindly to the silent treatment, sweetheart."

She stops and turns to face me, and I step into her. My hands cup her face, and her heavy eyes meet mine, and they're dilated. Like they were the night I fucked her in Glass. I frown, looking her face over. "Did you take something?" I demand.

Her lips curve at the corners. "Maybe."

"Ashtyn," I growl. My hand grips her cheeks, and a whimper escapes her parted lips. "What the fuck did you take?"

"I don't know," she says, her cheeks smashed into her teeth.

I release her and grip her neck instead. She moans. "What the fuck do you mean you don't know what you took? Who the fuck gave you something?" I demand. She was never out of my sight. Even the bathroom...she had stormed out of the show, and I found her up against the wall. Where had she been when I couldn't find her? "What was it?" I ask again. I know she knows. She's done enough drugs in her life to know what they look like. "Did you snort it or swallow it?" It could have been anything. From powder to a pill to liquid.

Instead, she just lifts her chin. Her heavy eyes look unfocused, and her breathing has accelerated. She's so horny, and I was going to fuck her tonight but not now. I'd be too rough with her. I'd squeeze her fragile neck and not let go until her eyes rolled back into her head. But even I know that's not safe if she's on something.

I let go and run my knuckles down her throat, feeling her swallow against my tatted skin. "Turn around."

She does so, and I reach up to unbuckle the leather harness I put her in to keep her shirt and spiked bra on. I had plans tonight but they have changed. I remove the harness and grip the bottom of her shirt lifting it up and over her head. Then I unfasten the bra and push it off her shoulders.

A whine comes from her parted lips, and I smile, turning her to face me once more. "Good night, sweetheart."

"You're not going to punish me?" she asks softly.

I pull the sheets back, then undo her shorts and remove her underwear. Once she's naked, she crawls into bed, and I pull the covers up over her body. "Oh, you'll be punished, Ash. But I want you to remember it." Her heavy eyes close, and I sit down next to her.

I won't leave her here all night fucked up by herself. I'll stay with her to make sure she's okay. Then tomorrow, I'll make her regret ever knowing me.

I STAND ON THE BALCONY, WATCHING THE SUN RISE OVER THE tall trees while sipping on my coffee, when I hear her moan and start to move around in bed. Turning, I step through the open doors and into her bedroom. She rolls over, lifting herself onto her hands. Her hair falls to cover her face, and she groans, "Fuuucckk."

"Rough night?" I ask, taking another sip of my coffee.

She sits up and turns to face me, glaring. She's still pissed. Good, I'm ready for a fight. It's time to get some shit figured out, and I wanted to wait until she was coherent.

"Do you have any idea what I could do to you?" I ask.

She snorts, her heavy eyes closing and then opening. The harsh sunlight hurts her sensitive eyes. "Just do it already and get it over with."

"Over with?" I laugh. "Sweetheart, it's a lifetime punishment, not a spanking."

She throws off the covers and stumbles out of bed. My eyes fall to her naked body. Fuck, I'm so hard for her right now. Have been since I brought her back to me.

Her pretty blue eyes meet mine, and she holds her arms out wide. "Why the fuck am I even here, Saint?" I don't answer. I don't have to. The simple answer is because this is where I want her. She's mine. She snorts at my silence. "Move on...I did." With that, she goes to walk toward the bathroom.

I drop my coffee cup and grab her hair. Spinning her around, I shove her into the wall by the bathroom door and wrap my hand around her fragile neck. Her nostrils flare, and eyes narrow up at me, but she doesn't fight me when I place my face in hers. "We took vows..."

"Like that ever mattered," she snaps. "You married a dead woman, Saint. No one knew I existed." Her voice rises.

"I did," I shout in her face. "You're my wife—"

She gives a rough laugh that makes the hairs on the back of my neck rise. She truly doesn't give a fuck. "A Lord doesn't marry for love, Saint."

I release her neck and step back from her, needing a second to collect my thoughts. I thought there was a reason why she shot me and ran. Could it have just been that she wanted me dead and she knew that a divorce wouldn't happen? "You truly believe that bullshit? That I don't love you?"

Her bottom lip trembles, and her breathing picks up. "You proved that..." She pushes off the wall. "I asked you to save me, and you refused."

I frown. "Save you..." I trail off, remembering that day like it was just moments ago. They say that people tend to block out the bad things that happen to them, but I'll never forget the day she left me. "You asked me to kill you," I say through gritted teeth. "That's not proving love."

"And you couldn't do it." She pushes off the wall and shoves me, but I don't move. "Huh? Which one of us was the coward?" Her small hands hit my chest once again. "You son of a bitch. I never asked you for anything. I just wanted you to do one thing, and you couldn't fucking do it."

"I wasn't going to kill you!" I scream, my heart racing with how fucking worked up she's gotten me.

She takes in a deep breath, trying to control herself, and her pretty blue eyes fill with unshed tears. "I would have done anything for you, Saint. Anything." The first tear falls from her bottom lashes to land on her cheek. "I was trying to save you, but you wouldn't do the same for me. If you would have just let me go..." Her voice breaks, and she swallows.

I reach out to cup her face, and she goes to pull away, but I grab her face in both of my hands to force her to look up at me. "What do you mean, save me?"

Her watery eyes search mine before she whispers, "It doesn't matter, Saint. It's over. You won."

"Ashtyn—"

She pulls herself free from me and turns, walking into the bathroom door. She slams it shut, and I hear it lock. I go to ram my shoulder into it when her bedroom door opens behind me. "Saint?"

"What?" I snap, turning to see it's Kashton.

"We've got a delivery."

Letting out a breath, I decide to let her cool off while I go and rip some brand off a Lord's chest. Poor unlucky bastard will have to endure my bad mood.

FIFTY-FOUR

ASHTYN

A knock comes at my door, and I sit up before the door opens. Jessie enters. "Your presence is wanted in the office."

I've been confined to my room for the past week. We flew back to Pennsylvania, and I haven't seen the guys once. It's been driving me nuts, and I know Saint is aware of this. He's punishing me for our fight the following morning. And honestly, I hate it. I will never tell him the truth because it won't change anything. It's over and done. He lied to me. Why should I divulge information to him?

Getting out of bed, I make my way to their office. I step inside and see Saint standing in front of the floor-to-ceiling windows, his back to me. His cell to his ear. "That's not what I fucking said!" he snaps, spinning around. His eyes meet mine, and I stiffen at the way they pin me in place. "Get it fucking right, or I'll carve it into your fucking head." He ends the call and pockets his cell. "What do you want, Ashtyn?"

I swallow nervously at how cold he said my name. "You..." I clear my throat. "Wanted to see me."

"No. I didn't." He falls into his seat, dismissing me.

I nod to myself and turn to leave.

"I did."

Stopping, I look over at Kashton, who stands from his desk. Walking over to me, he holds out a cell phone.

"What the fuck is this?" Saint snaps.

"It's a phone." He hands it to me. "It's got four numbers in it. The three of ours..."

"And the fourth?" I ask softly.

"Jasmine's."

My eyes widen. "What—?"

"Abso-fucking-lutely not!" Saint shouts, coming over to us. He goes to take it from me, and I step back. "What the fuck are you doing, Kash?" he barks out.

"You heard her in New York. She contacted the police and filed a report. She needs to know that Ashtyn is okay. And if she does, maybe that will keep her from sticking her nose where it doesn't belong." The way his voice softens with the last sentence, I feel like he's trying to protect her. I'm just not sure from who. I would never hurt her. She's the type of friend that I always wished I had.

Saint runs a hand through his hair. "Fine," he grinds out and gives me his back, walking back over to his desk.

I don't waste a second and already have her number pulled up before I can lie down on my bed.

It rings a few times as I nibble on my nails. Just when I think she's not going to answer, it stops.

"Hello?" she asks softly.

I flinch, realizing she's probably just gone to bed from a long night at Kink. I sit up. "Jasmine. I'm so sorry to call you so early. I wasn't thinking..."

"Who is this?" she asks through a yawn.

"It's Ashtyn...Brittany," I correct myself.

"Oh my God, girl," she gasps, now wide awake. "Are you okay? Where are you at? I'll come get you," she rushes out.

I smile and let out a soft laugh. "I'm fine."

"But...that guy you were with? Do you know him? Where the fuck have you been? I've been calling and texting you nonstop."

"Yeah," I sigh. "It's complicated."

"Complicated how? Like I need to show up with the police? Or I need to set the place on fire to burn the rats?"

I laugh softly. "It's fine. I'm fine. I promise."

There's an odd silence on her end, and I wonder what she's thinking about me. What did Kashton do to her in the women's restroom? I'm sure Bones barged in there after we left.

"Does this have to do with Whitney missing as well?" she asks, breaking the silence.

I slowly get to my feet. "What do you mean Whitney is missing?" I haven't heard that name in so long. She was on the run too from Tyson Crawford. Poor thing, she's lucky she got away. Whitney ran to Vegas and became a Queen. But I never spoke to her. We kept our distance. I was too afraid if she got caught, I'd be found.

"After seeing you and the stunt that Kash pulled, I called Titan to check on Whitney. I had been trying to get ahold of her since I saw the wreck your place was in, hoping she could help me find you. But she hasn't been answering my texts or messages either."

"What did Titan say?" I ask, having a tightening in my chest. "Is she okay?"

"He said not to worry about her. That she was where she belongs."

My stomach drops at her words. "He said those exact words?" I question.

"Yeah. I didn't get a good feeling about it, and when I questioned him further, he dismissed me." She huffs. "Typical man."

Where the fuck could she be? And where should she be?

"How are you doing? How are you feeling? Are you taking care of yourself?"

That sounds like such an odd question, considering I don't have control over myself. But I tell her, "Yeah." I don't want to worry her. She can't do anything for me.

"What about birth control? You're still taking it, right? I don't want them to knock you up and trap you."

"Of course." I snort. "God, could you imagine...?" I trail off, coming to a stop. "I have an IUD," I say more to myself than her.

"That's good."

But a memory comes to mind of how I woke up when I got here. I was naked, tied to a table, and they put me to sleep. I felt like I was out for hours, but all they did was place a tracker in me. Right?

What if...they had someone remove my IUD? What if they tied my tubes? A hysterectomy? Would I know that? From what I remember, all women must be sterilized here at Carnage. I'm no longer his. I'm a prisoner here. Like all the rest. No...could Saint do that? He was mad that I fucked other men when I thought he was dead. So I can see him making it impossible that another man could knock me up.

That thought makes me weak in the knees. Saint hasn't given me any contraceptives to take. He hasn't used a condom that I know of. He also hasn't fucked my cunt while I've been awake. Only my mouth. He's also the only one out of the three who I've been with. I know why Haidyn hasn't touched me. He hates me.

But Kashton? I nibble on my bottom lip before asking, "What's up with you and Kash?" Maybe Jasmine is the reason he hasn't touched me. Maybe he's in love with her or something. I almost laugh at that thought. Lords never love a woman.

"I don't want to talk about him." She dodges my question. "Kashton isn't important. You are, Brit—" She stops herself. "Ashtyn."

I want to ask her more questions about her and Kashton, but I know she won't answer. So I tell her, "I promise I'm fine."

"Where are you? I'll come and visit."

"No. No. No. Don't do that," I rush out. I'm not sure what has been said between the Lords and Bones, but it was obviously getting heated at the show, and I don't want to cause any problems for her. Fuck the Lords and Bones, but I won't put her in harm's way.

"Ashtyn, you don't sound like a woman who is okay." She huffs.

"I...I don't know where I'm at." I lie to her, and my throat tightens.

She's quiet for a long second before she speaks. "I'm saving your new number, and if I don't hear from you at least once a day, I'm coming to find you. Got it?"

A smile spreads across my face. "Got it."

SAINT

I'M SITTING AT MY DESK WHEN THE DOOR FLINGS OPEN, slamming into the interior wall. My head snaps up, Kashton grabs his gun, and Haidyn jumps to his feet.

"What the fuck, Ash?" Kash barks, dropping his gun to his side. "You want to die today?"

"Where is Whitney?" she demands, ignoring Kashton while glaring at me. "And what did you do to me when I arrived? Other than the tracking device?"

The room falls silent, and my teeth clench. I look over at Kashton, and he runs his hand through his hair, letting out a long breath. Giving her that damn phone was the worst thing he could have possibly done. I don't know Jasmine, but she's going to fuck shit up. Kashton just wants some sort of lifeline to her since Jasmine has apparently blocked his number. I'm not sure what he did to her in the bathroom back in New York, but it was enough to piss her the fuck off.

"Fuck Whitney," Haidyn states.

"Haidyn!" I growl.

He steps out from behind his desk and walks over to Ashtyn. She glares up at him with her shoulders squared. "Bones isn't the one who ratted you out. Whitney was."

"No." She shakes her head.

"She's here. In a cell in the basement. Ask her yourself." He goes on.

"Haidyn!" I shout. What the fuck? Her talking to Whitney is the last thing I fucking want to happen.

He turns to face me. "Let her see." Haidyn shrugs carelessly. "Whitney gave her up to save herself." He turns back to Ashtyn. "She's a coward, just like you. No wonder you two were besties." With that, he storms out of the office, slamming the door shut behind him.

The room fills with her heavy breathing, and when her eyes meet mine, I can see unshed tears in them.

"You didn't answer my other question." She lifts her chin, trying to act like she's not about to cry.

I cross my arms over my chest and just stare at her. I'm not going to either. Let her think whatever she wants.

The first tear falls from her bottom lashes, and she turns around, giving me her back, and rushes out of the room.

"Fuck!" I hiss.

"Saint—"

My phone ringing interrupts whatever Kashton was about to tell me. I'm not in the mood to talk to him right now anyway. "Hello?" I snap into the phone.

"Hey, just wanted to let you know we're about five minutes out," the Lord states on the other end.

Goddammit, I forgot they were coming today. "Okay."

FIFTY-FIVE

ASHTYN

I run down the hall to see Haidyn waiting for the elevator. "I want to see her."

He chuckles. "Don't believe me?"

Reaching up, I grab his shirt and pull on it. He spins around and steps into me. "Watch it—"

"I want to see her." I interrupt him. "Now."

He rubs his chin, then nods. "Okay."

We enter the elevator and take it down to the basement in silence. Stepping off, I follow him down the long and cold hallway, through the plastic strips that hang in the doorway. We pass a few prison cells that have full concrete doors. The only way to see inside are the little slots that they feed them through. Water and bread are all they get. Well, that's what they were fed when I was here last time.

He comes to a stop at a cell and punches in some numbers on a keypad. When it unlocks, he pushes the door open, making me flinch due to the loud squeeze that echoes through the basement.

"Go ahead." Haidyn gestures with his hand. "But I'm not sure she'll tell you anything."

I move to stand in front of the open door, refusing to go inside it. I'm not that desperate for information. A brunette lies on a stretcher, like the one I remember being strapped to. She's also wearing a strait-jacket, staring up at the concrete ceiling.

My feet move me forward into the cell, and my pulse races. "Whitney?" I ask roughly.

Her head snaps to the side, cold eyes meeting mine and stopping me in my tracks. I swallow the knot in my throat when I see the 666 branded on the side of her face. It's bigger than the one I have on my body. It looks fresh—red and irritated.

She sits up, and I take a step back, half expecting her to run at me. "What...what did they do to you?" I ask softly. Is she here because of me? Did I do this to her? She's the only one I ever contacted after I left. I felt so alone. I was depressed. I just needed someone...

FOUR YEARS AGO

I sit on the floor in my hotel room, staring out of the floor-to-ceiling window. A bottle of pills next to me and there's another bottle to my right but it's full of vodka. I throw it back and only part of it makes it into my mouth. The rest runs down my naked body.

The door slamming shut makes me flinch. I just fucked a man for money. That's not the part that makes me feel worthless. It's the fact he wasn't Saint. I know Haidyn and Kashton used me, but it never felt wrong. Saint was always right there with me.

This was different. Lonely.

I pick up the burner phone that I have and stare at it. I've dialed Saint's number so many times just to see if anyone answers. It's the unknown that's eating me alive. Did I kill him? Did he survive? If so, is he looking for me?

It doesn't matter. He can never find me. It doesn't matter if I'm no longer pregnant. I can't go back and undo what I did. What I was accused of...

I lie down on my back and hold my phone up in front of my face with shaking hands and dial the one number I know I can trust. It's a gamble, but I just need to know...

"Hello?" the female answers and my heavy eyes fall closed as a tear runs down the side of my face.

"Whit-ney...?"

I never could bring myself to ask her if Saint was alive, and she never offered that information. As far as I knew, she didn't know. Her senior year, she had been given to a Lord—Tyson Crawford—and when she needed to escape the world, she came to Las Vegas and became a Queen. The Kings made sure that our information stayed discreet. I'm not saying they care about us, but they care about their clients who pay a lot of money for their services.

She jumps to her feet and rushes me. Her movements aren't fast but they catch me by surprise, and I freeze in place. Before she makes contact with my body, Haidyn steps in front of me and reaches out, gripping her neck. He picks her up off her feet, spins her around and slams her into the concrete wall.

I gasp, my hands coming up to my face.

"We've talked about this, Whitney," he says calmly while she gasps now lying on the floor. "Now...what do you say?" He grabs her dirty and matted hair, yanking her to her knees forcing her to face me.

My wide eyes meet his before they drop to her sunken ones.

"Fucking bitch!" she sneers.

"Whitney, I never meant—"

"Luke should have killed you!" she screams, thrashing in his hold.

Who the fuck is Luke?

"Just like my sister. I should have let him kill you both!" Her shrill voice hurts my ears, and I reach up, placing my hands over the side of my head as my eyes sting with unshed tears.

This is what Carnage does to you. It makes you go crazy.

SAINT

I RUSH DOWN THE HALL AND ENTER WHITNEY'S ROOM, PUSHING Ashtyn out of my way as Haidyn yanks Whitney off the floor by her hair. He slams her down onto the stretcher, and I help him strap her down while leaving her in the straitjacket.

She's screaming and thrashing the best she can, but she's weak.

We get her tightly secured, and I turn to look at Ashtyn. This is why I didn't want her down here. Nothing good could come of this. What the fuck could she possibly ask that Whitney would tell her the truth? Whitney is not on her side. Never has been and never will be.

Ashtyn steps back into the hall, and her wide eyes meet mine. I say nothing, and she turns and runs back toward the elevator. I head after her only to stop right outside the door when I see her standing in the hallway. Tyson Crawford and his wife stand in front of her.

Whitney screaming behind me fills the cold space as Tyson reaches out and pushes his pregnant wife behind him, blocking Ashtyn's view of her.

I see Haidyn come up next to me, and Ashtyn takes in a shaky breath. "You should have killed me when you had the chance," she whispers to Tyson.

He holds her stare and opens his mouth to speak when Lake steps forward. "I can answer any questions you have."

"No," Tyson snaps at his wife.

She smiles at Ashtyn, ignoring Tyson. "Everyone deserves to know the truth about their life." Lake goes to pull away from Tyson, but he yanks her back with his hand in hers. Pausing, she steps in front of him and kisses his lips before pulling her arm free and walking toward the elevator. I allow Ashtyn to follow.

Honestly, Lake knows just enough that might pacify Ashtyn for now. There's still so much more that she doesn't need to know. It wouldn't do her any good, just harm.

"You think that's a good idea?" Tyson asks me, shoving his hands into his jean pockets once the girls are in the elevator and headed upstairs where it's safe.

I shrug. "Can't be worse than Whitney."

He walks toward us, and we turn to all three enter Whitney's cell. "Has she given you anything?"

"No," Haidyn answers. "We've had her in the jacket for three days and nothing. I don't think she'll give up any information."

"Ty-son," she chokes out, yanking on the restraints and looking over at him. "Please…"

He gives her his back to face us. "And Luke?"

I shake my head. "He said he turned in Ashtyn and Adam's mother, but that was all we got out of him." I'm not sure I trust a damn thing he says anyway.

"What about her cell phone?" He goes on.

When she was brought in, she had two phones. One was destroyed and we kept the second trying to find any information we could on Ashtyn. "Nothing," I say once more. There weren't even any text messages between her and Ashtyn. Just a contact with a number.

The thought of a phone makes me think of Jenks. I haven't heard anything from him about the cell I gave him to go through. I need to call him.

Two hours later, I'm sitting in my office after Tyson and Lake left when my door opens, and another visitor enters the room.

"Hey, man. Gavin called us to come in?" Sin states, entering with his pregnant wife on his arm.

I stand from my desk. "Yeah, he texted me," I say, nodding to him. "He should be here any minute." Devin is our doctor here at Carnage. But when we took in Sin's mother-in-law, I struck a deal with him. She's pregnant, and they're going to take the baby once she delivers. I promised he could bring in Gavin—a doctor of the Lords. It was a simple gesture that made him feel comfortable and gets me what I want in the long run.

The door opens once again, and I expect it to be Gavin, but it's not. It's my wife. "Ashtyn, can you give us a second?" I say, clearing my throat. I've ignored her, hoping she'd crawl to me asking for forgiveness. For what? I don't know. I just need her to need me, but I know the truth. She doesn't. Not anymore. She now knows what freedom feels like, and she's just a prisoner here.

Sin's wife drops his hand and turns to face mine, and my pulse races, knowing what's to come. "Ashtyn?" Elli breathes. "Oh my God, it's been so long."

Ashtyn smiles brightly at the bleach blonde, excited to see a familiar face. "Yes it has. How have you been?" She holds her arms out wide and hugs the pregnant woman. "You look fabulous. Congratulations..." They strike up a conversation, and I look at Sin.

He's standing there staring back and forth between them, scratching his head. "You know my wife...?" he asks, sounding just as confused as he looks. When Ashtyn doesn't answer, he looks at Elli. "You know her?"

She gives him a warm smile. "Yes." Laughing, she points at my desk. "I saw a picture of you and the Spade brothers on Saint's desk a while back and thought it was you."

Sin looks at me, and I just stare at him. "How...?" He looks back at the women. "How do you two know each other?" The girls are about four years apart, so they wouldn't have attended Barrington at the same time.

"Laura, Elli's mother, was my mom's therapist," Ashtyn answers, sounding less enthusiastic about admitting that fact. Then she turns her attention back to his wife.

He turns to face me fully, and I watch his face grow tight. "Excuse us, ladies." I walk past them and out into the hall, knowing I need a second alone with him.

The moment the door shuts behind us, he faces me. "What the fuck, Saint?" Sin barks.

"It's not what you think..."

"So you didn't set me up in hopes that my wife would exchange her mother for me?" he snaps.

I sigh, not exactly. "I didn't know Elli's father was going to bring her in, offering Laura in hopes to get you back," I growl. Sin made an arrangement with us. He turned himself over to us in order to set Elli's father free from Carnage. Did I know who Elli was? Yeah. Did I want her mother here under our roof? Absolutely! I hated that woman. She had hurt Ashtyn before, and she wanted to get rid of her. I still think she was the one who helped Ashtyn escape from Carnage. I was going to torture that information out of her, but the bitch showed up pregnant, and until she has that baby, I won't touch her.

He gives a rough laugh, not believing me. "Fuck you, Saint." Sin goes to open the office door, and I grab his upper arm, stopping him.

"You were willing to do anything for your wife. I will do the same for mine," I inform him.

He yanks the door open and enters the office. "Elli, Gavin will be here any minute. Let's go."

"Yeah." She nods to him and then hugs Ashtyn again. "I'll call you. We'll hang out." Elli tells my wife, and her face falls as if I will never let her have any friends. Once Laura gives birth, Sin will never bring Elli back here.

I don't blame him, but I don't regret what I did. Sin willingly gave himself up for his wife, and I respect that.

He takes Elli's hand and ushers her out of the office, leaving me with Ashtyn. We haven't spoken since our fight a week ago. I've avoided her and her me.

We stand in silence, and she licks her lips. "Elli told me they are here to see her mother?" Her eyes meet mine. "Why is Laura here at Carnage?"

"Because this is where she deserves to be," I answer.

"So...she's a prisoner?"

I say nothing.

"May I see her?"

"No," I growl. "Stay the fuck away from her." We've got her secluded right now anyway. She's needed around-the-clock care to make sure the bitch makes it to full term with the baby. Sin would slit my throat if anything happened to the child he and Elli will raise as their own.

"Saint—"

"Stay the fuck away, Ashtyn!" I shout, getting irritated.

Letting out a huff, she spins around to leave when I speak. "I'm leaving tomorrow and will be gone for two days."

Her hand pauses on the doorknob.

"Haidyn will be here with you," I tell her, wanting her to know she'll have a babysitter so she doesn't get any crazy ideas.

Her body stiffens, and then she yanks it open and storms out.

FIFTY-SIX

ASHTYN

I have a half brother. That new information doesn't surprise me. What does is that he's connected to Whitney and Laikyn. I spent an hour with her yesterday when she and Tyson showed up.

She didn't seem to have much information for me, but she was willing to tell me what she knew, and that was more than Saint and the others have done.

She asked if I remembered the girls who went missing. When I told her yes, she informed me that Luke and my mother were involved, and that the guys think that's why my mother was killed. It makes sense. My brother said that he was being framed. Maybe that was Luke trying to blame it on Adam. But that brings up another question—how was Whitney involved? I spent a lot of time with her and never noticed anything. But would I have? A lot happened in my life that I still hid from Whitney.

Then I find out that Laura and Whitney are both here at Carnage. They've been right underneath me all this time, and I had no idea. I hated Laura, but that doesn't mean I think she deserves to be down there. Did I agree with the things she did and said to me?

No. But I know the Lords, and maybe they controlled her? Maybe the Spade fathers forced her to make me do my sessions? And she knew things that no one else did...if not for her, my life would have gone much differently, and I'm not sure that would have been better. If I had stayed here and told Saint I was pregnant and it wasn't his child, me and the baby wouldn't have had a chance. That's all I wanted—to give my child a chance at a better life. I even failed at that.

The truth is I don't know what to think anymore. At this point, I'm not sure what is up and what is down.

Besides my mother, I don't know what happened to my family. Hell, as far as I know, Adam is down in the basement as well. Would they do that to one of their brothers? Yes. I have no doubt. If you don't honor your oath, you're punished. It's that simple.

It was great seeing Elli. I was never close with her, but I remember seeing her when my mom would drag me to her sessions with Laura. Her practice was out of her home, and I'd see her often while sitting in the hallway when my mother would need a moment alone with Laura.

My mother told me to stay away from her because she was a bad influence. I'm not sure why she thought that, but we never hung out. She was younger than me.

I sit on the floor in my bedroom, just staring at the damn clock that continues to tick loudly. I've been in here since I stormed out on Saint yesterday in their office. I'm trying to clear my mind and figure out where I go from here, but I know the answer. Nowhere.

We took vows, I willingly became his wife, but I will rot here as his prisoner. He hasn't even given me my ring back. I know he saw that I was wearing it at Glass when he showed up. And I took it off later that night before I got in the shower. He was lying to me here when we got into our fight after New York. He doesn't care. He's a Lord; he's been trained what to say and when to say it to make you feel special or hated. And like he said, I'm easily manipulated.

Nothing has changed. And it never will. He'll keep shit from me, and I'll do the same to him. Sometimes, the truth just doesn't matter.

The seconds on the clock move ever so slowly, the sound so loud it makes me cringe with each movement.

Tick, tick, tick, a constant reminder that there is no end in sight. Just an endless amount of torture. I'm in a loveless marriage, I get ignored, I get used...it's a typical marriage in our world.

You're nothing special. My mother had said to me. I hate that she was right more than anything.

At least when I first got here, he fucked me. As stupid as it sounds, it made me feel useful. Now he's ignoring me. That's my punishment.

Tick, tick, tick. The clock mocks me, and my watery eyes look up at it. *Tick, tick, tick.* Second by second, I sit here in a room and his is down the hall. I haven't even been inside of it. I might as well be locked up in the basement. At least then, I'd know where I belong.

Tick, tick, tick. I get to my feet, pick up the chair that sits at the round table by the double doors to the balcony, and throw it at the fucking wall. It hits the clock, shattering it before it falls to the floor.

I'm breathing heavily, looking over the broken glass, and I realize I'm that clock. Broken. It's just time that I quit trying to be a good girl. He's made up his mind, and I have done the same. But him bringing me back had me second-guessing my decision four years ago. I need to get back to her. Fuck him and fuck this life. It doesn't get any better.

I've always been a puppet. For him, for my mother, for the Lords. We're just meant to be used. Sex makes you feel things. Another line my mother once told me. After I left Saint, I told myself that was a lie because the other guys I were with never made me feel what Saint had. She was right again.

Sighing, I walk away from the shattered clock and make my way to the bathroom. I need a bath, and then I'm going to find something to get high with. Or drunk. I need something, and I don't care if Saint finds out or not.

I STAND OUT ON THE BALCONY, OVERLOOKING THE DARK NIGHT. It's amazing how far you can see when there's light but nowhere to look in the dark. The fact that I ever thought I'd have a life with a man who loved me for me and wanted me to give him children is stupid really. From the moment I was hidden here, I knew my life would never be the same, and I was an idiot to think it'd ever be anything different. Better.

We don't all get the same chances in life. I was raised that we have the better life, but it was bullshit.

I hear my door open, and I don't even bother to turn around and see who it is. I don't have to. It could only be one person, and he's the last one I want to see right now.

He remains silent as he walks out onto the balcony and comes to stand beside me. Placing his forearms on the railing, he leans over, overlooking the woods.

"What do you want, Haidyn?" I ask tightly. He's done nothing but avoid me since I returned. I know why, and I get it, but why pretend now?

"I want to take you to dinner."

I snort.

"I'm serious, Ashtyn."

The sincerity in his voice has me facing him, and he does the same, turning toward me. I stare up into his dark blue eyes, and he reaches out his hand, his knuckles brushing the hair from my tear-streaked face. He doesn't say anything, and I hold my breath when he leans forward and softly kisses my forehead.

"Get ready. We leave in thirty minutes." With that, he turns and exits my room, giving me no chance to argue.

Maybe Saint left me behind for this very reason. To spend time with Haidyn. If Saint knew the truth about my past with his brother, that's the last thing he would have done.

My hair is still damp from my recent bath so I quickly dry it and decide to put it up in a ponytail. Once done, I put on some foundation, blush, mascara, and gloss, calling it good. I'm walking out of my closet after getting dressed when my door opens promptly at eight thirty.

Haidyn enters and comes to a stop. He shoves his hand into the pockets of his black dress slacks as his eyes drop to my heels and run up over my exposed legs. They slowly rise to meet mine, and I nervously rub my sweaty hands on my thighs.

"Ready?" he asks.

I nod, turning to my nightstand. I go to grab my cell but pause. Why do I need it? Saint's not going to contact me, and I already did my daily call with Jasmine. So I turn and head for the door as he follows me.

We make our way down the hallway and to the elevator. Silently, we ride down to the first floor. We pass Jessie as we exit the front double doors, and he stops to have a word with Haidyn, but they speak too quietly for me to hear what words they exchange.

Haidyn holds the door open for me, and I softly thank him as we step outside onto the porch. A black Escalade SUV is parked out front in the circle drive. A man stands at the back-seat door and opens it for me. We both thank him as we climb in.

It's captain seat style on each side facing the center. I take the seat with my back to the driver. Haidyn sits across from me.

The car begins to move, and Haidyn pulls his cell from his suit jacket to text someone. My first thought is that it's Saint. He's telling him how bad I look. Or how mopey I've been since Saint left me.

I take a deep breath, trying to calm my nerves. "Why are we here?" I blurt out in the silence.

He looks up at me from his phone. His fingers pause over the keys. "Because of our fathers—"

"I don't mean life." I interrupt him. "Right here. Right now." He knows I'm not talking about the Lords. "Why are we going to dinner, Haidyn? You've avoided me since I've returned. Why the sudden interest?" I cross my arms over my chest.

His eyes are trained on mine, and I shift in my seat. The Spade brothers have a way of making you feel naked when you're fully dressed. He drops his eyes to his phone and returns to texting. After a few seconds, he pockets his cell and looks back at me. "I wanted a better life for you."

My stomach drops. They sound so much like my mother. "I...I don't know what you're talking about." I roll my eyes, acting like his words don't bother me.

"I've always loved you, Ashtyn."

My pulse races. "Haidyn—"

"Not in the sisterly love sort of way because that would be gross. Considering I've fucked you." His eyes drop to my crossed legs, and I shift in the leather seat. "Also, not enough to want to spend the rest of my life with you." I frown, and he chuckles. "Romantic, right? You were supposed to be my chosen."

"No—"

"You were." He interrupts me. "Your father had a meeting with mine. I walked in on them discussing our future. I said I wouldn't do it. At the time, I knew that Saint was obsessed with you. He was always watching you, and when you weren't around, you were all he ever wanted to talk about. Every move you made, he knew, therefore we all knew as well. You couldn't hold a conversation with him that didn't turn to you at some point."

I scoot closer to the edge of my seat.

"My father didn't give a shit what I wanted." He laughs. "Surprise. You were going to be mine. I thought I wasn't going to have a choice. But one day, I overheard a phone conversation. Saint had already gone to your father, and it was decided that you would be given to Saint."

"What was the deal that my father proposed?" I ask.

"Does it matter?" He shakes his head, answering his own question. "Not anymore."

"Of course, it does," I snap.

"What? You going to leave Saint?" He laughs at his own question.

"You already tried that once." His eyes drop to my chest this time, and I take in a deep breath. "A little piece of advice. If you plan on trying that again, make sure to kill him. Otherwise, you'll never get away with it."

I sit back in my seat and huff. Glaring out of my window, I watch as the trees go by too fast to count.

"Why do you think I did what I did that night?" he speaks again.

I look back at him before my gaze drops to my hands.

"You never thought about it?"

About why he did what he did? No. I was raised not to question the Lords. There are no rhymes or reasons. It just is. "I just thought—"

The driver interrupts me. "Sir?"

"Yeah?" he asks, looking over my shoulder.

"We've got company. Two black SUVs and a black cargo van."

Haidyn spins around to look out the back glass. "Shit," he hisses. "Get over here and put your seat belt on," he barks at me.

I scramble to get over next to him and buckle up, my heart suddenly racing. "Do you know who it is?" I rush out.

"No." He gets down on his knees and pulls out a drawer that seems to be underneath the seat I was sitting in. Several guns are inside, and he pulls one out. He checks the chamber and the magazine before returning to his seat. "Lose them," he commands the driver while removing his suit jacket.

"Yes, sir," the driver says and then hits the gas.

My seat belt tightens across my chest.

"Ash—"

We're hit from behind, slamming us forward. The seat belt sits so high on my neck that it chokes me.

"I said fucking lose them!" Haidyn snaps at the man.

"Trying to, sir..."

We're hit again, and Haidyn's arm lands across my chest to hold me back as if my seat belt isn't going to do its job.

"Here." Haidyn leans over the back bench seat. Then he's

removing my seat belt and placing something over my head. "What is this?" I ask, my hands shaking.

"It's a bulletproof vest." He pulls the Velcro across my chest and stomach so tight I can barely breathe.

"Where's yours?" I ask when he sits back in his seat, but he ignores me. "Haidyn?" I grip his hand, digging my nails into his tattooed arm. My wide eyes meet his, and he looks much calmer than I feel. "You need..."

"I'm fine, baby girl. Put your seat belt back on," he orders before moving to the other seats that face us. He leans over into the front of the SUV and talks quietly with the driver. One hand holds the gun while the other points out to the road as he gives instructions.

My wide eyes look around to see what's going on, but the SUVs and the cargo van are gone. Nothing but the dark night around us. I let out a shaky breath and sit in my seat. Running my sweaty hands down my bare thighs. My feet bounce up and down, and now I wish I had brought my cell with me so I could call Saint. Even if I know he won't answer, maybe it would make me feel better.

Haidyn looks at me over his shoulder. "Put your seat belt on!" His eyes glare at me.

"It's fine. They..." The sound of crunching metal cuts off my words. My body is thrown forward, and I feel like I hit a brick wall. Something covers my face, taking away my sight. A loud ringing takes over my hearing, and I feel like I'm rolling down a hill.

I can't breathe. As if a weight is sitting on top of me. My sight is still restricted. Voices start to clear the ringing sound, and I blink rapidly to see Haidyn on top of me. His hands are on either side of my face. He's got blood running down his.

His body pins mine down while something sharp digs into my back, and I wonder if that's why I can't breathe. His mouth moves, but I can't hear anything he's saying.

My hands try to push him off me, but when he doesn't budge, I hit the thing strapped to my chest. I rip one of the Velcro off, and he sits up, undoing the others.

I manage to suck in a breath, arching my neck the best I can, and my lungs burn.

"Ashtyn?" he shouts. "Ashtyn. I'm going to pull you out."

I don't understand what he means or why we're lying on the ground. But before I can say anything, he grabs my arm and yanks me through broken glass. Then I'm looking up at a sky full of stars. The world seems to spin around and around.

"Ash?" Haidyn's voice makes me flinch. Then hands are on me. I'm pulled to a sitting position, and I stare into his blue eyes. There are four of them. "What hurts?" he demands. His hands push some strands of hair from my face that my ponytail no longer holds up.

Hurt? Am I supposed to be hurting?

"Breathe!" he commands, and I try to push him away, but he grips my face in both hands, placing his face in front of mine. "Fucking breathe, Ash. Come on, baby girl. Take in a deep breath for me."

My vision goes blurry, and I realize I'm crying. When I blink them away, he comes back into focus. His pretty eyes dart back and forth between mine. I part my lips and manage to suck in a sharp breath. It feels like I've swallowed a ball of fire, making me choke. I begin to cough.

"That's it." He nods his head. "Deep breaths. One after the other."

"Hai-dyn." My body trembles in his hands.

"Don't fucking talk, Ash. Just breathe for me."

My hand goes to my burning chest, and I yank at my dress. "Burns..." I manage to say between gasps.

"You're okay. It's okay." He runs his knuckles down my face, wiping my tears away.

"You're bleeding," I whisper.

"I'm fine. Don't worry about me."

"Hai—"

I'm yanked up from the ground by my hair, and a scream is ripped from my mouth at the sting in my already pounding head. An arm wraps around my neck from behind, pinning me to a strong body. I try to fight, but I'm too weak.

Haidyn slowly gets to his feet and lifts his hands into the air. "Let her go."

My hands dig into the arm choking me as my body fights the best it can. The process has my dress rising up my thighs.

A dark laugh makes the hairs on my neck rise. "Haidyn. It's good to see you again."

"Let her go!" he shouts, stepping forward.

Something hard and sharp pushes into the side of my cheek. "What would Saint have to say if he knew what you've done to his girl?" the man who holds me asks.

Haidyn's jaw sharpens as his eyes go to mine, then rise to meet the man behind me.

"Get in the van," the man orders Haidyn.

"I'll go with you, but she stays behind." He nods to me.

"Hmm, as tempting as that is, that's not happening."

Haidyn runs a hand down his bloody face. "Then you can go fuck yourself."

The man laughs once more before he holds out his right hand, and a loud noise has me covering my ears. I blink to see Haidyn standing in front of us, and the next moment, he's lying on the ground, face down.

I start kicking and screaming. My throat's on fire as I don't even recognize my own voice. "Get him in the van," the man orders, dragging me across the broken glass and metal that covers the road.

"HAIDYN!" I scream, watching two men pick him up.

I'm thrown into the back of the black cargo van, and I go to jump out, but my hair is grabbed once more, and I'm shoved down onto my stomach. A shoe digs into my back as the side of my face is smashed into the floor that smells like vomit and piss. I'm kicking and screaming the best I can as my arms are grabbed and brought behind my back. Something wraps them, securing them tightly. Then I'm hauled to my feet and shoved onto a bench.

I watch as two men toss Haidyn inside, and he lands on his back. He's been shot. His button-up is soaked in blood, and I fall to my knees next to him as the doors are closed.

"Haidyn?" I cry, fresh tears clouding my vision. "Help him." I fight whatever they tied my wrists with, knowing I need to apply pressure to his wound, or he'll bleed out.

"If he dies, he dies." Someone chuckles.

I raise my head to look up at a man sitting on the opposite bench. He's got a black mask on and a leather jacket with matching gloves. Who are these men? "Saint and Kashton are going to kill you for this," I spit out. Me? No one gives a fuck about me. But Haidyn? He's a Spade brother. A Lord. And no one goes after a Lord.

He slaps me across the face so hard it knocks me over. My body lands across Haidyn's. Laughter fills my ears as pain explodes behind my eyes. "You should worry about yourself, bitch. We've got plans for you, and you're not going to like any of them." More laughter.

A hand gently touches my hair, and I expect it to yank me to my feet. But when it doesn't, I look up through watery lashes to see it's Haidyn's. He's weak, but his eyes are open. I watch his chest rise and fall slowly, and I sniff. "I'm sorry, baby girl," he whispers.

I begin to cry harder, my shoulders shaking as my nose runs. I'm still having trouble breathing, and my chest aches.

"Shut her up," a man calls out.

I'm yanked from Haidyn and forced to sit on the bench, and I watch his hand fall to his side as his eyes close.

"Open wide, bitch!" A man laughs before something is shoved into my mouth, not even giving me the chance to fight.

SAINT

Kashton and I are two hours into our flight. I'm sitting on the couch, answering emails on my laptop while Kashton watches porn on his without earphones. The woman fake moaning while the sound of the guy's dick fucking her sloppy wet pussy fills the private jet. Prick. Like I want to listen to that shit right now. I'm fighting with Ashtyn; therefore I haven't fucked her since we returned from New York. But what's new? Story of my life.

An email notification pops up on the screen, and I choose to ignore it while I finish typing out what I was in the middle of. Once done, I open it up.

Sweetheart.

"What the fuck is this shit?" I bark out, getting Kashton's attention.

"What?" he shuts his laptop.

"Not sure." I grab the remote off the table and turn on the flat screen that hangs on the wall. I pull up my email and go to the most recent one, pressing play.

A humming sound fills our private jet from the speakers that hang above us as a large concrete room comes onto the screen. The lights buzz, and boots slapping on the floor echo.

"That's Carnage," Kashton states, getting to his feet.

The camera is placed on what looks to be a counter. It shows a metal table in the middle of the room. It's got strategically placed medical restraints—black and white leather belts around it—from one side to the other—to strap something down. Or more like someone. I know because we've used it before. On people we've tortured. On Ashtyn.

The door on the opposite side of the room squeaks open. The noise is so loud it hurts my ears. A man enters the space. He's dressed in all black. Combat boots and cargo pants with a chain linking his belt loop to a back pocket. He's got a gun strapped to his thigh. Looks to be a .45 in a holster. A long-sleeve T-shirt with a vest over his chest and back. It reminds me of a bulletproof vest that a SWAT member would wear. But it doesn't say that. He's got a mask on that covers his face.

"Who the fuck is this?" Kashton demands. I don't answer because my guess is as good as his.

He walks over to the far counter and opens drawers and cabinets, placing items on a rolling cart next to him. He knows where everything is, which makes me nervous. Reaching up, he presses the button to the radio he has on his vest. "Bring her in," he commands, letting go of it. His voice is altered, so I can't tell who it is.

I really wasn't sure what we were watching until now, and my heart races with nervousness. Fear. Of what we're about to watch.

"Fuck," Kashton hisses. "We're going back." He storms toward the front of the plane to give the pilot his new orders.

My eyes stay glued to the fifty-inch TV, praying this is some joke. That the *her* being brought in won't be Ashtyn.

The guy on the screen grabs a few more things from a drawer and pulls out a few packaged items. He rips the package open and places the them on the cart, arranging them so everything has its own place.

The door opens once more, and two men enter. They're dressed identically to the guy already in the room. Not a single piece of skin showing on their bodies.

One walks backward while he holds the ankles of a woman. The other guy walks forward, his arms wrapped around her upper body.

My fear that it wasn't going to be Ashtyn has my breath catching when I see the woman they're dragging in.

She struggles in their grasp. Her body rocks back and forth as she bucks and tries to free herself, but it's useless. The only thing she wears is a hood over her head. She's naked and the 666 I branded on her is clear as day. Our fathers made me do it to remind her who she was, that it was her cross to bear in a way. Now it's a beacon for anyone who wants to hurt me.

"Shit," Kashton hisses, running back to me and catching sight of the TV.

She struggles helplessly, and by the sound of her lack of voice, I'd say she's gagged underneath the hood that they have tied around her neck.

They shove her into the side of the table, bending her over it while one of the guys holds her down with a hand at the back of her neck. The other removes a knife from his pocket and cuts the zip tie that holds her wrists behind her back.

Before she even gets the chance to fight with her hands, they toss her onto the metal table, slamming her down. She goes to roll over and pull her knees up into a ball on her side, but the two men waste no time strapping her down in the restraints. White leather cuffs are wrapped around her wrists and secured down by her side to the table. Black leather belts are secured around each ankle, forcing her to keep her legs open. Another one is strapped across her upper shoulders, securing her chest and head down.

"When was this taken?" Kashton demands.

"I...I don't know." My eyes quickly drop to my laptop. "I just got it. How far out are we?" I ask him.

Shrugging, he shakes his head. "Don't know. Told him to turn the fuck around. He wanted to argue, saying we couldn't. I punched him in the goddamn face and said just fucking do it." He drops to the chair next to mine and grabs my laptop, getting to work on the email to see if he can track it.

"She's ready for you," the first guy who entered says into his radio.

Time seems to slow as I watch her lie naked and strapped to the table as they watch her. My eyes scan her body, noticing she has bruises on her thighs, a cut on her arm, and dirt on her knees. What the fuck happened since I left her?

A fourth guy enters the room, dressed like the others, wearing a mask and gloves. Not a single inch of skin is showing. ACE is written across his vest. He walks right up to the table, and his mask tilts down to look at her. "How was she?" he asks as the original guy rolls the cart over to him.

"Fucking handful." One laughs, reaching down and slapping her breast.

She arches her back the best she can and fights the restraints, the sound amplified in the cabin over the engines.

Ace slowly pulls another strap out from the other side of the table and lays it across her lower stomach. "Feed that through," he tells the other guy who slides his end through the metal ring and then hands it back to Ace. He pulls it tight, pinching her skin, and buckles it as well. "That should be enough. Not like she'll put up much of a fight." They all laugh. "Will you, *sweetheart*?" he asks, leaning his mask-covered face down toward the hood that covers hers. "Let's get started."

She continues to thrash around the table as he dunks what looks like a washcloth into a glass bowl full of liquid. He wrings it out and then runs it over her heaving chest and flat stomach. She's got dried blood on her, making me even more confused. What the fuck happened before they brought her into this room?

Then he moves it to her pussy, making her jump and fight once more. She's wearing herself out. She's doing what they want her to do. Once satisfied, he begins going over each leg.

He's washing her. Then he tosses the washcloth back into the now bloody bowl and picks up a dry one. He dries her off while her struggle gets weaker and weaker every second.

He tosses it to the side, and it falls to the floor. Then he walks over to the counter and grabs a knife. My heart hammers as he goes back over to her and places his hand on her hip. "This is going to hurt," he tells her. "But as long as you stay still, it'll be over sooner rather than later."

Her body jerks as he presses the tip into her skin, forcing it to split.

It's the first time I've heard somewhat of a noise from her gagged mouth. It's almost a faraway scream, making my chest tighten. Her body tenses, pulling tight on the restraints that hold her down.

Blood runs down the side of her body before he presses two fingers into the now open skin and removes the one thing I had that guaranteed I would never lose her again. He drops the tracker to the floor and stomps on it with his black combat boot.

He then turns back to the cart and picks up a black device that makes Kashton jump to his feet. I can't seem to find the strength to stand. He presses it to her skin and gives her three staples, trying to close the wound he just opened as she shakes violently, the gagged screams seem louder than the last.

"Such a good girl," he tells her, and her naked body sags into the metal table. "You deserve a reward for that." Picking up something off the cart, he then pops the top on a tube of lube. He pours it all over the pink egg and then stands. He runs his fingers between her legs, and once again, she fights. He begins to finger fuck her, forcing her body to rock on the table. Her neck and back arch, and her hands fist. "That's it." His distorted voice coos. "Such a good whore. Aren't you, sweetheart? You had no problem coming for me before. Come on my fingers, love. Come all over them. Show me how much you like it."

"Who in the fuck is this, Saint?" Kash shouts.

It has to be... "James," I answer.

"No way. We killed him," Kashton argues with me. "Plus, even if he had still been alive when we left with her, how the fuck would he have access to Carnage? Or know where her tracker was?"

"There's no one else it could be," I grind out. *Someone she's fucked?* That list could be long, considering she'd been on the run for four years. I never asked for a list because I liked the idea that she'd ever only been with me, Haidyn, and Kashton.

"Where the fuck is Haidyn?" He pulls out his cell and starts calling him. "Voicemail," he growls, throwing it to the floor of the plane.

The man removes his fingers and slaps her cunt, making her flinch. He steps back, and she sags into it. After a second, he slides the egg into her. After wiping his fingers just inside her on her bare chest, he picks up his cell and hits a few buttons. She starts rocking back and forth, fighting once more, fighting the vibrating toy inside her.

He picks up a marker and removes the lid. He writes WHORE across her upper chest. Then FUCK ME next to the 666 on her pelvic bone. BITE ME on her right thigh and USE ME on her left thigh.

"Look how pretty you are." He tosses it to the side as well. Reaching up, he grabs her breasts, and her hips buck. "Fuck, I've missed these."

"It has to be James," I whisper, not believing it could be anyone else.

"Here...how about a little more. I want you to enjoy it." Grabbing his cell, he turns up the vibrator, and she's practically convulsing on the table at this point. "That's more like it."

The other three laugh, reminding me that they're in the room. They stand at the foot and head of the table in their masks, watching her. Enjoying the show. The third leans up against the countertop with his arms crossed over his chest.

"We're almost done," Ace tells her, but I doubt my wife can hear him. Between the hood over her head, the gag in her mouth and the vibrator in her cunt, her senses are heightened. "You're doing so good."

His mask looks up to the head of the table when he speaks. "Go get the crate." Then he looks at the one who stands at her feet. "Help me out." He unclasps the ankle that's next to him while the guy follows his lead.

She kicks her legs since they're free, but Ace grabs them, wraps his arm around her knees, and shoves them up to her chest. "Hold them," he barks as she tries to fight him.

The other guy rushes to the side of the table to take his place. Once Ace thinks he has it under control, he walks over to the counter and opens a top drawer. He removes a butt plug and lube. He pours it all over the black silicone. So much so that it slides down the sides and onto the floor. "I'm being generous, love," he tells her as if she fucking cares. "Some don't get this courtesy."

Walking back over to her, he stands at the end of the table, legs wide, and runs his fingers along her ass.

"Shit," the other guy hisses, locking her legs in place as her hips buck off the table, making it rattle.

"Got her?" Ace asks, sounding impatient.

"Yeah." The other man's mask nods. "I'm good."

"Just lie back and relax, sweetheart," Ace tells her before he pushes the butt plug into her ass, making her body rattle the table as it fights. Ace chuckles once it's in and stands up straight. "You didn't mind when I fucked it, baby." He slaps her ass cheek, and his laughter grows. "You begged me, remember? Your ass was up in the air, and you were on the verge of tears. You were so fucking needy for me to take it."

He reaches up and motions with his glove-covered fingers for the other guy to release her legs. He pushes them down, and they redo the ankle restraints before she even has a chance to fight them.

Ace walks back over to the side of the table, facing the camera. He reaches out and runs his glove knuckles down her chest, making her back arch up off the table at his unwanted touch. "We had fun, didn't we, baby?" he asks her, slapping the side of her breast.

He reaches down at her neck and undoes the hood's string. There's a reddened mark from how tight it was on. He pulls the hood slowly off her head. A cloud of dark hair covers her face, stuck to her skin from tears, snot, and drool.

She's sobbing behind her gag, and he places his mask-covered face down to hers. "Shhhh. Shhh, darling. You're okay," he tells her, his hands pushing her hair from her face so he can see her.

He grips her cheeks and turns her head to the side, forcing her to look toward the camera. Red-rimmed blue eyes stare at mine, and my breath catches in my lungs.

"What the fuck?" I hear Kash bark, but I ignore him.

"Remove the vibrator," Ace orders the guy who stands at the end of the table. He reaches between her tied legs and pulls it out, making her slump against the table, and he holds it up. "Show her. Show our whore how much she liked it."

The guy walks over to the head of the table and holds the wet egg over her face, smearing the wetness onto her cheek, and she shakes her head, screaming into the gag that's buckled tightly around her face, pinching her cheeks.

"So fucking good, huh?" Ace asks and slaps her cheek before rubbing the drool, snot and tears all over her face. "Such a good fucking whore." He laughs, and she arches her neck, body shaking from her sobs.

Her eyes close tightly, and tears run down the side of her face.

"Don't worry, sweetheart. I'm going to put it back in." He turns her face to look up at him, and he slides two fingers down between her tied-open legs and pushes them into her.

She blinks rapidly, fresh tears falling from the corner of her eyes.

"I should keep you for myself, but this isn't about me." He removes them, and a sob wracks her naked body.

The door squeaks open, making her jump, and the guy who left earlier enters once more, pushing what looks to be a wooden box into the room that sits on a rolling cart. "See that, baby? That's all yours."

Then he looks at the guy who rolled it in. "Get it ready," he orders. "I'm going to plug her cunt back up." He goes to the end of the table and easily slides the egg back into her. Grabbing his cell, he presses a few buttons, and her hips begin to lift off the table, fucking the toy inside her while she sobs uncontrollably.

The other two remove the top and side of the wooden box.

My eyes go back to Ace, and he's got a syringe in his hand. Pulling the plunger, he fills it with a clear liquid. Then he walks over to her and sinks it into her neck. "It's not going to make you pass out. Just relax you," he tells her, and she blinks, her eyes already getting heavy. "Enjoy having all of your holes filled, sweetheart." He runs his glove-covered knuckles down her tear-streaked cheek.

Her body relaxes into the table, and he undoes her restraints; she no longer fights. Instead, her head falls to the side, her heavy eyes on the camera. She doesn't even blink. She looks dead. The only sign she's alive is the soft movement of her exposed chest.

He rolls her over onto her stomach, bending her legs to where her heels touch her bare ass. He wraps a belt around them, securing them tightly. He picks her limp body up and places her in the middle of the box on her stomach. Her heavy eyes are still on the camera as her head is to the side.

Her arm dangles out of the side of the box, and one of the guys picks it up, pushing it behind her back, where Ace does the same. They wrap a rope around her wrists, tying them together and then securing the extra to her ankles.

"Place the top on," Ace orders.

And the other two lift the wooden top, placing it over the three sides. There's a metal hook screwed to the top of it. Ace pulls out a double hook that I once gave her and places it through the rope that ties her wrists together, connecting her tied wrists to the top of the crate. She won't be able to move inside it. At all.

He then lifts her head up by her chin. Drool runs out of the gag, and her heavy eyes are unfocused. "Be a good whore and come all over that toy. Can you do that for me?'

She doesn't respond in any way. He lets go of her face. Her head falls to the bottom of the box, and she blinks. Her lashes are slow to open this time.

"Close her up," he commands as he turns to face the camera.

The two guys put the side piece on, and just like that, she's gone. Tied up and put away in a box like a doll. To be stored in the attic. A lock is put in place as if she has any chance of freedom.

"Do I have your attention, Saint?"

My name echoes in my ears as I watch the other two wheel her out of the room, the door closing behind them.

"I only gave her enough to keep her comfortable for about an hour. It'll start to wear off. She'll eventually realize she's been buried alive in the Pennsylvania woods." *Her worst fear.* "She'll then panic. Do you think she'll run out of oxygen first and suffocate? Or do you think she'll vomit and choke on it? Doesn't matter, really." He laughs. "This was all recorded an hour ago. I waited for you to get two hours away before I sent you the video. It'll take at least two hours to get back. She should be coming around anytime now. You'll look for her, of course." He steps closer to the camera. "I hope you find her. I truly do." He steps even closer. "Because I want you to know what it feels like to hold the woman you love dead in your arms." And with that, he turns and exits the room.

"FUCK!" Kash throws his laptop across the room, and it hits the screen that still shows the footage of inside the room. It's empty other than the table she was strapped to and the cart that he used to hold all the devices he used on her.

I stare at it. Not sure what I expect to happen but waiting for something. Anything.

"Saint?" Kash shoves my shoulder, and I blink.

I fall onto the seat and pull out my phone. I dial up the one number I can think of to help. He answers on the first ring.

"Hey, Saint..."

"I need your help." I rush out, getting to my feet, and start pacing. I place him on speakerphone when he speaks.

"Name it."

"I'm sending you a video." I nod to Kash, and he starts typing away on my laptop since he destroyed his. "I'm in the air. Too far away. But I need you to watch it and tell me if there's anything you can do. Something we might have missed."

"I have the guys here. Can they watch it as well?" Tyson asks. I'm not sure who the fuck he means by *guys*, but I'll take all the help I can get.

"Yeah." I swallow the knot in my throat.

"Got it. Starting it now." I hear the sound of the video in the background as they stay silent. I continue to pace back and forth, feeling a fire burning in my chest. I was terrified, but now I'm pissed.

He waited until he knew I couldn't get to her. He wants me to suffer, but she's the one suffering right now. Her fear is being buried alive. And that's exactly what he made sure to do to her.

"Saint?" Tyson calls out.

"Yeah?" I snap out of it.

The sound of doors opening and closing tells me they're getting in the car before the roar of the engines comes through the speakers. "Where was she last?" he asks.

"Carnage," Kash answers. "We had to leave so she and Haidyn stayed behind."

Just then my laptop alerts me of a new email. Kashton's eyes meet mine as he sits in front of it.

"What is it?" I ask.

"We just received an email labeled **Haidyn**."

"Fuck." Tyson sighs, knowing exactly what that means. "We're headed to Carnage. Finn thinks he has an idea of how to track her. I'll call you as soon as we get there."

Kashton hangs up, and then I turn to face the cracked TV. It still works just has lines through it. Kash puts a new video on, and we watch it play out.

It's of the entrance of Carnage. The surveillance cameras are pointed down at the front double doors. They slam open, and she's thrown over a man's shoulder. She kicks the best she can, but her hands are tied behind her back. She manages to knee him in the face, and he drops her.

She's got the ball gag in her mouth, and she tries to scoot away, but he grabs her by the hair and yanks her to her feet before tossing her to another guy. He carries her out of sight, and two new men enter Carnage. They are on either side of an unconscious Haidyn. His feet drag behind him, his shirt covered in blood. His head is down, so he might be dead, but I can't tell.

"Cut the cameras," a guy says into the radio on his bulletproof vest, and it goes black. I continue to stare at it, and new footage appears. It's like the one room Ashtyn was in, but this is a different one.

Haidyn is brought in and placed on a table. He's strapped down just like she was—ankles, wrists, and one across his chest.

The door opens once more, and Devin enters the room. "Jesus," he hisses when he sees Haidyn, running over to him and demanding, "What happened?"

One of the guys holds a gun to the back of Devin's head. "Save him."

Just then, Haidyn opens his eyes. Taking in a shaky breath, he looks around aimlessly.

Nodding, Devin moves over to the cabinets. "I just need to sedate him."

"No!" a guy barks out.

Devin turns to face the room. "I can't help him unless he's sedated. I have to cut him open—"

"You've got two choices." The man interrupts him, moving the gun and pressing it into the side of Haidyn's head. "You either cut him as is, or you give him a shot of adrenaline."

Devin looks at Haidyn and then at the guy and nods. He begins to rummage through the cabinets and drawers, tossing items he needs onto a metal tray. Then he grabs more restraints from a cabinet underneath the table.

"What the fuck is that for?" one of the men asks.

"What you have on him now won't be enough," Devin explains, connecting a leather belt to the side of the table and throwing it over Haidyn's waist. "Once the adrenaline hits, he'll be hard to keep down. I need him as immobile as possible, especially if I cut him open." He tightens the belt and then places two more across his legs. He pulls a mouthpiece out of a drawer and turns to Haidyn. "Open," he orders.

Haidyn's eyes find Devin's, and what he says makes the hairs on my neck stand. "Ash-tyn?"

One of the guys laughs. "That bitch is as good as dead. You'll be lucky to join her."

Haidyn opens his mouth to say something, and Devin shoves the mouthpiece into it, not wasting any time. Then he takes the needle, plunging it into Haidyn's bloody chest.

FIFTY-SEVEN

SAINT

We're landing and in the car within an hour and twenty minutes. Way too long but as fast as we could get back. We enter Carnage when my cell rings. I answer on speakerphone. "We're here..."

"We found her. Sending you a pin now."

I hang up and look down at my cell. We race to the back of Carnage and run through the woods. My heart hammers in my chest.

Voices come from deep within the trees, and I'm sucking in breath after breath as I watch the guys grow closer. Ryat stands next to the broken box, shovel in hand. Tyson is down on his knees next to a body.

"ASHTYN!" I scream, running faster, not sure where I got the rush from, but knowing I have to get to her.

"Saint." Tyson stands and turns to face me. He moves in front of me, hands on my chest, bringing me to an abrupt stop.

She lies on her stomach, head to the side, dark hair hiding her face. Her arms are still tied behind her back and secured to her ankles in a hogtie position. "Untie her!" I bark at them as they just stand around staring.

"Her neck is broken." Sin whispers, kneeling beside her while looking up at Ryat.

"No!" I shove Tyson out of the way and drop to my knees next to her.

"Saint?" Tyson places a hand on my shoulder, and I push it off.

"Someone give me a fucking knife," I demand.

"Here." Ryat kneels on the other side of her and opens his pocketknife. He cuts the rope that binds her wrists to her ankles, and they fall to the ground. I pick her up in my arms, and her head falls to the side. Sin was right...her neck is broken. My shaky hand pushes her dark hair from her face, and I take in a deep breath, pulling the body to me.

I drop my head to hers and let out a cry of relief. Dropping the body, I stand and look at Kashton who also stares at the dead woman. When his eyes meet mine, he frowns. "Where the fuck is she?"

"So this isn't Ashtyn?" Jenks asks. He, Alex, Finn, and Colton stand quietly to the side.

"No!" I growl, my shaking hand pushing my hair off my slick forehead. "How the fuck did you find her?" I point at the dead woman. I'm not sorry she's dead. I'm just glad it's not my wife. But the fact that this was a setup makes my stomach knot more than it already was. What was their plan? Did they think I'd find her so quickly? Was this just a ploy to keep me busy for however long while they took my wife out of the country? It hasn't even been two hours since they sent the videos, but they had been pre-recorded. How and when did they switch out the bodies?

"After watching the video, I decided to try to track the vibrator..."

"Excuse me?" Kashton asks, frowning.

Finn holds up his cell. "The vibrator is linked to an app. Anything linked to an app requires some sort of Wi-Fi, which allows me to track the signal."

"Can you track the cell it's coming from?" Kashton asks.

He shakes his head. "I tried, but it's no longer in service."

"FUCK!" I take a step back from the woman.

"We're not going to give up." Tyson steps in front of me. "We'll find her."

But the question is, will she be dead? I don't ask that out loud because we're all thinking about it.

"It has to be an inside job." Kashton is the one who speaks next. "We've got to find out who the fuck got access to Carnage and how."

As much as I hate it, he's right. I need to find her, but I also don't want to be looking blindly. I need answers, and I'm only going to get them if I know who has her.

"But where do we start?" Sin is the one who asks.

I look at him, and I'm thankful that we didn't kill him when he gave us the chance. And the fact that he showed up to help when he knows I was using him as bait. My eyes drop to the dead woman at our feet, and I get the first glimmer of hope. It makes the corners of my lips twitch. I love a good bloodbath. "I know just where to start. Bring her."

ASHTYN

THEY SAY DEATH IS PEACEFUL. THEY SAY THERE'S A WHITE light and that you have this sense of serenity. A calmness washes over you as you accept that it's all over.

Is that only if you go to heaven?

Because I'm pretty sure I'm dead, and everything hurts like hell. I'm freezing. Like a bone-chilling coldness that has my entire body shivering. My jaw is sore, my teeth locked down tightly on the ball shoved into my mouth. Lips cracked and face swelling.

I hear voices and music in the distance. It takes everything I have to lift my head. A light shines ahead of me, and I can see through the back of a house. The floor-to-ceiling windows allow me an inside view of the three-story mansion.

I'm not sure how I got here or how long we've been here. But I woke up like this what seems like hours ago. From the looks of the trees that surround me, I'd say I'm in the woods. My wrists are tied together with rope and secured above my head to what looks like a metal pole that runs between two trees. It pulls my torso tight.

My legs are spread wide open, rope wrapped around each ankle and secured to cinder blocks that I'm standing on. I try to pull free, but all it does is feel like I'm tearing my muscles.

I whimper as drool runs from my gagged mouth, and I sniff, trying to breathe, but my nose is stuffy. Something crawls up the back of my leg. For all I know, it could be a snake or a spider. I'm praying for the snake. Maybe it'll make its way to my neck and wrap itself around me, suffocating me. The thought makes me think of Saint and what he watched on the tape that the guys recorded back in that room at Carnage. Has he seen it yet? Was it live? Does he even know that I'm no longer there? And Haidyn? Where the fuck is he? Did they kill him? He had been shot and wasn't talking much when they separated us. God, I hope not. I'd hate to be the reason they hurt him.

A back door to the house opens, and two guys step outside onto the porch. I tremble as they walk down the concrete steps, passing the Olympic-size swimming pool, heading right toward me.

There's not a lot of light where I'm at, but the back of the house gives off enough that I can see enough. They're dressed the same as before—black pants, black long-sleeve shirts with matching gloves and masks. They've got their voices altered so I can't tell if they are the ones from earlier or not. I hate that the most, that they're hiding who they really are. I'd prefer to see their true faces. Only a coward chooses to hide himself.

"I say we let her go, and we play a fun game of hide-and-seek," one suggests as they come to a stop in front of me. I don't have to see their eyes to know they're running over my naked body. "First one to catch her gets her mouth. The other gets that sweet cunt."

The other man laughs. "Why chase the bitch when we can have her right where she is?"

"You're no fun." The first one pouts.

My hair is grabbed, and my head yanked back, making me cry out into the gag. My spit flying out around it. Hands dig into my already sensitive cheeks squeezing painfully and tears fall from my eyes.

"No. I think we'll fuck her right where she is." He lets go and lowers his hand to his black jeans.

The sound of his zipper being lowered has me fighting harder against the rope. My body twists back and forth with what little it allows. The blood rushes in my ears and the rope around my ankles tighten with each small movement cutting off the circulation.

"Hold her head in place. I want her eyes on mine while I fuck her," he tells the man behind me. "Fuck, I can't believe I'm going to get to fuck Saint's bitch."

The one behind me laughs, and I pull against the restraints, screaming into the gag. I try to tear my head free, but he just yanks it farther back, forcing me to stare up at my tied hands above my head. The drool at the back of my mouth slides down my throat, choking me, and I cough into the gag, my body convulsing as I try not to die.

"That's the sound I want to hear."

"What the fuck do you two think you're doing?"

I'm let go, and my head falls to hang down so the drool can leak outside of the edges.

"Sir...we...."

"Get your asses inside," the new one barks.

I hear their shoes shuffling as they step on twigs and leaves over my heavy breathing.

"Let's make you a little more comfortable," the new guy says, and I blink rapidly to free the tears from my eyes to clear my vision.

A second later, the gag is unbuckled at the back of my head. I try to spit it out, but my arms are pulled so tight above my head that the leather straps are stuck between my arms and embedded into my cheeks.

He steps in front of me, grabbing the gag, and yanks it free of my mouth.

I spit out the excess saliva pooled in my mouth, my face stinging from how tight it was. "Ple-ease." I begin to sob.

"Shh." He grips my chin and shoves my head up. "See that house ahead of you. There's over twenty men in there. And guess what they want?" He doesn't let me answer. "You."

I sniff.

"If any of them come outside, I'm going to let them have what they want. Understand?" He lets go of my chin.

I nod the best I can. If I get their attention, they get to rape me. Just like the two that he just stopped.

"Let's try a test." He reaches out, pinches my nipples painfully hard, and yanks on them.

I throw my head back and grind my teeth, holding my breath at the pain from my skin stretching.

"Good girl." He lets go, and I sag in the ropes, fresh tears falling from my swollen eyes. "I like this." His hand goes to my 666 brand, and I flinch at the soft touch of his knuckles. "I knew then that Saint was in love with you. He was nice enough to knock you out. I wouldn't have."

How does he know that?

"I sure as fuck would have kept you awake. Watched you cry and scream. Beg me to stop while I made sure it was the most painful experience you'd ever had. But then again, you like that, don't you?"

I do. I did. But Saint understands how far to take it. He's never truly hurt me. Not like that.

His glove-covered hands reach down to his pants, and he unbuckles his belt. I pull on the ropes. "No..."

"Shh. Remember, Ashtyn. Anyone comes outside..." he trails off, and I start to hyperventilate. My breathing is coming quicker and quicker. I feel like I'm going to have a panic attack. I'm standing up straight, but it feels like something presses on my chest. "It's just another test," he says, ripping his belt from his jeans. Then he slaps it across my chest.

The sting feels like a million fire ants biting me at once, and it takes my breath away. Just when I manage to get one in, he hits me again. This time across my upper thighs.

I shake in the ropes as the leather hits me once more across my ribs, wrapping around to my back.

"That's good, Ash." He walks behind me, and I sag.

Finally able to catch my breath, I begin to sob. The belt lands across my back, and I try to arch it to get away before he hits me again, but I can't escape it.

Humiliation washes over me that I ever liked this before. To be treated as such. Memories flood my mind of when Saint tied me up in front of Kashton and Haidyn in the woods at the party and how much I was getting off on it. This time, I want to die.

He hits me five more times in various places before I see the belt fall to the ground in front of me. I'm sobbing; tears, snot, and drool run down my face while my entire body shakes uncontrollably. My skin is on fire, and the fact that I'm now sweating makes the pain even worse. He comes to stand in front of me. Reaching into his back pocket, he pulls out a small size of lube.

"I think he may have gotten you pregnant." He laughs.

"N-o." I can't even speak properly anymore. The single word was slurred as if I've been drinking all night. If he were to cut the rope, I'd fall to my face unable to stand on my own two feet. It's like that night Tyson came to my house all over again. Although this time, I know Saint won't be showing up to save me.

"That's what a Lord does, Ashtyn. He picks a bitch, and he makes sure to knock her up. Breeding is a requirement." He pours the lube onto his glove-covered fingers and places them between my open legs. I try to pull my knees together, but the rope around each ankle prevents that. He shoves them into me easily with the help of the lube. "There's been a story going around for years that the Lords add *supplements* to the younger generation's food."

He pushes his two fingers farther up into me and moves them around. The pain takes my breath away, but I have no choice other than to take it when all I want to do is scream for help. He removes them to add three this time just as forceful.

"They require all the Lords going through initiations to live at the house of Lords, where they are offered three meals a day by a live-in chef. Now granted, the Lords are always coming and going freely. So they could eat out, but after four years of staying at the house of Lords, they're bound to eat there at some point. But here's the thing..." He adds another finger, and I can't hold the whimper that leaves my trembling lips. "I've been told they only do it to the highest rankings of Lords. I mean, crazy, right?" He laughs, removing them, and I bite my tongue to hold in a sob. "But totally believable. They used to force the bottom-feeders to undergo vasectomies. So why not enhance the powerful ones to have twins? There's always power in numbers. And let's face it, people die. So twins offer more of an opportunity."

I take a deep breath and lift my watery eyes to meet his black mask. "Why...are you telling me this?" I manage to ask, my voice rough since my throat has gone raw from crying.

"Because I want you to understand why I have to hurt you."

All I can do is shake my head.

"Did Saint let you keep your birth control, or did he remove it?"

I stiffen at his question. How would he know I had an IUD? Is that what Saint did when he knocked me out? My lack of response makes him laugh.

"You have to lose this baby, too. Just like the last one. I can't undo a wrong, but I can make a right. A fresh start so we can move on and have our family. Just like we were meant to have."

My stomach sinks at his words. "It's...you." I manage to whisper. How did he find me? I pull harder on my restraints and a sob bubbles up my throat. "Saint will come after you. He'll make sure you're dead as well." Even if Saint doesn't love me, he will be enraged if I'm pregnant and someone killed his child.

"I'm not afraid of Saint. I have a plan for him too."

He walks behind me, and I try to lean my head back to see what he's doing but my fucking arms are in the way. "Another test." He chuckles and then I feel his hands on my ass.

I struggle, buck and try to kick but nothing helps. It only makes the ropes tighter, my muscles ache and my skin burns. I'm sweating profusely and my shoulders are screaming.

"I'm going to fuck your cunt, Ash. I'm going to make you feel good." I drop my head to sob.

I feel the tip of his cock at my pussy and I scream out as he goes to push into me. He stills and I hold my breath when one of the back doors opens.

I see a hand on the doorknob, and I stare at it as my heart pounds after a second it closes, and I sob in relief.

He wraps an arm around my waist from behind, pulling my ass back and then he's pushing into me. I try to let him, knowing the less I fight, the easier it'll be, but I can't. Instead, I tighten and try to pull away at the pain he causes.

I stare at the sticks and fallen limbs as he pushes his cock into me and takes what he wants. His grunts fill the night air and tears roll down my face knowing I can't fight him. He won. I wasn't strong enough.

When he finally pulls out, I hear him zip his pants and he walks around to stand in front of me. He picks up the gag that lies on the dirty ground.

Panic grips my chest, and I sniff. "I promise." *Gasp.* "I won't..."

He shoves it into my mouth, and I try not to gag at the taste of dirt but fail. "This is for your own good, Ash." He pushes the leather straps between my tear-streaked cheeks and arms. Pulling it tightly around my head, he buckles it in place and adds, "I'll let you hang here for the night while my cum leaks from your pussy and down your thighs. Just like it was meant to be."

I cry into the leather ball, and my watery eyes widen when I see him pull a black hood from his back pocket. He shoves it over my head and pulls a string, tightening it on my neck like before. "Get some sleep, sweetheart." He calls me by Saint's nickname, and I shake my head the best I can, but of course, it's no use. "I'll wake you in the morning for another test."

FIFTY-EIGHT

SAINT

I make my way down to the basement and pull my key out to unlock the prisoner's door. The sound of squeaking metal wakes him. The man sits up on the concrete floor and begins to crawl backward when I enter. He pushes his back into the far wall.

"Where is she?" I get to the point. I don't have a single second to waste. I've seen what they did to her when they thought I was watching. I can't imagine what she's going through right now. The fucked-up part of me wishes they'd send me another video. Just so I can see that she's alive. The what-ifs are the worst part. I need to know she's breathing. That she's not lying in a corner all alone, bleeding to death and praying that I make it in time.

The man chooses to ignore me and brings his knees to his chest to shield his naked body from me. "Bring her in," I order.

Kashton and Sin enter the room and drop the woman's body to the floor in the center. She's on her stomach so I kick my boot out, pushing her onto her back so he can get a better view of the dead woman. Her body has started to harden. Rigor mortis is setting in. It usually can take up to six to eight hours to take over the entire body. But it seems to be happening faster.

"Whitney?" He gasps, getting to his hands and knees, he crawls over to her where she lies. "What the fuck did you do to her?" he demands.

"They killed her—"

"No." He interrupts me as if that's impossible.

"They broke her neck and buried her in the woods after they switched out Ashtyn's body with hers."

He shakes his head the best he can, still not believing me.

"Who the fuck did this?" I shout, losing my patience. I don't have time for this. "Where is my wife?" I grip his hair as hard as I can, trying to rip his scalp clean off his head and rip him off her body.

He chooses to remain silent. I look at Kashton and nod my head. I see Ryat and Tyson approach the open door and enter the small cell.

Kashton pops the lid on what Ryat gives him and pours the contents all over Whitney's naked body. Then Sin pulls a lighter out of his pocket and hands it to me. I strike it on my jeans and toss it onto Whitney, and she instantly goes up in flames. The fire heats up the small concrete room.

He screams out but once again pushes himself up against the wall. I go over, grip his hair once again, and drag him closer to her, pushing his face as close to the fire so he can feel the heat but not burn him alive. I need answers before I can kill the bastard.

"Where. Is. She?" I growl through gritted teeth.

"I...don't...know..." he says between sobs, fighting my hand that keeps a grip on his hair.

I look at Kashton, and the look of annoyance he gives me tells me that he too thinks Luke is telling the truth. But if it's not him, then who? Who the fuck has access to Carnage and the security system? Why kill Whitney? She's the only connection to Luke.

Now a list of men who want to hurt me? That list is a mile long. They aren't after Ashtyn. It's me they want to hurt. And they know that the only fucking thing I care about in this world is her.

I turn my back and go to the door. Kashton, Tyson, Ryat, and Sin each walk out. I watch Luke stare at his wife's burning body as I shut the metal door and lock it.

"WAIT!" He rushes to the door.

"Do you know how long it takes for a body to burn?" I ask him.

He shakes his head, crying while his bony fingers curl around the bars, trying to yank it open. The smell of burning flesh already fills the hallway outside of his cell.

I smile. "You're about to find out." Then we all walk away, leaving her in there with him, screaming for us to put her out. The heat alone will be excruciating. I'll wait until tomorrow to give him his daily amount of water. Maybe he'll have more to say then. Even once she stops burning, the smoke will linger, and the smell...it'll be hell in there. Literally. I'd say it'd kill him, but he can get fresh air through the door. And if he dies, he dies.

We all enter our office, and I walk to my desk. I catch sight of the picture on my desk of the four of us from years ago. The one Elli had seen when she visited. It's our senior year at Barrington. She's got a smile on her face. The guys aren't smiling, but you can see how protective they are of her. I knew that if anything ever happened to me, they would make sure she was taken care of. That's all I ever wanted. To make sure that she got everything I ever wanted her to have—the world.

Now she's gone. Naked, bleeding, and probably crying. She needs me, and I'm nowhere to be found. Maybe Haidyn was right...I should have never brought her back here. She deserves a life outside of here. Without me.

Grabbing my computer, I throw it across the room, and it shatters one of the floor-to-ceiling windows.

"Saint." Tyson places his hand on my shoulder, and I jump, spinning around to see them all just staring at me.

"What's the word on Haidyn?" I ask.

"Devin still has him in surgery," Kashton answers.

We saw the video with the guy holding a gun to Haidyn's head while Devin gave him a shot of adrenaline. We watched him wake up and Devin dig the bullet out. Then the video ended. Once we arrived, everyone who was involved in both videos was gone.

"Maybe he can tell us something..."

"It could be days before he's awake." I interrupt Kashton. But a part of me knows that he might know something.

"What can we do?" Sin asks.

I run a tatted hand down my face. "We're going to check every cell. Every person that is here at Carnage."

"For what exactly?" Ryat is the one who asks this time.

"Anything. Ask them what they know. If you even think they're lying, we take something from them." This place isn't called Carnage for nothing. I'll collect heads and hang them on the fucking wall. Make my wife a bouquet with them for her return because I will bring her home. I've done it once; I'll do it again. No matter what it costs me.

I KICK BOTH DOORS OPEN TO THE HOUSE NOT CARING ABOUT giving myself away. I know she's here. Finn was able to track her down an hour ago. It took me that long to get here.

Two men sit on couches in the living room, and I'm able to put a bullet between each of their eyes before they're able to get me.

Another one jumps out from a side door, and he gets a shot off before I put one in his knee. He drops to the floor, and I land another in his chest.

A guy rushes me from the hall, and I put two into him. A third goes into the back of his head as he falls to the floor, making sure he's taken care of as well.

I head toward the hallway that he came from and come to a quick stop when I see her at the other end of the hall.

"Sa-int." She speaks my name, but it sounds like the first word she's said in days. Her wide eyes go to my left arm, and I look down at it to see blood drip from my fingertips. I've been shot, but I don't feel it. Not yet. My adrenaline is too high. "You're—" A man stands behind her and places a hand over her mouth. The fact that she doesn't fight him tells me what I feared. She's weak.

"I'm fine," I assure her. She's naked, dirty, and trembling.

The man behind her grabs a hold of her matted hair. I swallow when I see him lift a gun and press the barrel into her hollow cheek. She looks so skinny. It's only been a day, but it looks like she's been starved for weeks.

I drop my gun to my side. "Ashtyn." I manage to say her name, but it's soft as my eyes sweep over her naked body. She's covered in bruises and cuts like she's been beaten. My worst fear comes to life.

"Don't take another step, or I'll give her a new hole in her face for me to fuck," the guy holding her orders.

My teeth grind, and I look over her again once more. She's not shaking or the least bit scared. Is she drugged? Or did I take too long, and she's come to terms and accepted a life of being raped and beaten? The thought makes me pissed at myself, and my heart breaks for her.

"Get on your knees," he orders.

"I'm not—"

"Get on your fucking knees!" he shouts, pushing the barrel of the gun further into the side of her face, smashing her cheek.

"Okay. Okay," I rush out, lowering myself to my knees, and I interlock my fingers behind my head as if I'm being arrested.

"Saint, don't—"

"Shut the fuck up, bitch," he growls at her.

"No," she shouts, and the guy behind her places his free hand over her mouth once more.

The next second, I feel a gun at the back of my head as a voice commands, "Hands behind your back."

I do as I'm told, knowing I have to buy some time. The guys will be in here any second to save her. Kashton knows she is the main priority. A zip tie is pulled tightly around my wrists, locking them behind my back.

"That's better," the man holding her says cheerfully. "Now let's get started."

"Let her go," I demand, and they both laugh. "I said let her go!" I scream, my voice echoing through the house. "You don't want her. You want me. Here I am. Take me."

"I have something better planned." The man lowers his gun from her bloody face and grabs her right hand. He places the gun in it and wraps her fingers around the trigger.

"No. No. No," she rushes out, and he laughs once again.

"Shoot him."

"No. I won't..."

"You've done it before. Come on, shoot him."

"NO!"

"Ashtyn?" I bark, getting her watery eyes to focus on mine. "Do it."

Her breath catches, and she shakes her head.

"Come on, sweetheart. Be a good girl and shoot me."

Sobs wrack her naked body. I hear the cock of a gun and watch the man behind her point it at the back of her head. "Shoot him, or I shoot you."

"Do it," I growl, and she shakes her head. "Fucking shoot me, Ashtyn. Come on!" *Come on, sweetheart. Do it for me.*

She just stares at me, tears running down her bloody and swollen face. "I...can't," she says softly.

"Please," I beg, my chest tightening. I walked into the house, ready to die to save her. "It's okay." I nod.

She licks her busted lips. "I love you."

It's the last thing she told me when she shot me at Carnage. I give her a soft smile, accepting my fate. "I love you too, sweetheart." I take a deep breath, knowing it'll be my last, but I watch her close her eyes and turn the gun on herself as she pulls the trigger.

The sound is deafening to my ears.

I'm shoved to the floor, and someone sits on top of me. My scream echoes through the hall. She falls to her knees, and the man behind her laughs. "Fuck. That was poetic. True love right there." He kicks her back, and her body falls to the cold floor.

I'm screaming her name, hoping that she responds in some way, but she lies there unmoving. The man kicks the gun out of her hand and in our direction. "For a bitch, you've got some balls." He fists her hair and leans down, gently kissing her tear-streaked cheek.

Her lifeless eyes are still open, and I pray she's just in shock. That she didn't kill herself for me. I was the one prepared to die. It's always been me. Not her.

"It makes me horny." He chuckles

I try to fight, but something is on my back, pinning me to the cold, hard floor. The gun is still held to the back of my head. "Watch your bitch get fucked like the whore she is."

"Don't fucking touch her!" I shout so loud my throat burns afterward.

The man in front of me laughs, undoing his jeans. He pulls his dick out and spreads her legs with his, pressing his gun to the side of her bloody face. "Tell him, Ash. Tell him I've been fucking you every day for a week now."

A week? Has it really been that long? Did I really fail her that badly?

She says nothing, her eyes still straight ahead.

I try to get to her, but I can't move. It's like something is wrong with me. My body is unable to move. Maybe it's from being shot. "ASHTYN!" I shout, needing her to snap out of it. Fight. Do something. Show me that she's alive.

But my chest squeezes as I watch blood all of a sudden puddle underneath her body. It drips from her nose and her lips. The side of her face smears it as he positions his dick between her spread legs, and he pushes into her with a grunt. "She's still warm, Saint," he adds, gripping her hair. He yanks her head up so her lifeless eyes meet mine.

I'm screaming, my body fighting the man on top of me, and I watch her body rock back and forth on the cold and hard hallway floor, unable to help her. Unable to save her. I'm a poor excuse for a man. Fucking pathetic.

"Saint?" I hear her voice, but her lips don't move. "Saint?" More blood covers the floor. So much so that it's almost reached me where I lie face down. "Saint?"

"It's okay, sweetheart," I say, my throat closing up on the lie. Nothing about this is okay. "I love you, Ashtyn," I say it more for myself than her. Fuck, she has to know that, right? She's always been it for me. Even after she shot me. Nothing she could do to me would stop me from loving her. "I love—"

I blink, catching something out of the corner of my eye, and I look over to see Kashton standing at my desk. His eyes go to the wall that I was staring at. It was like watching a horror movie play out in front of me.

"What?" My eyes bounce around the room to see that I'm still in our office at Carnage. My hand goes to my left arm, and I run it up and down to see that I'm not covered in blood and no bullet wound of any kind. "Ashtyn?" My eyes meet him.

He lowers his eyes and shakes his head. "The guys haven't found anything yet."

It felt so fucking real. Watching her lie there dead while a man raped her. That feeling of helplessness was crippling.

His eyes narrow on mine. "It's been three days, Saint." He softens his voice. "You need some sleep before you drive yourself crazy."

I hate to be reminded that I've failed her. Three days since I was sent a video of her being tortured. Three days since I thought I found her dead in the woods. Three days without my wife, and it feels like a lifetime. But he's right. I have to take better care of myself if I'm going to be who she needs. I have to be prepared for everything and think smarter. That thought proved that she'll need me once I find her, and I can't be half myself. That won't be enough.

"Haidyn?" I ask.

"He hasn't woken up," he answers, clearing his throat.

ASHTYN

THE ONLY SIGN THAT I STILL HAVE ARMS IS THAT I CAN LOOK UP and see my tied hands above my head. Otherwise, my arms and hands are numb. My right shoulder screams, and my legs have cramped up. I can barely breathe most of the time. I've cried so much that my eyes constantly burn.

For four days, the masked man has come out and raped me. Every time has been the same...removes the gag, whips me with his belt, and rapes me. Then places the gag back in and the hood back over my head. Even during the day. My skin is on fire from my sunburn. There's a few hours during the day when the trees don't provide shade, and the sun hits my bruised and cut skin.

I'm in so much pain that I don't even know when the last time I was able to sleep was. I'm just in total darkness most of the time with the damn hood. Even when it's on during the day, it gives me zero light. All I have are my thoughts, and they're driving me mad.

Right now, I hang from the pipe between the two trees, and water drips off my shaking body. He hosed me down, saying I was a disgusting whore who needed to be cleaned. A part of me wishes he would have left the hood on and let me drown.

Voices hit my sensitive ears, and I don't even care to look up and see who is coming. It won't matter. There's no stopping them.

My wet hair hangs around my face, and drool drips from my cracked lips as I look down at the ground. A set of black boots comes to a stop in my line of sight, and I flinch as he bends down and unties each ankle. Standing, he kicks the cinder blocks out of the way, and I hang from my tied hands.

A groan escapes my open mouth at the new position. The rope that ties my wrists to the pipe is cut, and I drop to the ground with a gagged cry. Pain explodes throughout my body, and I lie face down, unable to move. I don't have control over my limbs.

The gag is removed, and something new is replaced over my head and fastened around my neck. "When the cat's away, the mice will play."

Laughter fills the woods and I'm grabbed and rolled onto my back. I look up to see the masked men standing over me. One drops to his knees above my head and pins my still tied arms down to the uneven ground. The second one straddles my legs.

"We're going to give you a little something. Make this a little more fun for you." He pulls a syringe out of his pocket and removes the cap with his teeth.

I close my eyes. I'm too tired to fight or even speak.

"It's only going to hurt for a second," he says before a burning pain shoots through my body.

My cracked lips open and a scream escapes my mouth as I arch my back. The sound of birds flying from the nearby trees follows.

"That's it." The one lets go of my arms and then cuts through the rope, freeing them.

The other stands up off me, and I roll onto my side, holding my chest as I feel like my heart may explode. "If you last twenty minutes, I'll be surprised." He chuckles. "We'll give you a three-minute head start. Don't want to end the game too soon."

I pry my swollen eyes open and look around aimlessly. I feel drunk, like the world is tilted on its side, but I realize I'm still lying on the ground.

Using my left hand, I push myself up to a sitting position as my back screams in protest. I can't feel my right hand at all. My feet tingle, and my stomach rumbles. I'm so hungry.

Something around my neck gets my attention, and I reach up to feel a collar. My trembling fingers move to the back, and there's a lock on it. Pulling on it, I hear a bell of some sort. It's me. They've given me a cat collar like Saint had. But the leather is thicker and heavier.

"You're wasting your time," someone says, and then a boot is shoved into my back, pushing me forward.

I get to my feet and fall. My legs are so weak they tremble.

"Why isn't it working?" the other asks, and I have no clue what he's referring to.

"Maybe she needs more. I didn't want to overdo it," the first one says.

"Run, bitch!" one orders.

Getting to my hands and knees, I begin to crawl away from them. The stupid bell rings as my body moves mechanically. I fall on my face, and they laugh.

"We'll give you ten minutes," one states. "It'll be better if you actually have the strength to fight us." The door shuts, letting me know they returned to the house.

I lie on my stomach, my head to the side, staring at a squirrel not far from me as my heavy breathing moves the leaves that cover the ground. Taking everything I have, I get back to my hands and knees and crawl as far as I can as fast as I can.

I'm a fucking turtle. Tears sting my swollen eyes, and I hate myself for crying. I've done it so much in the past few days.

The door opens once more. "I think you're ready," one says.

And I dig my hand into the ground, feeling the dirt under my nails.

"It's okay, Ashtyn. We're going to play with you first," one taunts.

I scramble to get behind a large tree and press my back into it as they laugh. Looking down, I see a small puddle of water. It's from the guy hosing me down this morning after he whipped me. I push my hand into it, digging my fingers into the mud and grabbing a handful. Bringing it up, I cover the bell connected to my collar. Squeezing my hand around it, I try to fill the small holes with mud. If I can pack it full of it, you won't hear the bell when I run.

It doesn't work like I want it to. So I lie down, getting my face and neck as close as I can to the puddle and grab another fistful. I do it a few more times until there's not much left, and I shake the collar. Tears of relief fall from my eyes when there's no ringing.

Getting to my shaky legs, I press my back into the rough tree and take a deep breath. It's now or never. They gave me the opportunity

I've been needing. No one will ever find me out here. Wherever the fuck here is. I have to do this on my own. Save myself.

I push off the tree and run as fast as I can in the opposite direction of the house and farther into the woods.

Have you ever had those dreams when you're running for your life, and one of your legs doesn't work? You drag it behind you? That's what I feel like right now. I have no shoes, no clothes, and no fucking clue where I am, but I'm running for my life. I can feel my pulse racing and blood rushing in my ears.

I refuse to look back. It'll just slow me down. I'm sucking in breath; my side aches, and I can't hold back the sobs of relief at how close I am to freedom. I try to be quiet, but it takes everything I have to stay on my feet. They hurt so bad as I step on sharp objects and twigs. I trip over a log covered in leaves and land on something sharp that takes my breath away.

Rolling onto my back, I blink looking up into the night, seeing all the stars twinkle as my shaky hand comes to my side. I whimper when I feel something sharp sticking into me. It's glass.

Looking to the right, I see the reflection of brown glass. It looks like part of a broken beer bottle, and if I had to guess, I'd say it's part of what's embedded into me.

"Ashtyn? Here, kitty kitty." I hear the altered voice. "Come on, *sweetheart*, be a good pussy, and let me catch you."

"Dude, that's so fucking stupid." The other laughs.

They don't sound really close, but the fact I can hear anything tells me that I'm too close. Slowly, I get to my feet and keep going in the direction I was headed.

I'm exhausted. All I want to do is sleep, but if I stop, I'm dead. I hobble my way through the trees, dragging my right leg and holding my bleeding side. I'm having problems breathing, and my throat is closing up on me.

I can't die here, not like this. Making it to a clearing, I sob harder when I step onto the blacktop. It's a road. Two lanes and curvy. I start to walk down it, looking over my shoulder to make sure they're not on my ass. Lights come around the corner, and I stand in the center of the two lanes, prepared to die if they don't stop in time. It's the only chance I have at this point.

I hold my heavy arms up and wave them the best I can when it comes to an abrupt stop, almost hitting me. I fall to my knees, my head hanging, when I hear car doors open and close.

"Jesus Christ," a man hisses.

I lift my head, but I can't see anything since the headlights are even with my already blurry eyes.

"Where the fuck did she come from?" another one demands.

"Pl-ease?" I manage to get out. "They're...coming." Who knows how far out they are.

"Get her in the car." Hands grab at me and yank me to my feet.

I whimper as I'm picked up and cradled to a hard chest. Car doors open and close as I'm placed inside.

"Phone," I manage to say through cracked lips. "I need—"

"A hospital." One interrupts me.

"No." I start to fight, and he lets go of me.

I fall to the floor and push my back up against the back-seat door on the driver's side, pulling my knees to my chest to cover my naked body. I could have just traded one nightmare for another. "I need a phone." I manage to say.

My hand is grabbed, and a phone is placed in it. Just like in the woods, my fingers won't work on the phone. It's as if my mind has no idea how to process a phone call. And a thought hits me: I don't know Saint's number by heart. I could call my cell number that Kashton gave me, but it's probably dead by now.

I can only think of one number at the moment. I ramble it off three times before I hear a phone ringing on the end of the line. It was placed on speakerphone, and it's held in front of my bloody face.

"Hello?" the voice asks.

I don't know any of the Spade brothers' numbers by heart, but I know hers. "Jas-mine." My voice cracks.

"Yeah. Who is this?" she asks, sounding worried. "Are you okay?"

"Ashtyn." I swallow the lump that forms in my throat. "I need you to call Kashton."

She sighs. "Ashtyn, I told you he doesn't matter..."

"Please?" I interrupt her, feeling my eyes grow heavy. "I'm lost...I'm about to pass out. I need...I need Saint..."

"Oh my God, Ashtyn. Where the fuck are you?"

"Call Kashton." I don't have the time or energy to go through everything. "Give him this number. Tell him to have Saint call..." If he can get these guys to take me to Carnage, then maybe I'll have a chance.

"Hold on. I'll add him to the call," she rushes out.

I close my eyes and let the drool run out of the corner of my mouth, too tired to swallow it. A second later, I hear ringing.

"Jasmine—"

"I have Ashtyn on the line. She needs Saint." Jasmine doesn't let Kash finish.

"Ashtyn?" Kashton barks out. "What do you mean...?"

"Kash," I say roughly. "I need..."

"SAINT!" I hear him scream, making me flinch. "It's Ashtyn."

I blink my heavy eyes. "Directions," I whisper. "Give them directions."

"Ash? Sweetheart? Where are you? Are you okay?" Saint's voice rattles off questions.

I try to talk, but my heavy tongue won't move.

"What the fuck, Jasmine?" Kashton barks. "Where is she?"

"She was here," she snaps. "She called me from this number."

"Whose number?" Saint demands.

"We found her," one of the guys in the car finally speaks. "She's in the car..."

"Where the fuck are you?" Saint barks out.

My heavy eyes fall closed, and this time, I can't open them back up. I can hear Saint's voice in the distance, but I'm not sure if I'm imagining it. For all I know, I'm hallucinating and still tied up in the middle of the woods.

FIFTY-NINE

SAINT

I shove the double doors open and rush down the front steps as a car pulls into the circle drive. Kashton, Sin, Ryat, and Tyson rush after me. The car comes to a stop, and I yank open the front driver's side door.

"Whoa." A guy who looks to be in his early twenties raises both of his hands. I yank him from the car and knock him to his knees. Kashton shoves his face down and presses a gun to his back. Sin removes a guy from the passenger seat.

"We're just helping her," a guy rushes out as Ryat pulls him from the back seat.

All three are held at gunpoint. I'm not taking any chances.

I rip the back driver's side door open, and she practically falls out, her upper body leaning halfway out of the car. She's got herself crammed behind the driver's seat and back seat on the floor. "Ash?" I bark out, kneeling next to the car. "Ash, talk to me." I reach for her neck and am thankful I can feel a pulse. Pushing wet hair from her face, I find her eyes closed. She's got indentions in her cheeks. They're from a gag. She's got a collar on, and she's covered in mud and dirt. "Come on, sweetheart." I grab her arm and have to pull roughly to get her out of the tight position she's got herself in. "Get them to the basement," I bark at the guys, carrying her unconscious body into the front double doors.

Gavin and Devin are already waiting for me. They've both been keeping a close eye on Haidyn, so the moment we got the call, I had them ready for her arrival. I lower her body onto a stretcher, and they start to rush her through the building and to the elevator.

I look over her body. She's naked, covered in cuts and bruises. Her wrists and ankles have rope burns. I open her eyelids to see bloodshot eyes. She looks dead, but the subtle movement of her chest tells me she's not.

It's enough for now. "Hang on, sweetheart," I say as the elevator dings, signaling we're on the hospital floor. A piece of glass is stuck in her side with fresh blood running down it.

We get to the hospital, and when we go through the double doors, Devin pushes his hands on my chest. "Stay here."

"No, I'm not—"

"Goddammit, Saint," he barks at me. "I don't have time to argue with you. Stay here." He pulls away and rushes after Gavin who wheeled her into an operating room.

I SIT NEXT TO HER HOSPITAL BED. SHE'S BEEN BACK AT CARNAGE for five hours now. My wife was lucky. If you could call it that. She had a dislocated shoulder and was severely dehydrated, but other than that, she'll be okay. The laceration from the glass in her side needed stitches but again, it could have been worse.

"How long until she wakes up?" I ask Devin as he enters.

"I'm going to start weening her off the sedation soon." He comes over to the opposite side of her bed and checks the machine controlling the meds that are administered into her IV.

He said they don't normally sedate for her injuries, but that they opted to because most likely popping her shoulder back into place would have caused her to wake up and be in pain.

"This is good news, Saint. She's going to be okay. No broken bones or internal injuries. It looks bad, but it's just cuts and bruises." Devin had said to me earlier.

Then we got the results, and things weren't *okay* anymore.

The rape kit came back positive. I knew it would. As much as I wished for it to be negative, I knew what was happening while she was gone. And I hate myself for allowing it. For not protecting her. I failed her again.

"It doesn't make any sense," I growl through gritted teeth and get to my feet. "They take her, shoot Haidyn, and then bring them both back here, film them separately, and then leave with her?" I shake my head. "Why?"

"I—"

"Then they let her go?" I pace, ignoring whatever he's about to say. I'm talking more to myself than him. "There's no way that she escaped." I don't care what anyone says, I won't believe that. They let her go, knowing she'd come back here to me. Is that why? Let her return raped and battered? Do they think I'll throw her away? Toss her to the side like she never meant anything to me? I spent four years searching for her, so nothing could happen to her that would make me not love her or give up on her.

And there were three men in the car? How many different men were on the videos they sent us? They were all dressed the same so those who were in the room with her, could have gone and been with Haidyn. I was sent two different videos. Who knows how far apart they were filmed because he waited two hours to even send me the one of Ashtyn.

The door swings open, and I spin around to see Tyson entering the room. He looks at Ashtyn and then me. The blank stare on his face has my pulse racing.

"What's wrong?" I ask, stepping toward him.

He swallows nervously. "It's Haidyn..."

"I'll stay here with Ashtyn." Devin says. "She's fine. Promise."

I run out of the room, wondering what the fuck is going on. My heart pounds when I see Tyson enter Haidyn's room down the hall from Ashtyn's. He holds the door open for me, and my stomach drops when I enter.

Sin stands up against the far wall, his face in his hands. Ryat sits in a chair, staring at the bloody floor. Kashton stands at the head of Haidyn's hospital bed, his forearms on each side of Haidyn's head, he's bent at the waist, Kashton's forehead resting on Haidyn's. Gavin stands next to the bed, paddles in hand.

A loud beep fills the silent room. I'm trying to comprehend what I'm seeing, but my heart doesn't want to believe it.

"I'm sorry," Gavin whispers and places the paddles on the cart beside him.

I watch Kashton's body shake as he fists his hands. Jasmine stands behind him, arms crossed over her chest as tears run down her face. I was told she arrived a couple of hours ago. After Ashtyn called her, she jumped on her father's private jet and flew right here. She wasn't going to leave until she saw her friend was okay. I'm not sure if the Kings know she's here, but I'm not calling to rat her out. I'll make the call if she gets in my way, but until then, Kashton can deal with it.

Licking my lips, my pulse races. Stepping forward, I look over Haidyn lying on the hospital bed. He's got blood running down his nose and my knees threaten to buckle at the thought of losing my brother.

Kashton pushes up off the bed and Jasmine touches his back. He spins around and knocks the cart over. Everything crashes to the floor and Jasmine yelps in surprise at the sound of it clanking to the floor. "GODDAMMIT!" he screams and then storms out, pushing his shoulder into mine, and she runs after him.

I step further into the room, and Gavin's eyes meet mine. "We did everything we could..." He reaches over and turns off the machine, bathing the room in a deafening silence.

The blood rushes in my ears like a freight train. My eyes are on Haidyn's peaceful, but bloody face as Gavin pulls the white sheet up and over it, covering my dead brother from the world.

SIXTY

SAINT

I'm storming off the elevator down in the basement. I can hear voices behind me, but I ignore them. I'm on a mission.

My wife and brother were taken. And now one of them is dead. Someone has to pay for that. It'll be the three pieces of shit who brought her back. Because those three make the most sense to me. If they're innocent? Then it sucks to be them. Talk about wrong place wrong time.

"Saint?" I'm grabbed and yanked back.

I spin around and come face-to-face with Tyson. I fist my hand, and he steps back, placing his out wide while Sin and Ryat stand on either side of him. "I'm sorry about Haidyn," he says softly.

I block him out. I refuse to believe that my brother is upstairs, under a sheet as if he never existed. The sour taste in my mouth makes me want to vomit. But I swallow it down. "Where did you put them?" I demand. "Where are the three guys you all brought in?"

"We separated them." Ryat is the one who answers. "Kashton didn't want them anywhere near one another because they would be able to talk."

I give them my back. "And Luke?" I snap.

"Same place he's been," Sin responds.

Making my way down the hallway, I shove the plastic dividers out of the way and storm through the pits. Then hit the hallway with the cells on either side. I dig the key out of my pocket and open Luke's cell.

He flinches at the loud squeak of the door being yanked open. "Get the fuck up," I bark, rushing over to him. His dead wife still lies on his floor, well what's left of her. The skeleton of her body is all that remains. It takes two to three hours for a body to burn. She's been lying there for four days now.

"N-o," he says hoarsely, pushing his body into the back corner.

I step on part of Whitney's body, feeling the bones crush under my weight stomping over to him. I grab his hair and yank him to his knees. "Who the fuck killed Haidyn?" I scream in his tear-streaked face.

He cries harder. His frail and bony body trembles.

I yank him over to Whitney and place my boot out in front of his bare feet, tripping him. He falls to his knees next to what's left of her, and I shove his face into the ashes sprawled out on the floor. He coughs and sputters as I rub his face in what was once his wife.

Yanking his head back, he screams, his hands coming up to his face and wiping her off while crying. "Who the fuck did this?" I shout, my hand tightening in his hair. I'm shaking as much as he is, but for different reasons.

"I—"

It feels like a hammer hits me in the face, knocking us both back into the far wall. The sound of a blaring alarm begins to go off and the floodlights come on throughout the basement. I cough, waving my hand in front of my face to clear the dust and probably Whitney's ashes that now swirl around the small room. "What the fuck?" I bark out, grabbing ahold of Luke that tries to get up beside me.

"A bomb." I hear Tyson cough, and I look up to see him and the others out in the hall through the wall that's been knocked down. All three of them getting to their knees, brushing debris off of themselves.

"Who the fuck set off a bomb?" I ask, shaking my head and trying to get the ringing to stop. Maybe it's the blaring of the alarm. Either way, it's given me a headache. Or it could be the fact that I was just slammed into a concrete wall.

Luke begins to laugh, and I shove him to his back, straddling his naked chest. I wrap my hand around his throat, lowering my face to his. It's still covered in Whitney's ashes. "Who the fuck set off a bomb in here?"

His eyes grow hard, and he stiffens underneath me. "You did exactly what they wanted."

"Who?" I shout. What the fuck is he talking about? He could be lying. Or he could believe every word he says—men have been known to go delirious while caged.

"Them." He gives me a wicked smile, and I see the dirt and ash in his gums and on his tongue. He has no teeth. Tyson ripped them out one by one. "You brought them into Carnage. Just like they wanted you to."

"The guys who delivered Ashtyn." Ryat is the one who speaks.

I look up at him. "Where did you put them?" The alarm stops, but the ringing in my ears continues.

"We spread them out...I put my guy down the hall." Sin states, pointing down the now rubble-filled hallway.

"How the fuck did they plant bombs?" I wonder. "Didn't you guys pat them down?" Jesus Christ, who the fuck are these men?

All three of them nod. "We did." Sin dusts off his jeans.

"We stripped them down to nothing," Tyson adds.

I frown and look down at Luke. "You're lying." Stripping those who come into Carnage has been something our fathers taught us to do. It serves a purpose. Gives them no defense. There's something very vulnerable about a man being stripped by another, hosed off and thrown into a cage like an animal. It's humiliating.

"It was a suicide mission," Luke speaks.

"Are you saying that they willingly swallowed bombs?" I question with a snort.

He gives a rough laugh, and I narrow my eyes on him.

"Are they shoved up their asses or something?" Sin asks, making Ryat laugh.

Luke doesn't find it as funny.

"They each have bombs?" I look at him. They brought three men in, that means two more are still to go off. Are they on timers? Triggers? How long until the next goes off?

"Four of them have bombs." His wicked laughter fills the room.

"But there were only three men." Tyson frowns.

"Who is the fourth?" I yank Luke's head off the floor only to knock it back into the concrete. "Who the fuck has the fourth bomb?"

His laughter grows, and I've had enough of his shit. "Sin, there's a box of gloves right by the door. Hand me two."

"What?" Luke's laughter stops, and he starts to thrash under me to get away. "What are you going to do?" he demands.

Sin enters with a pair of gloves, and I get up off Luke to turn him over. "Put your knee into his back. Hold him still."

Sin does as I say, placing his weight onto Luke's back, making him cry out, and I yank his arms behind his back, holding his forearms parallel, and I nod at Sin to take them. He pins them down for me.

"What the fuck?" Luke cries.

"He's about to be elbow deep in your ass, man," Sin informs him.

"It's not me!" he shouts, squirming. "I swear to God—"

"There is no God." I interrupt him. "Just you and me. Now be a good boy, spread your legs, and relax." I place my legs between his, shoving them apart and forcing his ass up in the air.

"Saint?" I look up as Ryat tosses me the tube of lube sitting next to the gloves. Honestly, I was going to use spit, but this will help speed up the process.

"You can't do this!" Luke screams, thrashing on the floor. "You can't do this to me, you motherfucker!"

"You kidnapped, raped, and murdered innocent women with barbed wire. I'd say an arm up your ass is getting off easy," Ryat tells him.

I pour it all over the black glove covering my fingers and hand before pouring it over his ass and legs, just dousing him with most of the bottle before tossing it to the side. Placing my hands on his ass cheeks, I shove them open as he screams louder than the ringing of the alarm that still echoes in my pounding head.

"Ash-tyn," he cries.

"What about her?" I growl, getting tired of this game.

He's sobbing and mumbles unintelligible things into the concrete floor while Sin has him pinned down.

"Ashtyn." Sin is the one who speaks, and my eyes snap to his. He swallows nervously and drops his eyes to Luke. He doesn't think he had one, either, but I had to check. His eyes meet mine once again before he speaks. "They brought her in. You don't think..."

"Is that true?" I shout at Luke. "Is that the fucking truth?" I'm screaming, my throat burns, and I shove Sin off Luke so I can toss him onto his back. He's still a sobbing mess. I wrap my hand around his throat and yank him to his feet with my lube-covered glove hand and slam his back into the wall that's partially missing. "Fucking answer me, you son of a bitch, or I will..."

"I don't know." Spit flies from his mouth as tears and snot run down his face through his wife's ashes that cover his dirty skin. "They just said there were four..."

I slam Luke's head into the concrete and step back, letting him fall to his violated ass. Think, Saint...It can't be her. Devin and Gavin ran every test there was. They would have seen a bomb. It would have shown up on x-rays, right? The CT scan? Ultrasound? There would have been some kind of red flags to make them dig deeper if they found something odd.

It's Luke. He's trying to distract me by using my wife. I'm not going to fall for it. I grab Luke and shove him to the floor once more. "Tyson, go find Kashton. Fill him in on everything."

"Done," Tyson states and takes off.

Sin walks out of the cell only to come back with a set of gloves of his own. I shake my head, pointing at the hallway. "Get out. Both of you go. I'm not going to be responsible for killing you guys if he's lying." I'm not that knowledgeable when it comes to bombs. So I have no clue what might set it off.

"I'm staying." Sin smiles with excitement, and I growl. I don't have time to fight him on this, and he knows it.

"Ryat, alert the hospital staff. Have people moved to the morgue." It's the safest place that I can think of right now.

Sin's face pales, and he too looks at Ryat. "Will you make sure Gavin moves Laura, please? The last thing I want to do today is explain to my wife that a bomb killed our child."

"On it." Ryat sprints off.

Sin removes his belt and kneels down by Luke, who is losing his shit once more now that he realizes this is happening. I hold his arms down his back while Sin fastens his belt around his wrists. Then he flips Luke onto his back. I undo my belt and wrap it around his thighs.

Sin places his knee into his neck and shoulder, pinning him down, he then reaches underneath Luke's tied legs, and pulls his knees to Luke's chest. The position lifts his ass and lower back off the concrete floor, giving me better access.

"Okay, Luke. Let's see if you were telling the truth." Sin laughs. "I never thought death by anal cavity search would be an option for me." Shaking his head, he adds, "I like my odds."

ASHTYN

I'M SITTING UP IN MY HOSPITAL BED AND DEVIN STANDS NEXT to me, handing me a cup of ice. "Try this first. If you can keep it down, then we'll move onto liquids."

Nodding, I take a piece of cubed ice, but I just let it melt in my mouth.

"That's good." He smiles at me when I swallow.

My throat is sore, but my body feels good. Of course it's numb from the pain pills, but I'll take it after the four days of being strung up outside while being starved and deprived of survival essentials. My head is a little foggy, but he told me it's the sedation wearing off from earlier.

The sound of an alarm goes off, and I flinch. "One second." He pats my thigh over the blanket and walks over to the door. He pokes his head out and looks both ways down the hall and then shuts the door, returning to me.

"What's going on?" I ask over the blaring alarm.

"I'm not sure." He removes his cell from his pocket and then places it to his ear as he calls someone. They don't answer because he puts it away after a second.

"Where's Saint?" I ask worried. I woke up about thirty minutes ago, and Devin was in here with me. He explained what happened and that he and Gavin removed the piece of glass, and I've got stitches. My right arm is in a sling because they had to relocate it. Sounds painful, but I feel nothing at the moment. When he started to talk about the test results of my rape kit, I shut down. He wanted to bring in someone to talk to me, and I refused. It won't change what happened. I want to forget, not let that motherfucker win by having to talk about it.

The hardest part will be Saint. How he'll feel about me now. How he'll treat me.

"Don't worry, Ashtyn. I'm sure he's fine." His cell rings, and he digs it out again, answering it. "What the fuck is going on?" he tries to whisper, but I hear him clear as day over the blaring alarm. "What?" he barks.

I pop another piece of ice into my cracked lips. I'm so thirsty, it's just not enough. So I pop two in this time.

The door swings open, hitting the interior wall, and a male nurse pops his head in. "We're moving everyone to the morgue," he rushes out, and then he's gone.

"What?" I look at Devin. "Why?"

He doesn't answer me, but the way his phone call just went, I think he knows and doesn't want to tell me.

The door opens again and this time I get nervous when Saint rushes in. Afraid to have the conversation about how another man used me—made me a whore. But my nervousness turns to concern when I see how dirty he is. He's got blood on his shirt; I'm guessing that's mine. But he's also got dirt on his face, neck, and arms.

"May I speak to you for a moment?" he asks Devin tightly.

"What's going on, Saint?" I try to adjust myself of the bed.

"Nothing, sweetheart." He leans down and kisses my forehead, and I get butterflies. I was so terrified he'd be mad at me. Hate me or no longer want me. "We'll be right outside for a second."

Before I can say anything, they both rush out and into the hall, letting the door close behind them. I lean my head back, trying to ignore the damn alarm and close my heavy eyes. I'm so tired. I'm sure it's a combination of the drugs and the past four days of my life.

I hear the door open but keep my eyes shut, knowing it's Saint and Devin returning. "Everything checked out, Saint," Devin says softly. "She's in no danger."

"Saint?" I hear a man speaking. "We've got to move Haidyn's body..."

"What do you mean *Haidyn's body*?" I ask, my eyes springing open.

Saint's jaw hardens, but he doesn't say anything to the guy.

"Saint?" I start to sit up but a sharp pain shoots up my side, and I roll onto it. Fuck, what happened to the pain meds? Are they wearing off?

"Lie down, Ash, for fuck's sake," he growls, coming over to me.

"What's going on?" I ask, and tears sting my eyes. Why isn't he telling me anything? "Where is Haidyn?" My throat closes, knowing what he's going to say. Why would they move us all to the morgue? And why did he say body? Does that mean he's dead?

The alarm continues to blare, but their refusal to answer my question is deafening silence. "Saint?" I demand, my voice rising.

"What the fuck does he mean?" My eyes shoot to the male nurse, and he stares at the floor. "Saint, please..."

"He's gone, Ash," Saint answers softly.

Haidyn's dead? I feel my chest tighten. They killed him? "Nooo." I choke out, sucking in air that makes my throat burn. I grab at my neck, my skin all of a sudden hot as if being branded all over.

"Calm down, sweetheart."

I'm gasping, my stomach knotting, and a weight sits on top of me.

"Give her something." He barks at Devin.

"No." I grab Saint's shirt. "I need to see Haidyn." I try to use him to pull myself off the bed.

"No, Ash." He pries my hands from his shirt and holds them in place in front of me. "You need to rest..."

"Where is he?" I cry. "I've got to see him."

"Devin!" he shouts. The head of my bed is lowered and Saint gets up to stand over me as he holds my wrists in his. I thrash in the bed trying to get up and ignore the pain in my chest.

Then I feel something warm in my arm, and my eyes grow heavy.

"That's it, sweetheart." He places my hands on my stomach and brushes my hair off my sweaty forehead. "You're okay."

I blink and fresh tears run down my face, and I let the darkness suck me under, trying to think how I'll live a life without Haidyn in it.

SIXTY-ONE

SAINT

She's out within seconds.

I smooth her hair out and wipe her tear-streaked face. That blaring fucking alarm is still going off.

"Saint?" the kid speaks.

"Turn off that fucking alarm!" I snap at him. "And where the fuck is Kashton?" I shout, losing my mind.

The male nurse takes a step back into the hall, out of her room. "I'll look—"

"I got you." Just then Tyson walks by, grabbing the kids' shirt and pulling him from the door.

"We need to get her moved," I order Devin, and he's already unlocking the wheels on the bed.

Getting to the morgue, we find a private room for her, and I pull up a chair and sit down next to her, holding her hand. The weight of the past four days is making my chest heavy. Honestly, I haven't had the chance to even process what I saw in Haidyn's room. I refuse to believe he's dead. I don't know where Kashton went, and my cell phone is dead.

I kiss her knuckles and run my thumb over her ring finger.

Reaching into my pocket, I pull out her wedding ring. I grabbed it from her place in Vegas and have held onto it since I brought her back. A part of me wanted her to ask for it, but she never did. The other part of me was satisfied that she wore it when I fucked her in Glass.

I've kept it in my safe in my bedroom since we've returned from Vegas but I pulled it out when she was taken from me four days ago. I slide it onto her finger.

Four years ago

I ENTER MY BEDROOM TO FIND HER LYING IN BED. THE COVERS UP to her neck and she stares at the ceiling. I branded her last week. She doesn't seem mad anymore, just broken. And it makes me wonder if that's what our fathers wanted. I'd rather her hate me.

"Hey, sweetheart." I sit down next to her, and her watery eyes meet mine. I cup her cheek. "I have a surprise for you."

"What is it?" She licks her plump lips.

I smile, trying to cheer her up. "Come on, I'll show you."

"We're leaving Carnage?" Her eyes light up, and I hate to say no and see them go blank again.

"Not technically," I say instead, and she frowns, but that light is still there. "Come on." I pull her to sit up, remove the covers and then help her to stand. "Go pick out something to wear for me." I gently kiss her lips. "You've got ten minutes."

She goes to the closet and returns wearing a soft pink off-the-shoulder sweater dress that rests high on her thighs with black tights and matching heels. She always loved to dress up for me to show her off. But when you have nowhere to go, it's pointless. "Do I need make-up?" she asks, dropping her eyes to the floor nervously.

"No," I say and walk over and take her hand. "You look perfect."

She blushes, and I slide my hands into her hair, tilting her head back and lowering my lips to hers. I kiss her tenderly, slowly tasting the only thing in this world that I can't live without. I'm a starving man, and she allows me to feast on her.

I deepen the kiss, and she moans into my mouth, her arms wrapping around my waist, and I groan into hers when her nails dig into my back. I want to grab her ass, lift her and push her down into the bed, but that'll have to wait.

Instead, I pull away and watch her heavy eyes open. Then I escort her out of the bedroom. She stays quiet as I walk her down the hall and to the elevator. When it stops, the doors slide open and she comes to a stop when she sees the stained glass double doors.

Her wide eyes meet mine. "Saint." My name trembles on her lips. "What are we doing here?"

"Do you trust me?" I ask, running my knuckles down her fragile neck, feeling her pulse race.

"Yes." She straightens her shoulders. Not a single second of hesitation. Even after everything I had to put her through, she trusts me.

I push the doors open into the cathedral, and she steps inside to see Haidyn and Kashton standing at the Lords altar.

She turns back to face me and I cup her face in both of my hands, her pretty blue eyes search mine as they fill with unshed tears. "Ashtyn Lane Price..." I start, and her lips part. "I'm in love with you." She blinks, and the first tear falls. "I've been in love with you all my life. This is me, a Lord, asking you to be my Lady. Will you marry me, sweetheart?"

Another tear falls, and she licks her wet lips before whispering, "Yes."

I'M BROUGHT OUT OF THAT MEMORY WHEN THE DOOR OPENS. Sin enters the room; an angry-looking Jasmine comes in behind him. "Kashton needs you," he says and nods to Jasmine in some sort of vague warning. I'm too tired to figure it out.

"Where is he?" I ask, running my hand down my face.

"Downstairs," he answers and again, it confuses me because we are downstairs.

"May I stay here with her?" Jasmine asks, her eyes on my wife.

"Yeah." I kiss Ashtyn's forehead and exit the room, closing the door behind us. "What the fuck was that about?" I question.

"Kashton is in the basement, killing people. Jasmine was trying to calm him down. He tossed her to me and told me to get her the fuck out of there." He looks over at me. "I figured it wouldn't hurt just in case another bomb goes off while we're down there."

Sighing, I pick up my pace, and he does the same.

ASHTYN

I'M SITTING UP IN MY BED EATING MORE ICE CHIPS WHILE I wait for some clothes. I was actually happy that Saint wasn't in my room when I woke thirty minutes ago because that means he wasn't going to stop me from seeing Haidyn.

I never really knew how Haidyn felt about me while growing up. We weren't as close as me, Saint, and Kashton were. Haidyn was closer with Adam than me. Kashton was friends with everyone. Then our senior year, when I became Saint's chosen, Haidyn's chosen hated me. I mean, I understand why, but it wasn't like I went after him knowing he was taken. It wasn't about me and her. Until she made it that way.

Senior year at Barrington

I'VE BEEN SPENDING ALL OF MY TIME WITH SAINT SINCE OUR VOW ceremony three weeks ago. The Lords throw parties constantly now that the seniors can get ass. I thought I saw a lot watching porn, but that's nothing compared to what I've seen these men do to women.

I had to pee so bad, and I couldn't wait to make it to Saint's private bathroom in his bedroom. It was on the other side of the house, which is the size of a hotel. So I decided to used the closest women's bathroom I could find.

I'm pulling my jeans up when I hear the bathroom door open, and girls' laughter echoes.

"God, did you see her? Can she be any more of a whore?"

I stiffen, recognizing the voice and knowing exactly who she's talking about. Me.

I open the door, and a set of green eyes meet mine in the bathroom mirror. "Fuck," she whispers, her eyes widening.

"What?" Sierra looks up and spots me in the mirror. She turns and walks over to me. I see motion at the bathroom door behind her but stay quiet. "We were just talking about you." She smiles.

"I heard."

"We're tired of you throwing yourself at Haidyn and Kashton. Honey, they don't want you."

I lift my chin but say nothing.

"Everyone knows you're a whore." She rolls her eyes. "Not like it's a secret."

I swallow the knot in my throat. Why is it the women that always make you feel the shittiest about what you choose to do with your body?

"I think we'll go throw ourselves at Saint." At the mention of Saint, the man steps farther into the bathroom behind her.

The other woman spots him and gasps but stays quiet.

"Yeah, Melony can ride his face, and I'll fuck his cock. And then when we're done, he can let you lick our cum off him."

I'm shaking, skin heated at the thought.

"Then you'll know what I taste like, bitch." She slaps me across the face, but I don't feel it. I'm too angry at the visual she just gave me.

Sierra spins around to exit and comes to a halt gasping. "Haidyn!" She squeals.

He wraps his hand around her neck and pulls her to him. She grips his muscular arm, fighting to breathe when he puts his face in hers.

"We fuck Ashtyn because we want to. And don't think you're fucking special. Kashton and I have offered you both up to Saint. He doesn't want either one of you." He lets go, and she rubs her neck, gasping to catch her breath. "But if you want to fuck someone else..."

"No." She shakes her head. "No...no...I don't..."

He grips her hair and drags her out of the bathroom. Kashton's chosen and I follow after them through the crowded hall and into the living room.

"Hooke?" Haidyn calls out.

"God, no. Haidyn, please don't..."

"What's up?" Hooke looks up from his phone sitting on the couch.

"Still want a piece?" He holds Sierra out in front of him like an offering. Her body trembling and crying.

Hooke tosses his phone to the cushion beside him, leans back and places his arms across the couch, grinning. "What can I have?" he asks, his eyes running up and down her body in a way that makes her tremble.

"Whatever you want," Haidyn answers, and she can't hold back the sob.

Haidyn spins her around pulling her back to face him.

"Please?" she begs, her hands gripping his T-shirt trying to cling to him now. "Don't make me..."

He cups her tear-streaked face. "Make me proud," he whispers against her lips, and she swallows nervously at the threat. Then he steps back and crosses his arms over his chest.

She bows her head and turns around to face Hooke, knowing she has no choice. She is Haidyn's, and he can do whatever he wants with her. Sierra takes a step forward, and Hooke speaks. "Strip. Give everyone something to look at while I fuck your mouth."

She whimpers, reaching down and grabbing the hem of her dress. She pulls it up and over her head and then pushes her underwear down her shaking legs. She takes another step forward, and he orders. "On your hands and knees. You'll crawl to me."

She falls to her knees and crawls across the floor to him where she stops to kneel. He reaches out and pushes two fingers into her mouth, and she sucks on them. Then he slaps her, making her cry out. "Beg me, princess. Beg me to fuck your face."

"Ple-ease?"

He slaps her again. Harder.

"Oh God...please?" she cries out. "Fuck my mouth, Hooke. I need you to fuck me."

"That's better." He undoes his belt, yanking it from his loops and wraps it around her neck. Pulling her forward, he removes his hard dick from his jeans and begins to fuck her face while men and women sit around listening to her gag and cry while they record it.

SHE MADE ME FEEL BAD ABOUT MYSELF. WHAT SAINT ALLOWED the guys to do to me. What I got off on. Haidyn sticking up for me felt good. He made me feel like I belonged. I know that sounds stupid as fuck, but I felt...loved.

After Hooke finished using Sierra, Haidyn took her to his bedroom and tied her to his bed where he left her while he came back and partied with us. I felt accepted in a way.

I celebrated by getting drunk as fuck and cocky. I started mouthing off to Saint, knowing it would piss him off and he'd punish me. My punishment was Haidyn and Kashton.

Two hours later, Saint carried me over his shoulder to his room where he had Haidyn and Kashton held me down while Saint tied me up and gave me an enema. Then he fucked my mouth while he let it set. Afterward, he untied me and allowed me to use the restroom. Then he tied me down once again on his bed and let Haidyn and Kashton fuck my ass.

She never looked at me again after that night, much less spoke to me. I considered it a win. Not only did Haidyn let another man use her, but he also then used me.

The door opens to my room, and Jasmine enters. "Finally found something." She comes over to my bed and places a pair of blue scrubs next to me.

I look up at her.

"I took it from a nurse."

"You took these from someone?"

She nods. "I told him to give me his clothes or I'd have Kashton rip his head off." Jasmine shrugs. "I felt like I had a fifty-fifty chance he'd buy it."

I laugh softly and nod. "Kashton would do just that."

"Here, let me help you." She places the top on and then helps me get the pants on and get to my feet. "Where are we headed?"

"I need to find Haidyn," I say.

"I know where he's at. I overheard someone mention him while I was trying to find you something to wear."

"I've got to go before Saint gets back and has me knocked out again."

She places my good arm over her shoulder and helps me walk out of the room. My body isn't in a lot of pain, but it is kinda sluggish. So I allow her to help me.

We leave the room and make our way down the hallway, taking another to the right. We come up to a door, and she pushes it open.

It's cold and eerily quiet. Rows and rows of freezers cover the back wall. I'm sure it's packed with bodies. There are five metal tables on wheels lined up in front of them. The one in the center has a once white sheet over it. But it's now bloody.

My eyes instantly sting, and I walk over to it on shaking legs. Gripping the edge, I pull it back, and a sob comes out when I see Haidyn lying in front of me. His face is soft, almost serene. I've never seen him look so peaceful. "Haidyn," I choke out, placing my hand on his face. He's cold.

I climb onto the table and lie down with him, trying to heat his body up with mine. "Please...I need you." He saved me. He was there when I needed someone, and I couldn't do the same for him.

The door opens and that nurse from earlier enters the room. "Ashtyn," he sighs, "you can't be in here."

"Get out." Jasmine snaps at him and I close my eyes, clinging to my friend.

"Miss..."

"My name is Jasmine, and she's telling her friend goodbye. Have some fucking compassion and get the fuck out!" I hear the door slam shut.

I sniff, my nose runs, and my chest tightens. "I'm so sorry, Haidyn. So sorry..."

The door opens again. "I said get..."

"Hello, Ashtyn."

My blood runs cold at the familiar sound of my name. Slowly, I push myself up to look over Haidyn's body to the man now standing in the room.

"What the fuck?" Jasmine barks.

His eyes move to hers, and he smiles. "Jasmine, it's been a while."

SIXTY-TWO

SAINT

I step over the fourth dead body down in the basement following the blood trail. Sin wasn't wrong. Kash is currently on a killing spree. He may be the joker, but when you piss him off, he is ruthless. It just takes more to get him there than it does me or Haidyn.

The thought of our brother in the morgue makes my chest tighten and hands fist. I'm going to get answers, and whoever did this to our family will pay. I'll make sure the last word they speak is Haidyn's name before I carve it into their chest.

But I've got to calm down Kashton first. He's obviously not asking any questions before he kills them.

We come to the pits, and a man crawls across the concrete floor, dragging his broken legs behind him, sobbing.

"Kash?" I say, getting his attention, but he ignores me and walks over to the far wall. He grabs a meat hook, his fingers curling around the handle.

"Please...noooooo," the man sobs, trying to move in the opposite direction, but he's too slow.

Kashton walks over to him as the guy rolls onto his back. He raises his hands to defend himself, but Kash leans over, shoving the hook underneath the man's chin and yanks him to his feet. Kash pulls the guy into him with the hand still gripping the hook while the other starts to punch the man in the face. The position has the hook cutting into the man, splitting the guys neck and chin. Blood squirts out and the guy makes gurgling sounds.

Tyson and Ryat stand to the side watching. Ryat looks impressed, but Tyson looks worried. Ryat and Sin knew Haidyn, but they weren't as close to him as me and Tyson were. Sin comes to stand next to me.

"Kash?" I walk over to him and place my hand on his arm. He lets go of the meat hook and the guy falls to the ground with it still stuck in his neck. By the way he gags, he's not dead yet. "What are you doing?" It's a stupid question because I know he's hurting, but this isn't going to get me what I need.

He's breathing heavily, and his eyes are wild. He's covered in blood.

"Did he know anything?" I ask, pointing at the man flopping around like a fish out of water.

Kash runs both his bloody hands through his hair, pushing it off his face. "He wasn't going to tell us anything anyway."

"You don't know that," I growl.

His eyes narrow on me. "I know that it was an inside job and the only way we're going to fix the problem is to kill them all."

I take in a deep breath, trying to calm my nerves. I'm about to lose my shit, and if we burn this place down, it won't do us any good. "We're—"

"You're right. It was an inside job," a male's voice states, but it's distorted like in the video.

My stomach drops when I see Ashtyn enter the room with Jasmine by her side. They both have duct tape over their mouths. Jasmine's hands are tied behind her back, and Ashtyn's are zip-tied in front.

"What the—?" Kashton steps forward but two men dressed the

same as the video are behind them, holding both girls by their hair.

Coming to a stop, the girls whine as they're forced to their knees, guns cocked and placed at the back of their heads.

The blood rushes in my ears. I've seen this. My worst nightmare. Both men are dressed in black pants, long-sleeve black shirts, and bulletproof vests. They've got gloves on and have guns strapped to their thighs. Matching masks cover their faces. Not an inch of skin or hair can be seen.

"What do you want?" Kashton yells, stepping forward, and the guy behind Jasmine yanks her head back, making her scream into the tape.

I hold my hands out when Tyson steps up next to me. Technically, we could take them. It'd be five against two, but it will only take a second for them to kill the girls, and I won't take that chance. I can't lose her again.

The guy behind Ashtyn pulls out a cell, and a second later, the phone rings as he places it on speakerphone. "Hello?" a man answers. Again, you can't make out who it is.

"We've got them. In the pits." He hangs up, and I curse that they've got their voices altered.

I look at Ash, and her head is down. She's dressed in blue scrubs and tears run down her face. How did they get to her? Was the bomb their plan? Get everyone to one part of Carnage while forcing our attention down here? It left them sitting ducks.

She sobs, her shoulders shaking, and I hate what I've done to her. I brought her back here. She was happy without me. She had moved on, and I couldn't accept that because I was too selfish.

"You're okay, Ash," I tell her. She raises her bloodshot eyes to meet mine, and they plead with me to save her. To be the man I was trained to be and fucking do something.

Kash steps forward, and the guy yanks Jasmine to her feet, wrapping his arm around her neck from behind. She screams out into the tape before he wraps his arm around her neck and begins to choke her while she kicks her legs out, struggling in his grip.

"Alright! Alright!" Kash raises his hands and takes two step back from them.

The guy lets go of her, and she falls to her knees, bowing her head and trying to catch her breath.

"Gentlemen." We turn to see a third man—guessing the one they called—enter behind us and my heart races. He's their twin. Dressed the same except he has ACE written across his vest.

I go to rush him, but his words stop me. "Did you like your gift?"

I tense at the way he laughs.

"I brought her back to you." He points at my wife on her knees, and I look at her confused and then back at him. "See...it took me some time to figure out how to do it, but here we are." He raises his arms out wide. "As much fun as I had whipping and raping your wife for the past four days, I thought I'd let her go and run back to you. Now you get to suffer the way that I did."

I haven't had the chance to speak to Ashtyn about what happened while she was away. But she didn't have to tell me. Devin read me the results. "What the fuck are you talking about?" I bark.

"Ashtyn is pregnant, right?"

"What the fuck are you talking about?" I avoid his question. One, because I don't know who the fuck this is. And two, because I don't know why he would think that. I mean, could be just a guess. She's a Lady, and we're supposed to reproduce.

He chuckles. "I thought *she* taught you better than to lie."

I look at Kashton, and he's white in the face. After Ash left and our training began, all staff was removed, and hers was brought in. Because she didn't want anyone favoring us. We were no longer Lords, just prisoners until she was done with us. He had to have been one of them. They were always dressed in cloaks and masks.

He looks at my wife. "You see, sweetheart, your precious Lord made sure he would get you pregnant."

She shakes her head, not believing it.

"Isn't that right, Saint?" He doesn't let me answer. "But no worries. I'm here to repay the favor. An eye for an eye."

"I don't know what the fuck you're talking about. What eye? What fucking favor?" As much as I want to slit his throat, the more he talks, the more time he gives us to come up with a plan. And that just keeps him busy. If he's talking to me, he's ignoring her.

He steps toward me. "I'm going to let you watch her lose yours, like I watched her lose mine."

Kashton looks at me like "what the fuck," and I start to laugh. "She's never been pregnant."

He looks over at Ashtyn. "Tell him, Ash. Tell him how hard it was on you when you lost our son."

I look at my wife, and her watery eyes are on the floor. "Look at me." Her shoulders begin to shake as her mumbled sobs fill the room. "Ashtyn!"

The man standing behind her grips her hair and yanks her head back. Her tear-filled eyes meet mine before they close and fresh tears run down her taped face.

The man laughs. "Not only did she keep that from you, but she had help."

She begins to sob.

That part doesn't surprise me. I knew that Laura had helped her.

"But don't worry, I took care of that for you too."

Laura? Did he kill Laura? I look at Sin, and he's confused as fuck. He has no clue how much Laura was involved in our lives in the past. I promised him I'd take care of her until the baby was born. "If you killed her..."

"Her?" Ace laughs. "Your brother, Saint. I killed your brother." He looks over at Ashtyn. "Haidyn knew she was pregnant with my child, and he also helped her escape."

ASHTYN

Four Years Ago

I RUN OUT OF HER OFFICE, NOT CARING THAT LAURA'S CALLING out to me. I can't hear anymore. So many lies. So much betrayal. And now a baby?

Sucking in breath after breath, I round a corner and run into someone. I scream as hands grab at me and lift me off my feet. I kick and fight, but they drag me into a room. It's one of the fathers. She called them to come get me and take me downstairs. They're going to kill my baby, force me to have a hysterectomy, and then throw me in a cell.

Saint won't protect me, not after what he finds out. A hand slaps over my mouth, muffling my screams, and I buck wildly since my nose is so stopped up I can't breathe through it.

"Shh, Ashtyn, calm down." A familiar voice growls.

My body instantly goes limp, and he releases my mouth. I sob as he sits me in a chair and kneels in front of me. "What the fuck is going on?" He places his hands on my shaking thighs and rubs them over my legs.

"I'm...pregnant," I cry, knowing I can trust him.

"Shit." He sighs, running his hand through his hair. "Does Saint know?"

I shake my head, tears spilling from my eyes, and I run my hand under my runny nose.

"I'll call him." He stands and removes his cell from his pocket, and I slap it out of his hand. "Ash—"

"No, you can't," I cry out, and he grabs my trembling shoulders.

"It's okay," he assures me softly.

He's so wrong. "No." I shake my head quickly. "He cheated."

His brows pull together. "What? No. He'd never—"

"He cheated." I gasp, trying to breathe, but my throat is closing on me. "You...can't."

"Ashtyn."

"Tell him." I grip his T-shirt and bury my face into it. He wraps his arms around me, and I begin to sob, repeating over and over that he cheated, hoping that he'll understand what I mean because I can't form a fucking sentence right now.

"I know what to do," he assures me. "Trust me."

I nod, knowing that Haidyn will help me. He takes my hand and rushes me down to the morgue. We go out through a back exit, and he's pulling me through the trees.

"Where are we going?" I ask.

"There's a tunnel back here that leads to a road. There aren't any cameras out here, so no one will see that you've left."

We come up to a hillside, and there's an old steel door. He lets go of my hand and removes a key from his pocket. He opens it up and pulls me into it.

"Hai-dyn?" My voice shakes as I stand in complete darkness. The sound of dripping water echoes. Then, seconds later, he turns a flashlight on and takes my hand, pulling me through the tunnel. There's already a car waiting on the other side. He helps me inside, and I bounce my knees, trying to figure out what to do.

Everything that Laura told me. I don't want to believe I'm pregnant and it not be Saint's.

HE PULLS UP TO A HOSPITAL, AND I TURN TO FACE HIM. "SOMEONE will see me."

"It'll be fine," he assures me, giving me a hoodie.

I keep my head down and let him guide me inside and to a room. I'm on autopilot. Numb. I'm Saint's wife. He married me. To be pregnant with another man's baby isn't allowed. Let alone he wouldn't want me after this. What will their dads do?

I stand in the room, my eyes on the floor as Haidyn undresses me from the waist down. He then lifts me to sit on the table. "Look at me, baby girl."

His hands are on my face as my watery eyes meet his.

"It's going to be okay. You're okay."

"Saint..."

"We'll figure it out," he says and then kisses my forehead. But we

both know that even if Saint wanted to stay with me and raise another man's child, the Lords would find out that he cheated. He went against his oath. He'd be stripped of his title and killed. Or worse, sentenced to Carnage for the rest of his life. I'm not worth that.

The door opens, and my breath catches in my lungs when I see the man enter. Pressing myself up on my elbows, Haidyn grabs me and pushes me down. "It's okay. You're safe here."

I shake my head, eyes wide. Is he crazy? "No..."

"This is Gavin," Haidyn tells me. "He's here to help, Ash."

"Haidyn." He nods to him, and I can't help but wonder why he looks identical to Devin at Carnage. Are they twins? Surely not.

He grabs my legs to put them in the stirrups, and I jump, Haidyn gives me a soft smile. Taking my hand, he keeps his eyes on mine while I lie down, shaking as Gavin pulls me to the edge of the table.

Tears fill my eyes and fall to the sides as Gavin starts talking me through the vaginal ultrasound until the only sound we hear is the heartbeat of my child.

"BULLSHIT!" THE SOUND OF KASHTON'S BARK MAKES ME flinch. "Haidyn wouldn't do that."

My watery eyes look up to see Saint glaring at me. I've never been more thankful to have duct tape on my face right now. So I don't have to explain what I did or tell him what Haidyn did.

"No." Saint shakes his head, also refusing to believe it. "She was never pregnant."

"Oh, she was." Ace laughs, and my chest squeezes. "Ashtyn's mother came to me. Said her daughter was a whore. Addicted to sex. She showed me a picture of her. Then she offered me a job. To fuck her daughter. It wasn't hard. She liked to party. So I went out, had a friend of hers drug her..." My breathing grows heavy. I wasn't sure how I never knew it happened. I was sore for days, but I wasn't sure why. "She bled all over my cock."

Shame washes over me as I kneel in front of all these men while they talk about me and what I allowed to happen. How stupid I was. Tyson has seen firsthand what the Spade brothers have done to me. No one cares about a woman who spreads her legs for fun. That's why we're taught to serve. It's not about us. It's about the Lords. My mother tried to explain that to me, but I refused to listen. Thought I'd be different.

"Then Luke fucked everything up when he had that hit put on Adam." Ace goes on growling. "And you guys brought her to hide her out here." He shakes his head. "Thankfully I had someone on the inside to keep me updated. Otherwise, I might have never found out she was pregnant."

Four years ago

"Congratulations, Ashtyn. You're pregnant."

I stare at her, my breath getting caught in my lungs. It can't be. I don't believe her.

She tosses the test into the trash can next to her and places her forearms on top of her desk. "What are you going to do if Saint finds out it's not his?"

"It's his," I whisper. I'm a hundred percent sure of that.

She arches a brow at me.

A fresh tear runs down my cheek, and I sniff. "I haven't been with anyone else."

"Ashtyn... we need to talk." Laura sighs. "I didn't want to tell you this, but you were raped."

I frown. "No." I shake my head. "Everything Saint has done to me has been consensual." I allow him to have his way with me. Even when I fight him, it's because I want him to overpower me.

"Not by Saint. But a man raped you. In your house before the vow ceremony..."

"No." I interrupt her. "I bled." I saw the blood. I was even worried about Saint going down on me afterward.

"I promised your mother I would look after you, and I'm afraid

I've failed her. I thought...I thought not telling you was the best thing, but you need to know that this baby may very well be from that night."

Tears burn my eyes, and I drop them to my lap. "I...Saint..."

"He cheated the Lords, Ashtyn. And he will be punished if anyone finds out what he's done."

I DIDN'T WANT TO BELIEVE HER. I RAN OUT OF HER OFFICE AND into Haidyn. He immediately took me to see Gavin, and the dates lined up. There was no way it could have been Saint's.

My eyes lift to Saint's and see he's facing Ace.

"You're lying." Kashton is still in denial. "We were there the night of the ritual. She bled at the ceremony. She hadn't been with anyone before Saint."

"That's what I never figured out..." Ace trails off. "How did you know that I fucked your bitch?" He laughs, and I flinch.

A silence falls over the pits, and the blood rushes in my ears, waiting to see if Saint answers. I never knew how he did it. I never got the chance to ask, and when he brought me back here, I never cared to ask.

"Altus had cameras in her house," Saint finally answers. "He recorded you raping her and showed it to me."

What? Cameras in my house? That's how Saint knew what had happened? Laura said that Saint knew but didn't tell me how. And that he had cheated at the vow ceremony. That if the Lords knew that I wasn't a virgin and Saint set it up to look like I was, he'd be stripped of his title. I couldn't take that chance.

"No." Ace shakes his head.

Saint fists his hands down by his sides. "I watched it. She was lying on her kitchen floor, begging me to fuck her. Calling out my name while you held her down pretending to be me and fucked her." Saint shouts, making me flinch, and I cry harder. "I made him a promise that I'd take care of it, and I did."

SIXTY-THREE

SAINT

I'm shaking I'm so pissed. "What the fuck do you want?" I demand. Enough shit. I need someone to make a move. "Huh? Want to kill me?" I lift my arm out and step forward. "Fucking do it."

Kashton shoves his hands in my chest and pushes me back while Sin grabs at me from behind. This is what I needed. A distraction. Even if I get shot, it'll give the others a chance to get the girls. "FUCKING DO IT!"

Ace holds out his gun, and I hear a muffled scream. It's Ashtyn. But I don't look away from the man with the gun in his hand.

"Be a fucking man." I smile at him. "Look me in the eye when you kill me."

Her screams grow louder, but still I ignore her. If I die here, I know she'll be taken care of. That's all I ever wanted for her.

"I'm not going to kill you." He laughs, his masked head shaking. "I'm going to lock you all up down here in the cells. I'm going to chain her up in the one right next to you. Let you listen to her cry and sob as I fuck her each day. While I feed her just enough to stay alive but not enough to keep your baby alive. Once your baby dies, I'm going to take her with me and leave you all here to rot in this hell that you love so much." He steps toward the girls, and I watch Kashton stiffen. "Bring her here." He reaches out with his gloved-covered hand and motions for my wife. "Now!" he barks when the man doesn't work fast enough.

I move toward her, and he holds his gun trained on me. "Don't fucking move!" he barks at me while Kashton moves closer to Jasmine and the other guy. "Bring the bitch over here!" he shouts.

I look at Ashtyn and her bloodshot eyes are narrowed, and she breathes heavily while glaring at me. She's pissed I offered myself up for her. I don't give a shit. When we both get out of here, I'm going to make love to my wife while I also beat her ass for keeping a pregnancy from me. I could have helped her. I could have fixed everything if she would have just said something to me.

The guy standing behind her lets go of his gun, and it hangs over his shoulder from the strap. Instead, he removes a knife from his pocket and flips it open. He grabs her hair and yanks her head back holding it to her neck. Her head is tilted to the ceiling, but her eyes remain on mine. Not an ounce of fear in her eyes.

I step toward them, ready to knock them both to the ground, and she gives me the slightest shake of her head. *What the fuck?*

"What in the fuck are you doing?" Ace shouts at the man. He goes to storm over to them, but the guy shoves my wife away from him and throws the knife at Ace. It lands in his leg, and he drops to his knees.

Everyone seems to move at the same time. I run and grab Ashtyn, dragging her away while Ryat takes the man behind her to the ground. Kashton body-slams the guy standing behind Jasmine, taking her down in the process. Sin and Tyson both grab Ace.

I rip the tape off Ashtyn's face and cut the zip tie holding her wrists together. "Fucking bastard." She slaps me, and I hold her to me. "Bas-tard." She begins to shake, sobbing against me. I sit on the concrete floor holding her to me. I knew what happened to her, and I was going to do whatever it took to make her mine.

I could have told her, but I chose to keep it from her. I didn't think that was something she needed to know. Am I a bastard for it? Yes. But when I saw her in her room three days later, she came onto me. Wanted me to fuck her. She wasn't aware of what had happened. I knew I had to take care of it. I didn't want to worry her. She was already so concerned she wasn't going to bleed for me, so why make it worse?

"What do you want to do with them?" Sin asks.

I look up to see both guys who held our women at gunpoint now on their knees, hands tied behind their backs. They're still fully dressed and wearing their gear.

"Strip them. Throw them in the cells," I order. I'll deal with them later. My wife and I have some things to discuss. Plus, I'm fucking exhausted.

"No!" Ashtyn jumps to her feet, turning to face them. "You can't do that," she gasps.

"Ash—"

"No." She rushes over to them before I can grab the scrub top she's wearing and jerks the mask off one of the guys, and silence fills the room when blue eyes meet mine.

"Hai-dyn?" Kashton whispers, speaking first, but Haidyn's eyes don't leave mine.

I walk over to him, and he lifts his chin to look up at me. I thought all this time, he didn't want to bring her back because he hated her after all the shit we were put through after she left. But it was because he helped her leave. He knew she was pregnant with another man's child and showed her how to escape me—her husband. He stood by my side when we took our vows.

"Saint—"

Fisting my hand, I punch him in the fucking face, cutting him off.

ASHTYN

"SAINT!" I SCREAM AS HE KNOCKS HAIDYN OVER ONTO THE concrete floor. "Saint, stop."

"This whole fucking time…" Saint shouts. "You knew why she ran. You helped her!"

"She deserved a chance," Haidyn yells, rolling over to sit up on his ass since his hands are cuffed behind his back.

"A chance at what?" Saint barks out.

"A life," he growls. "She always deserved better." He breathes deeply, and his eyes meet my watery ones. "She deserved to be a mom."

Saint turns to me, and his eyes drop to my stomach obviously knowing that I lost the baby. He steps toward me, and I take one back. His jaw clenches.

"How…how the fuck are you alive? You were dead?" Kashton asks. "Like no heartbeat. Dead. Body getting cold. Dead."

"I had help," he answers tightly.

Kashton raises his hands, running them through his hair aggressively. "By whom, the CIA?" Nervous laughter follows, and Haidyn just stares up at him. Saint stomps over to the other guy, who is still wearing his mask, and I hold my breath when Saint pulls it off to expose his face to the room.

Silence follows as everyone takes in the face that I haven't seen in years.

"What. The. Fuck?" Tyson speaks first.

"You've got to be fucking kidding me," Saint barks and then looks at me. "Did you know about this too?"

I don't answer because his question pisses me off. Instead, I look at Adam and see he's already staring at me. I don't know where my brother has been or why he was helping Haidyn, but I couldn't have been more grateful when I saw him walk into the morgue when I went to see Haidyn.

"ADAM?" I WHISPER, TRYING TO FIND MY VOICE.

"Adam?" Jasmine asks.

He looks at her and smiles. "Long story."

"You guys know each other?" My mind is playing catch-up.

"Yeah," he answers. "But that's for another day...we don't have much time." He rushes over to me and pulls me off the small table. He removes something out of his vest.

"What are you doing?" I ask my trembling hands going to Haidyn's tatted arm.

"Bringing him back."

"Back?" My pulse races. "What do you mean...?"

"Once he's up, we're going to need your girls' help." He interrupts me, and I nod, trying to wrap my head around what the hell is happening.

"I...I—" KASHTON TAKES A STEP BACK, TRYING TO PROCESS IT all, and Tyson helps Haidyn get to his feet and removes the cuffs.

The guy Ace moans on the floor, and we all look at him. Kashton walks over and removes his mask and I take a step back as if hit in the chest.

"Ashtyn?" Saint barks at me.

But I ignore him as I stare at the man lying on the concrete floor. "You..." I swallow the lump in my throat.

"Ashtyn?" Someone yells my name but my tear-filled eyes stay on the guy smiling at me.

"Hello, sweetheart." He laughs, and I flinch. "Tell him how much fun you had when you'd beg me to fuck you."

"Such a good whore. Aren't you, sweetheart? You had no problem coming for me before. Come on my fingers, love. Come all over them. Show me how much you like it."

His words play in my head after the car wreck when I was strapped to a table back at Carnage. The hood over my face, the gag, the hands....so many hands all over me. I was strapped down and unable to fight as he touched me. I didn't' know who it was. Honestly, I thought he was just making shit up.

"Noooo." I shake my head, tears sting my eyes.

"Get him the fuck out of here," Saint demands, and I flinch as his voice echoes in the concrete room. Sin and Ryat grab Ace and his laughter grows. "Strip him before putting him in a goddamn cell," Saint tells them before they drag him away.

Hands touch my face, and I whimper at the contact. "You're okay, Ash."

I blink, and tears fall from my eyes as I look up into a set of green eyes. It's Saint now standing in front of me. My chest is tight, and I'm gasping for breath. "I...slept with him." My words shake.

Saint sighs and steps into me, but I go to step back. "I...I let him—"

"Come on, sweetheart." He picks me up, and I bury my face into his shirt as I allow him to carry me out of the room.

SIXTY-FOUR

SAINT

I enter my room in the birdcage and lay her on the bed. I've been dying to bring her in here to be with me. She should have been here all this time. "You're okay, Ashtyn." She's shaking, her eyes wide, and I pull her into me.

I recognized the guy the moment Kash removed the mask. I had seen him before when I was watching her. Benny was one of her clients who came into Glass. She had been sleeping with him. I watched her one night meet up with him at a hotel.

It was one of the most excruciating things I had to witness. Watching my wife please other men. But I had to wait. I had a plan in place and couldn't deviate from it. Now I wish I would have rushed in and killed him right then and there. Not given a fuck about the plan and just taken her for myself.

Her cries fill the room, and I rock her back and forth until they subside and her body relaxes in my arms.

Kashton and I are sitting in the office when the door opens, and Tyson enters with his four men. Jenks drops something on the desk.

"What's this?" I ask.

"We took the phone that Benny had, and I crossed it with Ashtyn's phone you gave me. I was able to make a match."

"We knew that would happen," Tyson says.

"Yeah, but I also found a connection to a number that she had in her phone."

"Who?" I rub my forehead. It hasn't even been ten hours since I found out my brother betrayed me, and my wife had been pregnant when she left me.

"Whitney."

My head snaps up to see Haidyn now standing in the office when he answers me. I get to my feet and glare at him.

He is unfazed. "Benny said that he had a friend of Ashtyn's drug her. When they came to grab her, they traded her with Whitney. She was the only one who could put him in Ashtyn's house the night he raped her." He crosses his arms over his chest. "Her mother was dead, Laura was here..."

"Why didn't he touch Laura?" Colton asks. "He had the perfect opportunity."

"Because Laura was always on his side from the beginning," Haidyn answers. "If it wasn't for her, he wouldn't have known she was pregnant. She was his inside contact."

A part of me wonders if that's why Laura tried so hard to get my father to get rid of Ashtyn. She knew all along that she was raped and that I cheated at the ritual. She kept my secret because she knew I kept hers. I wasn't aware that her mother had anything to do with it, though. Benny said her mother planned it, but on the video, the masked man—being Benny—had called Laura and said it was done. It was her voice I heard on the other side of the phone.

I couldn't touch her, though. That's why when Sin came to me and we realized who we had inside of Carnage, I knew I'd give Sin whatever he fucking wanted in exchange for Laura. Even if that meant I had to take him in and torture him first. I'd kill a million Lords if it meant saving my wife. I was betting everything that Elli's father would bring her mother in. He spent too much time here to not want revenge.

Just then the door opens, and Adam enters. He's another one on my shit list. They are both tied at the top.

Kashton gets up and walks over to him, giving him a handshake hug. "Does this mean you're back?" Kash asks.

He shakes his head. "No. I don't belong here." Looking over the office, he turns to Haidyn, and they hug. "But I'll keep in touch." He looks at me, and I stay where I'm at.

If you ask me, he abandoned Ashtyn when she needed him the most. And to stay gone all this time. Why? What was the point of coming back now? How long has Haidyn been in touch with him? Did they have this all set up? So many questions that I refuse to ask because I'll look like I care, and I no longer do. I wrote him off a long time ago.

"How many did you collect?" Haidyn asks him.

"We've got eight loaded and ready to move," he answers.

Adam's referring to the prisoners we had here at Carnage. After Ashtyn fell asleep in my arms in our bed, I got back to work. I couldn't have her here unless I knew it was safe. We had moved everyone to the morgue and needed to get some back to the hospital. The buildings needed to be checked and cleared.

There were no more bombs. Just the one that went off. Benny had planted it when he had brought Ashtyn and Haidyn back here and killed Whitney. It was in the cell she had been occupying and just happened to kill one of the guys who brought Ashtyn back when Benny let her go. When Benny was here with Ashtyn, he had went to see Luke and filled him with shit knowing I'd go to him asking questions. He wanted Luke to throw me off and send me on a wild goose chase. There never were four bombs.

We did, however, keep the other two guys who brought my wife back. They will spend the rest of their lives here until I get tired of looking at them and put them out of their misery.

"Did he tell you anything?" Tyson asks Adam, referring to Benny.

Adam didn't ask if he could take him. I think he knows I wouldn't let him go. He deserves to be here, naked and chained to a wall with conjugal visits from others. The man likes to fuck, so I'll give him what he wants.

"No." He shakes his head. "I'd give him a few more days before he decides he wants to talk."

ASHTYN

I STAND OUT ON SAINT'S BALCONY OVERLOOKING THE courtyard. I woke up an hour ago by myself in a room I've never been in before. I knew it was Saint's immediately, but I was alone. I've stayed in here knowing that he'll be back and we'll have a lot to discuss. I'm not sure I'm ready to go over the last four years of our lives, but it's time to lay it all out.

The wedding ring on my finger is a constant reminder that I messed up. I vowed to be his, but didn't trust him to protect me. I doubted him. And I shouldn't have.

The sound of his bedroom door opening has me turning around, and my heart races at the sight of my brother. Four years doesn't seem all that long ago but somehow seems like forever at the same time.

"Hey," he speaks, entering the room and letting the door shut behind him.

I step off the balcony and into the room. "Hey," I say softly.

Looking around the room, he runs his hand through his hair nervously. "Ashtyn, I'm sorry—"

"It's fine." I interrupt him. We all fucked up.

"No. it's not." He walks over to me, and I look up at him. "I was going to come back for you. Please believe me."

I nod, biting my bottom lip.

"I...I was too late." He looks over my head and sighs. "Then Haidyn—" He stops himself from finishing that sentence. "I found out you escaped here." Reaching out, he takes my hands in his, and it feels off. We were never close, and I have a feeling that's not going to change. This is a goodbye speech. That I'm sure of. "Just know, I've known where you've been. And I wish I could have changed the outcome."

I pull my hands from him, stepping back, and he nods to himself, understanding that this is where I belong. I know that now. It took me four years of making stupid choices I won't make again to realize that. The world is a crazy place and so is Carnage. But I'd rather be here with the Spade brothers than out in the world with strangers.

Silence falls over the room, and after a second, he turns and exits the bedroom, leaving the door open. I walk over to close it but pause as my eyes catch Haidyn's. I go over to it and knock.

Seconds later, it opens, and he stands there. His blue eyes hard and sharp jaw clenched. He's got his nose ring in and has his black leather riding jacket on but unzipped. "What do you want, Ash?" he asks, giving me his back and walking over to his bed.

I enter and walk over to his bed sitting on the side. "Going for a ride?"

"Something like that." He zips up a backpack.

"Why did you have to pretend to die?" I ask.

"They wanted me dead, so I had to give them that," he says simply. "The only way was to let them think they had the Spade brothers outnumbered. One down and two to go was pretty good odds for them."

I nod in understanding. A silence lingers, and I feel the lump in my throat, my emotions still all over the place. That fear of losing him was terrifying. Then Saint hitting him so soon after his surgery. They're fighting. But I know it'll be temporary. They're brothers, and that's what brothers do. "Haidyn—"

"I don't regret it," he says, interrupting me, and I swallow nervously. Walking over to me, he cups my face in his warm hands. "I stand by what I said, Ash. You deserved better, and I'm sorry I couldn't help you."

"You did," I whisper. He helped me more than he could ever know. Leaving Carnage was hard, but losing the baby was harder. I wanted a chance to be better than my mother, than my life. But it just wasn't meant to be.

"Are you leaving?" I ask, my stinging eyes searching his. "Please, Haidyn...don't." My voice cracks, begging him to stay when he doesn't answer.

He gives me a sad smile and leans down, his lips gently giving me a forehead kiss. Pulling back, he whispers. "Be good, baby girl." With that, he grabs his backpack, throws it over his shoulder, and exits his room.

I sit on the edge of his bed, staring at the wall, my chest tight and heart heavy. How did everything fall apart so fast? Things had just started to feel normal, and now it's all fucked again.

Getting up, I walk over to his balcony, opening the doors. I hear his bike before I see him ride out of the garage and out of the gates. The black crotch rocket stops, and his helmet moves, and I feel his eyes on mine. My hands curl around the railing as he revs his engine and takes off, disappearing into the night. And I hate that last time I was here, I was the one to leave and now he's leaving me.

Why did it have to be like this? I love my husband, but that doesn't mean I don't care about his brothers. That they don't mean something to me too.

I blink the tears from my eyes and turn around to leave but come to a stop when I see Saint standing in Haidyn's room. His eyes search mine, and I blink fresh tears that blur my vision. "He left," I say, my throat tightening. "It's my fault."

"No, it's not, Ash." He steps out onto the balcony with me. "Nothing that happened was your fault."

"Why did you let him leave?" I ask, my bottom lip trembling.

"He'll be back," he assures me, pushing hair behind my ear.

"How do you know that?" I ask. This was my fear years ago. That our fathers would use me to push them apart. They're dead, and it still happened but only it was me that did it.

Saint smiles at me. "Because Carnage is his home," he answers. Taking my hand, he pulls me from the balcony and out into the hallway. He closes Haidyn's door, and I can't help but look over my shoulder at it as Saint pulls me into his.

I let him pull me into the bathroom, and he turns to face me. The air feels thicker in here, harder to breathe.

"Did Haidyn hurt you?" he asks, checking my wrists.

I don't miss the fact that he didn't ask about Benny hurting me while I was gone for four days. That's because he knows what happened while I was away. "No," I growl. "I offered to help him." I don't want him mad at Haidyn. "You know..." I lick my lips. "He was helping you too," I say, referring to Haidyn helping me get away.

"Ashtyn," he sighs, not wanting to have the conversation.

"Laura told me that you cheated when you made me bleed. How did you do that?"

He lets out a long breath. "The morning of, I cut myself and bled into a capsule. When I had you bent over the altar at the vow ceremony, I put the capsule inside of you and broke it."

My wide eyes are on his, and I wait for him to give me the punch line. "Saint...how could you do that? Why would you do that? Take that chance? You could have been stripped of your title. Or worse, sentenced to Carnage..."

He chuckles darkly as if what I said was a joke. "I was willing to take that risk to make sure you remained mine. I wasn't going to let you go."

"She could have turned you in." My mother may have set it up, but Laura knew about it as well. They were both in on it.

Shaking his head, he adds, "She would have had to explain how she knew. She was too involved."

"Why are you so mad at Haidyn, but not me?" I ask, trying to figure it all out. "I shot you," I remind him as if he could ever forget.

"I expected more from Haidyn," he answers. "He knew I could have handled it...fixed it somehow. Instead, he gave you an out."

"He gave me a chance," I whisper.

Reaching out, he places his hand on my flat stomach, and my chest tightens. His eyes meet mine, and I see the questions in his green eyes. *What happened to the baby?* But he doesn't ask. Instead, he says, "You know I would have raised him as mine, right?"

My eyes begin to sting, and my bottom lip trembles.

He cups my face, and I sniff. "It would have changed nothing, sweetheart," he whispers. "I loved you then. I love you now. You've always been it for me, Ashtyn."

My eyes close, and the first tear falls. I feel his lips on mine tenderly kissing me. "Come on, let's get you cleaned off and go to bed."

His hands fall to the hem of the scrubs I wear, and I lift my one good arm. My silent request for him to undress me. I spent four days with a man who whipped and raped me. Right now, I need a man who loves me. And I know Saint is that.

He lifts it up over my head, being extra careful with my shoulder before tossing it to the side and lowering my bottoms. He helps me step out of them. I stand naked in front of him, and he runs his tatted knuckles down my heaving chest. His thumb slowly and softly follows the welts and cuts from Benny's belt.

Looking down, I see whore written on my skin, and my breath comes quicker. Saint places his fingers under my chin, forcing my head up. "Eyes on me, sweetheart." He tries to distract me. "How's your shoulder?"

"Fine." It hurts since the pain pills have long worn off, but it's bearable. I'm tired of feeling foggy.

He turns and opens the glass door to the shower and turns it on. Then he offers me his hand to help me in. I wait under the warm sprayer as he gets undressed to join me.

SIXTY-FIVE

SAINT

I enter the shower, and her eyes sweep over my body. I haven't been naked around her since she's been back. She's been naked, but I've always just unzipped my jeans to fuck her.

Her watery eyes meet mine and then drop to my chest again. *I vow. You vow. We vow.* is written across my chest. Our vows that we took at the ritual and then again when we got married.

She runs the tips of her fingers over it and then across my scar where she shot me. Her eyes meet mine, and I cup her face. Her fingers trail over my Lords crest and then to the opposite pec to the 666 branding.

"When did you get this?" she asks.

"After you left." It was part of our training. We were branded as we brand our prisoners. My eyes drop to look over her body, and I hate to see the words that Benny wrote on her. I know they'll fade over time and eventually disappear, but the memories of what happened while he had her won't.

"Saint?"

"Yeah, sweetheart?" I ask while I run my fingers over her 666 brand.

"Am I pregnant?"

My finger pauses at her question, and I lift my eyes to meet her watery ones. "No," I say honestly. That was one of the tests that Devin ran after I pulled her out of the car.

"Was Benny telling the truth?" she whispers. "Did you remove my birth control?"

"I did," I answer honestly. After she was out, Devin removed her IUD. It was another reason as to why I kept her on pain meds for the first few days. If she was numb, she wouldn't think clearly. The Ashtyn I dragged back here is not the Ashtyn I wanted to love me. I didn't care if she loved me. Now that's all I want from this woman.

She licks her lips and sniffs.

"I'm sorry, Ash," I whisper. "I…I didn't know." I thought she left because Laura had gotten to her. I didn't know she found out what Benny did to her in her kitchen. And I sure as fuck didn't think that she could have been pregnant from him. The thought never crossed my mind.

She looks up at me through her watery lashes as the water hits us. "So we can have a baby?" She asks softly as if she thought I might have taken that chance away from her.

All I ever wanted with this woman was a family. "Whenever you're ready…"

She wraps her arms around my neck and pulls me down to her. My lips meet hers, and she opens up for me. I push my hands into her long dark hair, gently tugging her head back, and she moans into my mouth.

My hands fall to her thighs, and I grab them, lifting her, and she wraps her legs around my hips. She pulls her lips away from mine, and I rest my forehead on hers. "If it gets too much, let me know, okay?" Her body has been through so much the last four days, but I'm not going to turn my wife down. If she needs me, I'm going to be there for her. However I can be. I won't ever let her think that I can't be the man she needs.

She nods, licking her wet lips. "Okay."

Reaching between our bodies, I grab my hard dick and slowly slide into my wife. Her breath catches and eyes grow heavy when I start to move.

"Eyes on me, sweetheart," I order. I want her here with me in this moment. Not fading away, falling somewhere else. I grip her hips, pushing her back into the cool marble wall and lower my lips to hers as I remind my wife that she belongs to me, and I to her.

EPILOGUE ONE

SAINT

I'm standing outside of the two operating rooms. Both currently occupied with women. My wife is in one of them. I would offer to help, but I figured between her and Sin, they have it covered.

A shrill baby cry hits my ears, and I smile. One down. One to go.

A few minutes later, the door to my left swings open, and a good friend and fellow Lord exits with a proud smile on his face. "It's a boy."

"Congratulations, man." I pull him in for a hug, slapping his back and then he rushes into the room on the right.

I remain where I'm at until I hear the other baby crying.

My wife exits the room from the right seconds later, and she's smiling ear to ear. "It's a girl." Then she rushes back into the room that Sin had left.

They wanted the babies to have the same birthday. They figured it'd be easier on the kids. They are already going to have a crazy life living under the Lords, why make it harder on them?

I push off the wall and remove my cell from my pocket and dial up a number I've got saved but never called.

He picks up on the first ring, not knowing it's me. "Hello?" He sounds apprehensive answering a number he doesn't have saved in his phone. I don't blame him. He keeps his circle very small because, to the world, who he once was no longer exists.

"You know you're welcome here, right?" I say in greeting.

He laughs, knowing exactly who I am by the sound of my voice. "Yeah, I was supposed to be there, but I've been on vacation, and my flight got delayed in Chicago."

I snort. "Should have told me. I would have sent the jet," I say although I know he has his own. Or he did. Technically now, it's his daughter and son-in-law's on paper.

"Flying commercial keeps me humble," he jokes. "Reminds me where I came from." He laughs at his own words because we both know he never flew commercial in his life before now.

I step into an empty hospital room and walk over to the window that overlooks the courtyard. It's so pretty. Green grass, blooming flowers of various colors. During the holidays, the bridge gets decorated with lights and garland. The wives got a hold of it and said it needed some life. Funny, considering this is where people come to die. That'll never change.

"Why didn't you ever tell me?" I ask, unable to stop myself. Not sure when I'll get this opportunity again.

He goes silent for a second. "Would you have believed me?"

"No," I say honestly. You wouldn't believe some of the shit the people come up with that are brought in. They will say anything when they know they're going to die. "But you could have tried."

He sighs. "When your fathers were killed, so was my chance at freedom. But I never expected that to happen anyway."

"But we took over," I say through gritted teeth. He's just as stubborn as his son-in-law. Our fathers were crooked as fuck. They did things that even the Lords would not have approved of.

"You guys spent months in Carnage as one of us." He pauses. "Then after they decided you were ready, you were only focused on one thing..." He trails off, and I know exactly what he's talking about. My wife. "So I kept a low profile and just survived."

I run a hand down my face.

"But I can't thank you enough. You gave me my life back. Now I've got a daughter, a son, and grandkids." I can hear the smile in his voice.

"You saved my life," I whisper.

He chuckles. "You would have survived regardless. I was just in the right place at the right time."

I snort. Odd way of looking at it, but if you're in Carnage, you've got to have a sense of humor.

"Congratulations on becoming a grandpa," I add when the silence gets uncomfortable.

"Thank you for letting me experience it."

We hang up, and I pocket my cell and stare out into the courtyard once again. My mind remembers the first time I ever heard his voice.

"The first wave is tolerable...the second gets colder..." He pauses before whispering, "The third is the coldest."

It took Sin coming to us looking for Nicholas for me to realize who he was. I always thought my father was fucking Laura, and he might have, but the big secret was they were holding her husband for her. He never did anything wrong. After our fathers died, I went easy on him. Well, as much as I could because of what he did for me that night. I wish I would have set him free. Maybe it could have saved Elli from what she went through.

The door opens, and I turn to see Ashtyn enter the room with a glowing smile on her face. "A boy and a girl. Both healthy and with their momma who is doing great."

I walk over to her, cup her face, and kiss her passionately. Tasting the saltiness in her happy tears that she's cried witnessing both Laura and Elli give birth. They both had scheduled C-sections. Gavin performed one while Devin did the other.

I pull away, and her heavy eyes open as she breathes deeply. "How are my babies?" I ask, dropping my hand to her growing belly.

"Great," she whispers.

"Have you felt okay today?"

She rolls her eyes. "Yes, Saint." Laughing softly, she adds, "We've been good for weeks."

Her first couple of weeks were rough, but I still worry about her. That'll never change. I understand what Nicholas was saying because I feel the same way—I don't deserve the life I have. I get to lie in bed with my wife at night, holding her, loving her, and talking about our future while during the day, I'm covered in another man or woman's blood, making them pay for their betrayal. I'm not sure what I did to deserve the life I have, but I'll do anything to keep it.

EPILOGUE TWO

SAINT

EIGHTEEN YEARS LATER

I sit at my desk at Carnage when my cell rings. I see it's my wife, and I hit answer. "Hello, sweetheart..."

"Is *she* there?" she asks in a tone that tells me she's not in the same good mood that I left her in this morning.

"No." I look around the office that I share with my brothers and see I'm the only one here. My eyes drop to my watch, and I see it's a little after nine. "She should be in class."

"She's not. I just got a call from the school that she's absent."

My door swings open, and my eyes narrow on the brunette. She's got her long dark hair braided and hangs over one shoulder with a white ribbon tied into a perfect bow at the end. It makes her look sweet and innocent, but I know the truth. "She's here. I'll call you back."

"Do not let her sweet-talk you, Saint," my wife barks into my ear. "She needs to be in school."

"Uh-huh. I'll call you back. Love you." I hang up before she can yell at me. "Why are you here?" I lock my cell and set it down. "You were supposed to ride with your sister to school this morning." Tinsley is grounded from driving for two weeks. Having to ride with her sister is a punishment that she hates.

She rolls her blue eyes and plops down across from my desk. "Berkeley left before the sun came up to go meet with her boyfriend. She's trying some new rose quartz shit on him."

"Boy-boyfriend?" I ask, stumbling over my words. "Since when does your sister have a boyfriend?" I'm not even going to try and decipher what the fuck rose quartz means. I'll have to google that.

She waves her hand in the air. "It's nothing serious. Pretty sure he's married."

"Married?" I slap my hands on the table.

"We're eighteen, Dad."

I run my hands through my hair and take a deep breath. This is going nowhere. "Why are you here in my office?" I ask again. Let's start back at the beginning.

"I got suspended, remember?"

"Last week. Today is Monday. A new week. You should be in school."

"Look what I got." She ignores me and pulls out a rectangular box from her black backpack that has pink butterflies all over it. She's a walking contradiction in every aspect of life.

This is where her mother would tell her not to deflect and drive her ass to school. But curiosity gets the best of me. "What is it?"

"It's a souvenir."

I frown, sitting back in my chair. "For what?"

"I didn't even wash it." She laughs.

"Tinsley, that better not be what I think it is." I growl. She lifts her mother's eyes and smiles at me. "You can't take a knife to school." She knows this. We just went over this last week. With me, her mother, the principal, and the police officer that were present for our mandatory meeting.

"I'm going to mail it to him."

I run a hand down my face, holding in a sigh. I thought Carnage was going to be the death of me. But nope. It's my teenage daughter. "You stabbed him. I'd say the scar he'll have will be souvenir enough," I remind her as if she could forget.

"He put his hands on me, Dad," she snaps defensively.

"I—"

"He tripped me, and when I didn't fall on my face in front of everyone embarrassing myself like he wanted me to, he pushed me into my locker."

Being a dad is hard. I have to pick my battles with not only my wife but also a little version of her who thinks she's invincible. It's my fault. I'm definitely one of those parents who takes a hundred percent responsibility for the monster I created. "Tins, have you stopped to think that maybe he likes you?"

She gasps dramatically, placing her hand on her white school blazer. "Are you defending him?"

"No—"

"It doesn't matter if he likes me. That doesn't give him the right to be a fucking jackass." Getting to her feet, she leans over my desk and grabs a marker off it. I watch her write *watch your back, fucker!*

"You can't do that." I shake my head. "That's a threat." Jesus Christ, she's going to get arrested. She's lucky I'm a Lord. I had to pull out some major stops for her to stay in her private school. It's her senior year, I didn't want her to ruin it over some boy. No matter who he is.

She jiggles the box in her hand as her eyes meet mine. "I'm going to wait for him to open it. He'll probably be dumb enough to put it on his nightstand or dresser. Then I'll break in and stab him with it again."

"Tinsley." I get to my feet.

She flips her braid over her shoulder and gets to her feet as well. "I'll drop it off on the way to school. See you later. Love you." She throws her backpack over her shoulder and skips to the door like she's off to see a wizard on a yellow brick road.

"Tinsley." I growl.

She stops, one hand on the door, and turns to face me with a big smile on her face. I've been a sucker for that smile since the moment I held her. It's amazing how cute and evil something can be at the same time. I'm thankful that if she was ever in a situation that required her to fight, I have no doubt she'd win, but that's also what will throw me in an early grave. "Don't kill anyone today," I joke, trying to lighten the mood. I know her mother is being hard on her right now. I've always been the lenient one, which is crazy considering the life I live.

She laughs. "Don't worry, Daddy. I know how to get rid of a body." She winks and yanks the door open, rushing out of the office and slamming it shut behind her.

"TINSLEY?" I yell, running after her. I yank the door open and hear the door to the stairwell close. I open it up and race down it to the first level. Then I rush outside and hear an engine rev. *Fuck!*

Exiting, I see her on her crotch rocket, fastening her helmet. "Did your mother say you could ride that to school today?" I demand.

"Have to go, Dad. I'm late." She revs it up and takes off down the curvy drive.

I used to let the girls take turns riding with me when they were little. Just around here. Tinsley loved it, Berkeley not so much. Then Tinsley turned thirteen and wanted her own. Both Ashtyn and I said absolutely not. But for her fifteenth birthday, Uncle Haidyn bought her one. He spent the next year teaching her to ride it. Took her to get her M endorsement and of course she passed with flying colors. When that girl decides she wants something, she does whatever it takes to make it happen.

Haidyn also thinks it's cute that she's a pyro who likes to stab boys and encourages her craziness. Ashtyn told him that the next phone call we get from the school, he's going up there to get her out of trouble. He laughed and said he'd be there. I'm pretty sure Tinsley has him as her ICE contact in her phone. That way he can lie to us about what happens to her in case of an emergency.

The bike was one of many things that we took away from her when she got suspended. I know her mother didn't give her the key, which means she cracked my gun safe and got it out. I'd be surprised if she didn't tear the whole damn door off getting to it. She has a knack for destroying shit.

I take the stairs down to my car that's parked in the circle drive and fall into the driver's seat. A phone call won't do for Ashtyn. I'm going to go home and calm her down. I know just the thing.

Removing my cell, I pull up the app and turn it on. It makes me smile, knowing she wasn't expecting that.

I exit the gates of Carnage and drive across the two-lane road through the matching sets of gates across the street. Living in Carnage just wasn't what Ashtyn and I wanted for our family. But she understood that I had to be able to be here at the drop of a hat. So, we along with the others, bought the property across the street and built houses. That way all the wives and kids are close to us yet still out of Carnage.

I pull up to the driveway and enter our home. "Ashtyn?" I call out with a smile, holding my cell. When she doesn't answer, I expect to find her lying in our bed, face down with her ass up in the air ready for me to fuck it. When I left her this morning, she was in a good mood and begging to come.

The water from the shower covers my back as I pin my wife to the wall. I've got her wet hair twisted in my hand as I stand behind her. The bathroom is cloudy from all the steam and is full of her moans.

"Fuck, sweetheart." I pant. Lowering my lips to her wet neck, I suck the water off her delicious skin.

"Saint." Her hands flatten on the marble while I push the side of her face against it. I've got her hips pulled back, giving me a better

angle to her pussy as I fuck it from behind. "Fuck..." She trails off. "Right there."

The slapping of our wet bodies can be heard over the shower, and I'm glad I locked our bedroom door when I woke up this morning. There's always someone coming in and out of our house. If it's not Haidyn or Kash, it's someone's wife or children.

"What do you say, sweetheart?" I growl in her ear. My free hand drops to her right leg. I grip her slick thigh and lift it, allowing me to go deeper.

"Please—?" she begs breathlessly. "I need to come."

I smile before biting into her neck, forcing her head to the side with my hand in her hair. I suck hard knowing it's going to leave a hickey. I've been married for over twenty years and still feel the need to mark my wife. I'm never going to change. Just like the 666 brand and our vow tattoos will never go away.

And just when I think she's there, I slam forward, pinning her to the wall while I come inside my wife.

"What...the...fuck?" She's gasping when I pull out, and she slowly turns to face me.

I smile. "You gotta earn it," I say, knowing that I'm going to make her wait.

She slaps my chest, and I laugh. "What the hell did you do to deserve to come?"

My smile widens, and it grants me another slap. This time in the dick, making me bend at the waist with a grunt.

After I fucked my wife in our shower, I bent her over the bathroom counter and put a butt plug up her ass. I told her when I got home, I'd finish what I started. But when I enter our bedroom, I see it sitting on our bed, vibrating. "Ash?" I pick it up, turn it off on my phone, and enter the bathroom. She's not there either.

We've got two entrances to our closet, one on either end of the bathroom for his and hers. I enter hers to find her dressed in a black

silk robe, hair and makeup freshly done, digging through her clothes.
"What are you doing?" I ask.

"Getting ready," she answers without turning to face me.

"Where the hell are you going?" She didn't have anywhere to be today. That's why I filled her cunt full of cum this morning and then her ass with a plug. Once you have children, you have to get creative when it comes to sex. I've never ignored my wife. I'm still just as obsessed with her as I was back when I got to take her as mine.

"The school."

Not today. I want to take the principal and dean and trap them in Carnage. But they have no idea who we are. So for now, we play the game and just get Tinsley through this last year. If I allow my wife to go up there and make the scene like I know she will, I'll have to sweep in and fix it. And why do that when I can be balls deep in her instead? I'll save that for a day I'm in the mood to stir some shit. "She's fine, Ash." But I ask, "Does Berkeley have a boyfriend who's married?"

She gives a rough laugh. "No." It makes me feel a little better.

My wife spins around, and I wrap my hand around her throat, holding her in place. Her gaze is hard, and she tries to push me away, but I hold up the butt plug. Swallowing hard against my hand, she searches my face. "What did I say about this?"

She lifts her chin, and I smile. I love it when my wife challenges me. It gives me a chance to remind her how much she likes to be punished. "I told you to leave it in until I got home from work, or you'd be punished." *As if she forgot.*

"You came home early," she says.

Letting go of her neck, I place the butt plug on the dresser island in the center of the closet. "Clean it, put it back in, and meet me in the bedroom. For every minute it takes you, you get my belt to your ass."

She gasps. "Saint, we don't have time—"

"We've got all day." I interrupt her. I'll just skip work. Haidyn and Kashton can handle it without me.

"I—"

"Clock is ticking." I look at my watch, and she huffs, grabs the plug, and spins around, storming out of the closet. A win is a win, and I have no problem cheating in order to make it happen.

I open up the top drawer on my side of the island and grab everything that I need and then walk through the bathroom into the bedroom, ignoring her soft moans as she does as she was told.

We have a California king-size bed with a metal wraparound canopy. She keeps black drapes at each of the corners, tied back and open. There is a white bench at the foot of the bed, and I walk over and push it out of the way, needing to be able to stand where it's at.

I look up to see her now standing in the doorway to the bathroom. "Come here," I order softly, and she slowly walks toward me. I could ask her if the butt plug is in, but instead, I remove my cell and turn it on. She stumbles, whimpering, and I smile. "Good girl."

Taking her hand, I pull her into me. She's naked, and I'm still fully dressed. Looking at my watch, I say, "It took you five minutes."

"Saint," she whispers, licking her pretty pink-painted lips.

"Yeah, Ash?" I run my hand through her curled hair. I love when she's all done up for no other reason than to let me fuck it up.

"May I please come?" she asks.

I kiss her forehead. "After you earn it." Then I grab her arm, yanking her over to the bed's footboard. I smack her ass, and she crawls onto it. I grab her ankle, stopping her from going too far. "Face on the bed, ass in the air, and hands behind your back. I want your feet to hang off the edge and spread your legs wide open for me, sweetheart. I want to see how wet you are."

Doing as she's told, I pick up the rope and tie it around her upper arms, securing them tightly and then bringing it down to her wrists, where she's already got her fingers laced together. She knows the drill. All the hours she's spent tied to our bed while I forced her to come over and over again did the job. She never brought up her mother or Laura again. She knows that there is nothing wrong with being my whore and that there is absolutely nothing I wouldn't do to her body.

I take the remainder of the rope and toss it up over the top metal bar to the canopy and pull it down, tying it off to her already tied wrists.

"Saint," she moans. The rope pulls her arms up at an uncomfortable angle, making her arch her back more and placing her ass up in the air.

I undo my buckle, and she wiggles her ass when she hears it. I double it over and slap her pretty pink pussy, making her cry out. "That's one."

I turn up the vibrating butt plug as I plunge two fingers into her wet cunt. I can see she was sloppy when applying the lube because it's all over her ass, pussy, and inner thighs. She begins to ride them the best she can since her tied arms don't allow much movement.

"That's my good girl," I say, entering a third, my thumb rubbing her swollen clit. "Show me, Ash. How bad do you want to get off?"

She moans, digging her done-up face into our bed.

I slap her ass with my belt this time, and she yelps. "How bad, sweetheart?"

"Please, Saint?" she begs, her bouncing ass fucking my three fingers.,

I add a fourth and slap her ass once more. It's starting to turn red. You can see each hit, and her pussy is dripping.

"Please...oh, god..." She's practically crying now. Her voice so desperate and her body aching. "I need to come, Saint. Please..."

She clenches down on my fingers. I drop the belt next to her to turn off the vibrating butt plug, and she growls, yanking on the rope that ties her to our bed.

"Five swats, Ash. You don't get to come until you get your punishment." I remove my fingers, and her shaking body sags. "Then I'm going to remove this plug and fuck that tight ass of yours."

"Pl-ease—" she cries.

"Only after my cum drips from your ass will you get to come."

I was born a Spade brother, but I will die a husband and a father. And when I am buried in our cemetery and arrive at the gates of hell, I'll smile because I'll already know what to expect from the devil. A very short life with my family is worth an eternity of damnation.

THE END

LORDS TREE

THE RITUAL

RYAT ARCHER — BLAKELY ANDERSON

REIGN ARCHER   ROYAL ARCHER   RYANN ARCHER

THE SINNER

EASTON SINNETT — ELLINGTON ASHER

BREXTON SINNETT   ANNALEIGH SINNETT

THE SACRIFICE

TYSON CRAWFORD — LAIKYN MINSON

HOLSTON CRAWFORD   HARTLYN CRAWFORD

Carnage

SAINT CARTER — ASHTYN PRICE

TINSLEY CARTER   BERKELEY CARTER

ALSO PART OF THE LORDS WORLD

WANT TO DIVE INTO THE DARK KINGDOM?

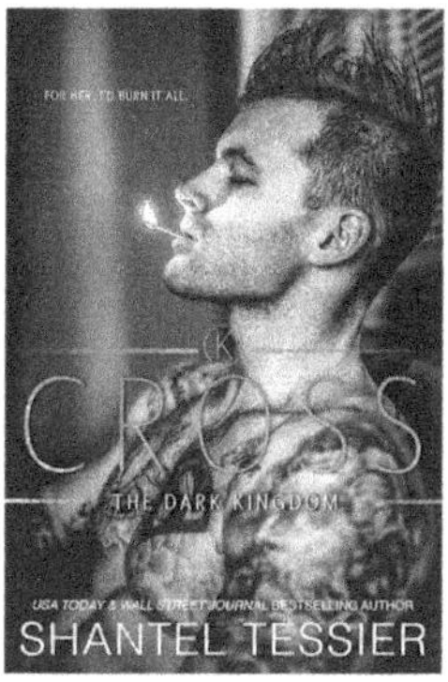

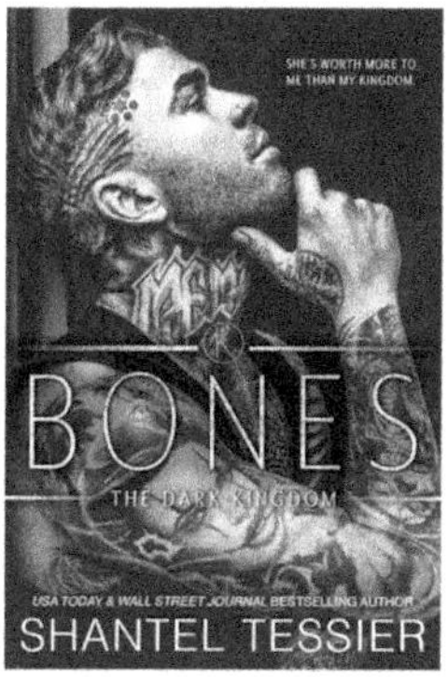

THE RITUAL

USA TODAY & WALL STREET JOURNAL BESTSELLING AUTHOR

SHANTEL TESSIER

RYAT

I enter her apartment, knowing that she's home alone. I made sure of it. Pushing her bedroom door open, I find her lying on the bed. She's on her back, her hands up by her head.

Eyes closed and breathing deeply. Passed out.

She took the GHB.

I figured she would. People in our world are always looking for a way to escape reality. I needed another taste of her, and there are rules for a reason.

Walking over to the side of the bed, I pull the covers off her to find she had changed into an oversized T-shirt before it kicked in. I fist the material in my hands, thinking it belongs to her cheating ex. Yanking it up, I see she's got on a pair of black lace underwear. Letting go of the shirt, I place my hand on her flat stomach and slide the tips of my fingers into the fabric. Teasing myself.

My cock is hard, straining against my zipper. I want to fuck her so bad. Ever since I saw her sprawled out on the floor, I wanted to take her dark hair in my hands and shove my dick down her throat and make her pretty blue eyes cry.

The rules of the ritual are simple.

The chosen must offer herself. She has shown me interest by showing up at the party. If there was any doubt what she was doing there—my bedroom proved she wanted something.

Even if it was just revenge on Matt. I'll take that. That's something I can use.

Typically, the chosen one and the Lord know each other. They've been friends, or they've dated. Few instances are like Blakely and me—when the Lord is forced to pick a certain chosen one. There are women at Barrington who would kill to be a chosen. Serving a Lord is an honor for them. Matt has kept her in the dark for a reason. He didn't want her to know what was going on. He thought it didn't matter, and she was a sure thing for him. Now that's no longer a possibility. So, his reasons for keeping her in the dark have changed.

I wouldn't say she would have been my first choice because I never thought of her like that. Is she hot? Yeah. But I knew she was off-limits. Even after I was given the order, I had reservations. That was until I started planting myself in her life. I've been following her for several weeks now. Then after the little taste she gave me—I've been salivating, wanting more.

If I had revealed myself to her in my bedroom that night, she wouldn't have allowed me to touch

her.

If the chosen one accepts, she is yours until you no longer have use for her. She won't

remember that motherfucker's name after I have my way with her.

Slowly, I hook my fingers into her underwear and pull them down her tan legs, letting my

knuckles graze her smooth skin. Gripping her thighs, I push them apart and crawl onto the bed to

kneel between them. I look over her shaved pussy, bringing the fabric to my face. I inhale, my

cock jerking in my pants. Fuck, I need to be inside her, but that can't happen tonight. Not yet.

The rules are clear, but they don't say anything about playing with her. They allow us just

enough to hang ourselves. The Lords are always testing us.

I throw the underwear to the floor and slide my hands up the inside of her thighs to her

cunt. I bite my lip, spreading her lips open for me. "Goddamn," I whisper, slipping a finger

inside her.

She's not wet, but I didn't expect her to be. Bringing my finger to my mouth, I suck on it

up to my knuckle and then slide it back in, gently testing the waters while my eyes go to her face.

Her head is tilted to the left, her dark hair covering her pillow, and her breathing remains

unfazed. I reach up with my free hand and shove her shirt up farther to expose her chest to me. I

smile at the fact she's not wearing a bra. Her breasts are fucking amazing. Round and firm, they fit in my hand perfectly with pretty pink nipples and small areolas.

Looking back down at her pussy, it's getting wetter. I remove my finger and add another one. She still doesn't move.

My girl has proven that I own her, and I can't wait to show her just what that means.

I start to get more and more aggressive. Her head moves to the other side, and a whimper escapes her lips. I didn't give her very much GHB because of her small size. I didn't want her to

experience too many side effects. I just needed her to be drowsy and impaired to the point I could play with her. Plus, it can increase an urge for sex.

She arches her back for me, her lips parting, and I watch the way her nipples harden as her pussy tightens around my fingers.

I readjust myself on the bed, placing my left hand by her head. I lean all my weight on it while forcing a third finger into her tight cunt. My cock twitches with anticipation to be inside her. To be the first there. To own her.

Her breath catches, and I gently kiss the corner of her lips. "Beautiful."

"Ryat." She moans.

"Yeah, Blake. It's me," I tell her, and she whimpers. Even drugged and only half-conscious, she knows I'm the one touching her.

I begin to finger-fuck her roughly while my thumb plays with her clit. Her body rocks back and forth, making her tits bounce and the bed squeak. She lets out a cry when her pussy clamps down, and she comes all over my fingers.

Something about having her like this—having total control over her body—is very powerful. Knowing she willingly took something I gave her without any knowledge of what it was. She's craving to be owned, to be dominated, to be mine.

I stop, and her eyes remain closed. Bringing my fingers to her mouth, I rub them over her parted lips, smearing her cum across them like icing. "Soon, little one," I tell her before I stick them in my own mouth, licking them clean. Tasting that fucking honey that I've been craving after she gave herself to me in my bedroom.

Pushing off the bed, I move to a sitting position between her shaking legs. I reach down and grab the collar of the oversized shirt and rip it down the middle. "I'll burn this," I say to myself, pulling her arms out of it, knowing that I'm one step closer to owning her and erasing any trace of Matt.

Reaching into my back pocket, I pull out the card and lay it on her nightstand. Now I wait.

CONTACT ME

Facebook Reader Group: Shantel's Sinful Side

Goodreads: Shantel Tessier

Instagram: shantel_tessierauthor

Website: Shanteltessier.com

Facebook Page: Shantel Tessier Author

TikTok: shantel_tessier_author

Store: shanteltessierstore.com

Shantel Tessier's Spoiler Room. Please note that I have one spoiler room for all books, and you may come across spoilers from book(s) you have not had the chance to read yet. You must answer both questions in order to be approved.

Printed in the USA
CPSIA information can be obtained
at www.ICGtesting.com
LVHW021637110424
777137LV00011B/497

9 798988 704942